for S
John

"The best succes... ...s Mac-
Donald tradition to come along in a ...
—*The New Republic*

"His dialogue rings with smart authority and reverberates in the memory long after the reader has closed the book."
—*The Philadelphia Inquirer*

"Mr. Greenleaf is a real writer with real talent."
—*The New Yorker*

"His dialogue is pungent, his observations mordant, his eye for detail concrete and telling. As both witty entertainment and modern morality tale, this is very satisfying indeed."
—*The Cleveland Plain Dealer*

BLOOD TYPE
"A fast walk on the wild side. Good, crisp writing produces characters who breathe."
—*Copley News Service*

"Tough, meaty prose, sly twists in plot, and immediacy of action make this a good choice."
—*Library Journal*

BOOK CASE
"Twisty and absorbing."
—*Kirkus Reviews*

"Moving, riveting and wonderfully and appropriately bookish in just the right sense of that much maligned word."
—*The Boston Globe*

DEATH BED
"All the right components are here—violence and sex, intellectual deduction and good guesses, wit and cynicism—plus lots of real surprises and that essential ingredient of the private-eye tale, a large pinch of morality."
—*New York* magazine

THE NEW
JOHN MARSHALL TANNER MYSTERY

BLOOD TYPE

STEPHEN
GREENLEAF

BANTAM BOOKS

NEW YORK • TORONTO • LONDON • SYDNEY • AUCKLAND

This edition contains the complete text
of the original hardcover edition.
NOT ONE WORD HAS BEEN OMITTED

BLOOD TYPE

A Bantam Crime Line Book/published by arrangement with
William Morrow and Company, Inc.

PUBLISHING HISTORY
William Morrow edition published 1992
Bantam edition/October 1993

CRIME LINE *and the portrayal of a boxed "cl" are trademarks of Bantam Books,*
a division of Bantam Doubleday Dell Publishing Group, Inc.

ISBN 0-553-56106-5

Published simultaneously in the United States and Canada

Bantam Books are published by Bantam Books, a division of Bantam Doubleday
Dell Publishing Group, Inc. Its trademark, consisting of the words "Bantam
Books" and the portrayal of a rooster, is Registered in U.S. Patent and
Trademark Office and in other countries. Marca Registrada. Bantam Books,
1540 Broadway, New York, New York 10036.

PRINTED IN THE UNITED STATES OF AMERICA

RAD   0 9 8 7 6 5 4 3 2 1

BLOOD TYPE

Chapter
1

Among other things, I'm a drinking man. Not an alcoholic, mind you—I don't imbibe till I pass out, or go on weekend benders, or wake with the shakes and shivers, or lose track of blocks of time in which I've done things I'm ashamed of when apprised of them—but I do take a drink most nights of the week. I like the places my mind visits when it's been primed with a half-dozen ounces of scotch and I like the person I become when my congenital tethers are loosened up a bit—I'm friendlier and funnier in such a state, less prone to the charms of gloom and doom. That I've been able to stay a drinking man rather than descending into a drunk is due less to my character than to my genes, the experts tell me. Which is fine, theoretically, except it doesn't explain why you can't find Melanoma Anonymous or Multiple Sclerosis Watchers in the phone book.

The primary task of a drinking man is to gauge the amount of fuel necessary to take him to the optimum state of being and keep him there. That's mostly a matter of practice, plus an appreciation of the variables—current psychological state, type of tipple employed, size and propinquity of most recent meal, congenial companionship or lack thereof, ambience of the scene of the undertaking. After thirty years of working at it, I get the quantity part right almost every time, except on the occasional evening when I don't want to get it right, I want to get it wrong. Such catharses excepted, the hard part for a drinking man is drunks.

In my experience, drunks are arrogant, assertive, and antagonistic; drunks are loud, lewd, and lecherous; drunks are dumb, dull, and demoralizing. Drunks demand excessive sympathy and dole out excessive blame. Drunks love the bottle more than they love themselves, and themselves more than anything but the bottle. If my only alternatives were to spend my time surrounded by drunks or give up drinking altogether, my choice would be the latter. Luckily there is a third option, which is to find a drinking man's bar that caters to nothing but. It took me a while, even in a drinking town like San Francisco, but a few years back I finally found a place that fills the bill.

The bar doesn't have a name. It's secreted in the back of a popular North Beach restaurant two blocks down the slope of Telegraph Hill from where I live and is filled with a noisy mix of domestic yuppies and imported tourists every night from six to midnight. The distant drone of these unknowing foils provides a perfect white noise for those of us who assemble, one at a time, like members of a secret sect, behind the partition at the back of the restaurant's main room—the partition with the posters of Tuscany and Tintoretto and Toscanini tacked to it—to enjoy our libations out of sight and mind of everyone but the few we regard as peers.

A dozen barstools, four tables. No waitresses, no ferns; no Muzak, no tipping. Peanuts and popcorn in bowls, pasta à la carte upon request, TV above the bar with a ball game on the screen and the sound blessedly turned off. No hookers, no drunks, no swells from out-of-town who've just discovered Fuzzy Navels and have something they want to sell you. And most of all, a bartender named Guido who doesn't speak even when spoken to and pours two ounces of what you want without being asked and keeps your glass topped up till you tell him you've had enough, which you keep track of because that's *your* part of the deal. As a token of their appreciation, the regulars call the bar Guido's even though the name doesn't appear on anything in the place, not even the Yellow Pages. Come to think of it, I'm not sure Guido is the bartender's real name.

The regulars number about forty, more or less, of which a score or so are present at any given time if the time is after noon and before closing at 2:00 A.M. I know each of them by name, but with most that's all I know or care to. There are a few exceptions—the criminal lawyer who collects fountain pens and first editions, the banker who writes turgid essays on free will and named his son after Immanuel Kant, the triple divorcée who's wearing herself out holding down two jobs in order to get enough money together to open a bar of her own. These are the ones I relate to, sometimes more, sometimes less, enough to care and be cared about. The divorcée, for example, brought me a tuna casserole the last time I was sick. I reciprocated by driving her to Yosemite on her birthday. It was the first time she'd seen the Falls or Half-Dome, and she's lived in San Francisco all her life. She talks a lot about going back.

My only real friend at Guido's, other than the times Charley Sleet, the cop, drops by after another bout with municipal mayhem, is Tom Crandall. Tom's a decade younger than I am, chronologically, but in spirit he's one of those people the New Agers call "Old Souls." In some ways, Tom's a vat of contradictions. He lives like a monastic, yet he's married to a torch singer. He's a fountain of information on a vast array of subjects, but rarely opens his mouth without being prodded. He drives an ambulance by day and reads history and philosophy by night except on Mondays, which is the only night of the week his wife has off. Tom always has a book with him when he comes to Guido's, and unless we lock onto a mutually absorbing conversation, he'll spend the evening reading. Since our respective vocations are essentially intrusive, what each of us respects the most is privacy—we only engage each other once or twice a week.

Tom and I talk about a lot of things, but seldom about our work. I've seen some nasty things in my dozen years as a detective, and Tom is hip-deep in them nearly every day, but by unspoken agreement we've decided Guido's should remain unsoiled by the subhuman aspects of our lives. We've both seen service in wartime as well—Tom as a medic, me as a rifleman—but we don't dredge that up, either. As I said, we're drinking men, not drunks.

For the most part, we leave our private lives alone as well. Mine doesn't amount to much, of course, so confidentiality isn't difficult—what's difficult is finding something interesting to say about it even when it's on a roll. Tom's situation is different. His wife is a celebrity of sorts, the featured chanteuse with one of the hotel bands on Nob Hill. She's on her way to becoming a local institution, referred to in the columns as San Francisco's answer to Julie Wilson and Barbara Cook. Because of their work schedules, she and Tom rarely see each other, which must have caused all sorts of problems, but if it had I didn't know what kind. All I knew was that whenever her name came up, Tom got vague and misty and maybe a little melancholy, then steered the conversation somewhere else. I figured if he wanted me to know more he'd tell me, the way he tells me what he thinks about Tom Wolfe—he hates him—or Philip Glass—he loves him—or George Will—he thinks he's a closet liberal.

Mostly Tom and I talk politics—local and global, pragmatic and theoretical. Of late, the sidebars had ranged from the inept management of water resources during California's five-year drought to the spread of AIDS among the city's homeless population and, most heatedly, to the issue of German reunification. Tom believes it's essential. I'm less sanguine, though my view is based on little more than Hitler and a hunch. Tom's is the result of an analysis that encompasses personalities from Charlemagne to Metternich and phenomena from the first Treaty of Versailles to the second partition of Poland. But that was last month. This month's agenda is war.

Iraq had invaded in August. We began bombing in January. Now, almost a month into what the media was calling the Crisis in the Gulf, the betting pools centered on the ground campaign—when would it start and how long would it last. As usual, Tom placed the war in a context that included citations from the Code of Hammurabi, the

Bible, the Koran, the United Nations Charter, and the spot-market price of oil. My memories of Vietnam led me to anticipate a protracted ground war with much suffering and many casualties on both sides. Tom's delving into Jane's encyclopedias of aircraft and weaponry led him to believe the war would be over a week after we attacked in force. What he envisioned was a slaughter on the order of the Crimean War. What he feared was that, like a middle-aged roughneck who's no longer top dog and picks fights with weaklings to prove his manhood, America would welcome the carnage and even revel in it. I wasn't sure which of us I hoped was right.

Tom usually arrives at Guido's about nine. I'm usually already there, at my stool at the end of the bar. But this time there was a deviation—Tom didn't have his book bag with him. I decided that at the very least the omission meant Tom was headed my way with something on his mind more immediate than the collective psychology of the Teutonics or the number of sorties that had been flown that day. A moment later, he was standing next to the stool beside mine, beer in hand, waiting for an invitation to join me.

When I motioned for him to take the empty seat, Tom collapsed onto it as though he had rocks in his pockets and a pack on his back. He was dressed as usual—Levi's and flannel shirt—and both above and below his thick black mustache his expression was dour and Lincolnesque, also as usual. Since empathy was epidemic in Tom Crandall, it wasn't odd to see him burdened by someone's plight, but for the first time I could remember, the object of the exercise was Tom himself.

Before he said anything, he drank deeply from his glass, licked the ensuing foam off his lips, crossed his long, thin arms atop the bar, and looked at me with eyes as wild as weeds. "I've got a question," he said gruffly.

"Shoot."

Since Tom seldom relinquishes a subject till he's worried it to a creative conclusion, I expected it to have to do with Bismarck or Hussein. But what he said was, "What the hell can you do about it if some son of a bitch sets out to steal your wife?"

Chapter
2

Spurred by silent-movie images of black-hatted villains abducting wide-eyed ingenues when the rent on the farm fell due, I felt an urge to laugh. But when I looked to see if Tom was serious, what looked back were eyes afloat on inkblots of exhaustion and bracketed by fine white lines of worry. I tried to get as serious as Tom was, but I didn't quite make it.

"Once upon a time," I began easily, hoping he was at least being hyperbolic, "they called it 'criminal conversation' or 'alienation of affections,' and you could sue the guy who tried it, even get an injunction ordering him to stop. If it was too late to keep her from running off, you could make him pay you a fair price."

"You said 'Once upon a time.' What does that mean, exactly?"

"It means the legislature abolished that particular cause of action back in 1939."

"Why?"

"They didn't want to clog the courts with any more domestic disputes than they already had. And because the concept smacked too much of indentured servitude: the analogy to rustling, the monetary measure of the wife's worth, the husband's proprietary interest in her affections—stuff like that."

Tom's argumentative bent asserted itself. "They measure her worth if someone runs her down and *kills* her, don't they?"

"Sure, but that's an event that seldom includes the wife's cooperation and complicity."

Although a surrebutter could be made, Tom's usual thirst for debate had been slaked by the subject matter. "So there's nothing I can do," he concluded glumly.

"Not as far as the law is concerned, I don't think. Oh, you might dig up a lawyer who'd help you run a bluff—file a claim of unlawful interference with the marriage contract or intentional infliction of mental distress or something. It would be thrown out of court, eventually, but it might be enough to make this character back off."

Tom shook his head morosely. "Not *this* character."

He drank till his glass was empty. Guido replaced it before it hit the bar. I sipped some Ballantine's and chewed some ice, then asked a question I seldom asked outside the confines of my office. "Why don't you tell me about it?"

Tom's only answer was to stare, blindly and blinklessly, at the bottles on the back of the bar. The prospect of making his problems public, even to an audience of one, seemed to roast his anguish.

But Tom was Tom, so he gradually retreated to reason and then to the rituals of our relationship. "Are you sure you don't mind?"

"Not at all."

His smile was only semisuccessful. "We don't do this, you know."

"Maybe that's because it hasn't been necessary before."

"Necessary." He sighed and shook his head, then looked at his beer but didn't touch it. "It's amazing what can become encompassed within that definition. Here I sit, married fifteen years, *happily* married as far as I knew, and suddenly it's become *necessary* for me to hurry to the local saloon so I can share the burden of my wife's dalliance with another man."

"Only if you want to, Tom. Only if you think it will help."

He blinked in surprise, as though he'd never considered otherwise. "Oh, it will help. It always helps to toss off some agony onto someone else—it's why behind half the doors in town lurks someone who calls himself a therapist." He tried to smile, but the mechanics broke down halfway through the process. "I'm afraid the subject won't be nearly as interesting as our conversation about the timber industry and the spotted owl. We're cutting trees faster than Brazil is cutting the rain forest, you know. I just learned that this week."

I smiled. "Why don't we talk about your wife?"

Tom drained his glass and turned toward Guido, who had already started our way with another draught in his hand. "Bring me a brandy in a minute, will you, Guido?" Tom said after he had his beer. "A double."

Tom hadn't ordered brandy for months, since the night before the morning paper had reported a particularly grisly rip-off retaliation in which rival crack dealers had gotten it on down by the Cow Palace and two of the losers had been decapitated. I hadn't asked, and Tom hadn't volunteered, but I knew he'd gotten the call to go out there that morning, and it had taken the brandy to get the carnage tucked into a place in his brain that wouldn't haunt him, at least not till he was home.

When the brandy was in front of him, he looked into its blood-red depths as though salvation might be beckoning. Like most people who look for messages in a bottle, Tom didn't find one to his liking.

"I've never talked to you about the war before," he murmured finally, not looking at me, not really talking to me, either. In common with most people who confess their sins to others, Tom was primarily trying to explain things to himself.

"And I don't want to talk about it now, really," he went on, "except to say that when I came back from Vietnam I was pretty messed up. Not only because of the war, I admit—there were things from my life before I went overseas that . . . well, let's just say I was fucked up. Drugs. Booze. Nightmares. The whole megillah."

He peeked at me then, just for a moment, to be sure I understood that the situation he'd abbreviated was none-theless extreme. "It's weird, but at the worst moments in my life, women have always rescued me. Of course, maybe that's *not* so weird, maybe it's what women do best; hell, maybe it's the answer Freud was looking for—maybe rescuing men is what women really want in life. I mean, it's not the worst job in the world, right?"

He paused to consider his insight. When it didn't seem to please him, he returned to his story. "When I was con-fused and crazy in high school, a girl came along and gave me, well, whatever it was I needed. Esteem, I guess. Or understanding. She liked me for the right reasons, was what it came down to, when everyone else was reacting to things that didn't matter. She was so sweet—God, I love it when they're sweet. She used to—"

Someone at the other end of the bar started laughing, and Tom broke off his reverie. He looked up the bar, then back at me. "But it didn't work out," he said simply. "I went in the army, things happened at home, and . . ." He shrugged. "Anyway, when I got back from Nam, I was even more screwed up than before, and along came Clarissa. It was enough to make me believe in God." He peeked at me again. "Almost."

I smiled at the qualifier. We had discussed religion *ad nauseam* over the years. Tom clearly wanted to believe in a higher power, perhaps even needed to, but his preexisting faith in the gods of reason and reality wouldn't let him make the leap, at least not yet. Me, I was still working on the problem, though since I read the newspapers more often than I read the Bible, the trend was generally the other way.

I was still pondering theological imponderables when Tom banged his hand on the bar. "How could I have been so *stupid*? "

The question was rhetorical, but I responded anyway. "I still don't know what you're talking about, but you're about as *unstupid* as anyone I know."

"That's not quite right," he growled bitterly. "What I am is *informed*. I know a lot of stuff, a *ton* of stuff—useless facts, misleading statistics, irrelevant information. My head's so full it creaks at the seams."

"What's wrong with that?"

"What's wrong is, I seem to know far more about the world than I know about my *wife*."

The words were slurred, less from the quantity of beer and brandy than from the pain of the revelation. The variables were catching up to him, and Tom was on the verge of getting drunk.

"I imagine you're not the first husband to feel that way," I said.

"No. And a lot of them end up wasting away their lives in places like this." From the look on his face, we might have been patronizing a cockfight.

Startled by his outburst, then chagrined at its implicit indictment of persons he regarded as friends, Tom looked around the bar as though he were wearing a new set of spectacles. What he saw seemed to alarm him.

"It was a miracle she married me, of course," he went on after a moment, the alarm become bemusement. "To this day, I don't know why she accepted my proposal. We're as different as two people can be. She's an *entertainer,* for God's sake. I have to get embalmed just to summon the courage to ask a gas jockey to check the tires."

The picture he'd painted of his marriage caused Tom to slip back into the funk that had brought him to Guido's in the first place, which was something different in degree and kind from the normal depressions that lurked around the two of us like pigeons around a park. Although there were a thousand reasons not to—my desire to preserve my friendship with Tom and the fact that I heard enough of other people's troubles during the day to cultivate them when my meter wasn't running, among others—I resolved to keep probing until I discovered the source of his torment. I didn't have anything to do the rest of the night, anyway. Or even the rest of the week.

"How did you meet her?" I prompted.

"We met in college. She was a senior at State and I was back from the war and earning a G.I. Bill living taking some courses in Asian history in the hope that what I'd seen and done over there would make sense if I put it in a context that didn't originate with the Defense Department and the CIA. Clarissa was a music major—she's known she wanted to be a singer since she was eight years old and her family trotted her out for every remotely appropriate occasion and made her sing 'Alice Blue Gown' and 'You'll Never Walk Alone.'"

Tom paused to enjoy what I imagined was an image of his wife as a budding Shirley Temple, but the vision didn't last. "I was trying to decide what the war meant— whether it meant eternal damnation for all of us because man's unquenchable inhumanity to man was the ineluctable stain of original sin, or whether it was just another exercise in barbarism so routine and unexceptional there might still be a place for me in the world, that I hadn't forfeited my right to function in what passes for civilized society the day I failed to put a stop to the castration ritual that certain members of my unit were so enamored with." He blinked. "I must say, by the way, that the recent events in the Gulf incline me toward the latter view."

Tom paused long enough to give me a chance to ponder what twenty years of physiological and psychological excess would do to the psyche, what Tom must have had to become in order to endure and even thrive in such a life, whether that was something better or worse than what I had become myself. Like most things I ponder, I gave up before I had an answer.

"Clarissa," he repeated softly. "We were in the same Global Studies class, only nodding acquaintances till we ran into each other at a concert in Stern Grove. I was a semi-roadie for one of the bands on the days I wasn't too drugged up to function, and she was a part-time singer with a group called Ozymandias. She was trying to be another Janis Joplin in those days, though her talents were more like Lena Horne's."

Tom sighed, more with pleasure than its opposite. "It was a Sunday. She was standing backstage waiting to go on, and I was fiddling with a balky amp and a drunken drummer, and we got to talking. I must have been less strung out than normal, because when I asked her to go out for a drink after the show, she said she would. It turned out we didn't live that far from each other—patronized the same grocery and, all that—and we started dating."

"Nice."

He met my look. "She saved my life, is what it came down to. Clarissa's the one who realized the only way I could survive with all the Vietnam baggage I was carrying was to keep doing what had kept me sane in Nam—keeping people alive. Literally, she meant: being the first one on the scene, the one who stops the bleeding and reduces the fracture and treats the shock and stuffs the guts back where they came from so someone somewhere else can figure out a way to make it permanent. And she was right. Medicine— emergency medicine, *street* medicine—gave me the kind of focus I needed to keep the compromises I'd made in the war from eating away at everything I believed about the world and about myself. She was right on, was dear Clarissa; I'll owe her for that forever."

Tom's lips wrinkled into a wry grin. "Of course, in her view the EMT phase was temporary. After we got married, she decided I could do better—med school, hospital administration, osteopathic college, *something*. She still brings it up; her ambitions are not solely egocentric." His smile turned charitable. "Clarissa thinks anything's possible if you make up your mind to do it. I, on the other hand, think all of us are pretty much etched in stone. I mean, if *est* or TM really worked, no one would have ever heard of Joseph Campbell or this Bradshaw character, right? So while I stumble around uncertain about everything from the implications of the budget deficit to the safety of irradiated food, Clarissa has made up her mind about virtually everything. And right now she thinks her mind is telling her that she's in love with another man."

Tom banged his snifter on the bar so hard I was afraid it would shatter in his palm. When it didn't, I went back to worrying that his soul was about to do the same.

When he'd wiped the spill and drained the dregs and signaled for another round, Tom looked at me and shrugged. "I love her, Marsh. I mean, we've never talked about this stuff before, but the main thing about me is, *I love my wife*. I want to be with her every minute. I don't come to Guido's to get *away* from her, like a lot of these guys; I come to get away from being home alone without her. It *kills* me that she sings her heart out for a bunch of drunken strangers six nights a week. I should be used to it by now, I know. But

I'm not. I guess I never will be. Which I suppose is part of the problem."

Guido brought another brandy. Tom sniffed and sipped. For a moment, I was sure he was going to cry.

"We've had a good marriage, you know? I mean, it's weird—she works nights, I work days—so we're not together that often, but when we are, it's great. The sex, the talk, the fun—everything. We've had problems, sure—money's tight, she wants a kid and I don't, I want to move to the country but she still likes the city, I want her to cut back her schedule but she says she's got to give it all she has while she still has her pipes. But we talk it through, and compromise, and it works out. Most of the time. How many great marriages do you know of, Marsh? Ever?"

I thought about it. Harry and Ruthie Spring. The Kottles, maybe. And ... "Three or four," I said optimistically.

"Well, we were one of them. Till *he* came along."

"So who is this monster?"

Tom sighed. "Richard Sands."

I squinted to get him into better focus. "*The* Richard Sands?"

"That's the one."

"*He's* the guy who's after your wife?"

"Yep."

"Why?"

Tom shrugged. "Because he loves her, supposedly. Because he was smitten the first time he heard her sing." His lip twisted sardonically. "'Because he needs her to make sense of his life.' And I quote."

I raised a brow. "You've talked to him about it?"

Tom shook his head. "Clarissa reports in. It's not like she's sneaking around behind my back—she tells me everything they do. They've got it down to a routine—he calls for her at the hotel after the second show, then spirits her away to his private club, where he uses his wiles to seduce her away from me till she's had her fill and asks him to take her home, where she climbs into the bed I've just vacated and gets her beauty sleep. Twelve hours later, the merry-go-round starts up again. And it's driving me fucking crazy."

"How long has this been going on?"

"Six months. That I know of. You ever see him on TV?"

I nodded.

"What did you think?"

"Lots of brass, lots of ego. Lots of money, lots of guts."

"A man who gets what he wants, in other words."

I nodded before I considered what it meant.

"Well," Tom said miserably, "what he wants is my wife, goddammit. So how am I going to stop him?"

Chapter
3

Although I both hoped and suspected Tom was exaggerating his problems, it was easy to understand the panic underlying his concern: His rival for his wife's affections was no ordinary swain. Richard Sands was a true tycoon, a corporate raider, a man who had used the relaxation of the rules and the buccaneer morality fostered by the Reagan administration, along with the brass and bravado that came to him naturally, to threaten, coerce, intimidate, and ultimately invade and occupy a series of corporate boardrooms up and down the West Coast. His real and threatened assaults on undervalued companies and overly complacent managements had yielded a fortune that placed him well up the *Forbes* listing of the world's richest men and made Sands the stuff of envy or outrage, depending on whom you talked to.

Sands wasn't a publicity hound like Trump or an obsessed crusader like Lorenzo; he was more a mystery man like Lungren or Buffett. Not much of his story was known, at least to me, but I did know Sands' rise was hardly rags to riches—his father had owned a small but lucrative business that catered primarily to the market for snack foods. Sands had attended Stanford and the Wharton School, then spent some years in Europe running the Hamburg branch of the family company, the Germans apparently possessing an unquenchable affinity for the charms of beer nuts and popcorn. But the snack trade soon became too tame for young Richard, and he set out after bigger game.

His initial success was at the form of legalized extortion known as greenmail. In the early eighties, Sands used a portion of the family fortune to accumulate stock in a company that specialized in updated versions of Murphy beds and convertible sofas. Two months later, he came away with $12 million in greenmail when the company bought out his position at a premium in order to prevent Sands from taking control of the board.

With the profits and publicity from that transaction, Sands was on his way. Two more greenmail forays yielded similar returns, along with a blip of adverse publicity when the founder of a target company killed himself rather than see Sands dismantle his dream. Casting about for bigger game, Sands hooked up with a protégé of Michael Milken's, and the two of them used Sands' brief but impressive record to persuade a host of mutual-fund managers and go-go S&L executives, whose jobs depended on achieving record levels of short-term performance regardless of long-term risk, to buy more than a billion dollars' worth of 16 percent junk bonds that constituted little more than a war chest for the raids of Richard Sands. Armed and eager, Richard Sands went hunting.

When greenmail became too outrageous even for the pirates of the eighties, Sands made the switch to LBOs. In a series of lightning moves, many involving established West Coast businesses, Sands helped managements take their companies private by buying up the stock at a price that was more than market but less than book value—advancing management's interests over those of the shareholders they were sworn to serve, in other words. Once the deal was done, Sands would aid the new owners in selling off enough of the company's assets to satisfy both the debt obligations incurred in financing the buy-back and the enormous fees that Sands and his battery of lawyers and accountants deemed their due for alerting management to the opportunity and arranging the funds to finance it. It took only a few years of such maneuverings to boost Sands' personal worth above eight figures and his reputation into the stuff of legend.

Sands wasn't stupid, obviously; he wasn't even crooked by the definitions most recently at work in the world. He'd played by rules that made millionaires out of twenty-five-year-old investment bankers and billionaires out of people like Boesky and Milken for doing nothing more valuable than persuading the government that it was foolish to follow a lot of Depression-era notions about antitrust and insider trading and fair disclosure and due diligence, let alone notions a lot older than those, notions of the sort you can find in the Bible if you consult passages other than the ones read on TV by slick-haired preachers who see the Good Book as a come-on rather than a code of conduct.

As far as I knew, Sands had never been indicted or convicted or even criticized very much, certainly not by the newspapers and politicians who operated within the generous ambit of Sands' corporate headquarters, a long, low slab of slate and cedar that lay along a reclaimed strip of land on the edge of San Francisco Bay directly east of the hill on which I lived. Over the years, Sands and his bright white helicopter and his pearl-gray limousine and his silver and gold Gulfstream had become as familiar to San Franciscans as the Golden Gate and, as Sands swept off in search of yet another corporate coonskin to hang on his well-hung wall, apparently inspired the same degree of awe.

Richard Sands was a San Francisco titan. Now that he'd conquered most of the Western world, what he apparently wanted next was the wife of the morose young man seated across from me, whose tears had finally begun to flow.

I patted the back of his hand, which lay on the bar between us, as helpless as a fish out of water. "Hey. It's not that bad. She's still *with* you, isn't she?"

Tom Crandall blinked at the tears, but the effort was ineffective. When he swiped at them with his palm, the streak across his cheek was made metallic by the reflection of the bar lights. "You know where I was this afternoon?" he managed after a minute.

"Where?"

"Down in the Tenderloin, helping my partner pull some poor bastard out of a fleabag on Eddy Street, then rushing him to S.F. General even though I knew he had AIDS and that whatever opportunistic infection had laid claim to him was so advanced that even if he was alive when we got him there he wouldn't be for long."

"Rough."

"Sure—there's lots of rough out there these days. AIDS is as bad a way to die as there is. But that's not the point at the moment. The point is, while I was doing business on Eddy Street, guess where my beloved Clarissa was?"

"Where?"

"Los Angeles." His grin turned sly, even close to evil. "Mr. Sands flew her there. For *lunch*."

"You're kidding."

"I wish. The occasion was the grand opening of some place in Malibu owned by a bunch of talent agents and movie stars. She says it could be a great boost for her if she fits in with the Colony swells. That's what they call Malibu—the Colony. Isn't that interesting? Do you suppose it's anything like a *leper* colony? And isn't it thrilling that the brilliant Mr. Sands has taken such an interest in my wife's career?"

The tortured ripple in Tom's voice caused several of the faces at the bar to turn our way, which in itself was saying something—one night a guy in the front room got stabbed in the throat by his wife, who was in turn punched in the face by his mistress, and no one in Guido's moved an inch.

I tried to be as comforting as I could. "Maybe that's all it is, did you ever think of that? Maybe Sands is just trying to get Clarissa a break in the business."

Tom's voice fell to a funereal pitch, albeit an Irish funeral. "You're like Chamberlain at Munich; you don't quite grasp the dimensions of the problem. Sands has *proposed* to her. Get it? He doesn't just want to sleep with her, or squire her around to the chichi watering holes, or turn her into his private plaything; he wants to make her his wife. "

"I thought he already had a wife."

"He does; apparently, like me, she's excess baggage. Either that or he's going to take them both to Utah and set up shop with the Mormons. Howard Hughes was big on Mormons, you know. Maybe it's a fetish with rich people."

I laughed. "You've got one thing going for you, at least—Clarissa's not eligible for marriage at the moment."

Tom waved at the suggestion. "Sands has that covered. He'll choreograph the whole thing—divorce on demand, all expenses paid; lawyers provided by him, one for each; a financial settlement that will be eminently fair to the miserable wretch she's married to—all very civilized and mature. Hell, I even come out of it with a profit, which would make marriage the only decent investment I ever made. In the meantime, he's shedding his spouse as well, so they're cleared for nuptial number two. After an appropriate period of recuperation and regret, of course."

I let Tom's bitterness swirl for a while, hoping the air would absorb or at least dilute it. But from the expression on his face and the clench to his fists, I could see his anger still fed on itself, and silence was an appetizer.

I spoke hurriedly, without thinking where I was going, which turned out to be a mistake. "It could be just talk, Tom. Maybe Sands thinks he has to talk marriage to get her to . . ."

"What? Let him into her pants?" Tom's lip twitched meanly. "I *told* you, he won't be *satisfied* with that. He wants to make it legal—hell, he's already got the ring. Five carats, I understand; formerly on the finger of Barbara Hutton."

I was amazed in spite of myself. "She's already wearing his ring?"

Tom shook his head. "Not yet. But it's there when she wants it."

"Clarissa's told you all this?"

"Are you kidding? Every night she comes home with a new chapter; she makes it sound like 'Héloise and Abélard Hit Hillsborough.' Last week he told her he'd buy her any house between San Diego and Seattle. If she wanted one that wasn't on the market, he'd do what it took to see that it was."

"That's just talk—rich guy bragging about his money. I don't think they can help it."

"Yeah? What about this? He says he's going to buy her a club of her very own. Clarissa's, featuring the vocal stylings of Clarissa Crandall. And that's not all. Seems that among his holdings is a small record label in L.A. that specializes in reissues of old standards—right up her alley. So he'll not only give her a venue, he'll make her immortal as well. Now how the fuck do I compete with that?"

His voice rose to the edge of hysteria. I said the only thing I could think of. "If she loves you, the rest of it won't matter."

Tom closed his eyes. "Come on, Marsh. Live in the real world. Love is sloppy sentimentality, an immature indulgence. You can't let it stand in the way of the good life."

"I doubt very much that Clarissa's that kind of woman. If she was, you wouldn't have married her."

In the face of my implicit praise, Tom's ire seemed to cool a tad. When he spoke, it was a hum of reminiscence. "She used to love me. A lot, I think, hard though that may be to believe. Then *this* bozo came along. He turned her head, Marsh; there's no getting around it." Tom blinked and indulged in rhetoric. "And who can blame her? No one in their right *mind* would choose a life with me compared to what Sands is offering."

"She picked a life with you before."

"But that was before she had a chance like this one. Look. I know it's not just his money she's after—she's not interested in Cadillacs or castles on the Rhine—it's what his money can do for her."

"Like what?"

Tom closed his eyes. "When we were young, we both had these ideals. I was going to start a free clinic. Clarissa was going to be a star and give lots of benefit concerts for the poor. All very liberal and altruistic. Except it didn't happen that way, for either of us; we've had to struggle just to keep our heads above water. But we've been working it out, at least I thought we were. Lowering our sights, coming to grips with what and who we are. It's been bumpy—

Clarissa is afraid her voice will go before she gets her best work on record, and then there's the age-old problem of what to do with me. But we were okay, or so I thought, because our marriage was the most important thing in our lives. But now it's not. Not for her, at least. How *could* it be, for her to *hurt* me this way?"

"What does Clarissa say about it?"

"She says she doesn't know what she wants anymore, she only knows she needs to find out who she is."

"A lot of women her age feel like that these days."

"But that's the *point*. Sands won't let her find herself; he'll gobble her up before she has time to look. Or worse, convince her that what she's looking for is him." Tom swallowed and almost choked. "I thought she *already* knew who she was, you know? I thought she was my wife."

Tom fought for self-control as I searched for some consolation to send his way. "She's not asking for a divorce, is she? She's just saying she's not sure."

Tom shrugged. "And in the meantime, Sands is hitting her with everything he's got. He's says he's tired of the rat race, wants to establish a foundation that will fund a medical center for homeless people and—here's a nice touch—that I can be the chief of emergency services, or some sort of consultant if regulations say the chief has to be an M.D."

I couldn't help smiling at the man's gall, and Tom couldn't help being incensed by it.

"The guy is telling Clarissa she's more important to him than anything he has, which the last I read came to almost fifty million." He rubbed his face so hard I thought he was going to draw blood. "You've got to help me put a stop to it, Marsh."

I sighed and shook my head. "You ever see the movie *Roger and Me*?"

Tom shook his head.

"It's a documentary by a guy named Moore. He—"

Tom scowled, angry at me for the first time ever. "I'm not in the mood to talk *movies*, for God's sake."

I persevered. "This guy Moore set out to talk to Roger Smith, the president of General Motors, about why GM was shutting down the auto-assembly plants in Flint, Michigan, and destroying the town. The movie was about all the tricks Moore came up with to get to talk to Smith."

"So how did he manage it?"

"He didn't. And I'd have about as much luck getting to see Richard Sands as Moore did getting to see the head of GM. Besides, I don't think Sands is your problem; I think *Clarissa*'s your problem."

He shook his head. "She can't help what she's doing. He's hypnotized her."

"But if he's really in love with her, there's no way you or I or anyone can stop him. I mean, it's not like you can buy him off. I don't know what I could do to help, even if I wanted to."

Tom looked at me bleakly. "Scare him, maybe? Threaten to sue?"

"I already told you, criminal conversation isn't a civil offense anymore, and he's got lawyers who would see through any other ploy in a minute. Plus, if you filed suit, the whole thing would come out in public, and the press would make it seem like the slimiest thing since Liz and Dick or Madonna and whatever the guy's name was she married for a minute. It's hard enough when these things are worked out in private; I don't think you *or* your marriage would have a chance if it was being played out in the papers every day."

Tom looked around the room, as though an idea might float by on a cloud of smoke. "Maybe you could, like, threaten him? Physically. Not really, of course. Just enough to—"

"Come on, Tom—guys like that have bodyguards three deep. I'd end up in the hospital or in jail, and Sands would step up his campaign even more."

"So what *can* I do?"

"Maybe you can challenge him to a duel," I said, but when Tom seemed to be considering the idea, I tried to find an answer. "The only thing I can think of is for you to talk to Clarissa and get her to see that this guy's no good for her. Even I know that the wife of a man like that gets swallowed up in his wake. After a month with him, she really won't know who she is."

"I've already tried to get her to see it that way. All she says is that she's been through so much pain trying and failing to make *me* happy, she's not sure of anything except she doesn't want to keep doing *that*."

"It sounds to me like she's got problems that don't have anything to do with you *or* Sands."

"Of course she does. She's getting old, Marsh—she's almost forty. A middle-aged torch singer is pretty much an oxymoron, you know."

"Maybe she should get into something else."

"She's been talking about it—teaching, songwriting, maybe even social work. The problem is, she's not considering them because she wants to, but because she's afraid she'll *have* to. If she marries Sands, she won't have to consider them at all."

There wasn't anything for me to add, so I let Tom work with it by himself for a while.

"I actually feel sorry for her," he said after a moment, "in spite of everything she's done. Show business is an awful life. She's out there all alone, seldom has a job that lasts longer than six weeks, has to compete with the new talent that comes along every year. She doesn't have much to show for her years in the business—no retirement plan, no record contract, no long-term bookings—and *I'm* certainly no security blanket. She's run to Sands because she thinks money will eliminate her problems, but she's wrong. Clarissa isn't the type of woman who can be happy as someone's consort, but by the time she realizes it, it'll be too late. For us, at least. I mean, I love her, but there are things I can't accept, you know? Some things a man has to hang on to or he can't call himself a man."

Tom convulsed silently, the brandy still his only lifesaver. "There's one thing I better mention," I said after he had control of himself. "I don't do domestic work. Haven't for years. I've turned down a lot of friends who wanted me to help them through a marital crisis, so I can't very well—"

"This isn't a *domestic* case, this is a *murder* case."

Oddly enough, I believed Tom saw it just that way. He had so little sustenance from the sources most men look to—money, power, fame—he was dependent on his marriage for the nutrients to keep him going. Tom had married above himself, he had always told me, an assessment that carried with it the fear that someday Clarissa would realize the fact and rectify the situation.

I was resisting the urge to back away from my refusal to get involved when Tom spoke up, all of a sudden endlessly calm and eminently reasonable. "I understand your position, Marsh. And I know there's really nothing you can do. I just needed someone to talk to about it." He shoved the snifter down the bar and looked around, a beatific smile elongating his lips. "I've enjoyed it here. You . . . Guido . . . the others."

As he tossed some money on the bar, I gave him as much solace as I could find. "If you think of something concrete I could do to help," I said, "or if you need to talk some more, you know I'd be happy to. Any time."

Tom responded with an eerie tranquillity. "Thanks, Marsh. For everything."

"Let me know how it works out."

"Sure."

"If I don't hear from you in a couple of weeks, I'm going to come see how you're getting along."

"Fine."

"Well, good luck."

He managed a brief grin. "I think I used up my allotment back in Vietnam."

Chapter
4

I spent the next several days mired in a depression triggered by my conversation with Tom Crandall. Part of my mood was generated by sympathy—Tom was as miserable as anyone I'd ever seen outside the walls of an institution, even though I'm in a business that traffics in misery, and I couldn't conceive of a scenario in which he would deserve what was apparently being done to him. Another part was frustration—Tom had come to me for help, had literally begged me for it although begging was as foreign to his nature as sadism, and for the life of me I couldn't think of anything I could do to alter the fact that his wife was evidently being poached from under his nose. But most of my problem was self-centered. Tom's troubles laid claim to my thoughts less because of what they said about Tom than because of what they said about me.

My failure to come up with a battle plan for Tom to employ in his war with Richard Sands reignited a malaise that's been with me off and on for several years. Charley Sleet calls it my midlife crisis, and because Charley is Charley and is therefore immune to the frailties of mortal men, he laughs whenever I say something that implies I'm undergoing some sort of inner reassessment. Charley may be right—the condition may be laughable and I may be just another slice of a syndrome—but that doesn't mean the malady isn't real.

For a long time, I tended to believe my state was purely psychological and thus susceptible to self-help. Analyze the problem, concoct a solution, put theory into practice: If results aren't immediate, the bookshelves are full of how-to's. But self-help hasn't worked, and neither has self-pity, and lately I've begun to think I'm wrong—clinical depression has been in the news a lot of late, along with drugs like Prozac that are supposed to render affective disorders obsolete by altering the neurotransmitters in kind and number or some such biochemical intrusion. Accounts like William Styron's, of battles with the storms of desolation, are increasingly bruited about, not always with the eloquence of Styron to be sure, but moving nonetheless. If pressed, I could come up with a pedestrian account of my own, featuring waves of worthlessness that make every episode in my past seem ignoble and inept, days of lethargy when nothing or no one seems worth the slightest effort, tremors of self-loathing that make suicide seem not only attractive but obligatory.

On the worst days, it occurs to me that I should seek psychiatric help. The problem is, to a self-sufficient soul like me, such a step is an admission of failure, further proof of an inadequacy with which I'm already overburdened. So I've held off, in the hope that my mood would improve on its own, that my depressions will vanish like the sniffles, that I won't have to change the recipe that makes me what I am. But like the track of a bad cold, my mood has spread to my chest, and now both my head and my heart are ailing.

Of course, Charley's right—what I've been feeling isn't unique. Many people my age, maybe most, undertake a midpoint readjustment. I know half a dozen marriages that are foundering after more than twenty years because one or both of the partners has become terrified, in the wake of an empty nest or a stalled career or the unsightly droop of age, that the arrangement that got them where they are is no longer sufficient to carry them across the final third of their lives. And I know several single people who have resorted to drugs or debauchery for much the same reason.

At such a point, people usually decide to do something before it's too late, and the first thing they do, the women at least, is talk to someone about it. Mostly they talk to other women, but because I've never married I'm occasionally regarded as lacking a vested interest in the institution, so some women decide to talk to me. My job has taught me how to listen, and I try my best to be of aid, but the dynamic of marriage is so different from my own unilateral existence, and the remedy for a faulty one so drastic, that I usually advise them to stick with it, talk it out and see it through; whatever you do don't jump ship, because the waters in Singles Land are not smooth sailing. In other words, I'm about as much help to these women as I was to Tom Crandall.

They're not much help to me, either, although they often want to be. It's not their fault—except for occasional grumblings to Charley Sleet or Tom, I seldom go public with my troubles. Like most men, I avoid confession whenever possible, for fear my weaknesses will be used against me and because I sense that, since I'm my own boss and am beset by no obvious horrors and lead a periodically dramatic life, some people feel I've got an enviable existence already and am being excessively grasping or inexcusably self-indulgent to suggest things could be better for me than they are.

But as anyone in middle age knows, it's not that simple: *Any* life can seem trivial to the person who lives it, and for months my thoughts have swirled with elemental inquiries—would I be more productive if I swallowed my pride and went back to being a lawyer; more complete if I asked my friend Betty to marry me even though we both profess to be happy with things the way they are; more significant if I wrote a book, built a boat, learned to speak Spanish; more useful if I joined the Peace Corps or volunteered at St. Anthony's or went to work for Legal Aid.

The answer to such questions depends on as many variables as does staying satisfactorily sober, however, so mostly I make a choice at random, work with it awhile, then decide I wouldn't live that life any better than I was living this one. In any event, the principles of inertia make such changes either unlikely or a long way off. For the moment, my best hope for a boost in morale seemed to be to abjure my rules about avoiding domestic disputes and make like the cavalry and ride over the hill and try to rescue one Tom Crandall.

Although Tom and I hadn't seen each other since our night at Guido's, he had kept me apprised of his state of mind, which seemed to be deteriorating rapidly. In a series of phone calls to my home and office—none lasting over twenty seconds, few involving any remark by me other than the opening salutation—Tom peppered me with observations.

The first call, in its entirety, went something like this:

"Hello?"

"He's been sending her love letters. How do I know? She reads me excerpts. She says she has a right to a private life, to have friends of her own, both women and men, to keep what she says and does with them a personal matter. Can she possibly be right? Can a marriage survive such secrets?"

"I imagine it can if both people want it to."

"How would you know?"

And he was right. How *would* I know? As I said, Tom Crandall was smart. Smart enough to wound a friend; smart enough to wound a wife.

There were other calls as well, hundreds it seemed, though there were probably fewer than a dozen. I came to regard them the way I regarded the briefings of generals Kelly and Neal—as reports from a war in which I was thankfully not a combatant.

Sometimes Tom spoke to me directly, but more often he left terse essays on my answering machine that invariably deposited a bit of Tom's pain for me to sprinkle atop the less-focused version of my own. For example:

"She lectures me on my attitudes. She says I worship women but don't respect them. She calls me a Victorian— she says I think women are weak and overemotional and incapable of true accomplishment. This from someone who demonstrates her own respect for her sex by playing footsie with another woman's husband."

And,

"*Do you think it's some kind of test? If so, what am I supposed to study? Where is the examination held? And who the hell is grading it?*"

And,

"*I asked her to tell me what's gone wrong with our marriage. She said we should spend more time communicating. Fine so far. But it's clear the exclusive subject of discussion is to be what's wrong with Tom.*"

And,

"*I'm thinking of tapping my own phone. Is it legal? How much would it cost for a gizmo that would make a record of everything she says to him? Can you get a rate on that kind of equipment for me? What can she do if she finds out?*"

And,

"*She has total recall of our years together. Of course what she recalls is less a marriage than a feudal system.*"

And,

"*I'm sorry I've made her do this, I really am.*"

And,

"*Did you ever study Chaucer? Do you recall the term 'cuckold'? Do you remember what a loathsome creature it evoked? Did you ever think you'd become one?*"

And,

"*How much longer do you suppose I can continue to believe her when she tells me they're just friends? Of course, their sexual shenanigans aren't pertinent, really. I'd much rather she was sharing her body than her mind with him.*"

And,

"*Are men as awful as women say? Are we, Marsh? Are we?*"

And, most recently and most distressingly,

"*I was in the army, you know. I spent nine months attached to Special Forces: nine months in the highlands with the most efficient killers this country could produce. I know a man who would waste Richard Sands for fifty bucks, no questions asked, just to show it could be done. In fact, he'd probably do it gratis.*"

At this point, I decided steps had to be taken. Tom's attitude seemed to be lurching from suicidal to homicidal, and though I didn't think he was capable of either step, I couldn't sit by and let it work itself out. After listening to Tom's most recent message, I considered my options for the rest of the evening, and in the morning I called a shrink.

Max Rosenfall is a forensic psychiatrist, on call to the top criminal-defense attorneys in town, a reliable reinforcement for the mentally ill in everything from insanity pleas to commitment proceedings. Although there were a lot of his ilk around, Max was one of the few I respected: Max wasn't a hired gun who parroted the pose of whoever was paying the bills; Max said what he believed, which was probably why juries invariably went along with his diagnoses and prognoses, outlandish though they often were—once Max convinced a jury that a young man had strangled his mother because he'd been driven temporarily insane by a video game. Even more surprisingly, Max had been known to say no to a fat fee if he thought the defendant was faking his symptoms or the family's reasons for putting Aunt Mabel in the nuthouse were more avaricious than compassionate. Unfortunately, after I'd reminded him of the instance when we'd worked for the same lawyer on the same case, then outlined Tom's situation for him, no is exactly what he said to me.

"I don't see that much pathology here, Marsh. Not unless you take this hit-man thing seriously, and even then, well, it's not an unnatural reaction, is it? The poor guy's got a problem—he's in love with a woman who is paying him back in spades for the dirt she feels he's done her. An all too common situation, sad to say, but one for which my particular branch of witchcraft has little to offer of immediate efficacy except to advise him to uncouple from her and take some steps to feel better about himself."

"This is the kind of situation that drove Othello mad, doctor. And he was only imagining things."

Max laughed. "True enough. So you should keep track of your friend to make sure he isn't slipping over the edge."

"There's nothing you can do?"

"Of course there is. I can do what you've been doing, which is to listen to his tale of woe, give him the chance to publicize his pain and his betrayal, then offer sympathy and concern and suggest some steps he can take to improve his self-regard. The difference is, I'd have to charge him two hundred dollars an hour and I'm not at all sure I could achieve much more than you already have or could if you tune back into him. Maybe you should put him in touch with a family therapist, set up an appointment that would preferably include his wife. It'll be cheaper, and probably more effective than the kind of prolonged analysis I deal in. But don't quote me on that or I'll be drummed out of the profession."

I thanked Max for his time and asked if there were any therapists he could recommend. He gave me three names. I called two of them, compared their fees and procedures, and prepared my pitch to Tom. I even made some notes, clichés mostly, phrases like "getting the lines of communication reopened" and "coming to grips with the underlying trauma," and pap like that. Then, when I envisioned the look on Tom's face when I began to read from them, I threw the notes away.

In any event, my preparations were all for naught. The message from Tom that was on my answering machine when I returned from Dr. Rosenfall's was shrill and histrionic:

"I was right—there's more to this than I thought. It's labyrinthine, Marsh; the ramifications are fiendishly complex. What it amounts to it is that Richard Sands is evil incarnate; I'm following a trail of blood that includes my own brother's. Prepare to be amazed."

I called Tom several times during the rest of the day and the day after that but never managed to reach him. After a couple of fretful nights, I stumbled out of bed and turned to the morning paper for diversion. In a two-inch filler at the bottom of page 9 and a more lengthy obituary set out in the second section, the *Chronicle* informed me and the rest of its readership that my friend Tom Crandall was dead.

Chapter
5

One of the more telling signs of age is that you scan the obituaries more closely than you scan the box scores. All too frequently I find a name that saddens me, in the case of a public figure, or pains me, in the increasingly common instance when the deceased is someone I know. Eight days after our night at Guido's and fourteen hours after the last time I heard his voice, I found my friend Tom—Thomas Clarence Crandall in the heading above the obit—a man the *Chronicle* labeled simply: Hero.

And hero he had been, not once but twice. The first instance occurred in the war, during a brief but terrible engagement that had earned Tom two Purple Hearts and a Silver Star for giving medical aid to a fire team that had been ambushed. Phrased in the argot of the citation, Specialist Crandall, despite many adversities and without regard for his personal safety, had crossed a minefield under hostile fire from a determined and aggressive enemy, located and administered to the wounded, become twice wounded himself, and continued to deliver medical aid and assistance until reinforcements had interdicted the ambushers and the dead and wounded had been transported to the rear. Specialist Crandall's actions were in keeping with the highest traditions of the service and contributed materially to the success of his unit's mission as well as to the mission of the forces of freedom in the Republic of Vietnam.

And that was the least of it, because Tom Crandall's heroism in war had paled before his valor in peacetime. This time the peril had been not man but nature—in the night and day following the earthquake of October 1989, for a period of more than forty hours, Tom and his partner had been hip-deep in the rubble of the Marina District, struggling to free people from structures that had collapsed as the ground contorted and convulsed beneath them.

Tom hadn't been able to hide his heroism—TV had caught his act. Again and again, as captured in the hand-held tremble of a Channel 4 camera, Tom had disappeared into a mound of mortar and brick and timber, passing debris back to his partner as he dug his way toward a plea for help that originated within the wreckage, risking further collapse of the building and the explosion of a ruptured gas main and any number of other calamities foremost in everyone's mind but Tom's.

He'd found one dead and freed four others over that period, accomplishing rescues few others would have considered. It was magnificent, to put it mildly—a physician who lived in one of the houses and had been on the scene the entire time was quoted as calling Tom Crandall the bravest man he'd ever seen. In contrast, the only comment I'd ever heard Tom utter about the entire affair was an expression of sorrow that he'd been too slow to save the one who died.

It wasn't surprising that Tom had told me almost nothing about any of this, not even his Silver Star. Nor that, although invariably reserved and unprepossessing, Tom was a certified hero. In my experience, such beings are often people who are not inherently brave—far from it—but are simply inherently dutiful. Whether the inclination is grounded in genetic encoding or merely a proper upbringing—in Sunday school or Batman comics or merely the family tree—I doubt anyone knows. Luckily for the rest of us, the filter we know as civilization has somehow allowed a few such people to survive.

As I read through the obituary, I was pleased that Tom was being duly honored for his exploits, but the feeling dimmed when I turned to the news article and read the circumstances of his death. Tom's body had been found in the Tenderloin, in an abandoned airline bus terminal at the corner of Taylor and Ellis. Death had occurred some time Thursday night, but the body hadn't been discovered until the next day. Since his job was to aid victims of disease and violence, and since there were more such victims per square inch in that area of the city than any other, Tom's presence in the Tenderloin was not surprising. Except Tom had apparently been alone when he died, not on call with the ambulance service, and the estimated time of death— 1:00 A.M.—was not his normal duty hour.

Stranger yet, the article initially implied that Tom had died from a mugging—his body was found in a place where such assaults had become de rigueur since the day hard drugs hit town—but in the final paragraph the police were quoted as saying that although a weapon had been found at the scene, foul play was not indicated. The *Chron* had trotted out, in other words, its usual euphemism for suicide.

Perhaps most surprising of all was that someone at the *Chronicle* had taken the trouble to dig up so many details about Tom's life and seen to it that they appeared on the obit page with a prominence more common to society mavens and movie stars. Among other things, as I began to wonder what had really happened to my friend, I resolved to find out who it was.

The obit said the funeral service would be held the next day, at a chapel across the bay in Danville where Tom's mother still resided. I detest funerals as much as anyone, but I decided to go nonetheless. In his thirst for a more thorough knowledge of his world and his insistence on a moral center to his life, Tom Crandall had been a hero to me as well as to the world at large, and fallen heroes deserve tribute. Plus, I had to admit, I wanted to see if his wife would show up for the services, and whether if she did she would arrive on the arm of the legendary

Richard Sands. In the meantime, I put in a call to Charley Sleet, to get a line on Tom's death from the police perspective, but Charley was where he always is—temporarily out of touch.

Chapter
6

The day was far too real for a funeral, the drought-driven heat of the San Ramon Valley too evocative of purgatory to give comfort to saints or sinners. After pulling into the parking lot next to the chapel in the north end of Danville, I sweltered in the irregular heartbeats of the Buick's idling engine as I watched the temperature gauge rise inexorably toward the red, an arc similar to the one I see every time I step on a scale.

Three minutes and a well-soaked collar later, I gave in to my compunctions and decided to forego the chapel service in favor of paying my respects at the gravesite, if the radiator didn't blow its top before I got there. In the meantime, I enjoyed the prelude that wafted my way through the heavy oaken doors of the small brick building, courtesy of the chapel organ. As a somber throng made its way from the parking area to the chapel entrance, I took an unobtrusive inventory.

There were more mourners than I expected. Although he had come across as a virtual recluse, Tom Crandall had obviously made a bigger dent in the world than he let on or perhaps was aware of. I couldn't know for sure, of course, but as I watched the crowd file dolefully into the chapel, I guessed it included several friends of his mother's, a couple of former teachers now retired, perhaps a former coach or commanding officer, probably an old girlfriend, and a couple of fellow grunts who, like Tom, had found peacetime more perilous than its opposite. I also spotted a few poor souls who knew only that there was a funeral that day and had decided to drop by and see if either the deceased or the mourners would generate some gossip. Although I was alert for the rumpled getup and boozy blear of an obit writer at the *Chronicle,* I didn't spot a candidate.

At ten minutes past two, an ambulance roared up, muffler bleating, siren off. As the disc brakes squeezed it to a noisy halt, the guy riding shotgun hopped out, smoothed the wrinkles out of his blue uniform with one hand and unkinked his tight black curls with the other, then pulled a stethoscope from his pocket and tossed it onto the seat he'd vacated. After a quick word with the driver, he dashed inside the chapel without bothering to close the door. His partner stayed behind, slumped behind the wheel, his only concession to the occasion the effort to close his eyes.

The ambulance service was Atlas, based in San Francisco, which meant the medic who'd hurried inside the chapel must have been Tom's partner. I remembered his name was Tony. I knew that he and Tom had been through a lot together, and that Tom envied Tony both his flagrant way with women and his seamless nonchalance in the face of danger and emergency.

I was about to ape the ambulance driver and catch some rest myself when a pickup truck rumbled to a stop in front of the chapel door. Battered and bruised, its paint worn to the color of mud, well past its useful life, it was precisely the kind of vehicle Tom would have driven to show his contempt for society's submission to the tyranny of internal combustion. But the man who emerged from the wayward Dodge wasn't anything like Tom, in aspect or in attitude.

Beefy in mass and autocratic in movement, with the set to his jaw and the glow in his eyes that complement the wrongheaded and the narrow-minded, the man marched into the chapel with less reverence than ferocity, intent on doing damage. When I tried to imagine a reason for his ferment or an object for his ire, I couldn't come up with an answer.

It was only after he had gone inside the chapel that I noticed a second person in the truck, so small her tight gray bun was barely visible above the seat back, so static she could have been a candidate for the last rites herself: Over the minutes the man was gone, her head never shifted a fraction. Only when the chapel door reopened and the man marched back to the truck and yanked open the passenger door did the gray head turn to watch. When it did, it confronted the tearful countenance of the woman the man had extracted from the chapel.

She was thirtysomething, plain going on frumpish, wearing a black frock that buttoned from hem to neck and flat black pumps worn at the heel. A gray ribbon around her neck supported a large gold cross and matched the one that drew back her straight black hair. Her eyes were wide and wounded by what had gone on between her and the man intent on shielding her from the fallout from the funeral.

As she approached the truck, the young woman looked back to the chapel for a final instant with what could pass for yearning, then hesitated as though she had decided to retrace her steps. But the man didn't give her a chance. He said something I couldn't hear, grabbed her arm and squeezed it, then tugged her toward the open door of the truck. The woman seemed to flinch, then resist, then yield to the greater force.

With just the briefest glance in the direction that included me, the young woman climbed grudgingly into the pickup. The gray-haired lady scooted to the center to give her room, the man slammed the door behind them hard enough to rattle the fenders, then climbed in the driver's side and sped away. The cloud he left behind was sufficiently toxic to make the ambulance driver open his eyes and wrinkle his nose and mutter an audible oath.

I was still trying to decipher the psychodrama I had just been privy to when the star of the show arrived. Her chariot was a long black limo I assumed had been dispatched by the mortician until I noticed the license plate—RS 2—and concluded her presence was courtesy of Richard Sands.

That didn't make me like her very much, and neither did the cut of her dress, which exposed enough cleavage to be more suitable for opening for Tony Bennett at the Venetian Room than watching them bury her husband.

Clarissa Crandall—tall, dark, large but far from hefty—got out of the limo, fluffed her cumulus cloud of hair, hitched her bodice to a more modest level across her breasts, smoothed the arc of a brow with the tip of an index finger, licked some shine onto her scarlet lips, and entered the chapel with the eagerness of a politician on his way to a press conference. Which left the limo driver, the ambulance guy, and me each trying to figure out who was who. In less than a minute, we decided we didn't care.

Twenty minutes later, the organ sounds returned, a peppy postlude this time, and ushered the mourners back to their vehicles. More than a few eyes were dabbed along the way, though none belonging to the widow, and several hands were clasped beneath words of condolence whispered to a stocky blue-haired lady who lingered in the chapel doorway, at once stoic and somber and sociable, each as the occasion demanded. I took her to be Tom's mother. When I looked for common features, I found them in the chin and mouth.

As unobtrusively as I could, I waylaid one of the objects of my interest—the medic, Tom's partner. He was movie-handsome and knew it, Neapolitan to the core. He was about to climb back in the ambulance when I caught up to him. "Can I talk to you a second?"

He frowned and looked at his watch. "What about?"

"Tom Crandall."

His black eyes measured me, to no clear conclusion. "What about him?"

"I was hoping you could tell me what he was doing on Taylor Street the night he died."

He shrugged without interest. "Tom got off on, like, your basic slime. You got an itch like that, you scratch it in the 'Loin." Tony wiped a drop of sweat from his temple and regarded me with an untroubled gaze. "Who are you? A cop?"

"A friend of Tom's."

"Name?"

"Tanner."

His eyes narrowed to the width of a scalpel. "The P.I.?"

"Right."

"Guido's."

"Right."

"Nice place, I guess. Me, I prefer Vesuvio or the Bohemian."

He started to say something else, but his partner pressed the horn. "Come on, Tony. We're AWOL, man."

"Put a patch on it, Harris." Tony looked back at me and rolled his eyes. "Fucking New Guy, gets diarrhea whenever we freewheel. Dispatch thinks we're chewing Chinese at Chan's." He climbed into the cab of the ambulance and slung the stethoscope over his shoulder. "I say what difference does it make? We don't tag and bag 'em, the city or Healthways will handle it. I mean, it's not like we're on commission, right? Not to mention it's Sunday."

"I'd like to talk to you some more about Tom when you have time. How can I get in touch with you?"

"Tony Milano, but in the book it's Anthony. Greenwich by the playground. Don't call me at work, 'cause if I'm at work, I'm in the rig, and they won't patch you through."

"Will you be home tonight?"

"Not if I'm lucky," he said, and smoothed his hair and rubbed his crotch. "And Tony Milano is as lucky as he needs to be."

The driver cracked his whip, and the rescue wagon roared away. I watched it go with the twinge I always get whenever I see someone doing a job I didn't have the nerve to do myself.

When I looked back toward the chapel, the cortege was already forming, Tom's casket in the hearse in front, his mother in the Chrysler that went second, the widow and her private limo next, the rest of us bringing up the rear. I hooked my Buick onto the end, hoping it wouldn't vapor-lock before we got there.

Ten minutes later, we snaked into a small cemetery nestled on a knoll beneath a glade of live oak and walnut trees just off the Danville Highway, not too far from Tor House, where Eugene O'Neill had lived for twenty years and written his best plays. By the time I crossed the creek and parked my car and hiked to the gravesite, the casket was in place atop the vault, and a flag had been draped over it. An honor guard stood at order arms, ready to fire a brief salute. I stood on the fringe of mourners and went into my customary trance while the minister did his thing.

Minutes later, the volley from the honor guard brought me out of it. As the lonely chord of taps echoed in the distance, the flag was folded and presented to the widow, who passed it to the mother without a word or glance, who clasped it to her heart. The honor guard returned to order arms, the preacher said a prayer, the casket was lowered toward its tomb. A young woman, presumably in hire to the mortuary, presented Clarissa Crandall with a snow-white rose. I'm not up on my interment protocol, but I think she was supposed to drop it in the grave. Instead, she looked at it as though it were a weed, then dropped it to the ground.

Moments later, the minister sent us on our way. Mine was down the hill toward Sands Limo Number Two, and I made sure I got there before the widow did.

"Mrs. Crandall," I said after she broke free of the knot of sympathizers who were plaguing her.

A brow arched. Her lips were as red as the stripes on her husband's flag. "Yes?"

"My name's Tanner. I was a friend of Tom's."

She looked at me the way my clients do on occasion, clients who regard private detectives as unsavory, even the ones who work for them. "Haven't we met?"

I nodded. "Guido's. About a year ago."

She twirled the golden lavaliere that frolicked between her breasts. "Ah, yes. My one and only descent into the abyss. Another shattered soul, Mr. Tanner?"

"I wouldn't call Tom's soul shattered, Mrs. Crandall. I'd call it overtaxed."

Her lips wrinkled like foil. "By me, I suppose."

I shrugged. "I wouldn't know."

"No, you wouldn't. Neither would his mother, and neither would the owners of the stares that were crawling all over me back there at that wretched chapel."

I let my gaze drop. "Maybe it's the outfit."

Her shrug made the outfit even more scandalous. "Sack-cloth and ashes would be preferable, I know, but I've got some stills to shoot this afternoon, and there isn't time to change." She duplicated my earlier glance. "You weren't exactly outfitted by Wilkes Bashford for the occasion."

I gripped my lapels and bowed. "Touché, Mrs. Crandall."

"It's Duncan now. I'll be using my maiden name for all occasions."

"Including wakes and second marriages."

She didn't know what that meant, and I wasn't sure myself. After she decided it didn't matter, she looked over my shoulder at the limo, to be sure it was ready to whisk her away from all this. "What can I do for you, Mr. Tanner? I have an appointment in the city in twenty minutes. Which means I can give you ten seconds."

"I was wondering what the authorities have told you about your husband's death."

"They've told me they're not sure what happened."

"Do they say when they'll know?"

She shook her head. "They don't seem very . . . agitated about it, however."

"They're hardly ever agitated about anything that happens in the Tenderloin. Did they do an autopsy?"

"I don't know. Why would they?"

I didn't have an answer I was ready to share with her. "Did Tom have a history of medical problems?"

"No."

"Had he had a physical lately?"

"I think they make them get one every year at the ambulance service."

"His was normal?"

"As far as I know. What are you suggesting, Mr. Tanner?"

"I'm suggesting the odds that he dropped dead in an abandoned bus terminal seem pretty long."

"But it happens."

"Yes, it does. So do muggings. So does suicide. I'm just finding it hard to believe that any of those things happened in *this* case."

Her eyes flared like an animal's near fire, and her lungs issued a hot burst of breath. "Well, you can scratch one item off your list—my husband was *not* suicidal."

I met her look. "I agree, as a matter of fact."

"Good. Is there anything else?"

"Did Tom have any reason to be wandering around the Tenderloin that night?"

She seemed irritated by the question. "Not that I know of."

I decided to irritate her some more. "Where were *you* the night he died, Mrs. Crandall?"

"At work. Not that it's any of your—"

"And where was your friend?"

She raised a brow. "Am I supposed to know who you're talking about?"

I gestured at the limo. "Mr. Sands."

"What difference does that . . . oh. I get it. You're implying Richard had something to do with Tom's death." Her look was scathing. "The short answer is, why would he bother? Mr. Sands has managed to get whatever he's wanted in this world without worrying his handsome head about my *husband*." She left it to me to decide whether Sands' trophies included her. "Now if you'll excuse me, I have to be beautiful for my photographer. And I suggest *you* find something to do besides drumming up business trying to make something sinister out of a tragic accident."

Clarissa Crandall twirled so rapidly her dress rose halfway up her thighs, then swooped into the limousine and disappeared behind a screen of black sheet metal and smoked window glass. I expected the limo to roar off toward the big, bad city, but a moment later a motor whined and the rear window rolled down.

Her expression was a stranger to the one she'd taken into the car. "There's something you should know, I think," she said quietly.

"What's that?"

"I loved my husband. I suppose you don't believe that, given what Tom has obviously told you about me. But I wanted you to know there's another side to his story."

"I'd like to hear it some time."

"Why?"

"It might help."

She looked beyond me, at the gravestones marching up the hill, including the ones decorated with Mylar balloons and plastic windmills, as though eternity were a frat party. "Help who? Help what?"

"Help me figure out what happened to Tom."

"What *difference* does it make?" She sighed and closed her eyes, weary in the lap of luxury. "Why are you bothering?"

"Because finding things out is the only thing I'm good at."

"That hardly seems enough."

"It is for me."

We regarded each other for a while, with a mix of sorrow and expectation. Then the window rolled up, and the limo was gone, and I was left behind in a quandary and a cloud of dust.

I looked around. Everyone else had gone except Tom's mother, who lingered near the grave as though she had it on good authority there would be a reprise of the Resurrection. In the hostile stare of a grave-digger who was slumped over the long handle of his shovel, impatient to get dust back to dust in a hurry, I strolled to her side. "Mrs. Crandall?"

The stout and tidy woman looked up at me, eyes buffed by sadness and memory. Her hands were clutching the flag to her breast; her mind was clutching at a miracle. "Yes?"

"My name is Tanner. I was a friend of your son's."

She blinked at the interruption and then at the intrusive sun. "I don't recognize you. Were you in Tom's class at San Ramon?"

I shook my head. "We were members of the same club, sort of."

"From the war, you mean?"

"No, just friends from the neighborhood. Over in the city. I saw Tom once or twice a week over the last few years."

She sighed. "Tom was a good boy."

"Yes, he was."

"The good die young, they say."

"I'm afraid this proves the rule."

Her eyes narrowed. "Was he happy at the end, do you think?"

"I'm not sure," I evaded.

When I didn't continue, she answered her own question. "I don't think he was," she declared firmly.

"Do you know what was wrong?"

She sighed. "The war, partly. Tom always worried about the war."

"Worried about what part of it, specifically?"

She looked toward a passing cloud. "Who can say? About whether he'd done right in going, I think; Tom always tried to do the right thing." She grimaced as though she'd felt a pain. "In my day, no one ever *doubted* wars were right. No one ever doubted anything. I suppose it's better Tom's way."

"Better—not easier."

She blinked away a tear.

"Was there anything else bothering him? Besides the war?"

Her lips stiffened as she looked around the cemetery, then softened when she saw we were alone. "That woman."

"Clarissa?"

She nodded curtly. "She was not *right* for Tom. She was too ... modern. Too pushy. I tried to tell him so, but ..." Her shrug suggested the effort had been both incessant and ineffective.

"Did you see Tom often in the past few years, Mrs. Crandall?"

She shook her head. "He was too busy. And she would never come out to the valley with him, so ..." Her hands rose and fell at her sides like fractured wings. "She made him choose, and he chose her."

"Did Tom have any friends still living out here? People he was still in touch with?"

She shook her head. "Only Ellen."

"Who's Ellen?"

She set her jaw. "Ellen Simmons. The one he *truly* loved. The one he *should* have married. The one that monster dragged away before the service even started. As if Tom had anything to *do* with that old business."

"What old business?"

She looked at me for the first time, finally conscious that I was essentially a stranger. "Nothing that concerns you. Or Tom, either one."

Chapter
7

Under the not-altogether-bogus guise of wanting to know more about my dead friend's origins, I lingered at the gravesite to try to pry more information out of his mother, lowering my voice so not even the trees and monuments would overhear. Her eyes fixed on the still-uncovered vault, her voice a leaden yet maternal drone, Mrs. Crandall uttered a simple eulogy: Tom had been an attentive son.

A happy childhood, a triumphant adolescence, a patriotic enlistment, were preludes to an increasingly distressing sequel. Troubled by the war, by his work, most recently by his marriage, after a bright beginning Tom had begun to founder. But not so much so that he couldn't find time to drive out to see his mother at least one Sunday each month, to take her to church, then to supper at the Lyons in Walnut Creek, then to the cemetery to put fresh flowers on his father's grave, which was not ten yards from the one her son had just been placed in.

"Was Tom's brother here, by the way?" I asked as her litany died away.

She clutched the handbag even tighter, as though there

were secrets deep within it. "Tom doesn't have a brother."

"You mean something happened to him?"

"I mean Tom doesn't *have* a brother."

I tried to recall the phone message precisely. "I thought Tom mentioned him recently. I must have misheard."

Mrs. Crandall had had enough of me. "I have to get back to the house; people will be coming by. I have to make snickerdoodles."

I started to take my leave, then turned back. "The woman you mentioned, the one Tom should have married. Does she still live out this way?"

Mrs. Crandall nodded, if possible even more distressed than before. "Ellen's still at home, more's the pity. She works at a bank in Oakland, but she lives with her folks on the old highway. How she stands it, I don't know—Orson Simmons is off his rocker; always has been. Poor Gertrude looks like death would be a blessing." Mrs. Crandall shook her head, her expression still suitable for extreme unction even though the people she had spoken of weren't eligible. "Tom broke Ellen's heart when he didn't come back to her after the war. It's the only mean thing he ever did."

"Absence doesn't always make the heart grow fonder." The surroundings and the sentiments had made me a greeting card.

Her lips stiffened. "The heart Tom had when he came back wasn't the one he took over there. That was bad enough. Then that *woman* got hold of him." She made Clarissa Crandall sound as corrupting as a cult.

After giving me directions to Ellen's parents' house, Mrs. Crandall started walking toward the Chrysler for the ride back to the mortuary. The trip to the car was a trudge; she took my arm to steady herself while I tried to believe I was performing a service instead of prying; along the way I almost tripped over a gravestone with a golf bag etched onto it. After helping Mrs. Crandall into the rear seat of the Chrysler, I thanked her for her time and returned to my Buick, glad to be going in another direction.

The San Ramon Valley has been a magnet for the fortunes churned out by the economic fission of the eighties, from the Rodeo Drive redux of downtown Walnut Creek to the inexplicably expensive homes clustered belly-to-belly in the Blackhawk subdivision to the festive jockocracy that flourishes around the watering holes in Danville. But it wasn't always so, and Mr. and Mrs. Simmons and their daughter Ellen lived in a board-and-batten bungalow tucked away in the corner of a walnut orchard in the flatlands not far from the freeway, a house that had doubtlessly been built back when Danville was as rural as Delano.

What the Simmons house lacked in style and sophistication it tried to make up for with precision. The grounds were simple but immaculate—hedges trimmed, lawn edged and mowed, flowers planted in perfect patterns. Each piece of gravel in the drive seemed to have been put in place by hand; the furniture on the porch was nailed to the floor to ensure perpetual symmetry; the window blinds were pulled to the same dimension: I hadn't seen that kind of regimental mania since I was in the army. Despite the effort at cut-rate respectability, I had a feeling this was a place the newer residents of the valley thought something should be done about.

When I knocked, the door opened immediately, as though someone had been standing guard out at the highway and had warned of my approach. Beyond the screen, Ellen Simmons looked at me with such frank curiosity I decided she must have seen me watching when her father pulled her out of the chapel and had been intrigued by the attention. Or maybe she was just interested in anything that might take her out of that house even for a moment, even something as scruffy and unpromising as a private eye.

She still wore her funeral attire—black dress and red-rimmed eyes—and still clutched a handkerchief in her fist. From the stretch of the dress across her bust and hips, I bet that after she took it off she would have it cleaned and pressed and return it to the person she'd borrowed it from. The crimson in her eyes was going to take longer to be rid of.

I introduced myself and said that I'd seen her at the chapel and asked why she'd left so quickly.

She answered my question with one of her own. "You knew Tom?" Her eyes bulged with hope and her hair got a quick pat: she wouldn't want to disappoint a friend of Tom's.

I nodded. "We lived near each other in the city."

She twisted her handkerchief and smiled, briefly and bravely. "I bet you're the detective."

"I'm afraid so."

"He thought a lot of you."

"I felt the same about Tom. So did you, I understand."

Her eyes rinsed themselves a bit more, but she was so used to it by now she ignored it. "You must have been talking to Mrs. Crandall."

I admitted it.

"She's a dear."

"She thinks you were the love of Tom's life."

"I know."

"What do you think?"

She hesitated. "I think he had a wife."

"Love's not always law-abiding."

Her look was intended to discipline me. "It was for Tom." Signs of resistance replaced the signs of mourning. "Besides, I don't know that it's any of your business what Tom and I were to each other."

"I think you're right." As right as Tom's wife and mother had been.

I let my apology sink in. When it had, her expression eased back to the original edition, which was drawn and melancholy yet somehow as plucky as a puppy's. "Mrs. Crandall told me Tom would often come by to see you after he'd been to see her."

She shrugged and bit a lip. "The last year or so, sometimes. Not often enough."

In those stark and bloodless surroundings, the nakedness of her desire was carnal. "What would have been often enough?"

She met my eye. "I imagine you can guess, if you're a very good detective."

We let it sit where it was for a while. Ellen Simmons worked on her eyes with her handkerchief while I worked less visibly on my tact. Neither of us made much progress.

Because she was well-brought-up, Ellen eventually remembered her manners and invited me inside, but was relieved when I declined. From the way she fidgeted when she issued the invitation, I guessed the housekeeping had slacked off since she'd heard the news about Tom. Nevertheless I was charmed. I hadn't met a woman who worried about housekeeping in years.

"I have a few questions, if you don't mind," I said as I moved to the shady side of the porch and she shoved open the screen door and joined me.

"Why? What's the point now that he's . . . gone."

"I'm not sure, to tell you the truth."

"Then what are you trying to do?"

"Preserve my options, I guess."

She hesitated, as though to measure my capacity to respond to her next question. "Do you think he was murdered?" she said suddenly.

I tried not to show my surprise. "I don't know. Do you?"

"Yes." The word was bold and heartfelt.

"By whom?"

"I don't know. That man Sands, maybe."

"So you know about that."

She nodded and borrowed Tom's words: "It was destroying him, what that man was doing."

"It wasn't a one-way street, though. Clarissa seemed agreeable to what Sands wanted, so why would Sands regard Tom as an obstacle? And anyway, a prominent man like that, why would he take the risk?"

Ellen shrugged. "I suppose it's silly. But I don't believe Tom just . . . *died*. Senselessly. That's what they're saying, right? That it was a mugging or something?"

"At this point, they're mostly fishing, I think."

"Tom was a soldier. He'd have known if he was in danger, and he'd have something done about it."

"Assaults come from strange places sometimes, Ms. Simmons. You don't necessarily get a warning."

She scoffed at my rebuttal. "Tom Crandall wasn't a *victim,* Mr. Tanner. After all he'd been through, he wouldn't just let himself be beaten up. He was *careful*. Brave and foolish, sometimes; but careful."

"What's your point?"

"I think someone *did* something to him. Someone he knew; someone he went to that place to meet." She paused, reviewed what she'd just said, and seemed more convinced than ever that the love of her life had been deliberately taken from her. "You must think the same thing, or why would you be here?"

"I do have a feeling that something doesn't add up," I admitted. "But it's only speculation. I don't have the faintest idea where to start to—"

"Of course you do," she interrupted.

"What do you mean?"

"You start by doing what you're doing now—asking questions."

I reddened like a schoolboy being corrected at the blackboard to the delight of his peers. "We'll know more when the M.E. issues his report about the cause of death. It might have been natural causes, you know. It happens."

"Not like that," she said confidently. "Not to Tom."

"Let's wait and see."

She put a hand on my arm. "Will you call and tell me what the medical report says? We don't take a newspaper— Father says it's filled with sedition and sacrilege—and I don't always have time to see the one at work."

I glanced at the room at her back, to make sure Father wasn't on a rampage to root out seditious sinners like me, then took down her phone number and promised I'd call. "Was that your father who came to get you at the chapel?" I asked.

She nodded.

"Why did he do it?"

"Daddy doesn't like the Crandalls."

"Why not?"

She hesitated, and her eyes lost focus. "There was trouble once. A long time ago. Father hasn't gotten over it."

"What kind of trouble?"

Footsteps sounded from inside the house, then Paul Harvey's voice oozed from a nearby radio and Ellen's spell was ended. "It doesn't matter what happened," she said firmly. "It doesn't have anything to do with this."

I waited for more, but it didn't come. That a similar disclaimer had been issued by Tom's mother made their stance either truthful or provocative. "Did you and Tom grow up together?" I prompted.

She nodded. "Second grade till he went to war." She pointed. "We went to a little school that used to be down where that church is. He walked me here after class during the entire junior high. I'd make lemonade from real lemons. We'd talk about birds and baseball." She tried to swallow and didn't quite make it. "When he went to war, he took both my Bible and my virginity with him. I never got either of them back. Not that I minded," she added wistfully. "The Bible did its work—Tom lived through it. It was my virginity that was wanting."

We exchanged long looks, mine more embarrassed than hers. Then she nodded in answer to a question I hadn't asked. "My first and only time. Amazing in this day and age, isn't it? And now I'm the proverbial old maid. When Tom and I were dating, that was the last thing in the world I saw in my future." She started to say more, then stopped herself. "I should go in; this kind of talk isn't seemly."

"Two more minutes."

Behind her, someone said something that made her stiffen, then retreat toward the safety of the screen. "I have to go. If I don't have dinner ready on time, I never hear the end of it. But I'm here every night by six, and on weekends, if you want to talk some more."

"Where can I reach you during the day?"

She shook her head. "The bank doesn't like me to do personal business."

The idea that Ellen Simmons would abuse her work privileges was incomprehensible. "Just one more thing," I said. "I was wondering if Tom said anything unusual the last time you saw him. Was he worried about anything, or frightened, or—"

"Tom was *always* frightened. He thought the world was mad, capable of viciousness at any moment. It's why it was so remarkable that he forced himself to minister to the worst of it." She hesitated. "No, not the worst. Only the least fortunate."

"But there was nothing specific on his mind the last time you talked?"

"Not really. Just . . . regret, I suppose is the word for it."

"Regret about what?"

She reddened. "Me, I suppose. My life and what's become of it. But his life, too, I think. He felt bad that it hadn't worked out better for either of us." Her eyes searched the distances; what they found was Tom. "He kept saying he'd done what he thought was right at the time, that if he'd known what he knew now he'd have done it differently. But he didn't, so there we were. Twenty years down the drain."

"What exactly was he talking about—what would he have done differently?"

"Not coming to see me after the war, I think. Not giving me a chance to . . ." She shrugged helplessly, the past incapable of narration.

"A chance to what?"

"Show him that nothing had changed, no matter what had happened. Show him we could be like we had been before he went away."

"Did he mention anything else? About his marriage, for example?"

She shook her head. "Not that last time."

"How about money? Did that come up at all? Did it sound like he had some kind of business deal going?"

She shook her head. "Tom thought money was directly proportional to corruption. I never heard him mention it except disparagingly." She blinked. "Sometimes I think the reason he didn't come by to see me more often was that I work in a bank."

I thought she meant it as a joke, but I wasn't sure. "Do you think he could have been mixed up in something criminal? Medical people have access to drugs, for example."

She adopted a pose as martial as the soldiers who'd fired their rifles across Tom's grave. "Never."

"Was he using drugs himself, do you think?"

"I am certain he was not." She looked at me. "Aren't you?"

Since I didn't see any point in denting her illusions, I didn't tell her that Tom had admittedly used drugs after he'd returned from the war. Given the stress he was under near the end, he could easily have repossessed that crutch.

Ellen prepared to close the door on me and my aimless musings. "Tom was a special man, Mr. Tanner," she offered in benediction. "If someone killed him, they should be brought to account."

I nodded. "But let's wait for the medical report. If it indicates something shady, maybe you and I can see to it that justice is done." When I looked at her again, I realized I wasn't the only one who regarded the proposal as a pledge.

"One last thing," I said. "Does Tom have a brother or not?"

Ellen Simmons looked at me for several seconds. "I don't know," she said cryptically. Before I could ask her to explain, the screen door banged like a gunshot between us.

Chapter
8

I got in my Buick and headed for the nearest onramp. Along the way, my mind began to flood, with images of Tom and with snatches of his conversation.

"America needs a good scare," he'd said once. "It's the only thing that will bring us to our senses. The problem is, the scariest thing in the world is us." And, "The Japanese will take whatever we're prepared to sell them, and we're prepared to sell them everything. That's because we no longer know what things are worth. Capitalism's Achilles' heel is that the only value it admits is money." And, "The most salutary step a politician could take—and it may be our only hope—would be to abolish commercial TV. But then how would he get elected without *saying* anything?" By the time I reached the onramp, these and similar aphorisms had become so immediate that I decided to return to the cemetery and say one last word to Tom myself—one last word in private.

The little graveyard was empty of family and friends; not even the grave-digger lingered: No one stood guard over the dead, who probably weren't worried about it. When I got to the site, I expected to discover the shovel had done its job and Tom had been interred, but what I saw was the hole I'd left an hour before and its attendant mound of earth. I crossed my arms and walked around the gravesite once, and then again, careful not to examine its contents, letting my mind wander away from reason and reality and drift toward the transcendental. At the same time, a part of me tried to think of something to say to someone who, in my less emotional moments, I was certain could no longer hear me.

What I settled for, in the end, was, "Sorry." And, "We'll miss you at Guido's." And finally, "It would be easier if I knew why." But the lines were evidently busy; I got no message in return.

In a mix of loneliness and the odd exultation that accompanies a surge of spirituality, I took one last look around to mark the spot in case I wanted to return some day, then started back to my car. But as I backed away from the grave, I tripped, stumbling over a clod that had rolled off the pile of dirt that was waiting to become Tom's blanket. I struggled to regain my balance, and inadvertently looked down. What I saw inside the grave made me drop to my knees and crawl to its edge and examine the contents more carefully.

Lying atop the casket that rested peacefully within its vault, as precisely placed as if they had been readied for the week's inspection, were some simple army artifacts: a faded bush hat, a pair of jungle boots, and, as shiny as its heavenly template even in the depths of the oblong pit, a single Silver Star. I had no doubt the articles were Tom's, no doubt they'd been placed in the grave with reverence, no doubt it had been done in secret. What I didn't know was who had performed the rite, or why.

When I got back to the office, I called Atlas Ambulance, the service Tom had worked for. When they realized I wasn't in the throes of medical emergency, they stuck me on hold for five minutes. Finally someone in authority got on the line, but only long enough to tell me he didn't know the answer to my questions—didn't know why Tom had been in the Tenderloin the night he died, didn't know of any particular difficulty he'd had on a call to that area or elsewhere, did keep files that would break out their emergency runs by location but they were private records and wouldn't be made available to me under any circumstances, not without subpoena.

The upshot was, if I was going to learn anything about Tom's work, it would have to come from Tony. I left a message with my Atlas antagonist for Tony to call when he got off duty, but the person who took it implied it was about as likely that Tony would get the message as it was that I would regrow hair on my bald spot.

The bout with the ambulance people was so enervating it was almost a relief that none of my other calls got through. Clarissa Crandall not only didn't answer, she left a slap of the supernatural in her absence: The voice on her answering machine was still her husband's, sounding firm and businesslike and very much alive, willing if not eager to receive my message. The unexpected visitation shoved me back to the gravesite for several minutes more. Afterward, my disposition was sufficiently sour that I was certain his wife had loosed Tom's ghost on purpose.

My next call was to Charley Sleet, but once again he wasn't at the Central Station and no one knew where he was or when he'd be back, which was par for Charley's course. The person who answered the phone at the *Chronicle* acted as if he didn't even know what an obituary was, let alone who might have written the one for Tom. And, as I'd predicted the last time Tom and I had talked at Guido's, I didn't even get past the first level of resistance when I called the headquarters of Sandstone Enterprises and asked to speak with its chairman and CEO.

The Sandstone call depleted my store of energies. After I made myself some coffee, I leaned back in my chair and began to drift.

If you can attend a funeral and not become immersed in thanatopsis, you're a better person than I am, or maybe you're just a clod. Anyway, I'd thought about death quite a bit as I made my way back through the Oakland Hills and across the Bay Bridge and through the tricky streets of the city on my way to my office in Jackson Square, and now I thought about it some more. I thought about peaceful death and violent death, anonymous death and heroic death, death in all its guises and gradations, culminating with the fact of Tom's death and the inevitability of my own.

I'd come close several years ago, to death of the violent kind. On my very first case after I'd switched from lawyering to whatever it is I do now, I'd been gut-shot in an alley just south of Broadway, gut-shot by someone I'd never seen before or since, gut-shot, I'd decided after a two-month inquiry, mostly by mistake. It had taken six weeks of hospital help and another month of homestyle convalescence before my innards were functioning properly and I was back to anything I could consider my norm.

I didn't have any out-of-body sensations as I lay bleeding in that alley, or see a lovely light or hear a heavenly harp; I just writhed in extremely uncelestial agony and tried to stem the flow. But during my recovery I'd learned a few things. I learned that I have an impressive tolerance for pain and an impressive intolerance of doctors. I learned I would rather run the risk of duplicating the torment of a gunshot than return to the even more excruciating pain of a law practice, even though the latter pain is purely psychological. And I learned that, despite my youthful indoctrination through a decade of sermons and Sunday school, I don't believe in an afterlife—not in heaven or hell or purgatory, not in reincarnation or resurrection or any of the other comforting versions of immortality that humans have devised to give them succor. I believe that when the liquid of life runs dry, we are as dead as our dogs and our dandelions.

Still, a part of my Sunday schooling must have taken, the part about effort and achievement, sacrifice and obligation, the Golden Rule and the eye of a needle, and other maxims that are even more a part of me than Tom's, which leaves me with the burdens of the doctrine but not the benefits. I'm a disappointment to myself as a result, some days more than others. Lots of people are, I suppose; it's too bad the Sunday schools don't spend more time teaching you what to do if you don't turn out to be quite perfect.

Fortunately a siren sounded at this point and ended my ruminations. I looked at my watch. It was after five—time for a drink, so I had a couple. Tony hadn't called. Neither had Clarissa Crandall; neither had Charley Sleet; neither had anyone at the *Chronicle*. The radio had nothing new on the war, which was still pretty much invisible.

When I looked Tony up in the book, I found a listing for a Milano on Greenwich that I figured for him, but all I got was his machine with a macho message directed toward the other sex, which apparently had little on its mind but Tony. I left my name and number, reminded him who I was, asked him to call me back. Since I wasn't in the mood to hear Tom's disembodied voice, I left his wife to a later time and place and tried the Central Station.

Charley Sleet sounded angry. Given the personnel problems in the police department, Charley was angry a lot of late. When he calmed down, I asked if he'd had dinner. He said he'd grabbed a burrito on the run about three hours ago. I said I'd spring for some pasta at Capp's if he could sneak away for half an hour. He said he'd stopped sneaking the day he got caught pawing through his sister's underwear when he was twelve and curious about what a brassiere looked like up close. I told him I'd meet him at Capp's in twenty minutes.

He was there when I arrived, burly, bearish, bald, sitting atop his chair at the communal table the way ice cream sits atop a sugar cone. As though to make sure I wouldn't change my mind, Charley had his order in before I was settled in my seat. I decided on the gnocchi, and we opted jointly for Chianti, which is the only wine I drink. I'd seen less red at a knife fight than the waiter had on his apron, but he had a jug of the grape and some vegetable soup in front of us in less than ten seconds. Five minutes after that the jug was almost empty.

The couple to our left was discussing movies. Charley listened for a minute, then grunted. "I'm not much of a movie man," he said. "But I went to this Tracy thing."

"Good. Crimestoppers should compare notes."

"You see it?"

"Yeah."

"What'd you think?"

"Awful."

Charley nodded. "I couldn't see who they were or figure out what they were saying. Was that just me or was that the way it was?"

"That's pretty much the way it was."

"If this Beatty guy's so old he's afraid to show his face, what'd he make the movie for in the first place?"

"Five million dollars or so."

"Is there anything those Hollywood guys won't do for a buck?"

"How should I know? I don't know any Hollywood guys."

The couple to our right was discussing the war. We eavesdropped for another minute, then I looked at Charley. "We won't see another Democratic president in our lifetimes. Not unless the ground war gets bogged down."

Charley swore. "You think this will settle anything? They been at each other for three thousand years over there; the Arabs and Jews been scuffling every day since forty-seven. A year from now, it'll be the same fucked-up place it always was—neither Bush or Quayle or anyone else will be bragging about this thing, and Schwarzkopf will pretend he was a private."

Charley's plate was almost empty after a handful of bites, and he was back to business. "You don't buy unless you want something," he grumbled.

"Police work has made you cynical."

"Doesn't have to do with police work; has to do with you."

"I'm a taxpayer. I have a right to keep current with city business. I pay your salary, for God's sake."

"You pay shit," Charley said around the final mouthful of linguini. "What do you want?"

"M.E. report on a guy named Crandall."

"Who's he?"

"Friend of mine. Found in the Tenderloin on Tuesday."

"Homicide?"

"That's what I'm trying to find out. The *Chronicle* was talking suicide or natural causes."

"The *Chronicle* talks out of its ass."

Charley thinks the paper is too hard on the police force. I don't think it's hard enough.

"Crandall," he mused. "Wait a minute. I think I know the guy. An EMT, right?"

"Right."

"Caught the call on a couple of my people. Good guy."

Charley calls the victims of the crimes he's assigned to "my people." "Yeah. Tom was a good guy."

"A little on the sober side, like he had piles or something. 'Course, EMS work will do that to you."

So will police work; so will privately detecting.

Charley wolfed a hunk of bread. "How'd you know him?"

"Guido's."

"Yeah? I didn't peg him for a boozer."

"He wasn't a boozer; he was a philosopher. A lonely one."

"I thought he was married."

"He was."

Charley shook his head in puzzlement—Charley hadn't known a lonely instant until his wife had died and hadn't known anything else since—and mopped the dregs of his plate with another hunk of bread. I followed suit as well as I could—no one eats as fast as Charley—then drained the rest of the jug into our glasses.

"How was the linguini?"

"Just the way I like it."

"What way is that?"

"The way it was the last time. What you want from the post?"

"Cause of death. Mysterious circumstances. Evidence of foul play."

"You suspect something?"

"Not necessarily."

"But maybe?"

"Maybe."

"Who?"

I hesitated, more from embarrassment than uncertainty. "What do you know about a guy named Sands?"

Charley licked his lips. "The limo and jet and like that? The building by the bay looks like a cigar box?"

"That's the one."

"You're going to try to tag Sands with a homicide? In *this* town? Jesus, Tanner. Next you'll be after me to roust the archbishop."

Chapter
9

I got home a little after six. Made myself a drink. Turned on CNN for the latest from the front, even though the latest was the same PR pitch as last time. Heated something that had been frozen for at least a year. Opened a bag of Oreos. Fixed another drink. Cut into the frozen stuff and discovered it was still frozen in the middle. Put it back in the oven. Looked through the paper for an ad for a sale on microwaves. Made a resolution to get one. Made another resolution to locate someone who knew what to do with it.

Switched from CNN to ABC. Learned the Supreme Court had just decided to allow coerced confessions to be used against criminal defendants. Fixed another drink. Thought about the demise of the once-proud court, reduced to a gang of nerds with a rubber stamp—no, no, no, it stamped, no you don't have to fix it even though it's awful, no you don't have to make allowances for two hundred years of apartheid, no you don't have to rein in the excesses of the police, no you don't have to jail the pirates who have plundered the country and are putting its future in their pockets. In *this* brave new world, everyone's on his own and the Constitution is less a bill of rights than a bill of lading and the Court is as oblivious to misery as God. Except that God can be oblivious and still be God, but humans can't and still be human.

Thought about going to Guido's to ease the pain, but decided I was drunk enough already. Thought about Tom Crandall, then about Tom's wife. Realized I didn't even know where they lived, so what kind of friend did that make me? Looked them up in the book, learned they lived less than three blocks from my apartment. Felt bad that I had never been there. Wondered why I hadn't. Decided to go calling even though the only one who might be home was a woman who regarded me as an enemy.

By the time I reached Tom's apartment at the dead end of a little street named Price Row, I'd sobered up a little, which was fortunate for all concerned but it didn't make the trip productive—no one responded to my rings or my knocks or my loitering in the alley far past the likelihood of raising anyone but a nosy neighbor. After further sobering in the form of a double espresso at the Caffè Trieste, I went home and called Clarissa and got another jolt in the person of Tom's voice asking for my message. I reminded him that I'd already given at the grave.

I retreated to the TV. After considering the situation through a *Sixty Minutes* chat with their military and Middle East experts, who brought to mind the definition of an expert as anyone who's twenty miles from home, I made more coffee, then took a shower and put on my other good suit, the one I hadn't wrinkled at the funeral. Ten minutes later, I was in my car.

The Velvet Room occupies the top floor of a Nob Hill hotel that is more elegant but less renowned than its neighbors, the Fairmont and the Mark Hopkins, which is the way both its reclusive clientele and its European proprietors want it. Since the Fairmont closed down the Venetian Room several months back, if you're looking for quality cabaret in San Francisco, the Velvet Room is the only place you'll find it on a reliable basis. The place is small as showrooms go, but the atmosphere is intimate and sumptuous, the view stunning after dark, the house band always in top form, the food the stuff of legend in terms of both price and preparation. I'd never been there, of course, so my information was only scuttlebut. Although I was hoping to do my waiting on a stool, the bar was closed for the dinner show, so I had to opt for a table.

People who dine alone are inherently suspect, and people with the temerity to don the kind of clothing I was wearing, which was the threadbare and subfashionable kind, were regarded as crazed or criminal in places like the Velvet Room. After expressing his disapproval succinctly and nonverbally, the maître d' led me to my trough. Because I hadn't crossed his palm with silver or dropped a name out of Herb Caen, I had a better view of the kitchen than the stage.

The room was decorated in swaths of pastels, art deco but not excessively so, with cutesy bas-relief on the ceiling, sculpted lighting fixtures climbing the walls, cut flowers on the tables. The flatware was baroque and superb, the service attentive to the point of idolatry, the wine list thicker than the phone book. The candles in their cut-glass bases gave off a scent of lavender, and the menu was a sheet of heavy parchment. I tried to stay sober enough not to set it on fire.

The first of what turned out to be a gaggle of waiters appeared to cater cruelly to my every need. Although I decided to keep my needs to a minimum—a salad and a highball—I wasn't going to get out of the place for less than fifty bucks. The waiter recovered from my parsimony long enough to direct another waiter to bring me my drink, which I dawdled over as long as I could.

The salad came and went, the vinaigrette lingering in a dusty aftertaste. The scotch did the same, as did a basket of bread and a goblet of water. By the time ten o'clock rolled around, I was a little drunk and a lot tired and an object of speculation at more than one of the nearby tables. When one particularly starched young couple laughed at what I suspected were my manners, I gave them my evil grin, whereupon they turned their attention to the ceiling, which was a nest of tiny cupids that were laughing at me, too.

Despite my investment in the evening, I was close to giving it up as a bad idea. All I had was a feeling that Tom Crandall was not a suicide or a mugging victim, that he was one of those men who don't die without a reason, and the reason is that someone feels threatened by that most dangerous of combinations—knowledge and integrity. At the moment, that seemed to be enough. Or maybe I just wanted to see Clarissa strut her stuff. I ordered another drink and made music with the butter knife and the water glass. Tintinnabulation, Poe would have called it.

A few minutes later, the curtain across the stage began to ripple, and sounds of scraping and sliding, and even a brief curse, seeped from behind its drape. Yet another waiter made a pass, offering a tray of desserts that would have put me in a ward for the terminally hypoglycemic. I was still waving him away when the houselights went down and a single spot made a perfect golden circle on the thick blue velvet of the curtain that defined the proscenium stage.

A man with a bright white tux and teeth the size of playing cards trotted from its umbra into its center, smiled too broadly, waved at the scattered applause as though it were the dregs of an ovation, told a harmless joke about the weather and a not-so-harmless one about the mayor, then puffed with self-importance.

"Ladies and gentlemen," he intoned. "At this time, it is my pleasure to present to you the pride of the Velvet Room, the biggest and best big band on the entire West Coast, the toast of San Francisco—Mickey Stringer and His Orchestra, ladies and gentlemen, featuring the sultry stylings of the Temptress of Torch, the delightful and delectable Ms. Clarissa Cran . . . er, Duncan. Clarissa Duncan, ladies and gentlemen."

The band struck up a thumping vamp, the curtain began to levitate, the MC trotted off as though he'd just brought about the Second Coming as Mickey Stringer and his trumpet replaced him in the spotlight. As Mickey bowed and scraped, the band moved into "Perdido."

I knew Mickey a little, had seen and heard him many times when he'd fronted a quintet at El Matador before moving up the hill. A former sideman for Buddy Rich,

Mickey could swing and, based on the opener, still saw to it that his band did, too. As they made their way through "Stella by Starlight," I stopped thinking about Tom and began to wallow in the rhythms and memories of youth. But after Mickey wrapped up a driving version of "Ciribiribin," the drummer began a roll that built to a loud crescendo, and I was back in business.

Mickey seconded the MC's fulsomeness, the band fell into its vamp once more, and Clarissa Crandall ... er ... Duncan swept onto the stage like Cleopatra just off her barge and running. Her cocktail dress had been exchanged for a floor-length gown, velvet of course, skintight, slit to her hip, so low-cut it seemed impossible for it to do its duty if she so much as tilted. Her manipulation of the microphone was carnal; her smile was practiced and come-hither; her lips were as red as the blood that was racing madly through my heart as it hurried to my skull for a better view.

She was a different woman from the one I'd met at Guido's and confronted at the funeral, a woman with charms enough to have provoked infidelity in Richard Sands and deviltry enough to have driven a man like Tom Crandall crazy. I started to resent her just a little, the way I resent most beautiful women for the nonsense they inspire in men like me, but when she moved into "The Man I Love," I chose to believe it was her tribute to Tom and I liked her a little more.

She could sing—not as well as Sarah Vaughan or Nancy Wilson, more like June Christy or Marilyn McCoo—and I could see why she'd become a staple of the band and the city. But when she reached for the upper register, I could also see why she was afraid her voice had begun its slide.

After her second number, I tore my eyes away from the widow Crandall long enough to survey the crowd. They were as rapt as I had been, faces like flesh-tone Frisbees in the reflected light from the stage, the men openmouthed and entranced, the women squinty and skeptical and maybe a little nervous. Although I was looking for Richard Sands, I didn't see him or anyone else I recognized, which was fine—I'd come to the dinner show in the theory that Sands wouldn't appear till later, which would give me a chance to waylay Clarissa between sets and talk to her about her husband.

I glanced at my watch. The band had been at it for almost an hour, so it was time to make a move. I pushed back my chair and as unobtrusively as I could—which wasn't hard since Clarissa was well into Porter's saucy "Let's Fall in Love"—slipped back to the bar area. The couple I'd chided earlier seemed relieved to see me go. No one else seemed to notice.

When the bartender looked my way, I asked for directions to the rest room. He pointed toward an archway at the end of the room. When I went through it, I found myself in a narrow hallway, dimly lit, extending indeterminately both left and right. An arrow on the wall said the rest rooms were to the right, so I went the other way.

The hallway dead-ended at an unmarked door—heavy, locked. I got out an expired credit card and the tools I carry for such occasions and remedied the situation before anyone was the wiser. On the other side of the door, the corridor was well maintained—carpeted and wallpapered and well lit. It took a left turn about ten yards from where I was, which would put it behind the stage, which was where I wanted to be. I listened to make sure no one was coming after me, then went to the corner and peeked.

At the back of the building, the hallway widened into a larger area, wide and high-ceilinged, complete with flats and props and other backstage accoutrements. In the center, a set of sliding doors opened to the freight elevator, which was large enough to admit stage sets and audio speakers and the like. On either side of the big doors were several smaller rooms that I assumed to be the dressing areas. The door to one of them was open. When no one appeared either in front or in back of me, I rounded the corner in a swagger: I had business to take care of and wouldn't brook distractions.

Several tables were scattered about the windowless room, along with two dozen chairs and a couch and a young black man in a white waiter's jacket who was busy cleaning up before setting out the snack foods and setups that were waiting on a serving cart. The kid was bobbing and weaving to the rhetoric of the rap tune coming through his headset, and neither the vibes of my presence nor the beat of the band out front was sufficiently potent to penetrate it. I guessed this was where Mickey and the boys took a break. When I looked for a sign that a woman would be welcome, I didn't see one.

Two rooms down was a blue door with a white star in its center. Luckily it was only as locked as the other one.

It was undoubtedly Clarissa's dressing room, elaborately furnished, a set out of a musical about musicals where the star is always gliding about in a floor-length gown and a grandiloquent gesture, fending off admirers. The dressing-table mirror was surrounded by lights, the screen in the corner came complete with a dressing gown draped across its top, and in the ice bucket by the love seat real ice was chilling a real bottle of really good champagne. I guessed Clarissa saw herself as a throwback, a chanteuse, a thrush, a nightingale, maybe even a gangster's moll. I also guessed that her stage-door Richard had paid for all her props.

I sat on the love seat and took inventory. The cold-cream jars and makeup tubes and throat lozenges and perfume cruets were numerous and looked expensive. The gowns on the rack along the wall were styled like the one out front—a couple of them seemed exact copies. There were a dozen pairs of spike-heeled shoes on a shelf, a basket of mums in a corner, a silver service for tea on the coffee table. All the comforts of home, except for a sign that she'd ever had a husband. The music from the stage, piped through a pair of speakers on the wall, was as faint as the signs of matrimony. A moment later, the sounds were silent.

I was about to give in to my baser instincts and rummage through the drawers in the chest beside the dressing table when I heard noises in the hallway. Instead of rummaging, I went behind the door and eavesdropped.

"The tempo on the Porter sucked, Mickey," Clarissa was saying as she opened the door a crack. "It's not a race, for Christ's sake; all that happens in a race is people get tired."

"The day I start taking tempos from a girl singer is the day I shove my trumpet up my butt and start whistling 'Dixie' with my mouth shut."

"'The Man with the Golden Asshole.' Suits you, Mick. Maybe someone'll write you an anthem. The monitors are fucked up, too, by the way—I can't hear myself over that drummer boy you like so much."

"Fuck you, sweetheart. We start with 'Who Can I Turn To?' next set."

"Richard wants 'Tangerine.'"

"He wants it, he can play it. Unless he forgot his kazoo."

The final jibe grew faint as Mickey Stringer and his choler moved down the hall. Clarissa Crandall muttered something I didn't catch, opened the door to the dressing room the rest of the way, flipped on the ceiling light, and closed the door behind her. "Jesus," she exclaimed when she saw me, her hand flying to her throat, her eyes narrowing to bring me in focus. "Who the hell are you?"

"Tanner."

I was hurt that she didn't remember me, and more so when she tabbed me as a flunky. "You're from Richard, I suppose." Her voice grew bored, and so did her bearing. She examined the room perfunctorily. "Let me guess— you brought the champagne. Well, it's nice, I'm sure, but I asked him not to send any more guys around with gifts. It makes the hotel people nervous. It makes *me* nervous. So be a doll and tell him I'll see him after the late show, like always. We can . . ."

Our eyes met in the makeup mirror. What she saw in mine made her change her tune. "You're not from Richard," she amended, squinting again to diminish her myopia.

I shook my head.

"You were at the cemetery."

I nodded.

She turned toward me. "Who let you in here?"

"No one."

"You broke in?"

I looked at the door. "It's not broken."

She looked at the door as though she hoped some- one would come through it and then hoped he wouldn't. "Should I be frightened? What do you want?"

"Just some more talk about Tom. And to tell you I like your music."

The compliment was a nonevent. "Tom," she sighed heavily. "Can't we let him rest in peace? He'll be much happier with the angels than he was here on earth with the rest of us."

"You can forget him if you want. I think I'll keep him around for a while."

She hugged herself for a moment as though I and my mission combined to create a cold wind, then sagged into the chair by the dressing table. "I'm not a monster, Mr. Tanner," she said, looking in the mirror to confirm it. "I know you won't believe it, but I'm in a lot of pain over this."

"I'll have to take your word for it, I guess. Things looked pretty upbeat from out there."

"It's my job to be upbeat." Her hands dropped away from her chest, and her back stiffened at what she perceived as an insult. "What do you want? I have to get ready for the second show."

"A lot of people don't think Tom committed suicide," I said.

"I don't think so, either. I already told you that."

"Some people think he was murdered."

Her eyes fluttered. "Who? The police?"

I shook my head. "A friend. Of Tom's."

"Who is supposed to have murdered him?"

"The friend wasn't sure."

"Well, it's nonsense. Tom just died, that's all. People die in the Tenderloin every day."

"You're sure that's all it was? A mugging that went too far?"

She met my eye in the mirror. "Yes."

"No one had a reason to want Tom out of the way?"

"Don't be silly. Tom was a little man who led a little life. Why would anyone want to kill him?"

"Little men get murdered every day, Mrs. Crandall. You'd know that if you ever read something besides *Variety*."

"I asked you not to call me that," she reminded me. "And if you think Richard had something to do—"

I shook my head. "I agree with you about Sands. I can't see him indulging in homicide, either; he's got too much to lose." I believed it when I said it; then I remembered Tom's final phone calls and reclaimed the possibility but kept it to myself. "I thought maybe you could put me onto someone else."

"Like who?" she asked.

"I was hoping you could tell me."

"Well, I can't." She browsed among the makeup and picked out a lipstick tube that looked like a rifle cartridge.

"Nothing unusual in his life lately, nothing he was scared of, nothing that made him mad?"

"Just the usual," she murmured.

"You mean Sands."

She shook her head. "I mean Nicky."

Chapter
10

"Who's Nicky?"

"Tom's brother."

"When I asked Mrs. Crandall about him, she got a strange look in her eye and told me Tom didn't *have* a brother."

Clarissa Crandall laughed dryly. "*Everyone* gets a strange look in their eye when someone mentions Nicky."

"Why?"

"Nicky's been . . . difficult over the years. People wish he would go away. Permanently. After a while, they start to believe he really has. The fact that no one ever knows where Nicky *is* makes it easy for them."

"Tom never mentioned Nicky to me, except at the end when he implied something had happened to him. Do you know anything about that?"

She shook her head. "I doubt it was anything sinister. Tom felt guilty about Nicky. And when Tom felt guilty, Tom kept mum."

"What made him feel that way?"

Clarissa looked at me closely, canting her head as though

that would give her a better view. "That's a big subject," she said. "Families and stuff." She stood up and grabbed a gown off the rack and went behind the screen. "I have to change."

I took her place at the dressing table and tried to ignore what was going on behind the square of translucent fabric by keeping my eyes on the powders and paints that littered the surface of the table in front of me, bottles and jars and tubes containing compounds I had never seen before or heard of. After a while, I couldn't resist a peek, but when I glanced in the mirror, the only curves I saw belonged to the champagne bucket and the mums.

Except for the rustling of silks and satins, Clarissa was silent for a long time. "We both think there was something funny about Tom's death," I said to fill the void. "And we both doubt there was a reason for Sands to be involved, even indirectly. Which means we're both afraid there might be someone out there who decided to murder your husband." I paused. "And we both want to make sure the only one in the Crandall family he has a grudge against was Tom."

I listened to a second rustle of fabric, then the purr of a zipper and the click of a heel on the hardwood floor. When Clarissa reappeared in the mirror, she was as blatantly alluring as before, but this time the theme was red.

Instead of gathered into her sexy stage pout, her face was folded in thought. "You run into a lot of freaks in show business," she murmured as she regarded herself in the full-length mirror that was affixed to the back of the door.

"What kind of freaks?"

"Guys with hang-ups about women. Guys with obsessions about 'stars.' Guys who hear voices telling them I love them, or need them, or want to hurt them." She shook her head. "The last one kept sending me his undershorts. One pair a day, for three months. Soiled, of course. Disgusting." Her voice trailed off to a hush made heavy by the perversion she had just described. A moment later, she shuddered for an instant, still revolted by the fan's effrontery.

"What made him stop?" I asked.

"Richard tracked him down and persuaded him to cease and desist."

"How did he manage that?"

"I didn't ask. Would you?"

When I didn't answer, she came to my side and gave me a nudge. I yielded the dressing table and returned to the love seat. Clarissa replaced me in the chair and began dabbing and rubbing and painting her face. Each stroke made her look more brazen.

"There's a new one out there, I think," she said finally.

"A new what?"

"Freak. Guy with hair cut real short and a scar on his cheek. Big. Wears these awful clothes—plaid polyester and gray slacks with brown shoes and like that. He's been by every night, lately. Late show only. Always by himself. I mean, I'm good but I'm not that good. He gives me the creeps. And I don't see how he can afford it."

"Have you sicced Sands on him yet?"

She shook her head.

"Why not?"

"So far he hasn't done anything but drool. If I scare off the droolers, I'm out of business."

Clarissa tended to her face some more, then moved to her bust, slipping her gown off her shoulders so she could whiten her chest to mimic the flesh of a bottom fish, oblivious to the effect the rituals of her toilette were having on me, an effect that led me to make a silent apology to Tom.

"Do you have a name for this guy?" I asked as she was finishing.

"He makes his reservation in the name of Kirby."

"I'll check him out for you."

She shrugged her gown back onto her shoulders. "Suit yourself. Who's paying for all this attention, by the way? If you check him out tonight, it will cost you a twenty-dollar cover and a two-drink minimum at five bucks per belt. Who gets the bill?"

"Only the IRS."

She looked at me and raised a brow. "Hard to keep yourself in beer and skittles that way, isn't it?"

"Someone usually turns up to make it worth my while. And what's a skittle?"

"A game. Like ninepins."

"Really? I thought it was some sort of food."

She wasn't inclined to discuss the derivation of Celtic slang. "Wouldn't it be better to have your clients lined up in the beginning?" she asked.

"Sometimes people aren't nervous enough to be clients in the beginning."

"When they *get* nervous, what do they get nervous about?"

Our eyes met. "That I'm going to learn what they've been hiding."

"You sound like that's a universal ailment."

"As universal as perversity."

Since Mrs. Crandall was included in the scope of my doctrine, I expected a disclaimer of some sort. But all she did was look at her watch.

"Expecting someone?"

"Sometimes Richard stops by between sets."

"You going to marry him once it's seemly?" I asked, borrowing an adjective I'd last heard from the mouth of Ellen Simmons and before that from my grandmother's.

She shrugged. "He hasn't asked."

"That's not what Tom said."

"Tom liked to read between the lines. Besides, Richard is already married."

"Does that make a difference?"

She found me in the mirror. "Not to me."

There was a response to that, but I decided not to use it. While I was debating the point, Clarissa dropped her eyebrow pencil and swiveled toward me. "It wasn't my fault, you know. What happened between me and Tom."

"Whose fault was it?"

"Tom's, mostly." She saw my look. "All right, *both* of ours."

"Yours and Sands'?"

She shook her head impatiently. "Mine and Tom's."

"So what did happen between you two? Was it mostly Sands?"

She shook her head. "It didn't have anything to *do* with Richard Sands. Not at first. It's just that after a while my problems with Tom were so . . . enervating that I had a very large need to have my hand held and be told I was beautiful and intelligent and desirable and loved for precisely what I was."

"It looks to me like there's a whole room full of people out there who've been doing just that for the last hour or so."

She shook her head. "They don't count. It has to be someone who *knows* me, who's not just slavering over a celebrity. Tom knew me better than anyone, but he stopped telling me those things a long time ago. When Richard came along and offered to fill the void, I couldn't see any reason not to let him."

"Even if it made Tom miserable?"

Her voice hardened. "The misery went both ways. Believe me."

"It always does. And if all you want is to even the score, the relationship falls apart."

She closed her eyes, but a tear seeped forth nonetheless. A moment later, her brand-new makeup job was ruined.

"*You* knew him," she charged suddenly. "*You* know what he was like. I mean, he was good and true and noble and all that, but Tom Crandall thought it was a crime to be happy. He thought we all had to suffer till the last wretch in the world was saved. Well, I don't *see* life that way: I think you should try to be happy, no matter what. If there's something you can do about the things that make you sad, fine—do them. But if you can choose between being happy and being miserable, why the hell shouldn't you be happy? Who does it help to mope around all the time? Frankly, I doubt the starving hordes in Ethiopia give a shit, don't you?"

When she looked at me, I didn't say anything. Although the object of her rebuttal was her husband, an equally appropriate target was me.

"I spent a lot of years trying to make Tom see things my way," she went on. "I did two shows a night for the paying customers, then a show at home for my husband. But he was a tough audience. And after a lot of years when I thought that making him happy was the most important job in the world, I decided I didn't *want* that job anymore. All of a sudden it wasn't paying worth a damn."

"What do you think was wrong with him?"

Her shrug was dispirited. "The war was part of it—he had these flashbacks and nightmares, about things he'd seen and done. But he wouldn't go *see* anyone about them; he just sat around and brooded. Plus his job. People do the most horrible things to each other—to themselves, their kids, even their animals. I think the most upset I ever saw him was the night they were called out to get a guy who had slaughtered his dogs before he slaughtered himself."

"Tom didn't try therapy at all?"

She shook her head. "He said it was because we couldn't afford it. But I *think* it was because he was afraid someone would tell him he was going to end up like his brother."

"Which is what, exactly?"

She began the new eyeliner. "Paranoid schizophrenic. Clinically. He hears voices and sees ghosts and gets messages—the whole nine yards. Nicky Crandall is so hyper he can't stay in a room for thirty seconds unless he's on medication."

"When's the last time you saw him?"

"Nicky? It's been years."

"Did Tom keep in touch with him?"

"He tried, but it was off and on; Nicky didn't stay in one place very long. Tom would get postcards—the last one was from Walla Walla. The one before that was from Galveston."

"Did Tom mention his brother lately?"

She sighed. "Tom didn't talk about himself at all anymore. Not to me. Apparently he saved it for you and the rest of the boys at Guido's." Clarissa blinked away another tear and swore at it. "I didn't mean to hurt him, Mr. Tanner. But I was in trouble. He made me feel worthless, like nothing I could do would ever make him better, like I was wasting my time to try. I did what I had to do to save myself."

"Why didn't you just leave? Dangling Sands under his nose made it pretty tough on him."

"I should have, I suppose. But I kept thinking my friendship with Richard would make Tom realize how unhappy I was, and then he'd *do* something about it. He'd see what I was getting from Richard and start giving it to me himself."

"I think all he could see was Sands' money. I think

Tom saw you being attracted to a man with fifty million dollars, and that was one thing he could never give you."

"But that wasn't what I *wanted*."

"I have to tell you that in the circumstances, it would be hard for a man to believe that."

She nodded grudgingly. "I know that. But I had to do *something*. At least my friendship with Richard got Tom paying attention to me again." Her grin was defiant. "Lately Tom gave more thought to my life than I did. He had *lots* of ideas how I should be living it."

I decided not to mention that Tom had made much the same complaint about her. Which I suppose is why the divorce courts are at capacity.

"Let's get back to Nicky," I said, but before I could ask a question, there was a knock on the door. I expected Sands or one of his henchmen, but the head that entered the room was Mickey Stringer's. "Randy came up with a new chart on 'Misty' I want to go over, and—" He looked at me and frowned. "Tanner, isn't it?"

I nodded. "Hi, Mickey. Been a long time."

"Bimbo's 365."

"Bimbo's, right. The good old days."

"You got that right. What brings you by the Velvet?"

I glanced at Clarissa. "Just a fan."

"Catch the first show?"

I nodded. "The boys sound great."

Mickey smiled. "Those kids make me feel like a kid myself. I don't know how they kept from being dragged under by rock and roll and rap, but thank God they weren't. The guy—Jarvis—on tenor, he's got chops like I haven't heard since Getz."

I stood up. "I'll leave you to your labors." I turned back to Clarissa. "I'd like to stop by the apartment some time. Look through Tom's things. Maybe talk some more about Nicky."

She shrugged dubiously. "Maybe. I don't know. Call me."

"Do me a favor first."

"What?"

"Take Tom's voice off your machine."

She frowned, then colored. "I . . . of course. How awful."

I looked at Mickey. "I'd like a favor from you, too."

"Yeah?"

"Next time I'm out front, put 'You Go to My Head' on the play list."

"You got it," Mickey said, and slugged me on the shoulder. "Want me to tell them to comp you a table for the late show? Not a busy night, they like the seats filled."

I hadn't intended to stay, but what with the band and the singer and the lead I'd just come up with, it was an offer I couldn't refuse.

As I reached the door, I pulled a Columbo. "By the way," I said to Clarissa, who was making one last check in the mirror. "Do you know what happened to Tom's Silver Star?"

She looked at me without interest. "I didn't even know he had one till I read it in the papers."

Chapter
11

The second show was even better than the first. The band had loosened up, perhaps courtesy of the amenities in the back room, and the charts were out of the books of Ellington, Strayhorn, Herman, and Hefti, with time out for a svelte rendition of my request. For her part, Clarissa wrapped herself around a lot of Porter and Arlen, with a dash of Jimmy Webb and Carole King for good measure, and the crowd—nearly a full house now that the tab was only a cover and minimum instead of a five-course meal—was putty in her red-tipped hands.

After the up-tempo version of "Misty" that Mickey had wanted her to look over, Clarissa left the stage and I decided to depart as well—I wanted to see what would happen when Clarissa left the building. The problem was, it was a big hotel, with lots of ins and outs. Unless a limousine was parked in front of one of them, I didn't see how I could arrange to be on hand when Clarissa Crandall left the premises.

I was still loitering in the anteroom, trying to form a productive plan under the watchful eye of the cute-but-surly hatcheck girl, when I got a break in the person of a fellow patron. He was big, crew cut, with a scar like a putty smudge along his jaw and a brow that shaded his eyes like a granite visor. He was almost certainly Clarissa's most recent admirer, and I guessed that he'd know exactly where the object of his desire would turn up when it was time for her to leave, so when he took the elevator to the ground floor, I went along for the ride.

He left through the main entrance, as far as I could tell without the slightest suspicion of me or my motives. After giving him some lead time, I tagged along. I reached the sidewalk in time to see him turn into the alley behind the hotel, which was coincidentally the alley where I'd parked my car with a WORKING PRESS VEHICLE sign in the window. It was also the alley where, sure enough, a pearl-gray limo waited like a mighty stallion to do the bidding of its master. The windows were smoked to black, of course, so I could only guess who was inside, but the license plate read RS-1.

My burly guide took up a position out of sight of the limo behind the thrust of a loading platform. I, in turn, knelt out of sight of both of them, behind a van with the hotel logo on the side, wondering what the hell I was doing. When I looked his way again, I started wondering the same thing about my guide. He had pulled a red notebook from his pocket and was making a quick notation—though he seemed a little old for it, he was apparently going to try for an autograph, of Clarissa or Sands or both.

I heard a noise and looked back at the limo. The front door—passenger side—fanned open, and a well-dressed corporate type, as old as I am or worse, sporting the mandatory three-piece blue suit of the species, got out of the limo and walked toward the hotel. It wasn't Richard Sands, but it was undoubtedly his emissary.

The blue suit left the limo door ajar as he hurried toward the rear entrance, and when the driver leaned over to close it I got a glimpse of him—a bodybuilding bodyguard type, natty in blue blazer and gray slacks, his disarming eyes as active as a lizard's tongue. Given his job, he was doubtlessly a graduate of a karate academy and the

Bondurant school and a survival course that featured famil-
iarization with rapid-fire weapons and defensive maneuvers
against both hand-tossed and remote-controlled explosives.
It's not all upside for the rich these days.

When I looked to see how my guide had reacted to all
this, he was gone. I looked back down the alley just in time
to catch one last glimpse before he turned the corner and
started up the hill toward the front entrance, which was back
the way we'd come.

His behavior was odd enough to make me want to talk
to him. Before I could set off in pursuit, the rear door of
the hotel swung open once again, and Clarissa Crandall
appeared, back in the cocktail dress that had scandalized
the funeral, escorted with silent but efficient gallantry by
the three-piece suit who'd gone to fetch her. The suit stood
beside the rear door of the limo, and Clarissa climbed
in with the ease that comes from practice; then he followed after.

The driver cranked the engine, and the limo slid down
the alley as silently as a skiff. Uncertain of what I should
do or if I should do anything at all, I got in my car and
waited till the limo had maneuvered itself into the street
and headed down the hill toward Union Square. When it
was out of sight, I drove to the alley entrance, debating the
merits of following the leader.

I was still undecided when my path was crossed by a
small gray Escort driven by the guy with the hair the length
and color of cheap carpet, who occupied the tiny car the
way gin occupies a martini. Since he was hurrying after
the limo like a terrier after a Toyota, he must have been
expecting a treat of some sort, so when the parade was a
block away, I made a right and joined it.

The trip was leisurely but purposeful. Obeying the
speed limits, taking the most direct route, our file of three
descended Nob Hill, crossed the lengthy bias of Market
Street, and entered the revived reaches of SoMa. After a
couple of graceful turns and a double-back on Seventh, the
limo turned into what amounted to little more than an alley
and glided to a stop.

I stayed on the far side of Seventh while the limo
disgorged its passengers, who turned out to number only

Clarissa and the blue suit. The suit knocked on a door a single time, which was enough to get it opened in a hurry. The two of them went inside, the door closed, the limo sailed to the end of the alley then took a right and disappeared. Moments later, the guy in the Escort swam by like a shark and took the first turn he came to. I stayed where I was for a minute more, then backed to the middle of the block and parked. After sticking the Press sign back in my window, I reconnoitered on foot.

Cleveland Street was a mixture of decaying warehouses and reclaimed office space. The building I was interested in was an elegantly refurbished town house that sported carriage lamps beside the door, a red awning to the street, and a brass plaque on what had once been a gatepost. The cornerstone indicated its origin was pre-1906. There was no name on the awning or the door, but the light from the lamps was enough for me to read the plaque—SANDSTONE CLUB—PRIVATE. I lingered and looked and listened, but could detect no sign the place was occupied even though I'd just seen two people go inside. When I tried the door, it was locked.

My prying must have activated a sensor, because a moment later the door swung open and a bruiser who could have been a twin to the one who had piloted the limo looked out at me and scowled. "You have business here, pal?"

When I scrambled for an entrée, I didn't come up with much. "I'd like to see Mr. Sands."

"He expecting you?"

"Indubitably not."

"So beat it. He don't do business here, anyway."

"It's not for business, it's for pleasure. I know he likes the torchers, so tell him I can get him some early Julie London if the price is right."

The gambit puzzled him even more than it puzzled me. "What are you, her manager or something?"

"Why don't you just deliver the message?"

The door closed, but only long enough for me to glance up and down the street to make sure I was still alone. "Fuck you and her both," the bruiser said when he returned. "You're here when I check back, I call the law for trespass."

I waved away the rout. "Regards to Mrs. Crandall."

"Don't know the individual," the bruiser said, then disappeared behind the heavy door.

In the chill of evening, I looked up and down the narrow street. The thump of noise from a bar a block away was the only thing keeping me from believing they were remaking *On the Beach*. When I got back to Seventh, I took two steps toward my car, then turned on a well-worn heel and went the other way.

I found the Escort down the first side street I came to, its nose pushed past the corner building so the driver was in position to keep his eye on the club. I stayed in the shadow of a lamppost for several minutes before approaching the crew cut, who was so fixated on getting the lid off his thermos he didn't hear me till I tapped on the window.

"Daily or hourly?" I asked.

He spilled hot coffee on his pants. "Who the fuck? . . . get the hell *out* of here, buddy."

"I hope the retainer was five figures."

"What the hell are you talking about?"

"Mrs. Sands. What kind of arrangement does she have with you—hourly or daily? Or maybe she went for a flat fee."

His sneer made his teeth look as yellow as custard in the streetlight. "Who said anything about Mrs. Sands?"

"I believe that was me."

"What the hell business is she of yours?"

"Just trading war stories with a colleague."

He frowned. "You're a P.I.?"

I nodded. "I've even got one of those." I pointed to the Press sign in his window.

He scooted to where the light was better. "I know you. Tanner. The Kottle case."

"Among others."

"I'm Standish."

"Miles?"

He scowled. "I only heard that a million times. *Garth* Standish. Office in Laurel Village. Used to be with the San Jose PD. How'd you know I was working for Mrs. Sands?"

"Because the only other person who'd be interested in what her husband and Mrs. Crandall are up to is dead."

He shrugged. "I don't know nothing about a stiff. Domestic is all I do."

"She going to file on him?"

"Who knows? Maybe she's just keeping score."

"She got a lawyer involved?"

He shook his head. "She came direct."

"You look beat," I said after a moment.

He glanced at the thermos. "Yeah."

"You probably got other cases backing up on you."

"So?"

"So if you fill me in, maybe I can relieve you. Just for tonight. You look like you could use some sleep."

"What's in it for you?"

I shrugged. "Nothing. But I'm going to be here anyway. There's no point in both of us going without."

The deal began to bake. Standish glanced toward Cleveland Street. "The club thing is standard procedure. They come here after the show, have a few drinks or sniff some blow or whatever, he takes her home about three, three-thirty."

"Easy gig. Except for the hour."

Standish nodded. "I get three, maybe four hours' sleep a night."

"Not enough for a man your size."

He yawned. "So who you working for, anyway?"

"Can't say. You know how it is."

He reviewed his ethic; it didn't take long. "Like you said, you're going to stake it out anyway. I could get some decent sack time for once, and you could call me in the morning and tell me what time they left and I could put it in my report and no one would be the wiser." His look suddenly darkened. "She didn't double *up* on me, did she? Hire you to check my methodology?" He made the word sound Slovakian.

I shook my head. "I'm working for the dead man."

Standish was too tired to pursue it. His head bent forward until it rested on top of the steering wheel. "I don't get some rest, I'll fall over in a fit."

"You ever get inside the club?"

"Naw. Sands has more security than Quayle."

"You always pick them up at the hotel?"

He nodded. "She's got someone else on him when the sun shines."

"You ever see Sands with a guy who looks like this?" I described Tom Crandall.

Standish shook his head. "I only see him with broads."

"Anyone besides the singer?"

He shook his head. "Not regular."

"You got pictures?"

"Nothing racy. The only place they go is the club, and it don't even got windows. I could get glossies of Trump and Maples easier than I could *this* guy." His yawn was the size of Chicago.

"Go get your beauty sleep. I'll call you tomorrow with the times."

He regarded me with surprising dignity. "Don't fuck me up on this, Tanner. I'm only doing it 'cause you got a reputation. You mess me up, I'll return the favor."

"I'll keep it in mind," I said as he goosed his little car to life and puttered off down Seventh Street.

I went back to my car, pulled to where I could see the Sandstone entrance, and waited. For more than an hour. I was waging a major war with sleep myself when not one but three limos showed up from wherever they'd been grazing and took three different couples off to other destinations. The men were expensively dressed and powerfully poised, the women seemed present more for adornment than edification. The man who left with Clarissa wasn't Richard Sands, he was the three-piece suit.

Whatever the truth of the whole thing was, I decided they could all get along without me. As my Buick and I climbed the hill toward home, I wondered what Sands did at the club after all the rest had left, just him and his millions and the guy who guarded his body—wondered if he ever doubted it was worth it.

Chapter
12

When I got back to the apartment, there was a message on my machine from Ellen: She'd thought of something else to tell me about Tom. I should call her but not after ten—her father went to bed then, and the slightest sound would wake him. If she didn't hear from me tonight, she'd call tomorrow after work. I decided I didn't want to wait that long.

Just before noon the next day, I entered the Grand Avenue branch of the East Bay Bank in the heart of downtown Oakland. Ellen Simmons wasn't in sight in the rococo main room. When I asked to see her, the customer-service woman pointed downward. For a moment, I thought the gesture constituted yet another obituary, but I quickly recovered my reason and took the stairs to the lower level, where I found Ellen reviewing some checks in a cubicle near the vault that contained the safe-deposit boxes.

She wore a simple blue frock and a plain red sweater draped across her shoulders to ward off the subterranean chill. The expression on her face was even less lively than when she'd entered the funeral chapel, and I didn't improve the situation by materializing without warning in front of her desk.

When she saw me, she blanched. "I can't talk to you now," she whispered. "You shouldn't have come here."

"Maybe I need a safe-deposit box. To safeguard my valuables."

"I don't have anything to do with that. I don't have anything to do with people," she added when it looked like I was about to suggest another full-service option.

"You get a lunch break, don't you?"

She looked at her watch. "Only half an hour. At twelve-thirty."

"I'll go get sandwiches and meet you on a bench at Lake Merritt."

"I—"

"Ham or tuna?"

" . . . Tuna."

"White or wheat?"

"White."

"Coke or Sprite?"

"Milk, please."

"Chips or slaw?"

"Neither." She reddened. "But maybe a cookie. Chocolate chip?"

"See you in twenty minutes." I smiled. "Chocolate chips are seditious, you know."

She went from crimson to scarlet or maybe the other way around—I'm not good with colors—then went back to her stack of checks.

She was prompt, of course, and hungry—we devoured everything but the drinks in a matter of seconds. Content, even conceivably thrilled, by the alfresco lark, after the food had gone, Ellen took in our environment as though we were afoot in a foreign land: the trees, the lake, the rowboats, the carefree people strolling hand in hand in the noonday sun, the joggers enthusiastically punishing themselves, the children on their way to Fairyland. Nothing extraordinary, except that to Ellen Simmons it seemed a revelation.

"I never come down here," she murmured, more to herself than to me. "I wonder why."

I knew why: She hadn't done anything self-indulgent since she'd awarded her Bible and her virginity to Tom Crandall and seen her hopes dashed in the aftermath. "What did you think of to tell me?" I asked, after giving her more time to luxuriate in the view.

She licked a smear of mayonnaise from her lip. "I wasn't quite honest with you when we talked yesterday," she said with grave precision.

"You told a lie?"

"I'm afraid so."

"Shame, shame. What about?"

"Nicky."

"The brother."

"Yes."

"The one you didn't know Tom had."

She blushed for the hundredth time since I'd met her. "That was just me being cryptic. Nicky Crandall is very much alive."

"So I hear."

The response disappointed her. "So you knew that already."

"That he exists, yes. And that Tom was in touch with him before he died. But that's about all I know. How old is he, for example?"

"He's a year younger than me. Than I, rather."

"Which makes him . . . ?"

"Thirty-five."

"Where does he live?"

"I don't know, exactly."

"Here in the East Bay?"

She shook her head. "In San Francisco, somewhere near the Civic Center. He's living with a woman, I know that. Tom talked to her as well. I think he said her name was Jan."

"Tom's body was found near the Civic Center."

"Was it?" Her eyes were glazed and unreactive. In thrall to the serenity of the lake, she found coincidence and conspiracy incomprehensible. "The last time I saw him, Tom talked about Nicky quite a bit," she said after a minute.

"So how is that important, do you think?"

"I don't know if it is. But Nicky was like me—one of Tom's failures. Nicky might have been the biggest failure of them all."

"When's the last time *you* saw Nicky?"

She blinked. "Nineteen seventy-two."

"You seem certain of that."

She hesitated. "I have excellent recall."

"Still, it must have been a memorable occasion."

"Yes, it was."

A tear came to her eye. She dabbed at it but didn't smear her makeup because she wasn't wearing any. "*Darn* it. I've been crying so *much* lately. My boss can tell, and he's getting sick of it. He told me the next time it happened, he'd send me home."

Ellen took a mirror out of her purse and looked at herself. She didn't seem pleased with what she saw. Which made her standards the converse of mine—I liked what she saw in her mirror just fine.

"Let's back up a minute," I said. "How was Nicky a failure for Tom?"

She paused to consider her answer. "Nicky is sick. He has been for a long time. Tom—"

"Sick how?" I interrupted.

"Mentally. Schizophrenia is what everyone always said it was. He started acting odd in junior high school, and over the years it got worse and worse—wandering the streets at all hours, talking to himself, popping up in the middle of stores and churches and even people's homes to deliver some strange message that no one understood— by the time he was eighteen, Nicky had become an entirely different person from the one he'd been a few years earlier. It was awful for their mother, and very hard for Tom."

"I understand that over the last several years Tom and Nicky were only in touch periodically."

She nodded. "It's been that way since Tom came back from the war, pretty much."

"But they'd gotten together recently."

"Yes."

"So what did Tom have to say about his brother the last time you talked to him?"

She frowned in concentration. "Tom was worried about him, that was the gist of it. More so than normally, I mean. He implied something bad was going to happen to Nicky."

"You mean something other than his mental problems?"

"Yes. He said . . . let's see. His exact words were, 'I let it happen once; I won't let it happen again.'"

"What was it that happened the first time?"

She shrugged. "I don't know."

"Something Tom said to me in a phone message implied he thought something might have *already* happened to Nicky; that he might even be dead. Do you have any reason to think that's true?"

Ellen shook her head slowly, as though it had become weighty with recollection. "Tom was just sort of rambling that day, talking about his brother, and his wife, and how life had gotten so mixed up lately. He was quite despairing, about a lot of things, I think." Her eyes leaked liquid once again, and she looked skyward. "I hope my father's right— I hope there *is* a kingdom up there, a paradise for people like Tom."

I looked at her. "Do you believe there is?"

She shook her head slowly. "I have a hard time."

"So did Tom."

"I know." Her look was bleak. "He worried about that, too."

We watched a flock of pigeons make war over a crust of bread. "Everyone keeps telling me Tom would never have committed suicide," I said finally, "and in the next breath they give me a dozen reasons why he might have done just that."

Ellen shook her head with sudden vigor. "You have to take it on faith—Tom would never have taken his own life. He would have given it willingly for a thousand causes, but he would *never* have thrown it away for nothing."

"Not even to ease the pain you admit he was experiencing?"

She clasped her hands in her lap, tightly, as though the link would make her eloquent. "Tom thrived on pain. No, that's not it. He didn't enjoy it, but he needed it. Psychological pain, I'm speaking of. To be torn by conflict, racked with doubt, that was the only way Tom could tell he was functioning at the level he thought he ought to be."

"I don't know what that means," I said with more than a little meanness. "'I hurt, therefore I am,' or some such nonsense?"

Ellen closed her eyes. "To know what *any* of this means—Tom, Nicky, me—I have to tell you what it was like back when we were young." She opened her eyes and looked at me. "Do you mind a history lesson?"

"History is my business."

She colored again—her flesh was as variable as a chameleon's. "It's not *like* me to talk about this kind of thing, particularly to a stranger, though since everyone in my life *is* a stranger, except my parents, I don't get to . . ." This time the color was pink. "Anyway, I'd like very much to tell you about Tom. About *us*."

She crossed her arms and shifted to a more comfortable position on the bench. "When he was fifteen, Tom Crandall was everything that everyone else aspired to. He got top grades. He played sports. He was a singer, too; he and his friends had this rock band, and when they played for dances, the kids would gather around and cheer and cheer and . . . well, life was *like* that for Tom. What other kids dreamed about, Tom experienced routinely. He even played Brick in the senior play. I was Maggie. We were tremendous. The principal was scandalized." Just now her smile wasn't Maggie's at all, but that of an ingenue with a glass menagerie, awaiting a gentleman caller who had already come calling for the last time.

She paused to gather up more memory; when she had, her expression darkened. "The problem was, it came too easily. He did things other people envied, but he didn't have to work for them—it was more like he was blessed in some way. But Tom was smart, and perceptive, and he saw that because of what he was, some people worshiped him, but other people hated him, and he began to feel guilty about both of those reactions—to feel unworthy of his gifts, even ashamed of them. So he set higher and higher standards for himself, standards that *couldn't* be so easily achieved. Because Tom was Tom, they became standards no one could *ever* achieve."

"I think I know what you're talking about," I said, because it was true: Tom's personal code was as exalted as any I'd ever seen.

"Tom became obsessed with his shortcomings," Ellen went on. "They were shortcomings visible only to him, of course; no one else could figure out why he seemed so unhappy. They thought it was contempt, most of them— that Tom was 'stuck up,' to use the term of the day—but what no one understood was that Tom's contempt extended solely to himself."

"That's a pretty good prescription for a breakdown, eventually," I said. And for a suicide, I thought but didn't say.

Ellen nodded. "The good thing was that Tom kept looking for an answer, but of course any answer that would satisfy him was by definition extreme. He became a vegetarian. He worked nights at a hospital, cleaning up. At one point, he decided to become a monk, so he built a little fort up in the hills and stayed there for three weeks without seeing or speaking to anyone, just to see if he could do it." She shook her head with wonderment. "When he discovered he could, he didn't want to be a monk anymore."

"Sounds like Groucho: 'I don't want to join a club that would have me for a member.'"

"That's it exactly. He could have been a success at anything—doctor, lawyer, business—but that would have been too easy and too . . . trivial. So he drove an ambulance. And rescued people. And thought about life. And wished he was more than he was." Her voice broke. "And for some reason loved that woman."

The reference to Clarissa was as jarring as a curse in the rarefied context in which she'd just been speaking. "Did you ever meet her?" I asked.

Ellen shook her head. "I only know what Tom told me. In the beginning, she was a godsend; in the end, she was trying to destroy him."

"Literally, do you think?"

Her face hardened into a stubborn mask. "All I know is that Tom is dead. It's not for me to say whether that's what she wanted."

The words were melodramatic and encrusted with bile, and that wasn't a natural state for Ellen. I decided to move her away from the marriage. "How does your history lesson apply to Tom and his brother?"

It took her a moment to leave Clarissa behind. "Nicky was the opposite of Tom. It was like they were twins, except Tom had the good qualities and Nicky the bad. Tom didn't realize how exceptional he was, and Nicky thought he was special but he was really just . . . crazy. Tom had a hyperactive conscience, and Nicky had no conscience at all. He was mean, if you want to know the truth—always in trouble, always doing something to embarrass you, always being compared unfavorably to Tom."

"Which made Tom feel even more guilty."

She nodded. "Nicky started acting stranger and stranger. Looking back, it was because his illness had started to set in, of course, but Tom thought *he* was responsible, that no one gave Nicky a chance to be himself because Tom had led them to expect too much of him. So he set out to save Nicky from himself."

"How?"

"Oh, he got coaches to take him back on the team after he'd been kicked off and teachers to let him make up the tests he'd skipped and the principal to overlook his truancy. Things like that. Just before Tom went away, Nicky had gotten so bad that Tom convinced a clinic in Walnut Creek to admit Nicky as a charity patient—I think Tom did chores for the doctor, or something."

"What happened to Nicky after Tom went to Vietnam?"

"Not long after he got out of the clinic, he got in some trouble and left home."

"Wasn't anyone helping him? With medication or psychotherapy or something?"

Ellen nodded. "He was still seeing the doctor at the clinic, but it didn't seem to do much good. The Crandalls didn't have much money, so I'm not sure they could afford the proper medication. Anyway, Nicky got worse and worse, and eventually he made a mistake that turned everyone against him, so he left town and began to roam. After he got back from the war, Tom tried to keep tabs on him, but it was impossible."

"What did Nicky do that turned everyone against him?"

Ellen closed her eyes. "I don't know, but it doesn't matter. It's ancient history; I don't even know why I've told you all this. Living in the past again, I suppose. I tend to do that." She looked at her watch. "I've got to get back." She opened her purse. "What do I owe you for my lunch?"

"Don't be silly."

"Please. It's only right."

"No, it isn't."

She looked at me again, this time for so long I became uncomfortable. "You remind me of him," she said softly. "I suppose that's why you were his friend."

I don't know if she intended the reaction, but I regarded her statement as a trophy.

When I started to get up, she took my hand. "Would you do me a favor, Mr. Tanner?"

"If I can."

"Would you let me talk to you again some time?"

"Sure. Let me give you my card. You can call me whenever—"

"No," she interrupted. "This is forward of me, I know, but what I want is for you to take me to dinner some time and let me talk about myself. I just . . . never get a chance to *talk* about myself. And I have some things I'd like to say."

I smiled. "When do you want to do it?"

"Any time." She wriggled with embarrassment. "I'm at your disposal."

"How about tonight? Then you won't have a chance to change your mind."

She nodded somberly, as if we'd just agreed to post the banns. "Please pick me up at seven. I can't stay out later than ten, or Father will be upset."

Sometimes children have to upset their parents, so the parents will learn they're not children anymore, but I decided it wasn't the time to mention it.

Chapter
13

I was still drifting, without a client or a crime to propel me, pursuing little more than a sense that something sinister had happened to Tom Crandall. It occurred to me that maybe I was on the case because the possibility that Tom had taken his own life was too much baggage for me to carry, baggage stuffed with a lot of Tom's incapacities, but, because I called myself his friend and because friendship surely encompasses the obligation to know when the other is despairing and to try to do something about it, with my own ineptitude as well.

Since Ellen Simmons shared my view, albeit for reasons no more tangible than my own, and since she was a woman out of time—a child in some respects, with the charms and vulnerabilities the word implies—I had agreed to be her dinner companion that evening. Second thoughts were all around me as I watched her walk back toward her office—depositing her lunch bag in the trash along the way, picking up someone else's litter while she was at it—but I decided I couldn't disappoint someone whose life was already laden with disappointment.

Traffic in the Bay Area is a nightmare these days, partly from the leavings of the earthquake, partly from the time lag inherent in infrastructure, partly from the torrent of people still moving into the area despite its drawbacks, so it seemed silly to drive back over the bridge to the office only to turn around a few hours later and struggle through the rush-hour sludge on my way back to Danville. When I tried to think of something to do on the east side of the bay other than what I usually did, which was to browse some bookstores or tour the art museums, the best I could come up with was to have another chat with Tom's mother.

I found a phone booth and called the bank. When I got through to Ellen, she reacted as though she were on the line with Beelzebub—my willful breach of the edict against personal calls hinted that she'd made a date with the devil. Not until I told her what I wanted, and why, and promised never, ever to call her again at work did her words melt to a normal timbre. Or maybe her supervisor had left the room.

Ellen gave me directions to Tom's family home, and thirty minutes later I was there. The house was much like the one Ellen lived in—a small board-and-batten bungalow, a relic of the valley's origins—but in contrast to Ellen's militaristic environment, this one was negligently tended and irregularly maintained. Shades drawn against the afternoon sun, the house slumbered like an old gray cat at the end of a driveway that was marked at the street by a metal mailbox on a chain-link post and a rock that was painted white and emblazoned with the number 23322.

There was no car or other evidence of habitation in sight. Heavy and still, the air seemed undisturbed by living things, human or otherwise; even the trees in the surrounding orchard seemed somnolent. I remembered reading that the original walnut grafts—English onto black—are failing for some reason, probably for the reasons the rest of us are failing.

When I knocked at the door, a dog started barking; a moment later a second took up the song. For several minutes the canine chorus was all that greeted me. I looked and listened for signs of life other than four-footed, knocked on the door half a dozen times, wondered what I was doing there in the first place. As if to confirm the illicit nature of my presence, a siren sounded in the distance, adding its voice to the weird chorale, making it a comic opera. The siren got nearer; the dogs barked louder; I was the first to yield.

Halfway back to my car I heard a door scrape open at my back and the porch boards screech at each slow step taken by the person who had ventured onto it. I turned around. Mrs. Crandall, burly in her slip and slippers, was watching me with thick belligerence. The mongrel at her side duplicated her attitude exactly.

Although it was better than midafternoon, I'd clearly awakened her. She seemed dazed, befuddled, and more than a little frightened, as evidenced by the cast-iron skillet that dangled from the hand that wasn't dragging a thin white strap back onto her shoulder. I made as abject an apology as I could come up with and took two steps toward the porch. The dog growled; Mrs. Crandall brandished cookware.

"I told you the last time, I don't want you coming *around* here," she blurted in a fuzzy rasp.

The combination of grief and slumber seemed to have addled her senses. "I've never been here before, Mrs. Crandall. The only time we met was yesterday at Tom's funeral. After the service, near the grave."

She frowned. "Tom?"

"He was a friend of mine, remember? At the cemetery, we talked about the old days, before Tom went to Vietnam. And about his friend Ellen Simmons."

The siren had become loud enough to make us wait for it to whiz past on the highway that was twenty yards behind me on the far side of the lifeless orchard. "You're not here about Nicky?" Mrs. Crandall asked when the screech had diminished enough for her to prevail above it. "You're not one of the ones that was here before?"

I shook my head, wondering at the history that had led her to lie to me about her other son when I'd inquired of him previously. "I would like to talk some about Nicky, Mrs. Crandall, but I'm interested in the person who was here before. What was his name?"

"He didn't say."

"What did he want?"

"To take Nicky off. In one of those." She looked in the direction of the fading siren.

"He came in a police car?"

She shook her head. "An ambulance. A white one with red letters."

I tried to decipher what was going on and finally came up with an answer. "I think the ambulance you're thinking of was the one Tom used in his work, Mrs. Crandall. His partner brought it to the funeral yesterday, when he came to pay his respects. It must have been someone else who came about Nicky."

She shook her head. "He told me Dr. Marlin sent him."

"Who's Dr. Marlin?"

"Nicky's doctor. Back when he first went crazy."

"The one at the clinic in Walnut Creek?"

She shook her head. "Not anymore; he moved away."

"Why would Nicky need an ambulance, Mrs. Crandall?"

"He didn't need it; it needed him."

"Why?"

"To give him his medicine."

"When was this?"

After a long pause, she slumped and shook her head. "Time's been lost to me for a while." She looked up. "I thought it was night; I thought it was time for bed. I must have pulled the shades too soon." As though it had become a stone, she bowed her head until her chin rested on her chest. "It's a fearsome thing to be confused about day and night." To register his sympathy, the dog muttered a woeful moan.

I resumed my advance on the porch. "I'm confused about a lot of things myself."

Mrs. Crandall regarded me with dispassion. "You're young. You've got time to straighten yourself out. I'm too old to change a thing about me or the world, either one."

"No one's that old," I said, then wondered if I believed it. "I had lunch today with a friend of yours," I went on as affably as I could manage given the look in the mongrel's eye.

"Who?"

"Ellen Simmons."

Her eyes widened, and her grip on the skillet loosened. "*Tom's* Ellen?"

I nodded. "I met her at the bank where she works, and we had a picnic by the lake."

She considered my story, compared it with her estimate of reality, then nodded. "Ellen has an important job."

I envisioned the stark and servile basement where Ellen Simmons paged through her pile of checks. "Yes, she does."

"Ellen always loved Tom. Even after he married that woman."

I nodded. "I think you're right."

"I don't know what will happen to her now that he's gone."

"Maybe something good."

The answer caused her to blink and, surprisingly, to join forces with me. "God knows Ellen deserves a blessing. We've seen too much grief, the both of us."

I nodded again and let silence edge my attitude toward tenderness. "I don't want to bother you much longer, Mrs. Crandall," I went on when it looked like her pool of pity had drained a bit. "I was just wondering if you'd heard from Nicky lately."

My question seemed to surprise her, not because she didn't know the answer but because I didn't. "Nicky never comes out here anymore. Everyone knows that." The declaration was orotund with truth.

"Does he call?"

She shook her head, then became peculiarly precise. "I haven't talked to Nicky since nineteen seventy-four."

If Tom's implication that something had happened to his brother was true, his mother clearly had no knowledge of it. I was about to ask what happened to drive Nicky away some seventeen years before when she looked back at the house in awe, as if it had just made a prediction.

"Isn't that an awful thing for a mother to admit?" she asked herself. "Nicky's as dead to me as Tom is. Both sons dead," she repeated, her tone less sad than awed, as though for the first time she regarded her life as cursed. "I'm not a mother anymore. It's the only thing I ever was, and now I'm not even that."

She started to sob, in lumpy convulsions that she made no move to stem, proud and pathetic on her porch. The dog whined awhile as well, rubbed against her leg then growled as I went to her side and put my arm across Mrs. Crandall's nearly naked shoulders. Her flesh radiated through my jacket, not the warmth of contentment but the singe of anguish.

I waited for the convulsions to subside, then hurried to finish my business. "Do you have any idea where Nicky is living now, Mrs. Crandall?"

The tears had washed away her stupor and revived her wariness. "Why?"

"I'd like to talk to him."

"What about?"

"Tom."

"What about Tom?"

"I'm just wondering if Tom and Nicky had been able to get together before Tom died."

"Well, they did," she said defensively. "My boys always did right by each other. Tom still loved Nicky, even after—" Her mouth snapped closed, trapping her final words.

"After what?"

She shook her head stubbornly. "Never mind all that. It's been forgotten by everyone except that lunatic down the road."

"Mr. Simmons?"

"*He* knows what I mean. You don't need to."

"Did Tom tell you he'd seen Nicky recently?"

Mrs. Crandall nodded.

"What did he say about him?"

"He said Nicky was sickly. He said he needed help." She paused and looked skyward, at the only source of assistance she'd ever found effective. "As if he hasn't always needed more help than anyone could give him."

"Did Tom say what was wrong?"

"He just said Nicky was sick—so sick he might die." She frowned. "But Tom was the one who died. Now why do you suppose that was?" She paused, then answered her own question. "Maybe he caught something from Nicky. Maybe that's why that *ambulance* was here," she added in a squirt of her former logic. "Maybe it came for Tom."

The rhetoric had spun through her mind so rapidly I was afraid she was going to faint. "Maybe," I agreed, tightening my grip to steady her. "Did Tom tell you *where* he'd seen Nicky?"

She shook her head, her thoughts elsewhere. "Tom was a good boy. Why is it the wrong ones die, do you suppose?"

I had no answer that was grounded in anything but chaos, but I wondered at the source of her heartlessness concerning her second son. "Do you know anyone else who might know where Nicky is, Mrs. Crandall?"

"There's no one left that cares."

"Why do people around here feel that way about him?"

"Because Nicky did bad."

"Like what?"

She shrugged my arm off her shoulder. "Things that don't need talking about." She looked down at herself with dismay, as though she only now realized how she was dressed. "I have to get a housecoat on. Reverend Dobbins might come by. He said he would, to see how I was getting along. He won't like it if he thinks I've let myself go."

As she turned for the door, I tried for one last lead. "What's the reason Nicky doesn't come home anymore, Mrs. Crandall? Did he do something violent?" I took a second stab. "Did he kill someone?"

She started to hug herself as a shield from me, and seemed surprised to find the skillet in her hand. "Ellen," she said abruptly.

"What does Ellen have to do with it?"

"When Tom went off to war, Nicky decided he had feelings for her. I told him it wasn't right, that Ellen was Tom's and always would be. Nicky told me he couldn't help it, he wanted to keep company with her. I told him Ellen was spoken for, and if he started bothering her with that nonsense, I'd have him put away again." Her lip stiffened. "He knew I meant it, too. Which I did."

"Why did you have him put away the first time?"

She straightened her back to establish her rectitude. "Tom said it was the thing to do, so I did it."

"What did Ellen think about how Nicky felt about her?"

Mrs. Crandall raised her head as royally as a duchess. "I never saw the need to ask about it." Her eyes were hard and small; the subject was clearly closed.

"Do you have a photograph of Nicky, Mrs. Crandall?"

"Nope. Threw 'em out."

"Do you have any of Tom's war medals here in the house?"

"Nope. Someone stole 'em. I don't got nothing that's any use to anybody," she concluded dismally, and left me and the dog to share the barren yard.

Chapter
14

I dawdled through the remainder of the afternoon, wandering around Danville and Alamo and Walnut Creek, absorbing the changes that time and the eighties money flood had wrought. I saw scores of ridiculous houses, mammoth structures that aped everything from jungle huts to French châteaux, and the usual scab of businesses whose presence indicates that both a history and a heritage have been lost forever—the Giorgios and Guccis and Godivas that pop up in places like Carmel and Jackson Hole and Santa Fe and draw their ilk like feces draw flies until such places are unendurable by anyone who knew them when.

As a result of my meanderings, by the time I started back to pick up Ellen, I was in a lousy mood, made even more so by my suspicion that what underlay my funk was not as much a matter of aesthetics as jealousy—I couldn't afford to live in the San Ramon Valley if I hocked everything I owned for the down payment. I'd have to rob a bank, which, in light of the savings-and-loan debacle, turns out to be how a lot of people got there in the first place.

Ellen didn't answer the door when I knocked, her father did. His name was Orson Simmons, he announced with tawdry grandeur. He was as sunny as Lincoln and as friendly as Coolidge, and his rusty voice would have eaten through sheet steel. I anticipated trouble and got it before I was halfway through the door.

"Her mother and I would like to know more about you before we allow our daughter to leave in your company," he declared after inviting me inside the way a drill sergeant invites a recruit to do a pushup. When I didn't answer, he felt obliged to provide an explanation: "Ellen is not as prudent as she should be when it comes to men."

"She seems prudent squared to me."

"What does she *know* of you?"

"She knows I was a friend of Tom Crandall's."

He crossed his arms above the bib in his overalls. His hands were large and gnarled in odd places, as though he used them as tools rather than incur the expense of buying real ones. "You'd be mistaken to think that counts in your favor," he declared.

I shrugged. "And you'd be mistaken to think that it matters very much."

His face darkened to the tint of the gloomy room. The haughty attitude angered me, as hauteur always does, so I girded myself for battle. If I'd been in a good mood, I would have handled it differently, I suppose, which is not to say I would have handled it better.

"What do you do for a living, Mr. Tanner?" Simmons continued in the same vein, which was the vein I used in my lawyer days when I had a cop on the stand. Because I knew how it was going to go if we got into it, I looked toward the door at his back, hoping Ellen would charge through it and rescue us, but no such luck ensued.

"I'm a private investigator," I said, then decided to embellish and even alarm him. "I'm also a lawyer."

It's testimony to the status of my current trade that Simmons saw my former one as an enhancement. "I don't know if Ellen knows that."

"Not many people do."

"You don't practice the profession?"

I shook my head. "Not anymore."

"Why not?" His expression was that of a powerless man who had sought power his whole life and couldn't imagine anyone would willingly give it up, however minuscule the quantum.

"I'm allergic to German cars," I explained.

He got the joke, I suppose, though you couldn't tell from his expression, which remained as grim as a bull-dog's.

"I'll be frank," he declared, as though it were an achievement.

I suppressed an old rejoinder. "Feel free."

"We're concerned that you're too . . . mature for our daughter. She is not . . . experienced. She is easily confused and manipulated. I—"

That did it. "Look, Mr. Simmons. You seem to think something lascivious is going on here, but it's not. I'm not engaged to your daughter, I'm not even courting her. We're just going to have a nice dinner, share a bottle of wine, talk about truth and beauty and the prospects for high-definition TV and—"

"Ellen doesn't use spirits," Orson interrupted, his words as stiff and bitter as the drink I wished I had. "I hope you will honor her decision."

"Of course I will, if that's what it is. But let me tell you exactly how mature *I* am, Mr. Simmons. I'm forty-eight years old, which means at least two things—I wear bifocals and I'm too old to care if you approve of me or not. Ellen and I have a date, and I'm going to wait here for her unless and until she tells me not to bother." I gave him my blankest look: "So. Can Ellen come out and play, or have you chained her to her bed?"

"You have no right to insult me," he sputtered. "This is my house. Ellen is my only child. I—"

"Why do you think your rights include depriving her of a night on the town?" I interjected loudly. "If you want a pet, maybe you should buy a dog."

For a moment, I thought he was going to hit me or try to. For a moment, he thought so, too. But he was only angry, not witless, and my guess was that fighting back had usually gotten him in trouble.

"You know nothing about this family," he muttered. "I have lived on this property for three generations—before there was a freeway; before there was a high school; before the walnut groves died out. I deserve respect."

"So does your daughter."

"You know nothing about what her life has been. Ellen has been hurt by men. More than once. She needs—"

The door to the kitchen opened with a bang, and Ellen stomped into the room, dress flaring, hair swishing, eyes white hot and fastened on her father. "You said you wouldn't *do* this. You promised that for once you'd let me . . . go. Without a fuss."

"But this man—"

"This man is my *friend*. I asked him to take me to dinner. He accepted the invitation. I was grateful. So that's where we're going. I'll try to be home by ten, but don't wait up." She turned to me with a glorious smile that blinded me to her father's scowl. "Sound the trumpets, summon the chariots, notify the society page; Ellen Simmons has a date."

She took my arm, spun me around, and marched the both of us through the door. As locked in step as a drill team, we reached the haven of my car without looking back or exchanging a word.

I helped Ellen inside, then went around to the other door, but before I opened it, I glanced back at the house. Through the screen, I could see Orson Simmons, stalwart in the center of his home, head down, shoulders heaving, a monument to impotence and frustration. A tiny woman in a blue print dress hovered over him like a nurse, rubbing his back, whispering consolations, all to no avail. A moment later, he brushed her aside and disappeared into the kitchen through the freely swinging door. The woman he left behind seemed less startled than relieved at his departure.

I got in the car and turned the key. Ellen was soft and stoic against the far door, hands in her lap, eyes on the house, shawl snug around her shoulders. "They're not bad people," she said as I turned around and headed down the drive.

"I know."

"They just think I can't take care of myself."

"Partly because you *let* them think that."

"It's also because they think the world is such a horrid place that *no* woman is safe in it."

"It's not that bad out there, Ellen. Not yet."

"I know. I should have moved out long ago and gotten on with my life. But somehow it seemed too complicated. Or too cruel. And when I imagined what life on my own would be like, the loneliness seemed overwhelming. So I stayed put. And here I am—a spinster."

I smiled. "A spinster who asks strange men for dates."

She smiled gratefully and placed a hand on my thigh. "You're not a stranger. I feel like I've known you for a million years."

"I feel like I've been alive that long, sometimes."

"And I feel like I've been alone that long."

We slipped into a tolerable silence as I took the old highway into Alamo on the way to Walnut Creek. After we passed the cluster of Alamo Square, I looked at her again. "Did you know Nicky Crandall was in love with you?"

The question jolted Ellen out of wherever her thoughts had put her. "You mean Tom."

"I mean Nicky."

She frowned. "When was this supposed to have happened?"

"After Tom went in the army, Nicky wanted you to be his girl."

Her laugh was dry and brief. "I didn't know; he never said anything. Nicky mooned around a lot, was clearly in some other world, but I never thought that world included me. Who told you this? Nicky?"

"Mrs. Crandall."

"What else did she tell you?"

"Not much. She clearly favored Tom over his brother."

Ellen nodded. "She's only human."

"Do you know why Nicky never asked you out?"

"Why?"

"Because his mother told him she'd put him back in the nuthouse if he did."

Ellen digested the news in silence until I pulled up in front of the restaurant, a bar and grill that was a clone of a dozen like it in San Francisco. I'm sure there were better places in the area, but I don't keep track of such things, and besides, I wanted Ellen's attention on something more fruitful than food.

We were shown to a table in the back by a hostess whose black leather minidress was the friendliest thing about her. The decor was southwestern glitz, the clientele was cowboy yuppie and unembarrassed by it, and Ellen's eyes were big enough to swallow it all in a single disbelieving gulp. Her astonishment enlarged geometrically when she looked at the right side of the menu.

We ordered drinks from the cocktail waitress, then Ellen put a hand on mine. "I think what you said may explain some things," she said eagerly. "I think Nicky must have written Tom about his feelings for me. I think that could be why Tom never came back."

"I don't understand."

"I told you that Tom felt responsible for Nicky's troubles, remember? I think Tom must have thought that if he didn't come back, then Nicky would have a chance with me. A chance to best Tom at something for the first time in his life."

It seemed a reach to me, but Ellen clearly had needed some explanation, however bizarre, for Tom's faithlessness for a long time. If that's what I'd brought her, I was glad.

"It's a little Freudian," I said, "but if you think—"

"It's not Freudian, it's *Arthurian.*"

Her voice fell to a wistful drone as I remembered that not long ago I'd thought of Ellen Simmons in much the same terms. "I was supposed to marry Nicky, don't you see? It all makes sense: I was Tom's gift to his little brother. And Tom was so far away, he couldn't see how impossible it was."

"Because Nicky was crazy? Or because you could never love anyone but Tom?"

She thought about it. "Both. It took Tom a long time to realize how sick Nicky was, that Nicky's problem wasn't his brother but his mind." Briefly brightened by her newly minted rationale, Ellen's face suddenly fell. "Or maybe Tom thought I was crazy, too. Maybe he thought Nicky and I were suited to each other. Maybe *that's* why he—"

She stopped when she noticed her reflection in the mirrored wall across from us.

She considered it for almost a minute. "*Look* at me. I'm still a child. I dress like one and act like one. For twenty years, I've done nothing to prove Tom wrong."

The conversation had taken a crooked tack, one that had its roots in the past rather than the present, one I couldn't follow. I tried to bring us back to the here and now. "Nicky never told you any of this himself, did he?"

Ellen shook her head. "Can you imagine how *afraid* he must have been, of what his mother might do if he started seeing me? Nicky was paranoid enough as it was."

"Paranoid enough to kill his brother twenty years later? For putting him in the nuthouse?"

The question was heartless, both in intent and context, but it produced the unvarnished reaction I sought. "After all this time? Why would he? Besides, Nicky *loved* Tom."

"Says who?"

"I . . . they were brothers."

"So were Cain and Abel."

That thought carried us across my scotch and her margarita and through the meal itself, which came in minuscule portions and went without fanfare except for the running chatter from the waiter, who was working so hard at making us feel important he succeeded only in making us want to hang him with one of the ropes that were noosed and coiled above the bar.

When the plates were cleared and there was a mousse in front of Ellen and a cognac in front of me, our eyes made music once again. "One last point about Nicky," I said.

She'd had enough of the subject but was too polite to deny me. "What?"

"If you wanted to find him, where would you look?"

"A week ago I would have talked to Tom."

"And now?"

"I guess I'd talk to Dr. Marlin."

"The one who treated him back when they first suspected he had a problem."

She nodded.

"How would I go about finding him?"

"He worked for the North Valley Clinic back then, but I think he moved to San Francisco. Following the craziness, I guess." Her smile was thin and bleached. "They tore the clinic down a long time ago. There's a taco place there now."

"I'll try to track him down."

Ellen dipped into her mousse, and I sipped at my drink. "You were going to talk about yourself tonight," I said after a minute. "So, did you collect paper dolls or toy soldiers?"

Her look was rueful. "I'm afraid I got you here under false pretenses—there's so little to tell I could have covered it all at noon between bites of my sandwich. I'm a woman who's done nothing with her life but dream."

"Then tell me your dreams."

Her descent into melancholy was steep and continuing. "I'm afraid I've forgotten most of them. One tends to do that when they can never come true."

"Then tell me some other things about yourself."

"Like what?"

"What's your favorite book?"

"*Anna Karenina.*"

"Why?"

"Because it's sad and true and about love and longing and despair." She blushed. "A life much like the one I lead myself. Not physically, of course—there are no counts and countesses out our way that I know of. But my mind is full of notions that no one even thinks about anymore."

"So is mine."

"You want me to believe you're joking, but I know you're not. That's why I knew we could talk about things I never talk about." She took another bite of mousse. "Does it bother you that you're out of touch with the world?"

"Sometimes. How about you?"

"I feel horrible about it."

"You shouldn't."

"Why?"

"Because what you think isn't wrong, it's just out of fashion. But fashion is a circle—sooner or later what's out inevitably comes back in."

"But what I think has made me shut myself up for twenty years in a sterile little house with my parents fighting and snoring in the next room while I think grand thoughts and tell myself that I'm purer and more noble than everyone else, when all I am is stranded." Her attempt to grin was touching. "It's easy to be pure when no one tries to make you otherwise."

"Change that part. Move out. Circulate."

"How?"

"Just do it. Call a mover and move."

"But where? Houses are so expensive."

"Rent an apartment. Buy a condo."

"And then what?"

The blind began leading the blind. "Do things. Go places. Meet people."

She looked around. "At places like this? Goodness. It would be like the Virgin Mary meeting Mick Jagger." She colored while I laughed. "I'm sorry. That was profane."

"That was funny. You don't have to frequent joints like this. Go to concerts. Plays. Museums. It isn't *all* garbage out there."

"I know, but it's . . . difficult. I spend all day in a basement and all night in what amounts to a cloister. I've gotten used to darkness."

I took her hand. "It'll be easier now that Tom's dead."

She dropped her head. "Don't say that."

"Why not? It's true—Tom's dead. I'm sorry and you are, too. But he'll never come knocking on your door and say he's been a fool, he never should have left you, he wants to live with you forever. That's not going to happen now. So you have to make something *else* happen."

"It's too late," she sniffed. "It's—"

"You're already having dinner with a private eye, for crying out loud. Keep it up and you'll be playing polo with a prince."

She made a smile materialize. "I'd rather eat pizza with a private eye, I think."

"See? I told you your ideals were solid. Let's get out of here and hunt up that pizza. Pepperoni okay?"

"Is there any other kind?"

Which is exactly what we did, then spent the evening arguing politics: It turned out Ellen was more liberal than

I was, which made me worry that one of my worst fears was coming true and I was getting reactionary with age. It only helped a little when I decided Ellen's viewpoint was less a product of reason than naïveté.

On the way home, we didn't say much. I had no idea what she was thinking, and she probably thought she had an all-too-sordid idea of what was on my mind. When we pulled into the drive, the houselights were out but a security light nailed to a tree branch made the yard as bright as a ballfield.

I stopped the car and looked at her. After a moment of reverie, she looked back. "I had a wonderful time tonight."

"So did I. Do you ever get to the city?"

"No."

"Well, you should."

"I know. I will. I just . . . it's going to take some time."

"Well . . ."

"Well . . ."

"I bet there are some eyes peeking out at us."

She smiled. "Six, if you count cat's eyes."

"How many cat's eyes equal one human eye?"

"That's silly."

"I hope so." I put a hand on her shoulder. "I think we should give them a show. Kitty and all."

She froze, then melted. "I think so, too."

I got out of the car and went to Ellen's side and opened the door. I reached for her hand and helped her out, then guided her to the exact center of the drive. In the glare of both the security light and the Buick's horizontal halogens, I took her in my arms and kissed her.

Underneath her billowy dress, her body was surprisingly full and her undergarments surprisingly subtle, suggesting her sex life was subversive, in the form of sheer silk bras and tiny lacy panties that only she and the mirror would ever see. Tentative at first, the embrace lingered and contracted—it wasn't something I did often enough to make it routine, and, for all I knew, Ellen hadn't kissed a man in twenty years. Which was why, I guess, the kiss became something real and wanted to be a prelude to something more.

I finally pulled away.

"My," she murmured as she straightened her dress. "I'd almost forgotten how . . . I'd almost forgotten."

"If you get forgetful again, give me a call." In the warmth of her heaving breaths, I glanced at the house. "Are you going to get in trouble?"

"Probably," she said. "It's about time, don't you think?"

Chapter
15

On the way back to the city, I took a detour, up Fish Ranch Road to Tilden Park, then over to Grizzly Peak Boulevard, the road that snakes along the top of the Berkeley Hills and, when the fog's not in and the clouds aren't low, affords the best view of San Francisco you can get this side of a blimp. The conditions were ripe and the view didn't disappoint, so I pulled off at a wide spot to let the perspective sink to my marrow.

At this time of night, the glory was all you saw, of course, not the filth but the shine, not the contagion but the vitality, not the rags but the riches of a city that was still, after the earthquake and AIDS and the rest of the modern urban horrors, next to New York and Los Angeles the most favored destination of anyone in America with ambition and an idea. I wished it were always only thus, but some of those lights were police stations and emergency hospitals and homeless shelters, and some of those buildings housed con artists and money launderers and child molesters, and some of those bridges led to people with lives like Ellen's—suffered rather than lived, received rather than earned, acceded to rather than fought for. I lived such a life myself, periodically; that I hadn't lived it for a lifetime I attributed chiefly to the decision, made a dozen years ago, to earn my living helping people whose troubles, in every single case I'd ever taken on, were far greater than my own.

With that small solace sloshing through my mind, I put the Buick in gear and curled down the hill toward the bay. By the time I crossed the bridge and eddied through the Financial District and climbed Telegraph Hill to the rented room I called my home, I was too exhausted for either dreams or nightmares.

The next morning I looked up Dr. Marlin. It wasn't as easy as I expected—he wasn't in the Yellow or White Pages, nor the city directory either. I had to refer to my files, in the form of a listing of the membership of the San Francisco County Medical Association, before I got a line on him—Leonard R. Marlin, Psychiatrist; Healthways Clinics, a division of Healthways, Inc., 222 Van Ness Avenue.

I knew a little about Healthways. Its clinics were part of a statewide organization that was designed to provide low-cost, walk-in medical services to the low and middle classes on a cut-rate basis. The clinics were no-frills storefronts, staffed mostly by nurses and physicians' assistants and paramedics and others with less-than-M.D. levels of training, but M.D.'s were rotated through the system as well—doctors in private practice working with Healthways on a pro bono basis or members of the Healthways staff who had presumably gone into medicine for something other than wealth or prestige.

I'd seen a couple of the clinics around town but had never dealt with any of them, either personally or professionally. My own medical needs are taken care of by Dr. Clinton on a trade-out basis—he gives me free care, I put heat on the deadbeats who haven't paid his bills, at least those who have the wherewithal. Since I've been generally healthy except when someone with a weapon has made me otherwise, so far the doctor's ahead of the game. But doctors always are.

Since the only listing for Marlin was in care of the Healthways operation, I assumed he was a member of the staff. When I gave the headquarters a call and asked to speak to him, they were reluctant to pay me much mind. To save time, I came up with a ruse—I told them I was making inquiries on behalf of L. Arthur Wilkers, Esquire, Attorney-at-Law. L. Arthur happens to be the city's preeminent specialist in the defense of medical malpractice cases—savior of scrub nurses and anesthesiologists and hospital boards of directors, nemesis of the maimed and the mangled. I'd never met the man myself, but I figured the people at Healthways would know who he was. I also figured there was little likelihood that Wilkers would ever learn I'd used him as a passkey if I made this the only time I used it.

As I hoped, Wilkers' name was a tonic. Helpful if not unctuous, the woman on the phone informed me that Dr. Marlin did indeed have an office at the Healthways building, but this was the day for him to be in residence at the clinic on Turk Street. I asked for the address of the clinic, then asked the woman to call and say I'd be there in about an hour and would appreciate a few minutes of the doctor's time. She told me she'd see what she could do. Which turned out to be enough—I spent fewer than ten minutes confined to the waiting room in the company of a mélange of battered wives, feverish infants, rheumatic elders, and scrofulous dope addicts, along with a couple of people pretty much like me, whose aches had their origins in less visible afflictions.

The clinic was in the heart of the Tenderloin District, flanked by a check-cashing outlet on one side and a sex shop on the other and a plasma center across the street: payday all around. Although the clinic itself was new and well maintained, the neighborhood was its opposite—if you didn't need medical help when you set out for the place, the odds were that you would need some by the time you got there, at least if you were old and alone and walking after dark.

It was just before noon when the receptionist—as white as gauze in her starchy uniform—declared that Doctor could see me now. The news didn't please my fellow sufferers, most of whom had been awaiting an audience a lot longer than I had. My consolation was that they wouldn't be put out long—I suspected Doctor wouldn't have much truck with me once he learned what I was up to.

His office was like the rest of the place—clean, functional, aggressively impersonal, as if the clinic were treating widgets, not people, as if the patients were plagued with faulty disk drives rather than broken bones and septic tissues. I'm sure it was efficient, and in some sense effective, and much better than what had been there before, which if memory served was a joint called The Chicago Club. But if this is the brave new world, why do so many people want to live forever?

Dr. Marlin was making notes in a red file folder when the receptionist ushered me into his presence. He was six feet, stocky, square-shouldered, blondish, and well groomed—beneath his short white coat his camel sweater and navy slacks made a sporty and luxuriant foundation. The half-glasses on the end of his nose added a hint of intellectualism to the mix. As he flipped through the file, his movements were smooth and liquid, equally suited to palpating tissue or selling snake oil.

With a final flourish, Marlin put down his pen and pushed his glasses atop his head and regarded me with careful interest. "Nurse said something about Art Wilkers," he began affably, unbuttoning his white coat to free his sweatered chest. "Has some poor soul filed a claim?" His tone was bland and unconcerned, implying that only a crazy person would have a gripe against him, which, given his specialty, was no doubt true.

"Not that I know of," I said.

He frowned. "Then what is this about?"

"Nicky Crandall."

He raised a brow and scratched his nose. I was sure the glasses were going to fall off what with all the movement, but somehow they didn't. "Nicky? What's Nicky got to do with anything? Surely *he* hasn't complained—without me, Nicky Crandall would be . . ." He stopped himself before he committed an indiscretion. "What *about* Nicky?" he retreated.

"I'm trying to find him."

The stench of malpractice behind us, the doctor regained himself: His movements became benign, his voice dropped an octave, and he seemed to double in size and sovereignty. "What makes you think I can help you?"

"I understand you treated Nicky during the early stages of his illness."

Marlin shrugged easily. "That was a long time ago."

"You're saying you haven't seen him since?"

He rubbed a palm across his forehead, but the half-glasses still didn't dislodge. "I'm not saying anything—such information as I might possess would constitute a doctor-patient communication and be therefore confidential."

"I'm not asking about Nicky's medical condition, Doctor. I'm just asking for his address."

"Why?"

"Because I'd like to talk to him."

"About what?"

"First, about the state of his health. Second, about his brother."

Dr. Marlin sighed, as though the subject were as weighty as himself. "Tom."

"Yes."

"A fascinating individual."

"Yes."

"A tragic figure in many respects."

"Yes."

The doctor leaned back in his chair. "How *is* Tom?"

"He's dead."

That brought Marlin off his high horse. He sat up straight and took the glasses from his head and laid them on the desk beside him, as though they constituted some strange offertory. "Are you serious?"

"Very much so."

"My God. I didn't know. When did it happen?"

"They found his body Friday morning."

"Where?"

"Not far from here, actually. The old bus terminal on Ellis."

"How did he die?"

I picked at random. "The prevailing thought is suicide."

The doctor became inscrutable. "I see."

"Do you concur in the finding?"

"How would I know without seeing the postmortem? I'm not a pathologist in any event."

"I just mean that based on what you know of him, and your training in psychiatry, do you think Tom Crandall was capable of taking his own life?"

Marlin closed his eyes in deference to the concept. "Anyone is capable of self-destruction given sufficient provocation, Mr. ... ah ... ?"

"Tanner."

His eyes glazed with the sheen of officialdom. "And you are ... what? An insurance agent of some kind? Trying to void a policy through the suicide clause?"

I bristled. Marlin was someone who assumes the motive for everything is money; I'm someone who hopes that money means nothing to me. "I'm just a friend of Tom's who happens to be a private investigator. Over the past few days, I've been talking to some of Tom's other friends and family, and—"

"For what purpose?"

I opted for a benign response. "To see if they knew of any reason Tom would take his own life."

A brow lifted. "And do they?"

"They know of a hundred things that would be reason enough for some people. But none of them think they'd be reason enough for Tom."

Marlin's hands became a steeple beneath his chin. "And Nicky? What does he have to do with it?"

"That's what I want to talk with him about."

Marlin preened with expertise. "One seldom talks *with* Nicky. One learns simply to listen to him."

"When's the last time you saw him, Doctor?"

He started to say something, then stopped. "I'm afraid I can't discuss it."

"Then you're currently treating him?"

He shook his head impatiently. "I'm sorry. I really can't pursue the matter." He got to his feet. "Now if you'll excuse me, I have to—"

"Just tell me this," I interrupted. "Is Nicky here in San Francisco?"

"I ... yes. I'll give you that much."

"Does he know about his brother's death?"

"I have no idea."

"So he hasn't mentioned it to you?"

"Please. I've said too much already. There are ethical strictures in this area—severe ones. I, for one, take them seriously."

The doctor had the look of a huckster more than a physician, which means he had the look of someone to whom ethical strictures were bagatelles. "If Tom didn't kill himself, then he must have been killed by someone," I said evenly. "It occurred to me that Nicky might be a candidate for the role."

The doctor said nothing for a long time. "Are you asking me to say it's impossible?" he mused after a moment. "Well, I can't. Nicholas Crandall is a very sick young man."

"Do you have any indication that's what really happened? That Nicky murdered his brother?"

"Not at all. Why would I?"

"Tom had become concerned about Nicky in recent weeks. Do you have any reason to believe something has happened to him? You seem to have kept track of him over the years."

"I don't keep track of Nicky; he keeps track of me."

"Whatever. I thought maybe you could tell me what was going on between the brothers Crandall."

Marlin shook his head.

"Was Nicky sick?" I persisted. "Other than mentally, I mean? Tom seemed to think he was."

Marlin shrugged. "I have no idea. His health habits were abysmal, of course. A serious illness—pneumonia, venereal disease, even TB—would hardly be surprising."

"So you have no information that Nicky Crandall is ill. Or dead."

"Not at all."

"Will you at least tell me if there was trouble between the two of them? There seems to have been some twenty years ago. Trouble over a girl. I'm wondering if Nicky might have carried a grudge."

"What girl are you referring to?"

"Ellen Simmons."

Dr. Marlin's eyes slid toward the window to his left. When I followed his glance, I looked out into a tiny parking lot, empty but for a double line of cars and a young man in a tattered pair of jeans and a Guns 'n' Roses T-shirt who was talking with a well-dressed businessman who was about to enter a blue Mercedes. The young man—a street person or a duplicate—put his hand on the executive's arm. The executive angrily shrugged it off. As he did so, his face turned in profile, and I recognized him—the man in the blue suit who had fetched Clarissa Crandall from the Velvet Room and delivered her to the Sandstone Club.

I looked back at Marlin. "Who's that?"

Marlin blinked and looked at me. "Who?"

I pointed to the window. "The guy with the Mercedes."

Marlin didn't need more than a glance. "I don't know. Probably a landlord, from the look of him. You'd be surprised who owns some of these tenements."

"How about the kid?"

"Street trash, obviously," Marlin said impatiently. "Now. Where were we?"

"Ellen Simmons."

"Ellen. A delicate child. Whatever happened to her, I wonder?"

"Not very much," I said.

The doctor frowned, then started to ask what I meant, then thought better of it and tried to wrap things up. "I'm afraid I have work to do, Mr. Tanner. I *will* give you a small piece of advice before you go—if you are the one who informs Nicky about his brother's demise, you should be most careful."

"Why?"

"Nicky's relationship with Tom was . . . complex. I'm sure you know that schizophrenics frequently hear voices they regard as precatory—commanding them to perform deeds that are often violent or self-destructive. Well, the voice Nicky hears most often is Tom's. At times Nicky believes he *is* Tom, or that Tom has taken control of his mind, which amounts to the same thing. It creates a volatile situation, to put it mildly."

"Has that situation become violent in the past?"

"I'm afraid I can't tell you that."

"Had they seen each other recently, to your knowledge? And if so, where?"

The doctor was on edge. "Please. I have other patients. You must leave."

"Is it possible Tom's death isn't all that bad from Nicky's point of view, Doctor?"

"How do you mean?"

"Maybe the voices will stop now that Tom's no longer with us."

"I doubt it, although for Nicky's sake I would certainly hope so."

"Maybe Nicky hoped so, too," I said.

Chapter
16

The stairway to my office opens onto an alley. It's a narrow alley, as are most, and cars seldom try to navigate it. Nonetheless I discovered, as I trudged toward work just before high noon after my session with Dr. Marlin, that the tacit roadblock had been breached and my alley was completely clogged. What was clogging it was a Cadillac, big and black, as impenetrable as a knot of union pickets smack in front of my office door.

At first I thought it was one of my landlord's customers getting a preview of Carson's latest shipment of antiques off the boat from Leeds. But Carson doesn't even brush his teeth till noon, flush customer or no, so I stopped thinking about Cadillacs and their owners and mounted the stairs to the second floor, reminded once again that stairs were more of a chore than they used to be.

I opened the outer door, the one that's never locked. The lights were off, shades drawn, room befogged with shadow. No one was waiting on the couch or working behind the desk. Clearly the Cadillac had nothing to do with me.

The mail lay where it had landed after the mailwoman shoved it through the slot. Since my balance sheet was such that I needed some receivables to be paid posthaste, my attentions were diverted by the possibility that one of the envelopes contained a check. Which is why it was only as I was listening to the creaks in my knees as I bent to pick up the mail that an itch in my nose and a coagulation in the air suggested someone was sharing the room with me. Which meant the Cadillac customer was mine.

She was standing by the window, arms crossed, peering through a slit in the blinds at the sliver of Jackson Square that was visible from my suite. Amidst my plain and hard-edged furnishings, her figure was as noteworthy as a pouf. I gave a good impression of being speechless when she asked me if I was Mr. Tanner, and again when she asked if I had time to see her even though she didn't have an appointment. I would have made time to see her if my next appointment had been with the chief of police.

I invited her into the private office and didn't bother to hide my gape as I watched her high heels carry her across the floor and into the inner chamber. Without being asked, she slipped into the client chair as easily as bills slip into a change machine, her jewelry toying with the light the way magicians toy with coins. Her dress proved that she regarded her figure as an asset; her red hair fell in a curve that must have taken an hour to sculpt; the gold at her ears and throat could have paid the rent on the room for a year. The thighs that crisscrossed as she made herself comfortable were sheathed in silk as white and filigreed as a plastic sack of snowflakes. The scent in the air that had forecast her presence crawled into my nose again and stayed there. Because I wanted to show off, I summoned the strength not to sneeze.

I made it behind the desk without tripping over anything, her long legs included, and sat back in my chair and tried to pretend that women like this visit me every day. Neither of us bought it, though we didn't say so out loud. In a variation of hard-to-get, I thumbed through the mail as though I were expecting a pouch from my operatives in

Djakarta and Katmandu. When I didn't find anything more weighty than a flier from Sears or anything resembling a remittance, I tossed the mail aside and asked my visitor if she wanted some coffee.

"I'll have to make it," I added. "It takes six minutes. Do you think our business will take that long?" I asked, hope a lacquer on my words.

Her look was arch and aristocratic and some other things I usually resent, but this time they didn't faze me. "I suppose that depends on how badly you want a job," she said, her voice as expensively modulated as her Cadillac.

In response to her question, I gave some thought to my bank balance, then to Tom Crandall and to how much uncompensated time I could afford to devote to his case even if it was a case. Then I looked at the way her thigh smoothed out every single wrinkle in the stretch of gray jersey south of her lap. "Semi-badly," I said. Then something clicked, a connection was made, and I quit acting like a schoolboy. "You're Deirdre Sands."

She recrossed her legs and tucked the curl on her shoulder behind her left ear. "Apparently my fame precedes me. My press agent will be pleased."

"If it makes any difference, my interest in that job you mentioned just climbed a notch."

"To semi-plus?"

"To very-minus."

She took a breath, fiddled with an earring, took inventory of the room. Most people don't find anything worthwhile till they get to the painting above the desk. It's a Klee, an original, painted in 1919, given to me by a client in return for services I never talk about, worth more than everything else I own combined. People are always telling me to lock it away in a vault somewhere, and I'm always telling them only if they lock me in with it. I need to read Ross MacDonald every six months or so, and to hear a Mozart concerto every week. But if a day goes by and I don't lay eyes on my Klee, life starts slipping out of sync. I suppose I'm addicted to it in some strange ophthalmic sense, but it doesn't bother me, because I'm addicted to worse.

"I like it," Mrs. Sands was saying.

"The Klee?"

"The whole thing. Not too gaudy, not too tawdry, a functional environment with a dash of something exquisite to keep it from being banal. I've paid a lot of money to a lot of decorators who've failed to come up with anything remotely as appropriate."

"Coming from someone with your taste, I take that as a compliment."

She raised two hundred dollars' worth of eyebrow enhancements. "How would you know about my taste?"

"The Style page of the *Chron* runs a spread on one of your homes every other month. The last was your pied-à-terre on Outer Broadway, if I recall."

She smiled fondly. "My little flat. I go there to get away from it all."

Going to Outer Broadway to get away from it all was like going to Washington to get away from hypocrisy. "What brings you by, Mrs. Sands?" I asked.

She straightened her back and clasped her hands. What made it a triumph was the number of rings that were in the way of a good fit. "Mr. Standish," she said.

"The detective you hired to tail your husband after sundown." I reddened as I spoke, because he was also the detective I'd forgotten to report to as promised.

She nodded curtly. "I caught Garth in a little white lie this morning. When he finally explained the situation—the arrangement he'd made with you in order to catch his forty winks—I became curious as to the reason for your presence at the club at that hour. Since Mr. Standish seemed incompletely informed on the subject, I decided to inquire myself. I hope you're not going to be tedious about privileged communications; I happen to know that private detectives *have* no privileges."

"Privilege and private eyes are pretty much strangers across the board all right. But it's not a problem, because I don't *have* a client."

She raised that brow again. "Really."

"Sad but true."

"How interesting." She patted her purse the way other people pat their cats. "If we get along, perhaps I can remedy the situation."

It seemed time to come up with some professional detachment, so I leaned back in my chair and cut off the view of her legs. "Did talking like that come naturally to you, or did you take a night course in elocution?"

She laughed. Like the rest of her, it was unrestrained and sensuous. "I spent two years in Cambridge after I dropped out of college, working as a governess. Or nanny, if you prefer. Cambridge in England, that is."

"You were a *nanny*?"

She nodded. "It's my husband who was born to the purple, Mr. Tanner. I grew up in Albuquerque, on the wrong side of the cactus to boot. The college I dropped out of was UTEP."

"Amazing."

A brow levitated. "In what way?"

"It always amazes me when poor people get used to being rich."

She darkened for just an instant, then erased it expertly. "It's quite easy, really." She was trying to be blasé, but her smile had flattened just a tad. "As long as you keep moving."

We lingered over the image for a while, of the hooks and barbs of wealth being obliterated by perpetual motion, and by the end of the hiatus I liked her a little better. "Speaking of your husband," I said, "why are you having Mr. Standish follow him?"

"That's premature, Mr. Tanner. I came to ask as much of *you*."

"The answer is, I wasn't following your husband."

"Really?"

I held up three fingers. "Scout's honor."

Her lips pursed. "Then you must be interested in his friend."

"Mrs. Crandall."

Her eyes flashed blue steel for an instant. "I believe that's her name."

"You know damned well it is. So why did you hire Standish?"

She thought it over to see if there was any reason not to tell me. "To see if I'm in jeopardy, of course."

"Physically?"

"Don't be silly. *Conjugally.*"

"And what have you concluded?"

"That it's too soon to tell."

"You don't seem overly concerned about the situation. Aren't you worried that Sands might leave you?"

Her look became as focused as an assassin's. "I'm less concerned about him leaving than about what he might take with him."

"You mean who."

She shook her head. "I mean *what*. When I met him, Richard was worth barely a million dollars. As of last July, his fortune had grown to some forty-three million and change, based on commonly accepted accounting principles. Under the community property laws of this state, I'm entitled to one-half the accumulation, or so I'm told by my advisers. If my marriage explodes in my face, I want to make sure my share of the booty is still around to cushion the blow."

I looked at her closely. "You'd feel nothing at all if your husband left you for Clarissa Crandall?"

Her expression became blithe and distant. "Naturally I'd feel something. Relieved, for one. Rejected for another."

"If the marriage is as arid as you suggest, why don't you leave him first?"

Her nose wrinkled as though the wind had shifted and she had just gotten a whiff of the perfume herself. "I've been advised against it."

"Why?"

"There's a sticky prenuptial thing. Apparently I have to remain the wide-eyed innocent to have any chance of setting it aside."

"So says your lawyer."

"Yes."

"In the meantime, you're making sure Richard doesn't abscond with the community property."

"Exactly."

"So why come to me? You've already got Standish on the case."

Her eyes narrowed. On her lap, her hands made fists that resembled diamond-studded baseballs. "It would help matters immensely if I could show my husband is a bastard."

"That he's sleeping with Mrs. Crandall, you mean."

She waved a hand to reroute me. "No one cares who sleeps with whom anymore, Mr. Tanner—it's assumed everyone's sleeping with everyone."

"I didn't know. I guess I missed *Geraldo* that day."

She was irritated by my answer, so she stood up and went for a closer look at the Klee. When she got within range, her hip was an inch from my cheek. It was quite a hip. If I turned my head, I could lick it. I wondered if she would like it if I did. I decided she wouldn't notice.

When she'd found what she was looking for in the Klee, she returned to the chair and started looking for something in me. "Our daughter went off to college last fall," she said abruptly. "A freshman—exclusive school, co-ed dorm. The first week they had a floor meeting, and at some point it was proposed that by the end of the year everyone on the floor should have slept with everyone else. Heterosexually speaking, that is. When they put it to a vote, the motion passed unanimously. By the end of the year, everyone had kept the pledge."

"Your daughter told you this?"

"Her *boyfriend* did. He goes to school a thousand miles away. He seems quite proud of what Diana and her classmates wrought."

"I guess that's why they call it the liberal arts," I said as I compared her story to the endlessly chaste days of my own undergraduate experience. It really was a different world; maybe I should start watching *Geraldo* after all.

"If not sex, what is it you *do* want me to pin on your husband?" I asked. "Some kind of financial shenanigans?"

Deirdre Sands narrowed her eyes and spoke like a spy. "I was thinking in terms of murder."

"I think I hope you're kidding."

Our eyes did battle for a while, until mine yielded to the superior or at least the franker force. "Are you asking me to frame your husband for a homicide, Mrs. Sands?"

She shrugged nonchalantly. "The beauty of it is, there's a good chance he's really *committed* one, don't you think?"

"We're talking about Tom Crandall, I take it."

"Of course."

"How did you know about him and me?"

"I have my sources."

"I hope they're better at gossip than Mr. Standish is at a stakeout."

Her lips wrinkled. "I'm here, aren't I?"

"You certainly are." I matched her grin. "What makes you and your sources think Tom Crandall was murdered?"

"This."

She dipped into her purse, then held out her hand. In it was a note, brief, to the point, written and signed in what was definitely Tom's hand: *Your husband's atrocities must be exposed. If you are willing to assist me, call this number. But be aware that he* will *be brought to judgment, with or without your help.*

The phone number was Tom's; the discomfort was my own. I looked around the office, then out the window. "Have I stumbled onto a movie set, Mrs. Sands? This has a decided air of unreality about it."

"My life has been unreal since the day I met Richard at a pool party in Piedmont. This is merely the next chapter in the fantasy. Which is rapidly becoming a horror story."

I held up the note. "I'm supposed to take this seriously?"

"Its author obviously did. I'm willing to pay you handsomely to find out if he was right."

"Do you have any idea what he was talking about in the note?"

She shook her head. "Do you?"

"Not if he was talking about something more immoral than your husband's dalliance with his wife." I paused. "Do you really think your husband is capable of murder, Mrs. Sands?"

Her gaze was marbled with mischief. "My husband is capable of anything. If you don't believe me, read the financial pages."

If it had been someone else sitting there, I probably would have sent her on her way, to an operative like Standish or the nearest free clinic for a healthy shot of Thorazine. But I was getting old, and beautiful women no longer slowed when they crossed my path, so I took a different tack. "Tell me about the note."

"I would have come to you sooner, but my secretary only gave it to me yesterday. She thought it was just another crank—Richard and I get hundreds of them. You'd be surprised how many lunatics think the fact that you have money and they don't puts you in their debt."

"I'm not only not surprised, I even think they're right."

She sniffed with irritation. "Let's not get into that, shall we? Discussions about noblesse oblige are boring."

"Your wish is my command."

"Sarcasm is also boring. As I'm sure you know." Mrs. Sands readjusted her legs. "As I was saying, when she saw in the newspaper that Mr. Crandall had been found dead, Matilda brought me the note and asked if she should do anything with it. I made inquiries. They eventually pointed to you. So here I am." Her eyelids fluttered, and her bust inflated admirably. "Will you help me, Mr. Tanner?"

"Help you what, exactly?"

"Prove my husband is a killer."

I shook my head. "But I'll let you hire me to find out who killed Tom Crandall. If it turns out to be your husband, I'll make him pay a price for it."

She bit a lip. "I suppose that will have to do."

"My rate's forty an hour plus expenses. Will that be a problem?"

Her smile was as mercenary as her regard for her spouse. "*All* my problems should be so picayune."

Chapter
17

Deirdre Sands gave me a five-thousand-dollar retainer and a hand to squeeze as she walked out the office door. She also gave me a husky laugh and a vigorous nod when I asked if she piloted the Cadillac herself. And she gave me, just maybe, a hint that she and I could have some fun sometime, if both of us were in the mood. The implication was that Deirdre Sands was *always* in the mood, an implication that had taken her a long way in the world. As her heels tapped their purposeful way down the stairs at the end of the hall, I wondered why her husband had soured on her.

The phone started ringing before I got back to the desk.

"This is Guy Heskett at the *Chronicle*," it said when I picked it up. "I've got a note to call you. Something about an obituary. It'll save us both some time if I tell you up front that I don't *do* obituaries."

"You did one for Tom Crandall."

The high, almost feminine, voice floated in surprise. "How did you know?"

"I didn't till you called."

"Oh. Right. I . . . What was Tom to you?"

"A close enough friend to know he was deserving of the tribute you paid him."

"He deserved a lot more than that. But what's your interest—you want a few extra copies of the paper?"

I opted for the direct approach. "I was wondering if you'd been in communication with Tom in the last month or so."

"Why?" His thin voice acquired a reporter's husk.

"Because some people are finding it hard to make sense of Tom's death."

"When does death *ever* make sense?"

"Lots of times, in my experience. This doesn't happen to be one of them."

"Have you seen the M.E. report?" Heskett asked after a moment.

"Not yet. My source hasn't gotten back to me."

"Well, mine has."

"I didn't know they did follow-ups to obituaries."

Heskett debated whether to tell me what he knew. "Our news story said that a weapon was found at the scene."

"I remember."

"Guess what it was."

"A slingshot."

"A syringe."

"Containing?"

"Epinephrine. Adrenaline, basically. Used to treat anaphylactic shock. But this particular dose was handmade and king-sized: a hot shot big enough to blow out the brain of an elephant. Which is what it did to Tom—he died of a massive cerebral hemorrhage."

"That's what killed him? An overdose of adrenaline?"

"That's what the M.E. says. And since Tom had access to the stuff in his EMU, the coroner's inclined toward suicide."

"That makes him the only one in town who tilts that way."

"I don't buy it, either."

The line went dead for a moment as we tested our stance and its implications. Heskett was the first to test it audibly. "Tom was a depressive personality."

"True."

"But not a nihilist, I don't think."

"Not quite."

"So not a suicide."

"Not even close."

"Which leaves homicide."

"You mean a mugging," I suggested, knowing it wasn't what he meant at all.

"With a syringe? Come on. I mean premeditated murder."

"You said it, I didn't," I pointed out, as though someone were taking notes. "So how did you know Tom? Were you in the service together?"

Heskett's laugh became a titter. "Hardly. I spent the war years in Vancouver and a decade more besides. I met Tom a year ago. I was doing a story for the *Recorder*."

"The legal newspaper?"

"Right—my former gig. They had me running down rumors that the city paramedics were on retainer to some personal-injury attorneys around town. Cappers, they're known as in the trade."

"So were they?"

"The city crews came up clean. I'm not saying they never plucked a few bucks out of some stiff's wallet, or copped a wristwatch or a ring or two, but I never found any link to the lawyers."

"Be hard to nail down, wouldn't it?"

"Hey," Heskett bristled. "I'm a good reporter. I got into the bank accounts of about a third of the EMTs to see if they were making unusual deposits, which they weren't except for one guy who had a way with the ponies. And I couldn't come up with a single accident victim who admitted being pressured by a paramedic to consult any particular attorney about their injury situation. Whatever might have gone on in the past, I'm pretty sure by the time I got into it, there wasn't any graft in the city rigs except some petty thievery."

"So you met Tom on assignment."

"Yeah. I'd run across him initially on an earthquake follow-up; you know about that, right?"

"Right."

"Well, when I got into the ambulance thing, I remembered Tom's name and gave him a call and arranged to follow him around for a couple of days, just to get the feel of the life." Heskett sighed. "It was like getting a feel for vivisection, let me tell you. But it was great getting to know Tom. These days you don't run into all that many people who make use of a moral compass."

"Tom may have worn his out."

"I don't know about that, but man was he refreshing. I'd just spent five years covering *lawyers*—you know, guys who choose up sides on the basis of who's paying the most bread—and here comes someone who doesn't have two dimes to rub together yet has a real live personal ethic. Not some situational shit, or self-serving pap about free enterprise and the perpetuity of the poor and all that, but a code he actually tried to *live* by. The last person I ran into with one of those was my philosophy teacher at Oberlin. Crandall made me feel like I was talking to Alfred North Whitehead, plus he helped me move up to the *Chron.* "

"How did he manage that?"

"I was at a dead end on the ambulance thing when Tom hinted there might be something fishy in the Healthways units."

"Healthways has ambulances?"

"Healthways has everything."

"So was there a problem?"

"They *definitely* had personnel who were dirty. I know for a fact that one of their drivers got a thousand a month to tout Vic Scallini onto any prime P.I. claims he rolled on."

Vic Scallini was one of the more successful and less ethical of the personal-injury specialists in the state, with offices in both L.A. and San Francisco and an ego that spanned the gap. The respectable members of the profession had ranted about Vic and his champertous methods for years, but the state bar had never reined him in.

"Yeah, this Healthways guy was dirty all the way," Heskett was saying. "Dickerson his name was. Slipped Scallini's card to the victims or relatives at the scene, maybe a C-note along with it, then followed up with a call recommending they see Vic to learn their litigation prospects. Scallini had Dickerson on commission, one percent of the recovery if Vic got the case and won it."

"One percent of a million-dollar verdict is a lot of money for an ambulance driver," I said.

"For a newshound, too. And a P.I. as well, would be my guess."

We shared some economic wistfulness. "So the Healthways guys were definitely capping?" I asked.

"That and worse. One former Healthways EMT told me that when it was a close case and it looked like no one would be the wiser, his partner would keep driving around town till the injured person died, rather than getting him to the E.R. right away, because the lawyer he was capping for liked death cases better than injury cases."

"That's because you can't get punitive damages in this state unless the victim dies."

"How did you know?"

"I used to be a lawyer myself once upon a time."

"Why'd you give it up?"

"I was making too much money."

Heskett laughed. "That's the kind of crap Crandall used to spout."

I basked in the compliment for about three seconds. "So did you nail this Dickerson?"

"Couldn't lock it up tight enough for my editor to run with it. Whatever the guy did with his money didn't show up in the bank books, and without a subpoena of Scallini's ledgers there was no way to prove the connection. But we went with some of the tamer stuff, and even that caused a bit of a stir, and I parlayed the story into my job on the city desk." Heskett paused to take a sip of something. "So what's really going on here, Tanner—you got a suspect picked out? You giving me an exclusive?"

I hastened to dash his hopes. "I'm just trying to find out what happened to Tom."

"Why?"

"Because someone ought to know. You never got around to telling me if you talked to Tom in the last few months."

"Not a word. But I know someone who did."

"Who?"

"Dr. Alan Lodge."

"The guy in the obituary."

"Right. When I called him for a quote for the obit, Lodge told me Tom had come to see him a week before he died."

"For what purpose?"

"He didn't say, but he wanted to know if there was anything unusual about Tom's death. That was before I knew something was."

Heskett waited for me to corroborate his conclusion. When I didn't, he donned his reporter's voice again. "Listen. When you *do* get a line on what happened, be sure and plug me in. I smell a story here."

I refrained from admitting that the stench was familiar.

When I called Lodge's office, the receptionist told me the doctor was in Honolulu for a medical meeting and was staying on for a few days of vacation time.

"It's important that I speak with him," I said.

"Dr. Timkin is taking over his practice in Dr. Lodge's absence. I can make an appointment for you to see Dr. Timkin, and—"

"I have to talk to Lodge. Where's he staying in Honolulu?"

"I'm sorry, I can't give out that information."

"Then give me a number where he can be reached."

"I'm sorry, sir. I think you should talk to Dr. Timkin."

"Does Dr. Lodge call into the office every day?"

" . . . Yes."

"My name's Tanner. Please give him my name and number and tell him I want to speak with him about Tom Crandall as soon as possible."

"Tom Crandall. Is he a patient of Doctor's?"

"Tom Crandall is the bravest man Dr. Lodge has ever known."

Forty minutes later, Alan Lodge was on the phone from Honolulu. The noises in the background suggested he wasn't far from the beach. Or maybe he was in his room watching *Magnum, P.I.*

"Mr. Tanner," he began earnestly. "I'm glad you called the office; I've been meaning to talk to you." His voice was thin and timid, a far cry from the stentorian tones of most M.D.s. I began to see why Tom had entrusted him with one of his last requests.

"What did you want to talk about?" I asked.

"Because Tom asked . . . that is . . . this is difficult. But I suppose it shouldn't wait till I get back."

"*What* shouldn't wait?"

Lodge inhaled a lot of ocean breeze. "Tom came to see me some weeks ago. Before that, I hadn't seen him since the earthquake, when he . . . Anyway, he came to the office with a rather strange request."

"Which was?"

"He said that if anything happened to him, I should get in touch with you."

"Why?"

"So you could help me find his brother."

"Nicky."

"Yes."

"What did he want us to do when we found him?"

"He wanted me to give him a medical workup and report the results to you."

"Why?"

"Tom was afraid his brother was ill."

"With what?"

"He didn't mention anything specifically. He simply asked me to do a complete physical exam on Nicky and follow wherever it might lead."

"Why do you think he wanted you to report your findings to me?"

"I don't know. I'm sorry I didn't call about this the moment the reporter called to tell me Tom was dead, but I had this meeting scheduled and I needed a vacation badly, so . . . anyway, I'll be happy to pay whatever expenses you incur in finding Nicky Crandall, Mr. Tanner. I want to live up to my part of the bargain."

"What was Tom's part of it?"

He paused. "I thought you knew. Tom saved my wife's life. She was one of the people he rescued in the earthquake."

Chapter
18

After fixing a cup of coffee, I put in another call to the Central Station. It must have been a cold day in hell, because Charley Sleet was on the line a minute later.

"You were going to get back to me with the postmortem on Tom Crandall," I reminded him.

"Got it right here. Bunch of new guys over there," he groused by way of apology and explanation. "Takes them an hour to wipe their ass."

"Overdose of adrenaline, administered by syringe."

Charley is never nonplussed. "This is to prove I'm not indispensable, I guess," he grumbled.

"This is to ask if the department is going to list Tom Crandall as a homicide."

"Murder by syringe, huh? Not the weapon of choice for many muggers, Tanner. They got a needle, they generally stick it in themselves."

"Were there any other drugs in his system?"

Charley paused to check. "No."

"No other signs of foul play?"

"Not enough to interest a D.A."

"I'm pretty sure Tom was murdered, Charley."

"By whom?"

"I don't know yet."

"You don't have a perp, how about a motive?"

"I don't know that, either."

Charley emitted his famous growl. "You come up with an answer to one or the other, maybe I can crank something up. In the meantime, it goes down as self-inflicted."

"You know the Tenderloin better than anyone, Charley."

"A dubious distinction."

"Ask around. Talk to your snitches. If you hear anything, let me know."

"Anything about what?"

"I'm not sure. All I know is that Healthways has come up a lot over the last few days."

"First Sands, now Healthways. Those clinics do a lot of good down there, you know."

"I know."

When I didn't say anything else, Charley said, "I'll keep it in mind."

I thanked him. "One last thing. Check the computer and the morgue sheet to see if you've got anything on Nicky Crandall. That's Tom's brother."

"Why?"

"Why not?" I said, and hung up before he could sass me back.

It was time to talk to Tony. When I called his home, all I got was a reprise of the salacious nonsense that befouled his answering machine. When I called the ambulance service, they told me Tony had graveyard this week and wouldn't be on till midnight. Since Tony wasn't going to come to me, I decided on the next-best thing.

Tony Milano lived in the swale between Telegraph and Russian hills, under the phallic eye of Coit Tower, on Greenwich across from the North Beach Playground. Kids were screaming and balls were bouncing and rackets were pinging as I climbed the stoop and pressed the doorbell beneath the Romanesque archway that framed the entrance to the building. My guess was that the handsome structure had been in the Milano family for generations. I also guessed that if and when Tony became its sole surviving heir, he'd trade it in on some place more fashionable, which is to say on something worse.

If Tony was at home, he was probably asleep, given his change in shift, so I pressed the buzzer and held it there. A bevy of words suddenly ricocheted back and forth somewhere at my back, Italian words aimed and fired with the mock exasperation that seems to be their trademark in everything from courtship to comic opera. I gave my finger a rest, then pressed the buzzer a second time.

"Gimmeabreak, fer Chrissakes," a voice pleaded from somewhere overhead. "Whatta ya, a frigging Mormon?"

I backed onto the sidewalk to where I could look up and see Tony Milano, shirtless in the open window, holding back a drape and looking down on me with the calculated cockiness of the young Stallone.

I said my name and reminded him of where we'd met.

"The detective," Tony mumbled. "Whatsa problem, you need a date?"

"I'd just like to talk to you some more about Tom."

"If you're takin' up a collection to cover the frigging coffin, yer wastin' yer time 'cause I gave at the office."

"It won't cost you anything but time to talk to me, Tony. Guaranteed."

"Time's something I don't got a lot of, now I'm on nights. What I got I save for the ladies."

"Five minutes," I said. "We'll talk while you get dressed, and I'll be finished by the time you're ready."

Tony leaned out the bay window and looked up and down the block. "Hey. This is San Francisco. I don't get naked in front of nothing but a mirror or a broad, and the broad goes first to make sure that's what the fuck she is."

I shrugged. "I'll stay down here. We can entertain the neighbors."

The prospect didn't please him. "Ah, what the hell. I been thinkin' about Tommy a lot lately. Me and him, we ran the best EMU on the street. The fucking new guy don't have the brains God gave linguini."

A buzzer buzzed. I pushed through the door and climbed to the second floor and entered a room that was straight out of the *Godfather* movies. It was decorated in brocaded Old

World fabrics and featured squat and heavily stuffed furnishings, a litter of religious icons, and somehow, through the selection and arrangement of drapes and blinds and lamp shades, a scrim of ocher light that seemed to shine straight from Nápoli as well. Tony must have lived with Mom.

Towel tucked around his waist, toothbrush jaunty in his mouth, feet elegant in red-lined leather slippers, neck adorned in matching ropes of gold, Tony Milano opened the door and waved me inside in time to the Harry Connick ballad playing in the background. When I started to speak, he cut me off with a shake of his head and disappeared into a back bedroom, only to appear a moment later wearing skintight black slacks and white silk socks and a third gold chain, this one cinched as tight as a cleric's collar around his muscled neck. His pecs and delts bespoke of pumping iron, his hair of continual evaluation and regular lubrication, his teeth of Mendelian perfection. As he shoved his arms into a silver shirt and pulled it around his torso, his routine was so reminiscent of *Saturday Night Fever* I expected the beat to turn to disco and Tony to enlighten me on the glories of his love life at the pitch of a Bee Gee falsetto.

Luckily it didn't get that far. Tony went to a drawer, got out a bristly shoe brush, and bent to polish his already burnished boots. When the shine was imperceptibly improved, he looked up. "So. You trying to make like Sammy the Spade or what?"

"Something like that."

"You think I got something you need?"

"I don't know. Do you?"

He shrugged. "What's to know? Tommy goes to the 'Loin and gets hammered by a frigging blood bag, doesn't get help till the vitals are flat and he's history. Happens all the time. That's why they got a morgue."

"Did Tom take drugs, Tony?"

"Tommy? Are you kiddin'? Tommy said a Hail Mary if he had a beer."

"Do you know how he died?"

Tony shrugged. "I heard a mugging."

"Someone shot him up."

"With what?"

"Epinephrine."

"Yeah?"

"Yeah. You carry that stuff in your rig?"

Tony nodded. "For the allergies. Have to get authority from base to inject it, but yeah, we got it. How the hell did the blood bag get hold of it?"

"Some people don't think that's the way it went down. The police, for example, think Tom loaded one up and killed himself."

Tony swore. "That would figure, right?"

"How do you mean?"

"More stool time at Winchell's for the fuzz if it's Suzy in the side. But that don't make it true." Tony looked out the window. "I got to go."

"Do you have any reason to think Tom was murdered, Tony?"

"You mean like someone took him out?"

I nodded. "Like that."

He curled a pulpy lip. "Why the fuck would they do that? I mean, Tommy was as straight as my dick in the morning—he never crossed *no* one. The worst I ever seen him do was cop some AZT from a D.O.A., then give it out later on to some slime who needed it. A fuckin' Robin Hood, he was."

"What about the Healthways thing?"

"The time with the newspaper? Yeah, some of the medics got jammed up by that one. Jimmy Dickerson down the block—Jimmy Pickle, we call him—he had a mean on for a couple weeks after, but I don't think he traced it back to Tommy. Anyways, Jimmy's making twice the bread he was driving an EMU, so I can't see him in Tommy's face over the Healthways thing."

"What's Jimmy doing now?"

"Pilots a limo for some heavyweight. Like I said, a real pillow."

"Is the heavyweight named Sands?"

"Who knows? Me and Jimmy, we had a falling-out." Tony admired the image in the mirror, then consulted the watch on his wrist. "Hey. I got a lady waiting at the Greco. And this one won't wait long."

"I guess your job gets in the way of your social life

sometimes," I said, to keep it going while I made sure I had everything I'd come for.

Tony's black eyes shone as brightly as his boots. "You don't got a clue, do you, Pops? The ladies get wet just *hearing* about the shit I'm into. They think it means I care, right?—hauling blood bags off the street. What I don't tell them is, the job is mint 'cause I don't fucking *give* a shit."

"Did Tom feel the same way?"

"Tommy? He was better than a frigging priest, man; always trying to *console* the creeps. Not just to figure out what went down, either—Tommy not only had to know what, he had to know why. Then he'd start with how they could fix it up—do this, don't do that; go see this person or that office; take this test or that test—half the time he didn't wait till he'd finished the CPR before he started with the advice. Like somebody's fucking mother, he was." Tony laughed to himself. "As if the blood bags would actually *do* anything even if there *was* a way out of the sewer." Tony shook his head. "People get used to the smell of it, man; there's no use trying to change them. Me, I say load 'em up and haul 'em off, then hose down the unit and go after the next one before they clog the system like a two-week turd in a flophouse toilet."

"But not Tommy."

Tony shook his head. "The dude got *involved*, you know? Some frigging domestic thing, woman cuts her husband a new asshole with a blade the size of a ruler, Tommy goes back on his own time to see how she's getting along *without* the bastard. Half the time she's at the hospital— right?—begging the asshole to forgive her even though she can hardly talk 'cause of the teeth he wrecked." Tony muttered an oath that seemed directed in part at his departed partner. "You can't let it *bend* you like that, you know? I mean, you got to stay smooth or you'll end up down the drain with the rest of 'em."

Tony glanced disdainfully in the general direction of the Tenderloin, as though it was the repository of everything he despised. In the meantime, his philosophy lingered long enough for me to compare it to my own and find too many points of congruence.

"Was there any particular place or person Tom seemed interested in lately?" I asked quickly, as Tony rearranged his chains.

He shrugged. "Not that I remember. Only his little brother," he added after a moment.

"Tell me about him."

"Nicky? The Nick was a foamer, man."

"Foamer?"

"Foaming at the mouth. Running without a leash. A certified crazoid." Tony laughed dryly. "The last few months, whenever we'd roll through the 'Loin, Tommy would go hunt for the fucker, to see how the poor bastard was doing. And you know what little brother would do when he saw him coming?"

"What?"

"*Run the other way.* Brotherly fucking love, man; it's beautiful." Tony laughed derisively. "Tommy kept wondering what was wrong with the guy. Hell, *I* knew what was wrong with him; he was a fucking *loony* toon."

"Where was Nicky living, do you know?"

He shrugged. "I never went up there, man. Not after the first time we ran into the guy. Tommy, he seemed glad to see him, but me, I see right away I don't want to be on the same *planet* with the dude."

"You must know approximately where he lived if Tom went there frequently," I persisted.

"Somewhere in the 'Loin, that's all I know. I think he had a room somewhere on Ellis, maybe, him and some girl."

"What was her name?"

"Who knows? But she must have been crazy, too, right? Have to be a crazoid to fuck one."

"Did Tom ever say anything to you about his brother being sick?"

"He was sick, all right. Schizo to the max."

"I mean physically."

"Hey. *Everyone* in the 'Loin is sick. I take Listerine five times a day to kill the shit I *breathe* down there." Tony hitched up his pants. "That's all I got to say about Mister Nicky Crandall. Ever."

He walked to the door and waited for me to join him. I

took my time getting there. "You ever drive an ambulance for Healthways, Tony?" I asked along the way.

By the time I had my hand on the knob, Tony Milano was rigid at my side. "I got nothing to say about that shit— I got out and I'm *staying* out. You get your cock and mine *both* in a grinder you start sticking it into Healthways, man. You don't want someone hauling you off to General with the rest of the blood bags, you'll leave Healthways the fuck *alone*."

Chapter
19

Her apartment was on the way back to my place, the hour was late enough not to wake her the way I had awakened Tony Milano, and when I tried to call her, I got a busy signal. Interpreting the circumstances as an engraved invitation to come calling, I walked the three blocks to the Crandall residence and rang the bell.

Clarissa was in a pink housecoat, hair in a yellow towel, feet bare and blue-veined, face flushed with the heat of her shower and her race to the door. There was an open, anticipatory look on her face when she opened it, but it closed like a fist when she saw me. "You said you'd call first," she protested.

"You said you'd edit your answering machine."

She winced. "I forgot. I hope his *mother* didn't . . ." Her lip twitched twice. "But then she wouldn't, would she?"

Which had us on the wrong foot already. Her cavalier hostility toward anything to do with Tom still angered me, implying as it did a jaundiced view of her husband's life and what it represented and an irreverent dismissal of his death. When I thought about it, I couldn't remember a time Clarissa Crandall *hadn't* given me a bad impression, whether through the hearsay of her husband's anguished chronicles or the direct testimony of her own hard-edged aplomb.

"You seem to be bearing up marvelously, Widow Crandall," I said with more sarcasm than I'd planned. "Maybe you should give workshops in grief management. Advise the folks at the local hospice how to cope."

She started to lash back, then sighed, then softened. "I deserved that. Almost. It's just that it's been . . . difficult lately. This thing has knocked me for a loop."

"By 'thing' you mean your husband's death."

"That. The reasons for it. Mostly my reaction *to* it."

"You sound surprised that you feel bad."

"I'm surprised I feel anything at all." She gathered the housecoat about her. "I know you think I'm to blame for what Tom and I were going through, but you really can't appreciate what I've had to . . . what he made me think about myself." Her stuttered plea for understanding drifted into silence, as though it was too flawed to bear fruit.

"I've done enough domestic work to know that no one has a monopoly on fault between a husband and wife, Mrs. Crandall. No matter how it starts, at some point it's tit for tat."

"More like a heart for a heart." She looked for a smile and found only a miniature. "So maybe you can cut me some slack. Just a little?"

"Just so I don't have to do the same for Mr. Sands."

The smile hardened at the edges. "Mr. Sands cuts his own swath, Mr. Tanner. He doesn't need help from either of us."

"You sound a tad disillusioned, Mrs. Crandall."

"I don't know *what* I am anymore. Except exhausted." She tugged her collar away from her neck and shook her head as if the jolt would make her more perceptive. "So what are you doing here, anyway?"

"I thought it might be a good time for me to look through Tom's things."

"Remind me again why you think you have to."

"I'm still looking for a line on his brother. I'm hoping something in Tom's effects will tell me where he is."

"Why is that important?"

"I'm not sure, except so far all roads seem to lead to Nicky. Do you—"

She turned to look at the clock in the foyer, then quickly cut me off. "They're redoing the promo materials at the hotel. I have to make sure they get my part right—if I'm not there when they go to the printer, they'll misspell my name and use a ten-year-old glossy of Lainie Kazan. How long do you think you'll be?"

I shrugged. "Twenty minutes?"

"I can give you fifteen."

Like all celebrities, she spent much of her life negotiating over her time. I decided to take what she gave me and come back later if I had to.

Clarissa stepped away from the doorway and let me into the apartment. The foyer was small and dark and nondescript except for a massive mink coat that hung like a thick black flag from an antique rack in a corner, a flag for the forces of evil. The living room was a refreshing change, bright and airy, framed by a baby grand on one side and a pair of massive speakers and two attendant tape decks on the other. Some of it commercially printed, much of it in hand notation, sheet music was so prevalent throughout that the room seemed tiled in black and white.

The curtains were flowered and frilly, the furnishings thin and insubstantial, the books on the shelves exclusively about music and musicians, including a set of the original Grove; the photos propped on every surface formed a visual autobiography of the star. The atmosphere was so attuned to Clarissa and her talent that I wondered if Tom had ever been allowed to enter it. And how he could survive if that was the only atmosphere available.

Clarissa endured my inventory from the center of the room, arms crossed, fingers worrying the sash at her waist. "Tom's office is in there." She pointed toward a doorway at the rear of the apartment. "It was his bedroom, too, actually. Since we kept such different hours, we . . ." She abandoned the explanation couples always seem obliged to give when you learn they don't sleep in the same bed.

"I assume that's where you'll find whatever it is you're looking for," she went on. "I've been going through his things, getting ready to . . . dispose of them. You look like you and Tom were about the same size. If you see any items you like, feel free to—"

I shook my head. "I don't think so, but thanks. Dead men's clothing gives me hives. Besides, I outweighed him by forty pounds."

She cocked her head. "Really? You don't look it."

That she might have paid me a compliment discombobulated her momentarily. "His books, then," she managed when she was back in form. "I'm just going to haul them to the library sale or the dump, so you'd be doing me a favor to take some."

I shrugged. "Maybe one or two."

"There are some empty boxes in there, I think. Load up. All you want. Really."

I thanked her and headed for the door. "I'll be in the back bedroom if you need me," she said, patting her towel, uncinching the sash. "But I truly do have to leave in a short while."

"Have you thrown anything of Tom's away?" I asked. "Or put it somewhere else?"

She stopped fussing and looked at me. "Nothing that would interest you. Just silly things. Sexy things, mostly, back from when we used to do . . . stunts." She rubbed her face with a hand that was stiff with the work of grief. "God. It seems like a century since we were happy. I thought the romance would never end, until I realized it already had."

I glanced at the photos on the piano and specifically at a snapshot of her late husband that was featured in a silver frame. Tom was posed beside his ambulance, smiling with calm and contentment, as sunny as I'd ever seen him. "That's not the way he saw it," I said.

"He didn't see it at all. That was the problem."

With a grimace more painful than I intended to provoke, Clarissa turned on her naked heel and was gone. Freed from being a dead man's advocate, I went to the room she had indicated, flipped on the light, and began to look around.

It was a cell, of course—spartan, dark, and dreary, just the way Tom would have liked it. Small cot; smaller desk and typist's chair; reading light; typewriter; radio and chest of drawers. One wall was a window onto a light well, another a cardboard wardrobe containing Tom's normal rumpled raiment and two crisply pressed work uniforms. Rising up the remaining wall, five shelves of bricks-and-boards were crammed with the only indulgences the room enjoyed.

Except for a variety of texts on emergency medicine and some handbooks from a night course in hypnotism Tom had evidently taken at some point, the books were primarily history and political philosophy: Kant and Hegel; Rousseau and Locke; even Bundy and Boorstin and Kissinger. There were turgid-looking tomes on Greek city-states and Renaissance craft guilds and more sexy volumes detailing such cultural icons as the Dreyfus Affair and the Scopes trial. The few novels in evidence—Gore Vidal's historicals, Charles McCarry's internationals, Ward Just's politicals—were piled behind the closet door as though Tom regarded them as contraband.

The remaining nooks and crannies were stuffed with Tom's regular diet of brain food—pamphlets and brochures and news clippings and hearing transcripts on a variety of arcane subjects that had been of interest to him at some time or another. I made my way through the entire collection, extracting a couple of items for myself along the way, finding references to everything but his brother. Eventually I reached the volumes closest to the bed, which suggested they were Tom's most recent source of reference.

The materials were on mental health, primarily: dozens of volumes, from the pioneering works of Freud and Jung to more recent formulations of Laing and Miller, of such a wide array I couldn't decide whether Tom was trying to cure his brother or himself. The *Merck Manual* was among them, as was the *Diagnostic and Statistical Manual* of the American Psychological Association, third edition. The focus of the majority of the monographs was schizophrenia: journals outlining recently discovered genetic and biological indicators, clippings on the component of the mentally ill among the homeless on the streets, case histories of families who had endured the torment of the disease for years.

There were materials on other maladies as well, chiefly ailments common to the street and thus to Tom's profession—articles on treatment and prevention approaches to alcoholism; Randy Shilts' book on AIDS and a collection of issues of the *AIDS Treatment News*; a variety of works on drug abuse and methods of rehabilitation from addiction. Tom Crandall had clearly taken his work seriously; I wondered if many physicians in the city were as well informed.

I leafed through all the volumes and through the desk as well, looking for an address book or correspondence or anything else that might be a connection to Nicky Crandall. Along the way I learned that Tom had been a fan of Diane Arbus, that he must have known everything there was to know about the Peloponnesian War, that he had actually read and made marginal annotations in the works of Wittgenstein, that he laughed at Gary Larson. But I learned not a whit of Nick.

I was close to the end of my search when I came across a large manila envelope, unsealed but bound with a rubber band, stuffed in the back of a drawer. It was full of clippings, from publications ranging from the Berkeley *Barb* to *Punch* to *Foreign Affairs,* on subjects ranging from sexual practices to world government to the virtues of the primal scream. All of them dated from more than a decade ago, which made them Tom Crandall's version of billets-doux, I was certain, from back when the fire was hot and Clarissa was glad to be its fuel and Tom was expanding her consciousness.

I put the clippings back in the envelope and the envelope in my coat pocket and looked through the rest of the accumulation, but the only thing I found that could conceivably be a lead was a note—handwritten in pencil, undated, signed by someone named Jan: *Scanlon's. Tonight. Please.* Scanlon's was a bar in the Tenderloin, a derelict hangout the last time I'd been there, which was the last time I ever wanted to set foot in the place. I pocketed the note as well.

I was about to close out my task when something caught my eye. It was a bookmark or so I thought, barely visible at the top of the second volume of the *DSM*. When I opened it, what fell out was a snapshot, out of focus and underexposed, of a thin, abstracted young man whose eyes burned so brightly and mouth curved so dismissively it could only have been Nicky. He was unquestionably wayward and alarmingly awry—shirt torn, pants soiled, face scratched and bruised—but behind the surface carnage something compelling still burned brightly: an energy, an earnestness, an inquiring and urgent aspect that bespoke of life and love. In overall impact, the picture seemed to portray less a pathetic state of being than a continuing plea for help.

I stuck the snapshot in my pocket as well and went back to the living room. Clarissa was waiting for me, changed into a dark blue suit, white blouse with big blue polka dots, and heels to match the suit. She looked smart and sharp and formidable. I wondered if it was part of their problem that Tom had never looked any of those things.

The tape deck was spinning, and a sprightly jingle was dancing out of the speakers. I thought I'd heard it before, and when the refrain kicked in, I knew I had—the catchy tune promoted the array of bargains currently available at the grocery chain I patronized when it had a sale on soup.

I listened a while longer, then looked at Clarissa. "Is that you?"

She nodded. "It's a little deflating, but it pays a lot of bills. Funeral expenses included." Her look intensified. "Richard arranged the session for me."

"So he's your manager as well."

"In a manner of speaking."

"I imagine he can open a lot of doors."

"Any door I want. And the nice thing is, those are the *only* ones he opens."

I decided I'd heard enough about the spotless Mr. Sands. To redress the balance, I reached in my pocket for the envelope and held it out. "I thought you might want these."

She took it from me and looked inside. When she saw the clippings, she moaned. "God. I didn't need *these* at this particular moment."

"Sorry."

She blushed. "I didn't mean it that way. I *do* want them. Of course I do. They're the most . . . *sincere* thing anyone ever did for me." She sighed and shook her head. "God, I loved him. Not at the end, not after he let himself sink into all that despair and tried to drag me in with him. But what he was before. The day we met, Tom Crandall was the most electric man alive. He had more ideas in an hour than the other men in my life had in a year, and all I wanted was to be what he wanted me to be. Then a decade went by, and all he wanted me to be was miserable. So I decided to reclaim my life."

I let the complicated eulogy eddy through the apartment, which absorbed it so quickly it seemed starved for the sentiment. "Why did he lose that excitement, do you think?" I asked when the echo had died away. "What made him change?"

She shook her head slowly, suggesting the effort she'd made to answer the question long before I'd asked it. "I don't know. Most people thought it was the war, but that wasn't it. He'd gotten over those times when I met him, had come to terms with what he'd done. Then all of a sudden he seemed to decide that everything around him was crumbling. The world. America. The city. Me. We were a disappointment to him, all of us, an entire universe drowning in materialism and immorality and self-absorption and all the other things Tom saw as mortal sins. But I didn't *want* to drown. I didn't want Tom to, either, but since he wasn't doing anything to save himself, I went looking for a life raft."

"Enter Mr. Sands."

Her anger flashed. "What was I supposed to do, go down with the ship? I was only the first mate, not the captain."

Clarissa walked across the room and banged on the piano. The chord was dissonant and disturbing, but her version of events seemed close to what I had observed myself, so I didn't try to talk her into a different one.

"What about it?" she demanded finally. "Did you have any luck tracking Nicky?"

"Not much," I admitted. "Do you know a girl named Jan, by any chance?"

"No."

"I think she may be Nicky's girlfriend."

"Then I wouldn't know anything about her. Tom wouldn't talk to me about Nicky. It was like I wasn't pure enough to know about him."

"I don't think that was it," I said. "I think Nicky was Tom's Achilles' heel. I think Tom felt responsible for what his brother had become, for some reason. I think that explains Tom's determination to help him. I think his failure in that regard may even explain Tom's emotional decline."

"That's crediting Nicky with a lot of damage," she said without much interest. "Have you talked to him about your theory?"

I looked at her closely. "I think it's possible he's dead."

There was no reaction other than ambivalence. "I wouldn't know."

"I thought maybe Tom had said something."

"Not to me." She looked at me long enough to make me uneasy. "I don't expect you to understand what went on between me and my husband; I'm not sure I understand it myself. But I don't want to be a problem for you, Mr. Tanner. As I said, it isn't easy for me to think that the man I loved was so miserable he decided to kill himself. I'd be very pleased if you proved it wasn't true."

The irony of having Deirdre Sands as my client while being of aid and comfort to her husband's mistress was almost too juicy to resist disclosing at this point. But this was one of those cases where I knew so little myself I wasn't inclined to tell anything to anyone.

"I don't think he committed suicide," I said instead. "I think he was murdered."

I expected to shock her, but she accepted the alternative without flinching. "Why?"

"I don't know yet, but I think it had something to do with Nicky. And maybe to do with Healthways, too."

"Healthways? Why Healthways?"

"I don't know that, either. It just keeps hovering. Like a vulture."

"Richard's chief aide works for Healthways," Clarissa said absently. "I think he's the president, in fact."

"What's his name?"

"Lex Chadwick."

She led me to the door. When I asked her more about Chadwick, she described the person I'd seen that morning when I was talking with Dr. Marlin, the man with the Mercedes who was arguing with the street kid in the parking lot.

Chapter
20

When I got back to my building, there was another car blocking the alley: a limousine this time, bigger than the Cadillac, pearl gray in color. The license plate read RS-1.

When I got to the office, I expected to find the great RS himself, but the man planted like a pine tree in the center of the waiting room was the burly corporate type who'd picked up Clarissa Crandall at the Velvet Room and deposited her beneath the awning at the Sandstone Club, the guy Clarissa had just claimed was the chief mucky-muck at Healthways. His suit still came in three pieces, but today they were a flawless flannel in a banker's gray, dyed to match the car. His attitude was a match as well—imperious, impatient, and domineering: from his close-cropped hair to his thick lips to the thrust of his chest, Lex Chadwick had all the earmarks of a bully.

"How may I be of service?" I said when he moved aside enough for me to share the room.

"Richard Sands wants to see you."

"When?"

"Now."

"Where?"

"At his club." Chadwick looked at his watch, which seemed to have been fashioned from a gold coin. "He would like you there by five—he has a charity event at seven."

"You mean charity as in tax-deductible? Or charity as in social climbing?"

He dismissed the quip as beneath his dignity. Or maybe he didn't get it. "I mean what I say. So does Mr. Sands." Our eyes met; Chadwick had used his as a weapon before.

"What does he want me for?" I asked.

The question seemed to disappoint him. "You know who he is, right?"

"Who doesn't?"

"Then what difference does it make?"

I bowed to his logic. The prospect of meeting Richard Sands made me recall my conversation with Tom at Guido's. "I guess Mr. Moore should have turned the tables."

"What are you talking about?"

"Only a movie."

"How is that of interest to Mr. Sands?" Chadwick puzzled over it the way dogs puzzle over sleight of hand.

I pointed toward the private office. "Other than the painting in there, few things in my life are of interest to anyone. Except my curiosity, of course, which I suppose is why you're here. What's your name, by the way?"

"Why?"

"My mother told me never to get in a limo with strangers."

He started to debate the point, then didn't; lots of people had that reaction to my mother's principles. "Chadwick," he said.

"You seem a tad . . . rough-hewn for a corporate president, Mr. Chadwick."

His eyes narrowed, and he glanced around the office as though he suspected someone had squealed on him. "My position is not relevant," he said.

"I beg to differ; I'm beginning to think Healthways is *very* relevant."

"How?"

"Well, one thing that's of interest is what you were doing at the clinic in the Tenderloin this morning, talking with a kid who looked like Sid Vicious."

Chadwick found no humor in the image; I doubt he found humor in anything but bankruptcy. "I've never been at that clinic or any other clinic; I have a highly paid inspection team to monitor the field operations and a roomful of numbers crunchers to keep track of the bottom line."

"What's left for you?"

"Motivation," Chadwick said heavily, and flashed a sadist's smile.

It would have been easy to underestimate Chadwick—he looked and acted a little like the late Aldo Ray—but given his relationship with Sands, I sensed it would be a mistake. "Shall we go," he urged with mounting irritation, "or should I tell Mr. Sands you declined his invitation?"

I bowed. "After you, Lex." When I paused to lock the door, the expression on his face said, "Why bother?"

When I was comfortable in the cushy leathers of the limo, a bar popped open in front of me, and an array of liquid refreshment was at my disposal. I chose a Heineken, pried off the top with a pearl-handled church key, and got ready to enjoy the ride. It was the second time in a year that a limo had been sent to fetch me. Either I was moving up in the world or limos didn't carry the message they used to.

We couldn't have navigated the traffic more smoothly if there'd been flags on the fenders and T-men clinging to the sides. Along the way, we attracted a host of admiring stares and more than a few denunciations. I was ambivalent about the situation myself.

We made it to the club with time to spare. By daylight, the place was even more impressive than when my bleary eyes had first observed it—the brickwork more intricate, the brass appointments more brilliant, the red awning more arrogant, the contrast with the rest of Cleveland Street more stark.

As he ushered me inside, Chadwick grew almost garrulous. "Bet you never thought you'd get this far the other night."

"*Au contraire.* I'm a democrat; I believe that someday, somehow, all doors will be open to me."

"Some doors don't open unless you have the balls to break them down." Chadwick's riposte disproved the adage that wealth and refinement go hand in hand. I think only the British still believe it.

Once inside, Chadwick led the way toward the door at the end of a hallway that was lined with metallic wallpaper reminiscent of hammered dimes and carpeted with something that could have passed for calfskin. Without a visible assist, the door opened onto an office that looked to be designed and furnished out of Industrial Light and Magic—smoked skylights, copper-sheeted walls, chrome-and-flagstone desk, slate floor, leather chairs, onyx tables. It was the kind of room every man envisions creating for himself the day his ship comes in, at least the men who grew to manhood in the last half of this century and whose ship is owned in syndication and financed with high-yield bonds.

I absorbed the high-tech scene until my fascination was drawn to another source. Although a fire was blazing in a stainless-steel hearth and a neon chandelier was contributing some candlepower as well, the eyes of my host were the most incandescent items in the room.

Richard Sands was seated in one of the architectonic chairs that flanked the fire, telephone to his ear, stock tape winding across a screen at his flank, fax machine oozing a message in the background. "Sell when the market opens," he told the bright red telephone gruffly, his eyes still roaming over me. "The entire position. We can buy it back in a week at eleven—the earnings are going to be *very* disappointing. And that, Mr. Leamington, is a lock."

Sands didn't want or wait for an answer. After putting the phone in his pocket, he smiled the smile of a man with a big bet on a sure thing: the man who'd fixed the fight.

"Mr. Tanner."

"Mr. Sands."

"I'm delighted you could join me."

"It was kind of you to send your carriage."

He blinked the gray-tipped lids that matched the gray-tipped hair that lay neatly against his temples. His money had bought enough self-assurance to make him handsome, and his grooming was fit for a thoroughbred. But as with great horses, the measure of quality lay below the surface sleekness, somewhere near the heart.

"Drink?"

"Scotch."

"Laphroaig okay?"

"Fine."

Sands nodded and Chadwick disappeared, which gave me time to examine the man. He was smaller than I expected, and younger-looking. When I compared him to his news photos, I found the latter lacking with respect to the force of his presence and the power in his jaw. Sands was tan, lean, rich, confident—what most people in this day and age aspire to be. It was only when he sent Chadwick off to fetch the booze that I noticed his hand was shaking. Which reminded me that what most people covet these days comes at a high price.

I looked around the room a second time and didn't bother to hide my admiration. "So what is this joint, exactly?"

Sands raised a brow. "The club? A hideaway for my staff. My top people need a place where they can let their hair down without fear of being compromised. We have a competent kitchen and bar, workout room, Jacuzzi, and the library." He glanced at the wall. "You might be surprised at what's behind those leather spines: I've been told my collection of erotica is without peer in the Bay Area."

When he looked at me, I told him I'd take his word for it. He seemed let down that my interest wasn't more tumescent.

"Upstairs we have the rumpus room," he went on. "There's only one key, available by reservation. You can do anything from watch art films to play badminton to mount an orgy up there, and no one's the wiser unless you brag about it." He assessed his environment the way I had. "A profitable investment, on the whole; some of our most productive strategies have been concocted here." His look turned naughty, which on Sands was more than a little scary. "Someone ought to do a study on the relationship between money and sex," he mused quietly.

"I think someone has."

"Really? What did they conclude?"

"That it's pretty much the same as the relationship between partridge and quail."

"But they're essentially the same thing."

"Exactly."

While Sands was digesting my fabrication, I looked around yet again, this time focusing on the gilt-framed figure on display above the fireplace, her naked flesh swelling to the illusion of three dimensions in the golden beam of a track light. My first impression was that the painting could pass for a Reubens. My second, as I examined it more closely, was that the model could pass for my client.

"A little wine, women, and song for the troops, huh?" I said, averting my eyes in a spasm of embarrassment.

"You could put it that way, I suppose."

"And Clarissa Crandall provides the song."

Sands gave me a peek at his legendary ferocity. "Only when she feels like it—I would never *compel* her to perform, for me or anyone."

"How gallant."

Sands' jaw clenched until bubbles formed beneath his ear. "Be as smart as people say you are, Tanner; stay on my good side." He started to embellish the suggestion but was interrupted by a waiter who appeared in the doorway with my drink on a silver tray. At a sign from Sands, he delivered it, awaited my approval, then disappeared.

I looked at my host. "You're not joining me?"

"I quit drinking nine months ago."

"Nine months. Let's see. Was that the day they sentenced Milken to jail or the day they let Boesky out?"

Sands swore derisively. "Like most people unschooled in the intricacies of the financial markets and blind to the capital deficit that plagues the nation, you fail to appreciate Michael's genius."

"Oh, I don't doubt he's a genius. But I also don't doubt he's a crook."

Sands turned the color of the expensively packaged smut on the wall at his back. "The rules he breached, if any, are outmoded, even catastrophic, drags on the workings of the free market."

"The market hasn't been free since the invention of money. What you guys mean when you sing its virtues is that you're free to fleece the poor folk, which is what you've been doing in spades for the past ten years."

Sands was livid, but like all successful men he had learned to make anger an asset. "I'd love to enlighten you about corporate finance sometime, Mr. Tanner," he retreated expansively, "but we're not going to solve the nation's fiscal crisis tonight, are we?"

"Not unless we can regraduate the income tax."

He raised a brow. "I'm surprised you're such a reactionary."

"And I'm surprised you aren't ashamed of yourself."

Sands' face flushed once again. "God save us from tiny minds. How do you think this country would have fared if there hadn't been men like me around at pivotal periods like this? Men who took chances, pushed the limits, redefined the rules?"

"I don't know how we'd have fared," I admitted. "And neither do you."

"I—" Sands forced himself to stop, then looked at his watch. "You flatter yourself if you think I have time for this. I've got a Cabinet secretary on hold, for Christ sakes." He readjusted his necktie. "Why are you making Clarissa's life so difficult?"

"I wasn't aware that I was."

"You admit following her last evening, I presume."

"I admit wanting to hear her sing."

"You followed her here after the second show. We have you on our security tape, so don't try to deny it."

I shrugged. "It was late; I was concerned about her welfare. I wanted to make sure she got home all right."

"Bullshit."

I smiled. "Probably."

Sands tried to look sincere and succeeded in looking sheepish. "You misinterpret our relationship. My primary interest in Clarissa is her talent, which has been tragically underexposed."

"I agree with you about the talent. The part about the relationship is bullshit. To coin a phrase."

"Much as her husband liked to think so, we don't spend our time making whoopie; we spend it charting appropriate paths for her career. Next month, for example, Clarissa makes her debut in Las Vegas. She's opening for David Copperfield on the strip."

"Make sure he doesn't make her disappear along with the dromedary."

Sands actually pouted. "I'm in a position to do great things for Clarissa. Why are you averse to that?"

The question seemed genuine. "I'm all for Mrs. Crandall becoming a star. But I'm wondering whether the things you've done for her include removing certain irritants from her life. Irritants like her husband, for example."

The burden of answering my question seemed to tire him. "You don't really believe that, do you?" he asked softly.

"I have to work at it."

"I'm told you're pressuring the police to treat the event as a homicide."

"Only if it's appropriate."

"I can assure you that it isn't."

"It's going to take more than that, I'm afraid."

"Why? What makes you think there was anything sinister about it?"

I met his look with what I hoped was equal insouciance. "A number of things. Including the fact that I'm in this room."

Sands closed his eyes for a moment, then went to the fire and warmed his hands even though the chilliest thing in the place was his regard for me. "I can cause you a lot of grief in this town," he muttered with what sounded like regret, looking up at the nude woman who seemed about to jump off the mantel and onto his shoulders in some sort of oriental calisthenic.

"I'm sure you can," I said.

"You would be wise to steer clear of me and my affairs and to cease your harassment of Ms. Crandall. If you do not, my people would like nothing better than to pressure you out of existence."

I smiled. "Professionally speaking, of course."

His stare was reminiscent of Hussein's. "Of course."

"I can't abandon a client, Mr. Sands. It's just not done."

"I was under the impression you didn't have a client."

"That was then; this is now."

Sands considered the possibilities. It took him quite a while—I imagine he had a million of them. "Is it Clarissa?"

"I can't say."

"What possible interest would anyone but Clarissa have in what happened to her husband?"

"You'd know better than I would, I imagine."

"Unless it's Sandstone you're after, and Clarissa is just a ruse."

"That's a possibility, all right. I'm a tricky guy."

"On the other hand, I've never known the SEC or the U.S. attorney to use outside investigators."

"Neither have I, now that you mention it."

"So it's got to be Deirdre." His look could have melted my fillings.

"Who's that?" I said, and left the room and the scotch and the portrait of my naked client in the umbra of his mighty scowl. As I climbed in the limo, I worked at remembering that Sands and Chadwick were titans of finance, not henchmen of the Godfather. Then I reminded myself that from a lot of perspectives, including my own at times, there wasn't that much difference.

Chapter
21

Although the city fathers and mothers have begun calling it San Francisco's new Barbary Coast, in reality the Tenderloin is just what Tony Milano said it was—San Francisco's sink trap, the place where the flotsam and jetsam of humanity congregate before being flushed into the sewer of the prison system or the whirlpool of drug rehab or the permanent leaching pond of a pauper's grave in Colma. It's an area wrenched with mental illness, ravaged by alcohol and drugs, riddled with poverty, awash in homelessness, pervaded with despair. Much of it panders not to the best of us but to the worst, in the form of grimy bars, slimy sex shops, pathetic strip joints, by-the-hour hotels, and the hustlers and whores and con artists such forms of commerce spawn. The Tenderloin is a walk on the wild side, a descent into the maelstrom, a long day's journey into night—I avoid it if I can. When I can't, I carry a gun.

Despite its reputation for degeneracy, the area boasts one conspicuous attraction. Its scabrous history and its degenerate present make the Tenderloin the only place in the heart of the city where property has remained relatively cheap. This fact hasn't escaped the notice of the most heedless and ambitious groups in the modern world—Asian immigrants and real estate developers. As a result of the most enduring achievement of our venture in Vietnam, legions of the former now swarm like a hyperactive virus among the lethargy and lassitude of the indigenous organisms, nesting in run-down hotels, eking out a living from small restaurants and grocery outlets as well as less legal means of commerce, somehow managing to survive and even thrive in an environment that would petrify the rest of us. Simultaneously, the more adventuresome realtors in town have begun to snap up the failing hotels and blighted commercial buildings that ring the Tenderloin's sclerotic heart, refurbishing them in the conviction that people won't mind stepping over lunatics and winos and weaving their way through prostitutes and panhandlers if at the end of the gauntlet they are presented with a hotel room that costs less than a hundred bucks a night or an apartment that rents for less than six-fifty. And of course they're right.

As part of a story on what they called the "New Tendo," a local newspaper recently conducted a survey of the area. Two years ago, there were sixty-three taverns in the Tenderloin; now there are only forty-five of them. The number of sex shops has likewise dwindled—from twenty-one to fifteen. The city fathers and mothers can legitimately regard this as progress, I suppose, but as I pushed my way through the door of Scanlon's at just after one o'clock on Wednesday afternoon, no one in the place seemed proud to be patronizing one of the surviving forty-five, or of anything else for that matter.

There were four men and two women sitting at the bar, a man tending to business behind it, and several hulks of indeterminate gender and geometry hunched over the tables in the rear. The light was suitable for a stag film, the smell for a meth lab, the sound for an autopsy—the ambience was apparently designed to make delirium tremens a tonic.

I took the stool closest to the door and waited for the bartender to notice me. After he had, I waited for him to decide that I'd waited long enough to let me know who called the shots—in joints like Scanlon's, the customer is always wrong.

He finally ambled my way, looking at anything but me, a greasy towel around his waist, the sleeves of a sub-white shirt rolled above his biceps, which were bulbous and elaborately tattooed, a combination that formerly suggested military service but now suggests a prison term.

"What's your pleasure?" he muttered in a tone that indicated my pleasure was the lowest priority in his life.

"Beer. Draft if you've got it."

"We don't."

"Heineken, then."

He smiled. The rims of his teeth were as dark as the booze in the bottles behind him. "Strike two."

"Henry's."

He lifted a thumb. His fingernails were dyed to match his bicuspids. "You're out, pal. Try somewhere north of Geary." He started to turn away.

"Bud. In the bottle."

He kept walking, elaborately nonchalant, as if business were so good he could afford to ignore me. But it was all an act—halfway down the bar he bent over and yanked open a cooler door, grabbed a bottle off a shelf, snapped off the cap on an opener screwed to the edge of the bar, and slid it my way with a shove that was carefully offhand and surprisingly unskilled. The bottle came to a stop halfway between us, which meant I had to get off my stool and fetch it, which may have been what he had in mind.

When I was back on my stool, I pulled two pieces of paper from my pocket, my movements as languid as a cellist's, and laid them side by side on the bar. One was real, the other phony. The former was a fifty-dollar bill; the latter was something called a Notice of Heirship. It had been invented and dictated by me an hour earlier, then typed inelegantly by my temporary secretary. I'd stapled it to the stiff blue backing that could make a laundry list look official, and folded it the way they fold wills before they slip them into pocket envelopes for storage in the vault. Given the gloom of the bar, I was hoping that from a distance the document looked potent enough to close the place down or have half the patrons jailed.

After his curiosity got the best of him, the bartender slid my way a second time, on duckboards that quacked when he stepped on them. To justify his presence, he asked if I wanted another Bud, but his eyes were jumping from the fifty to the bogus notice and back the way kids jump on and off a skateboard.

I shook my head at the inquiry about the beer.

He shrugged. I stayed silent. He wanted to reestablish his omnipotence by retreating down the bar once more, but the lure of my bait wouldn't let him.

"New in town?" he asked, plucking a glass off the back of the bar and rubbing it with a towel that looked like he'd used it to wax his car.

I sipped my beer and shook my head.

"Thought maybe you were a tourist."

I smiled. "I didn't know this place was on the Grayline."

"If they take a wrong turn out of the Hilton or the Parc Fifty-five, this is the first place they come to that looks like they can ask directions without seeing naked women humping cocker spaniels. We get about five a day like that." He laughed at an image that seemed to give him comfort. "They keep thinking no one would build a high-class hotel so close to a cesspool like this, so they're sure they'll eventually get out of it, but all they get is deeper in shit. By the time they're scared enough to look in here, they're pissed at everyone from their travel agent to the governor." He gave the glass another swipe. "People from Kansas can't believe human beings can live like this. Sometimes I can't believe it myself." He glanced at the notice one more time. "So what kind of business you in? Lawyer?"

"Investigator."

"Who with? D.A.?"

"Whoever pays the freight."

"So what's that mean, exactly, an investigator?"

"It means I look for things. Things or people."

"Which is it this time?"

"People."

His eyes flicked toward his customers, none of whom seemed to feel more imperiled than they'd been when I arrived. "Which one?" the barman asked.

As though this was just another day in just another job that was dense with the mundane, I put a fingertip on the Notice of Heirship and angled it so I could read it. "Nicholas Crandall."

"Crandall." He nodded. "That must be Nicky."

"Must be."

"What's he done this time?"

"What did he do the last time?"

The bartender gestured toward the back of the tavern. "Tossed a beer mug through the TV screen. Got tossed out on his ass about ten seconds later."

"What'd he have against the TV?"

"Claimed one of the Simpsons was insulting him. Guy at the bar said the only thing the Simpsons insult is the intelligence of the people watching. Nicky said when you couldn't see him, Bart was trying to get Jan to take off her clothes."

"Who's Jan?"

"Nicky's squeeze. So anyway, Nicky tosses the mug and I toss Nicky. You want to do some investigating, investigate how a whacko like that stays out of the nuthouse."

I didn't have to investigate, I already knew the answer—tight budgets and low taxes and a world that spends more to hurt people than help them means we don't have nuthouses anymore.

I was about to start plumbing the bartender's knowledge of Nicky Crandall when the door at my back opened to the accompaniment of a blinding flash of daylight. As my eyes were protecting themselves from the onslaught, somebody called out, "Ice Man been in this morning? Huh, Gary? I need to find him, bad. He dissed me, man—didn't show for his appointment."

The bartender squinted, then swore, then pointed. "*Out*, you slimy son of a bitch. I told you—no more of that shit in *my* place. Take your hustle somewhere else, you fucking ghoul."

I turned to look, thinking it might be Nicky Crandall who was being ousted, but it was only a youngish street kid, one of hundreds afoot in the Tenderloin these days, forced to sell their booty or their bodies to feed their habits even if their only habit is to eat and sleep.

I assumed it was no one I knew or cared about, but as my eyes adjusted to the light, I saw it was the kid I'd seen in the parking lot the day before, arguing with my new friend Chadwick. The more I looked at the kid, the more impossible it seemed that he and Chadwick inhabited the same universe, but despite his anarchistic and hyperactive aspect, the connection stayed pat.

"Fucking Dracula," the bartender muttered as I was wondering whether to readjust my priorities and start questioning the kid. Before I could decide which course would be more productive, the door swung closed behind him and, with a collective sigh of thanksgiving, the bar received the darkness as its due.

When I looked at him again, the bartender was brandishing a ball bat in his hand, sawed off just below the trademark, transforming it into a tape-wrapped cudgel. Which explained the speed of the kid's departure.

"Dracula?" I asked.

"Ah, the guy keeps coming around trying to scrounge up people to give blood to this place up the street."

"The plasma center."

The barman shook his head. "Dracula hustles for the something something blood bank, the joint up on Golden Gate. I mean, people got to have blood, sure, but blood's the only thing some guys around here got to sell that anyone wants to buy. I don't like Dracula promoting freebies for the fucking blood bank when the plasma center pays twelve bucks a pint. It don't seem right, you know?" Amazingly, given the place and time, the bartender had to suppress a shudder.

"What's the kid's real name?"

He shrugged. "Dracula's all I know him by."

"Know where he hangs out?"

"Sleeps above the blood joint, I heard."

"Where is it?"

He pointed. "Up by the Self-Help Center."

I spent some time trying to decide what it meant or if it meant anything. When I couldn't see significance in any direction, I returned to the business that had brought me there. "I take it Nicholas Crandall was a regular around here."

"I wouldn't say *anything* about *that* guy was regular. But yeah, he came in pretty often till I eighty-sixed him. His girl, Jan, cleans up three mornings a week, before we open." He looked at the papers on the bar for the umpteenth time. "That a warrant?"

I shook my head. "Notice of Heirship."

"Meaning what?"

"Meaning Nicholas Crandall has inherited some money."

"Yeah?" He stopped wiping the glass, looked at it with justifiable skepticism, then took it to a tub of soapy water and drowned it. "How much money?" he asked when he got back.

"That's confidential."

"Inherited from who?"

"His brother."

"Tom?"

I glanced at the paper as though I'd never heard the name before. "Thomas Crandall. Right."

"I heard he died. A shame, as a matter of fact."

"You knew the deceased?"

"He's been in a few times. Usually looking for Nick. Or Jan, which is the same thing."

"Tell me more about Jan."

The bartender shook his head. "Life's a goddammed card trick, you know? I mean, there's Nick—goofy as anyone who ever walked—and he ends up with a broad like Jan. I mean, she's a little bent herself, but still—makes me half-hard every time she wrings out the mop, boobs roll around in her shirt like apples in a sack." He laughed less in lust than in awe. "The rest of the day is downhill, let me tell you. But she wouldn't let me lick her clit if I was dying in the desert. Saves it all for Nick."

"Any chance she'll be in this afternoon?"

He shrugged. "If Nick's on one of his missions, she'll probably look in to see if he's back. But maybe not; after the TV thing I told him I'd deck him if he as much as peeked in the window." He glanced to his left; what he saw made him issue an amendment. "Not that I could tell if he did."

"Does Nick live close by?"

The bartender started to say something, then stopped and crossed his arms. "What's in it for me if I know?"

I looked at the fifty. "The change." I looked at the notice. "Plus however grateful Mr. Crandall might decide to be when I tell him you helped me get in touch with him about the inheritance."

The barman glanced around the bar, then lowered his voice to a whisper. "I don't rat on my regulars."

"Of course not."

"I mean, privacy is privacy. It's kind of my stock-in-trade."

"Mine, too."

"But there's money in this, right? I mean for Nick."

"Right."

"So that means—" A thought suddenly disturbed him. "'Course, you might be lying."

I shrugged. "Anything's possible."

"Most people who come in hunting someone *are* lying."

"I'm sure that's true."

"So how do I know you're not?"

I smiled. "You don't."

He tugged the towel tighter around his waist, then picked up the notice and looked it over; I think he even read it. "Hell, this is legit; *got* to be. I mean, you couldn't *fake* something like that. Right?"

"Right."

"And my TV got busted all to hell, so it's not like I don't deserve some . . . repar . . . whatever you call it."

"Reparations. Recompense. Remuneration."

"Yeah. Right. All that. So what the hell. Him and Jan crash in a flop on Turk. Above the sex shop with the neon tits out front."

Chapter
22

The bus terminal at the corner of Taylor and Ellis was terminally abandoned: overgrown with weeds, littered with trash, smudged with graffiti, posted with NO TRESPASSING signs, ringed with a cyclone fence in an ineffective effort to keep transients from establishing residency. In its heyday, it had been the downtown terminal of the airport bus line, the place where people who didn't want to spring for cab fare were taken when they opted for mass transit instead. But the airlines and the chamber of commerce finally realized it wasn't a boost for tourism to dump visitors to the city in the middle of what amounted to a free-fire zone, and the tourists were given other options. I walked the fenced perimeter until I found a way through it, then scuffed around in the debris and the dust inside the terminal, remembering Tom, thinking about Ellen, trying to make sense of something that seemed increasingly to have madness at its core.

I'd dealt with insanity several times in my work—most dramatically a few years back when I'd confronted a guy called the Maniac who'd been a Pied Piper of psychosis over in Berkeley for a while—but despite or maybe because of my experience I am and always will be afraid of mental aberration. Although Tom Crandall had been the mildest, perhaps even the sanest, of men, his murder had taken me into the depths of the Tenderloin, which is to say into a crucible of derangement. As I watched the flow of people up and down the street, some more normal than I, some tied to reality by the slenderest of threads, most on their way to Glide Memorial for a free meal, I couldn't shake the feeling that madness would erupt in a violent and definitive way before Tom Crandall's story was fully written.

The apartment on Turk was just as the bartender described, a crib on top of a smut shop that called itself Pluto's Porn Palace. When I got there, the shop was doing a brisk business, though mostly in the form of browsers— I doubt there was a magazine in the place that hadn't been thumbed through by someone and slavered over by some- one else and, most likely, become destined to be shoplifted by yet another connoisseur.

The proprietor glanced up when I asked him how to get to the apartment upstairs, pointed down the street to the left, and went back to what he was doing, which seemed to be fitting a blue French tickler over a pink plastic penis of what I hoped was more than life size. I regarded it as an achievement that he didn't try to sell it to me.

The door to Pluto's left had the number 52 hand-painted on it. There was a metal security screen across the entrance, but the lock had been jimmied so many times the iron around it could have served as a sponge; when I gave the grate a shove, the only resistance was inertia. The door to the building was similarly vulnerable.

Inside, the stairwell was dark and dank. The mailboxes along one wall looked regularly pillaged. Fumes of urine and cheap wine combined in their usual compelling fragrance, and the steps were littered with the usual postmodern trash—condoms and beer cans, syringes and Styrofoam, liquor bottles and burger boxes, and lumpy tubes of excrement both animal and human. The sole bit of flair was a tattered edition of one of the pub- lications featured next door—this one was called *Big Boobs*. Buoyed by the minimalist simplicity of the title, I waded through the slush, keeping my hands in my pockets and my eyes on the steps, and climbed toward the second floor.

As it turned out, Nicky Crandall's apartment was easy to spot—halfway down the hall, a bright white doorway loomed out of the gloom as dramatically as the prow of the Dutchman's ship. When I was still ten feet away, I could read the names—Nick and Jan—which had been painted on its surface in bright orange letters with the same sentiment that makes people carve initials into trees. The door was the only clean surface in the place, a distinction that could have only been maintained by fierce devotion. The acolyte must have been Jan; the elegance of the effort made me eager to make her acquaintance.

I knocked twice, then twice more. Something creaked, then scraped, then groaned. Then something else approached the door.

"Nicholas?" The voice was delicate but assertive, simultaneously eager and afraid.

I didn't respond.

"Nick? Is that you, babe? . . . *Nick?*"

I mumbled something indecipherable, something I hoped would help me pass for the person I'd been taught to believe that Nicky was. The response was immediate and insistent.

"*Run*, Nick! *Run!* They're *waiting* for you. Don't let them get—"

The warning was stifled in midword. A moment later, sounds of moaning were accompanied by a series of muffled thuds. After a moment of leaden silence, I heard someone struggling with the dead bolt.

The snow-white door burst open, and a man dashed into the hallway. In white uniform with red trim, he looked like a soda jerk more than a burglar. The word "Healthways" was stitched at the breast and back, but his eyes were more suited to mayhem than either medicine or malteds.

He looked at me, and I looked at him. "Who the hell are you?" he demanded. His sharp features suggested both competence and cruelty.

I pointed down the hall. "Apartment twelve."

"Yeah?"

"Yeah."

He looked right and left. "You see anyone out here just now?"

I shrugged. "Only Nicky."

He looked at me again. "Where'd he go?"

I pointed toward the stairway.

The man gave me another look, as if something would crawl across my face and tell him if I was lying, then went back inside the apartment without closing the door. "Let her go," I heard him say. "Come on, Ron; we got to catch him." And finally, "We got no *time* for that shit; come *on*."

The first guy and a second who was his twin in all but size and hair color ran into the hallway and headed for the stairs. I waited till they were out of sight, listened to their descending footfalls, then looked back at the apartment they'd exited in time to see the white door begin to close.

Before it latched, I used a foot to stop it. "Get *out* of here," a voice, girlish but determined, screamed at me. "I'm going to call the cops if you don't leave. I *mean* it."

"I'm not them," I said.

"What?"

"I'm not from Healthways."

The pressure against my foot diminished. A few seconds later, the door opened enough to let a single blue eye assess me. "Who are you?" the voice asked.

"My name's Tanner."

"What are you doing here?"

"Trying to find Nicky Crandall."

Her laugh was dry as sand. "You and everyone else in the world."

"I need to talk to him as soon as possible," I said.

"What about?"

"His brother."

"Tom?"

I nodded.

"Why don't you talk to Tom himself?"

Which was my second surprise of the afternoon. Apparently Jan, if it was Jan, didn't know of Tom's demise. I wondered if Nicky was similarly ignorant, assuming Nicky was still alive.

I asked her her name, to clear up at least one thing. "Jan," she said with pride. "What about it?"

"It would be easier to explain if you let me in."

"Yeah, well, I've had enough company for one day."

"So I noticed. I was hoping I'd get credit for faking them out."

She hesitated. "Was Nick really out there before?"

I shook my head. "I fibbed."

She hesitated again. "Wait a minute."

Her eye left the door but returned seconds later. "The ambulance is gone; I guess you're okay."

She opened the door. The face that looked at me in frank appraisal was tight and drawn, pallid and afraid, thin and anemic, yet close to lovely all the same. Blond hair spilled down her forehead like strings of overcooked pasta until it was brushed away by a surprisingly swarthy hand. Her wary eyes were sky-blue pinpoints above cheekbones that were as sharp and white as artifacts. Beyond the caution and exhaustion, her eyes held a store of strength that seemed to be on call.

"Are you all right?" I asked.

She nodded. Her lips were dry and barely pink; when she spoke, they moved only occasionally. The top button on her blouse dangled from a loose thread, presumably courtesy of Healthways.

"Who are you again?" she asked wearily.

"Tanner."

"So what's the program? Did Tom tout you onto Nick about something?" She smiled at a private joke. "Are you here to straighten him out?"

I shook my head.

She looked at me more closely, as if she hoped I came with a warning label. "You're not a cop, are you? You *look* like a cop. Or a father," she added, her voice as flat as a cabbie's.

"Neither."

"You from West Side Mental Health?"

I shook my head and tried to take control of the situation. "What were the Healthways guys doing here?"

"The usual—looking for Nick."

"What did they want with him?"

Her shrug was more casual than the incident warranted. "They claimed Dr. Marlin sent them."

"So Marlin is still treating Nick."

She shrugged once more, as though treating Nick were an abstraction. "I guess. Lately he just sends the ambulance around."

"Why?"

"So they can give him tests and stuff, supposedly. To make sure the medication's working."

"That's all there is to it?"

"I guess." Her eyes flattened, and her voice grew heavy. "Nick thinks it's a conspiracy, though, so maybe you shouldn't take my word for it."

"Whose word *should* I take?"

The question was difficult for her to answer. "Maybe you should just ask Healthways."

"I probably will," I said, then looked around the apartment. "When's the last time you saw Nick?" I asked when I didn't see any sign of him.

"Yesterday."

"Are you sure?"

"Why wouldn't I be? He *lives* here."

Her response came as a relief—Tom's fear of his brother's demise seemed to be unfounded. "Do you know where I can find him?" I asked her.

Her lips stiffened. "Do you know Nick?"

"No."

"Well, if you did, you'd know that once Nick goes out that door, no one on God's green earth knows where he's going. Not even Nick."

"He's that bad?"

The energy beyond her eyes surged to the foreground. "I didn't say he was bad; I just said he was unpredictable."

"Even when he's on medication?"

Something in my tone made her look turn arch. "Hell, mister, down here we're *all* on medication—how else do you think we could *stand* it?"

"Does that include you?"

Her look dared me to believe she was different from the rest of the denizens. "What do *you* think?"

"You look pretty squared away to me."

Her lip curled. "I'm on Prozac. It's very hip, if you don't know—Daddy pays a fortune to the shrink who writes my scrip." She paused and looked around, as though aware of her marginal surroundings for the first time. "I'm doing okay, most days." She thrust out her arms. "The last time I went off it, I did this."

The scars on her wrists shone as brightly as silver bracelets; the sheen in her eyes indicated the deeper wounds still hadn't healed.

"Nick got me to the clinic before I phased all the way out," she continued with pride. "He was really there for me."

It was the first good word I'd ever heard about him. "Have you been with Nick long?" I asked.

"Five years. I don't know if that's long or short."

"Long, I'd say."

"Yeah. I think so, too. Sometimes it seems *real* long— we've been on the road a lot." She blinked back the trend toward a rocky reminiscence. "What do you want with Nicky, Mr. Tanner?"

"To talk to him about his brother."

"Like, what do you want to know?" she asked a shade defensively. "Tom didn't come by this week, so if he's in some kind of trouble, Nick won't know anything about it." The subject galvanized her. "The next time you talk to him, tell him to try not to miss again. Nick gets all agitated when Tom doesn't visit. He takes it personally, you know?— claims Tom has gone over to the Other Side and stuff; I hear about it for days. If Tom could just get a *message* to us when he can't make it, maybe Nick wouldn't get so worked up."

"I'm afraid you don't understand. It's not Tom who—"

Riding a manic roll, she didn't let me finish. "But he'll come *this* Sunday for sure—he never misses two weeks in a row. So why don't you come by Sunday morning? I'll make pancakes. Nick almost always stays around on Sundays— he likes Charles Kuralt. He thinks the Other Side is after him, too."

"Who's this 'Other Side' you keep referring to?"

She shrugged. "Nick says people are watching him. Keeping track of where he goes and what he does so they can poison him. It's why he leaves before sunup, so he can give them the slip." She got a strange look on her face, as though she realized that what she was saying might be regarded as odd in some quarters. "They take Sundays off, Nick says. That's why he can stay home that day."

"Do you believe someone really *is* after him?"

She took the question seriously. "They were just *here*, right? I mean, just because you're paranoid doesn't mean you're wrong."

She didn't seem to realize she'd paraphrased an old joke. "Has anyone but the Healthways guys come looking for Nicky lately?"

She thought about it. "Only Dracula."

"What did he want?"

"The same thing he wants from everyone—blood. I tell him he's wasting his time, but . . ." She shrugged away the issue.

I gestured toward the room behind her. "Can I look around for a minute?"

For some reason, the request worried her. "Do you have to? Nick doesn't like people messing with his things."

"If I was going to do something weird, I'd have already done it, don't you think?"

She still hesitated. "I never know *what* I think anymore," she said finally, her energies on the wane. "It must be my medication." Hostage to confusion, she backed away and let me wander.

Like the door, the apartment showed evidence of effort. The surfaces were neat, the dishes cleaned, the furniture cheap and battered but tastefully arranged and skillfully mended. The only overt sign of mental illness was a drawing on the wall, a contorted rendering of a woman who looked in the grip of monstrous agony.

When she saw me looking at it, Jan commented as though I'd been admiring a candy dish. "Nick did that. It's me when my medication runs out, he says. Helps keep me straight."

"Nice," I said, and in an *in terrorem* sense it was.

I walked to the bookcase. In it were several New Age tracts I guessed belonged to Jan, some popular novels, and, more important, several of the same medical texts I'd found in Tom's room, primarily the tomes on schizophrenia and the various street diseases. I began to wonder who was teaching whom.

On top of the bookcase were several plastic bottles filled with some kind of liquid. I gestured toward them and asked Jan what they were.

"Nicky saves his piss," she said without affect. "That box over there has fingernail clippings. There's a bag of hair in the closet and even creepier stuff in the fridge. He was saving his shit till I made him throw it out."

"Why does he do it?"

"Nick says it's evidence."

"Evidence of what?"

"Of how they're trying to poison him, I guess. Nick's hard to follow, sometimes."

"How long have people been trying to kill him?"

She shrugged. "Ever since we got to town, it seems like."

"But you don't know who they are?"

Jan shook her head. "Not for sure."

Our smiles were carefully circumscribed. Jan asked if I wanted some tea, but the look on her face made me think she had doubts she could come up with any. When I declined the offer, she gestured toward the studio couch along the wall, which was made up for day use but must have served as their bed come nightfall.

After I was seated, Jan sank to the floor across from me, curled her legs beneath her, and looked at me with eyes that expected bad news. "Are you sure Nick isn't in some kind of trouble? They bust him a lot, you know—disturbing the peace, disorderly conduct. Especially when he's hearing his voices." She looked at me with sudden anger. "Especially when the voice is his *brother's*."

"I don't know if Nicky's in trouble or not," I admitted. "But if he is, it's worse than disorderly conduct."

Her eyes widened. "What do you mean?"

"I'm sorry to have to tell you this, but Tom Crandall is dead."

She froze, then groaned, then hugged herself. "That's not . . . possible."

"They found the body less than two blocks from here. He was killed some time Thursday night."

"God. Nick will . . ."

"What?"

"I don't know. Anything." She glanced at her wrists, suggesting one of the possibilities.

"Was Nicky home that night?"

She thought about it, then nodded. "We watched the new *Star Trek*. He gets signals from the bald guy, too." She was as matter-of-fact as if she were reporting a ride on the bus.

"Did he go out at all that night?"

She shook her head. "But I did. Nick sent me to the store for beer, and I got hassled by some street guy on the way back and had to ditch him, so it took a while. By the time I got home, Nick was upset, so we went down to Market Street. Nick likes Market Street."

Which made Nicky unique to the city. Which also left him without an alibi. "What upset him, do you know?" I asked.

She shrugged. "Nick gets upset. It's what he does."

"What did Nicky and Tom talk about when they got together?"

"I don't pay attention, to tell you the truth. Nicky likes me to keep quiet when Tom's around, so I read or sew or something and stay out of the way. They talk about the old days a lot, I think."

"Can you be more specific?"

"Not really. Jesus." Her voice rose, and her eyes grew desperate again. "Why didn't someone *tell* us? He's his *brother*, for God's sake. Was there a funeral and everything?"

I nodded.

"And they didn't even tell him," she repeated.

"Maybe they tried. Do you have a phone?"

She shook her head.

"That's probably the problem. But it made the papers. I'm surprised someone didn't see it and tell Nick about it."

"Not many people down here use the papers for anything but a mattress." Jan's back suddenly straightened. "Maybe that *is* what happened. Maybe someone told him, and that's why he took off."

"What did he say when he left?"

"Just that there was something he had to do. But there's *always* something he has to do. Usually something crazy." Her grin was slightly crooked.

"How did Nicky feel about his brother?"

"He thought Tom was the second Son of God."

"Seriously?"

Jan looked at me. "Well, yeah. It's what he thought. I know it sounds goofy, but he really did."

"So they had a good relationship? They didn't fight?"

"They fought all the time. Nick kept trying to explain things to Tom, about the Other Side and all, and Tom kept not believing him. It made Nick mad. Not mad— *frustrated*."

"What kind of things couldn't Tom understand?"

Her look became inscrutable. "Why Charles Kuralt wants Nick to eat nothing but frozen food. Why Bart Simpson wants in my pants. Why the Other Side wants Nick's blood. Why Nick's father is being held for ransom in Turlock."

"I thought his father was dead."

"He is." She hesitated with uncertainty. "I think."

I sighed. "Medication doesn't help all this?"

"The clozapine? Sometimes. When he takes it. The problem is, Nick *likes* his voices. He *likes* having secret talks with Peter Jennings. He *likes* getting signs from Sylvester Stallone. There were seven separate signals for Nick in *Rambo II* alone." She paused to right herself. "Or so he says."

"It's none of my business, but why have you stayed with him so long?"

Her voice lost its neutral drone and became more musical. "Because he needs me and I need him." She saw my look. "He's never done anything bad to me, mister. He's never hit me, or cursed me, or made me feel bad about myself. And that's more than I can say about any so-called *sane* man I ever knew—my daddy included."

"How do you think he'll react if I'm the one who tells him his brother is dead?"

"I don't know, but it will be hard for him. Tom was, like, his whole life, in a way. We've been all over the country, but we always come back to Tom. I think in a way Nick was Tom's life, too," she added stubbornly, as if to prove that at least in one sense the brothers were in parity.

"I still don't know exactly what went on between them," I said. "Why they were so at odds."

"Part of it had to do with a girl, I think. And it had to do with Dr. Marlin, too." She looked around the room, as if to confirm that Nicky wasn't there. "I'd better find him. If he hears about Tom and I'm not there, he might do something awful."

I remembered my adventure at the grave. "Did Nicky have any of his brother's war souvenirs? His Silver Star, for example?"

Jan nodded. "He wears it all the time. He has this hat he puts it on."

"Then he already knows what happened to his brother."

She frowned. "How could he?"

"I don't know, but he does."

"Jesus," she said simply, then looked at me in fear. "He may *never* come back. He may . . ."

"There's no use speculating," I said to quell her panic. "Just sit tight till you hear from me. I'm going to keep looking. How can I reach you if I need to?"

"Scanlon's. It's a bar on Mason. The bartender's name is Gary—he'll take a message."

I gave Jan my card and asked her to call me if Nicky showed up. From the dubious way she looked at it, she expected to have more important things to do than worry about me.

"One more thing," I said.

"What?"

"Is Nicky sick? Physically sick, not just mentally?"

When she met my eyes, it was with fully charged versions of her own. "Nick thinks he's dying. I don't know why, or if he really is, but that's what he thinks. What I don't get is, if Nick is so sick, why wouldn't Dr. Marlin *do* something about it?"

"Maybe he is. Maybe that's why he sends the Healthways guys around, to make sure the treatment is working."

Jan made a face and touched the dangling button on her blouse, to remind me of just how helpful Healthways had been. My apologia for Dr. Marlin was halfhearted in any event. The only thing I knew for sure about the doctor was that he'd lied to me about not being in touch with Nicky Crandall. Most likely he'd also been lying when he denied knowing Tom was dead, a fact Nicky had known as well. One question was, who had told whom about Tom's death? Another was, how had that person learned about it in the first place?

I didn't think Jan could answer either question, so I asked her another. "Do you know whether Tom ever had Nick tested for any kind of medical problem?"

She thought about it. "He may have. They were talking about some kind of blot test or something one time."

"Inkblot?"

"Maybe. I don't remember for sure."

"That's a psychological evaluation."

Jan shrugged. "Whatever. I wasn't paying attention. Sometimes I don't have the energy to keep up."

"What else does Nick say about it?"

"The sickness? He says the Other Side is doing it. He says it's a plot to destroy him. He says they made him sick on purpose."

Chapter
23

The Tenderloin branch of the John C. Fremont Memorial Blood Bank was a nondescript storefront near the corner of Golden Gate Avenue and Leavenworth Street, across from the Tenderloin Self-Help Center. The windows were covered with computer paper so no one could see inside, the hand-lettering on the sign taped to the reinforced steel door read DONATIONS ONLY—NO FEES PAID, and the banner overhead read FREMONT MEMORIAL. I entered with trepidation.

The woman at the reception desk was dour and defensive despite her snow-white uniform and the tag above a breast that identified her as Ms. Glad. The look on her face when I approached was closed and wary and perhaps a trifle terrified. Given the neighborhood, I found the reaction reasonable.

At her back was a single large room divided into half a dozen cubicles by a series of freestanding dividers draped with white muslin. The cubicle I could see into contained a chair and a cot and a blood-pressure cuff hanging from a coat rack like a roasted chicken in a Chinese grocery.

The place looked efficient and antiseptic though certainly not plush, but for most of the clientele of the Tenderloin branch, this was doubtlessly the most elegant establishment they'd been invited to in years.

While I waited for Ms. Glad to look up from what she was doing, I imagined a roomful of donors, arms pierced with needles, tubes leading to plastic bags being inexorably engorged with red while a roomful of hearts were pumping to meet the increased capacity of the circulatory system they served. For some reason, it wasn't a comforting picture.

Ms. Glad said something I didn't catch. I didn't catch it because I was wrestling with a memory of the last time I'd given blood, which was when I was in basic training at Fort Lewis a quarter-century ago.

They'd promised a morning off for anyone who donated, which seemed a genuinely good deal as opposed to the Hobson's choice that most training-camp propositions amounted to. So I'd signed up. And been trucked to the post hospital. And patiently waited my turn—the longer the wait, the more time away from training. Finally they called my name, directed me to a cot, told me to lie down and roll up the sleeve of my fatigues. Antiseptic applied, then a rubber tourniquet, then a slight prick at the inner elbow followed by instructions to open and close my hand to keep things moving.

No problem, except that it took forever. The technician—not a doctor or nurse, just an enlisted man like me—kept checking back and telling me to make fists faster while muttering snide asides about my blood pressure. The contributors at my flanks came and went their sanguine way, not once but thrice, as my heart and my fist still slaved away, my quota not yet reached. I started to sweat, to feel pain in my arm, to want the hell out of there, morning off or no.

Finally what appeared to be a real live doctor came over, looked at my arm, looked at the bag I was laboring to fill, told the technician he'd missed most of the vein, and ordered him to shut me down. Which he did, to my relief and his embarrassment. After freeing my arm, he rolled up his tubes, put a patch on the hole in my flesh, and bent to unhook my still-unfilled receptacle from the apparatus from which it dangled. Newly brave and smugly superior now that the fault was not my own, I sat up and watched him work, just in time to see him spill it.

Three-quarters of a pint of blood, *my* blood, washed across the floor like so much crimson wax, to my dismay and to a chorus of cries and curses from the people in its path. The last thing I remembered, before I fell to the floor like a stone, was the color and consistency of the horribly lovely fluid that bathed the technician's hands as he tried to catch the bag and flubbed it: E-4, in baseball parlance, too.

I woke to the prick of smelling salts and the chill of a cold sweat. The doctor asked me how I was, and I told him I was fine, which I was, oddly refreshed by my swoon. But as I got off the table and headed for the door, the eyes of my fellow trainees avoided me as assiduously as I've avoided giving blood from that day to this.

"Have you contributed with Fremont before?" Ms. Glad asked once more.

"No."

"Then we'll need you to fill out this form." She thrust a paper at me. "This will also inform you what testing will be done on the blood you donate." Her look intensified. "Please be advised that the declarations are made under penalty of perjury, and failure to answer truthfully may result in criminal and/or civil penalties."

I looked at her. "You mean because of AIDS and stuff."

"Among other things."

"I don't have AIDS."

"That's fortunate—it's a felony for a person who knows he is so afflicted to donate blood. But AIDS is not our only concern."

"I fill out the form, then what?" I asked, still unclear what I expected to learn during this adventure or the price I was willing to pay for it.

Ms. Glad was beginning to be worthy of her name. "Return the form to me. If you meet the screening standards, one of our trained technicians will assist you in making your donation."

"You said 'technician.'"

"Yes."

"And 'donation.'"

"Indeed."

"I'm supposed to get paid for this. Donation doesn't sound like getting paid."

Ms. Glad was irritated with me. "Apparently you didn't read the sign. Fremont Memorial does not compensate its donors."

"Why not?"

"Health and Safety Code Section One Six Two Six makes it unlawful to use blood obtained from a paid donor in any transfusion undertaken in this state. If you are in need of compensation, the plasmapheresis center will pay if you pass their screening. I believe the rate is twelve dollars per unit."

"How come they can pay and you can't?"

"Because plasma is different from whole blood—the collection process is more lengthy; the demand for plasma derivatives can't be met by voluntary services like ours; plus plasma derivatives can be heat-treated in ways that whole blood cannot, to further reduce the risk of contamination."

"Why would anyone give blood to you for free when they could sell it to this plasma place for twelve bucks?"

Her smile turned beatific. "The benefit our donors confer on their fellow San Franciscans, in terms of insuring an adequate supply of whole blood for our citizens who find themselves in need, far outweighs the more materialistic rewards at the plasma center."

It sounded weak to me, especially given the financial state of the donors most likely to patronize the Tenderloin branch. When I started to ask another question, she pointed at the form. "If you will complete the paperwork first, I'm sure I can answer your inquiries more precisely."

She gestured toward a table in the corner. A man was already sitting there, unkempt and unwashed, laboring over his form as though he were deciphering the Dead Sea Scrolls. I joined him without disturbing his concentration and set about filling out my own. Downwind from my compatriot, I held my breath and did my duty.

Personal history—unremarkable. Medical history—routine, although there was no box for gunshot wounds.

Sexual preference—weekly. Drug abuse—caffeine, alcohol, refined sugar. Risk groups—bachelorhood. Current medical condition—breathing without assistance. *Are you a male who has had sex with another male EVEN ONCE since 1977? Have you engaged in sex for money or drugs since 1977 or had sex within the last twelve months with someone who has, EVEN ONCE?* Gee, I don't remember.

When I'd finished, I looked across the table. My companion was still locked onto his task, frowning at the vocabulary and the print size, clutching his pencil like an ice pick as he checked off boxes left and right, which made his past at least as disheveled as his present.

When I returned to Ms. Glad, I must have looked dubious. "Did you have trouble with any of the questions?" she asked, implying that only an idiot would answer in the affirmative. "A good rule is, when in doubt, just say 'no.'"

"Okay . . . 'no.'"

"I meant on the form."

"And I meant what I said."

Her eyes widened. "You mean you've decided not to contribute?"

"That's right."

"Why, if I may ask? Is it a matter of money?"

"The problem isn't money," I replied. "The problem is safety."

She had heard the word before, and not in a pleasant context. "I see."

"You hear things about the blood supply these days. About it being risky."

"Alarmists, I assure you. As the form indicates, we test our product thoroughly before distribution."

"You mean for AIDS and stuff."

"AIDS. Hepatitis A, B, *and* C. HTLV I. We run tests for things you've never heard of. The fact is, the blood supply in this country is as safe as it can be." She lowered her voice and leaned forward. "Besides, you're forgetting something."

"What?"

"Any risk that remains in the blood supply lies with the *recipient* of the product. You, sir, will simply be a *donor*."

"You can't get AIDS from donating blood?"

She summoned the full force of her vocation. "There is no record of such an instance."

"You'll pardon me if I say that's less than entirely reassuring. I wonder if I could talk to the boss around here, maybe get some more—"

A noise behind me indicated my blood buddy had finally finished his form and was impatient to deliver it. I decided to let him finish his business before I fenced with Ms. Glad some more. "I think I need to think it over," I told her.

Ms. Glad looked at me and then at the transient. "Very well. But there will be no fee; we never negotiate."

I returned to the table to wait for a chance to probe the operation further, mainly so I could get a line on the Dracula character, who was apparently acquainted with both Nicky Crandall and Lex Chadwick.

As I sat down, I heard the other man ask if head lice were a virus. Ms. Glad blanched, then glanced at the form, then shook her head with increasing vigor and said something I couldn't hear.

"You mean I *flunked*?" the man protested with as much injured outrage as his battered psyche could muster.

"I'm afraid at the moment you don't meet our requirements," Ms. Glad answered kindly. "You shouldn't regard it as an affront."

"Dracula said I'd pass for sure."

Ms. Glad grew stern. "Dracula, as you call him, is not qualified to render that opinion."

"He works for you, don't he?"

"I believe he occasionally performs services as an independent contractor."

"Indep—" The man lacked the energy to complete the phrase. "So I'm out."

"I'm afraid so."

"If I don't get paid, *he* don't get paid. Right?"

"I'm afraid *no one* gets compensated at this institution," Ms. Glad pronounced primly. "We are a nonprofit organization."

The man squinted at her with a sudden flash of brotherhood. "Me, too."

Ms. Glad smiled despite herself. "I wonder, have you seen a physician recently, sir? There's a clinic down on Ellis Street, I'm sure they—"

The man held up a hand. "I been there before—all they want is to stick me with a needle. I used to be a junkie; I had all the needles I can stand."

"But you seem . . . ill."

The man shrugged. "I'm better than I used to be," he said, and shuffled off to the bosom of the Tenderloin, leaving Ms. Glad and me regarding each other in a mix of amazement and thanksgiving.

I joined her at the desk. "They come in several times a week, some of them," she murmured, her thoughts still on the transient. "They'd sell a pint a day if we let them." She sighed, then blinked at her sorrow. "Have you reached a decision?"

"I have."

"And?"

"I'm too chicken."

"It's virtually a pain-free procedure."

"It's just that I had a bad experience once."

"With a transfusion?"

"With a trained technician."

I had decided to ask if Nick Crandall was one of their regulars when a finger poked me on the shoulder. I turned to see the taller of the Healthways paramedics who'd confronted me at Jan and Nick's apartment.

"Catch him?" I asked affably.

He glowered and shook his head. "No trace. Which makes us think maybe he wasn't there at all. We think maybe you were playing games with us."

"Why would I do that?"

"That's what Don and me were wondering."

"It's a puzzle all right. Let me know if you come up with an answer."

The paramedic crossed his arms. "What the fuck you think you're doing here, pal?"

I looked around. "I'm thinking of giving blood. I'm sure as a health-care professional you applaud that."

"You claim you're giving blood. Before that you claimed you lived in the same dump as Crandall. I think you're lying both times." He looked at Nurse Glad. "He been processed yet?"

"He changed his mind," she said tentatively.

The medic nodded. "He does that a lot. For instance, I bet he's changed his mind about where he lives."

"You're right. I was confused before."

"Yeah, well, what confuses me is why you're poking your nose in Healthways' business."

I met his bluster with some of my own. "And I'm confused about what Healthways' business is."

The medic started to fence with me again when his partner peeked through the door. "Let's roll, Ron. Base says *they'll* handle it."

The tall one started to debate the point but finally yielded. His attention swiveled to Ms. Glad. "Where's Dracula?" he asked gruffly.

"I haven't seen him today."

"You tell him to come by the clinic. We need to talk to him."

"I'll give him that message."

Ron nodded and headed for the door. Before he reached it, he turned back. "I don't want to see you again, pal."

"Then I better start taking better care of my health."

"You do that while you got the chance," he said, and was gone.

I looked at Ms. Glad. "They're more like MPs than paramedics."

She wouldn't engage in gossip. "Healthways has a very aggressive health-services program."

"What do you suppose they want with Dracula?"

She made a face. "He's such a repulsive creature, I don't know why anyone would get *near* him." She looked at me. "What *are* you doing here, anyway?"

I smiled. "You ever hear of a man named Nicholas Crandall?"

"The name isn't familiar."

"You'd know if he was a regular donor, right?"

"Probably. Why is he important?"

"I really don't know," I admitted, and not for the first time. "Who runs this place, by the way?"

"You mean this particular center?"

I shook my head. "The whole operation."

"The Fremont Memorial Blood Bank is a nonprofit corporation, doing business exclusively in San Francisco," she recited. "We are the second-largest blood bank in the area, next to Irwin Memorial. We were established in 1986, when the Red Cross ceased collecting blood in the city. Our chairman is a man named Norman Glasswell. Our headquarters are on Divisidaro, near Sacramento."

"Does Richard Sands have anything to do with Fremont?"

"Not that I know of."

"How about Lex Chadwick?"

"I believe he's on our board."

"You'd better tell Glasswell that there's something fishy going on around here," I said.

Ms. Glad looked even more worried than when I'd come in. "I think he knows that already."

"What do you mean?"

"I'm not sure. I just know there's a problem of some kind. The blood people in the Bay Area are very concerned. Even the FDA is looking into it."

Chapter
24

I went back to the office and made some calls, mostly without success. Dr. Marlin wasn't at Healthways or anyplace else anyone would admit to. Ellen Simmons wasn't at work or at least wasn't being allowed to come to the phone. Although I tried half a dozen other numbers, the only one who talked back was my stockbroker.

Clay Oerter was my broker only in the sense that I'd lost enough money to him playing poker to figure he owed me a favor in the form of some top-of-the-head information from time to time. To give him his due, he seemed to think so, too.

"Clay."

"Marsh."

"How's the market?"

"Off seventeen. Apparently the war boom is ending except for the run-up on Raytheon. How's the mayhem?"

"Bullish as usual. Tell me about Healthways."

"Healthways. Hmm. Well, for one thing you can't get a pure play in it anymore, not that I'd recommend it if you could."

"Background, *s'il vous plaît*."

It must have been my accent that made him laugh. "Back in the sixties, Healthways seemed like an idea whose time had come. So thought its founder at least, a man named Eric Rattner. Rattner was a veritable Renaissance man—physician, philosopher, patron of the arts, humanist, philanthropist, even an erstwhile playwright if I remember correctly. He'd made a ton of money in downtown real estate and decided to plow most of it back into his first love, which was health care. Specifically, Rattner wanted to insure the delivery of quality medical services to people who couldn't afford to pay for them. What he did was put together a vertically integrated HMO funded not by employer contributions or private subscriptions but by the state and federal governments."

"An HMO is what?" I asked.

"Health Maintenance Organization. A privately financed health program, basically. Rattner didn't originate the concept—Kaiser had been around for years before Rattner started cranking up—but Rattner was the first to try to integrate an HMO from top to bottom and most definitely the first to direct his efforts toward the poor and unemployed rather than the middle class. Basically, instead of having individuals or employers come up with the money to fund the system, Rattner relied on Medicare and Medicaid and MediCal to pay the freight, gambling that the efficiencies of vertical integration coupled with a ruthless program of cost controls could make the concept work."

"I know about the clinics. What else does Healthways do?"

"The clinics were the first step—the walk-in med centers you see in major cities on the West Coast. The next step was to open a string of emergency hospitals smack in the middle of the ghettos—primary care only, very few beds, no long-term treatment. Then Rattner set up an extensive outreach to the surrounding community through a fleet of EMS units."

"Ambulances."

"Right. But these were ambulances with a difference— the Healthways units not only provided emergency services, they also provided follow-up monitoring and even at-home care in some circumstances—house calls, if you will. They undertook some pretty intensive wellness training, too, through educational and testing programs in the local schools and workplaces and social service agencies."

"Sounds like a good deal."

"It was a good deal from a medical point of view. From a financial point of view, it was marginal. The kicker was supposed to be when Rattner linked the neighborhood operations to a small drug company he set up to concentrate on manufacturing generic medicines that poor people use a lot—hypertension agents, analgesics, antibiotics, nutritional supplements, stuff like that. At about the same time, he bought up a small hospital-supply business so he could get some control over the outrageous costs of *outfitting* the operation."

"Clever."

"More than clever—brilliant. And daring. What Rattner figured was that the last two enterprises—the drug company and the supply outfit—would be profitable enough to absorb the losses generated by the more prosaic elements of the enterprise."

"Was he right?"

Clay sighed heavily. "The Healthways story is a tragedy, pretty much. After he went public, the stock soared for a while—up to forty times earnings back in the early seventies, a real flyer. But it was a dream, mostly—everyone on Wall Street certainly *hoped* it would work, if only for the reason that if it did then they wouldn't have to worry so much about all those *poor* people anymore. But just as Rattner got all his ducks lined up and was ready to subject his concept to the rigors of the market instead of the fantasies of investors, several things happened. The country went into the recession of seventy two. Plus, benefits and coverage under Medicaid began to decline dramatically as a result of budget cuts—in the beginning the program covered something like three-fourths of the people below the poverty line; now it's less than forty percent. Plus, our kind old Congress decided not to let Medicaid—the poor people's program—pay as much for certain services as Medicare—the old people's program—paid for the same procedures. All of which meant Healthways couldn't keep up with the raging inflation in health costs because its clientele was on the short end of the political stick. And finally, Eric Rattner had a stroke. He lingered in a vegetative state for years while his brainchild crumbled to dust around him. Died about five years ago, I think. Came close to being another Kaiser or Carnegie. Now no one knows his name."

"But Healthways is still operating. I was at one of their clinics yesterday."

"Right, but it's not Rattner's baby anymore. Healthways stumbled along under its own power for a while—it took a few years for the social-service bureaucrats to realize it wasn't working and to use any excuse they could come up with to deny funding. The stock fell to nothing—Healthways was on the brink of receivership for years. Then a year or so ago the whole kit and caboodle got bought out for peanuts in a not particularly spectacular takeover move." Clay chuckled dryly. "It probably won't surprise you to learn that the new owners have slightly different motivations than poor old Rattner."

"Like what?"

"Turning nonprofit HMOs into profit-making health-care corporations is a big deal now—Healthways is only one of several examples. In their last appearance before the analysts, the Healthways people claimed to anticipate earnings jumps of at least twenty percent per year through the rest of the decade."

"How are they going to get them?"

"I don't follow the stock that closely, but it seems to me there was some talk about additional efficiencies in the hospitals, new drugs in the pipeline, an anticipated growth in their market—the usual bullshit. A great way to invest, when you think about it—a pure play on poverty." Clay's laugh was uncharacteristically mordant. "Let's put it this way: The analysts were underwhelmed. The stock hasn't made a move in years."

"The new owner of Healthways wouldn't happen to be Richard Sands, would it?"

Clay whistled. "Your perspicacity never ceases to amaze me, Marsh. If you put that sixth sense to use in the market, you'd make a mint in no time."

I laughed. "I'll start buying stocks when Wall Street stops letting guys like Sands treat the market like a private sandbox."

"Hey. That was the eighties. Nowadays guys like Sands are barely hanging on. I hear he left for Toronto this morning, trying to get a bridge loan to take him over his next interest payment."

I was surprised: Apparently my client had misled me about the extent of her husband's fortune. "Sands is really on the edge?"

"Fingernail City. He's sold off two subsidiaries in the past six weeks, and rumor has it there's more to follow. Tidy balance sheets, too; lots of upside potential once we get out of the recessionary psychology we're into now. Sands let them go for a song."

"Why's he strapped all of a sudden?"

"Nothing special that I know of, just the credit crunch that's the handmaiden to the bank and S & L crises, in addition to the recession, of course—plus his debt overhang. The Street says his bankers read him the riot act—no more rollovers on the notes; word is they came to the meeting with their foreclosure specialists. Sands countered with his bankruptcy boys, of course, but Sands was the first to blink. So it's off to Toronto on a shopping spree. I hear if he doesn't connect in Canada, the next stop is Singapore."

"What would it take for Sands to turn it around?"

"A miracle in the form of several million bucks of cash flow, primarily. Happened every day in the Reagan years—if you needed dough, someone was always there to make some for you. Rights, warrants, junk—all they are is new forms of money."

"The Constitution says only the *government* can print money."

"What Constitution?" Clay asked with mock innocence. "Anyway, Sands is scrambling. I wouldn't bet against him, either: He won't go down without a fight, and if he *does* go down, he'll take lots of people with him. I hear folks are bailing out of Sandstone in droves. And melting their memory chips behind them."

"One more thing," I said.

"Shoot."

"Tell me what you know about blood."

"Are you serious?"

"Yes."

"Blood. As in the blood *business,* you mean?"

"Right."

"Well, it's big, for one thing. Several billion a year in sales of blood and blood products. A person has a ninety-five-percent chance of needing either a transfusion or a blood product at some time in their life. A pint of blood that's given for free to the Red Cross can be worth over five hundred bucks when it's broken down into by-products—plasma, platelets, stuff like that—and sold off to hospitals."

"What's the word on safety?"

"You mean the AIDS problem, I suppose. Well, there's no question that the blood banks—the Red Cross and the private banks both—didn't respond quickly enough to AIDS. Randy Shilts lays this out in his book—basically, between the time AIDS was discovered in 1983 and the time the blood people finally began testing for it, which wasn't till 1985, a lot of bad blood got into the system. Hemophiliacs were the chief victims since they use so much of it—over half the hemophiliacs who were getting blood back then ended up with the virus."

"How about now?"

"Well, testing has improved, I guess, and screening of donors is a lot stricter—no one's pretending AIDS isn't a problem anymore, that's for sure—so the supply is pretty safe these days, as I understand it."

"But not completely."

"People screw up sometimes, is one problem. A report not long ago took the Red Cross to task for laxity in its testing procedures. Seems that over a six-month period back in eighty-eight, they released a couple of thousand units of product that hadn't been properly tested. The FDA just shut down some private banks in Oregon and South Carolina because of similar problems."

"Scary."

"Sure. But if you're really worried about it, the big thing these days is autologous donation—storing your own blood for emergencies. Michael Jackson supposedly travels with several units of his stuff on ice, just in case." Clay laughed. "I'm not up on all the bloody details, Marsh—maybe you should see a doctor."

Chapter
25

It was too late to scare up a doctor for anything but a bridge game, so I tried Ellen Simmons again, this time at home. Her father answered the second ring—I guessed it was a full-time task, monitoring the ebb and flow of information in the household; like all authoritarians, Orson Simmons was maintaining control through the imposition of ignorance. I still wondered why Ellen submitted to such an atmosphere and why her father found it necessary to be a tyrant.

"What is your business with her?" Simmons demanded after I said my name and asked to speak to his daughter.

"Pretty much the same as it was the last time."

"For your information, her mother and I found your public demonstration of affection to be highly offensive."

"Sorry. Next time we'll do our demonstrating in private. Then you can use your imagination. Tell Ellen I'll be there in an hour."

Hoping Ellen's nocturnal habits were as invariable as she'd claimed, I hung up in the middle of Simmons' bluff and bluster, then found my car and aimed it down the hill. Time and traffic being what they were, it took ninety minutes to get there.

Ellen was waiting for me on the porch, knitting in her lap, her body curling to and fro in one of the matched cane rockers that were the only comforts the house was blessed with. She approached the car so quickly I didn't have time to fetch her.

"I was afraid you'd decided not to come," she breathed as she climbed in the passenger side and locked the door behind her. I wondered if the person she was trying to lock out was her father.

Her dress was bright and crisp and Easterish—full and flowery and almost low-cut, topped with a crocheted shawl I bet she had made herself; I also bet it was the first time she'd worn it on an occasion other than reverential. Her lips were still her natural pink, but her hair was wound atop her head in the fashion of some yesteryear, her cheeks were inflamed with blots of rouge, her wrist clanked with the sounds of charms on a silver bracelet. She was all dolled up and eager to please, but for some reason I felt bad, maybe because I wasn't the Lochinvar she hoped I was.

"Traffic," I said to explain my tardiness. "I always forget how awful it is. Do you drive to work?"

She shook her head. "Bus. I catch it out there." She pointed toward the Danville Highway. "Twenty-five minutes, door-to-door."

"So what do you do with all those minutes?"

She colored and stayed silent.

"Come on, what? *The Banker's Journal? Road and Track?* Needlepoint? What?"

"I write poetry." She grinned sheepishly. "You can laugh if you want. Most people do."

"What most people do is dumb. So what do you write—free verse? Couplets? Limericks?"

"Sonnets, mostly."

"Sonnets are great; I like sonnets."

"Really? Whose?"

"Ah . . . Shakespeare. He wrote good sonnets."

"Who else?"

" . . . Ah, mostly Shakespeare."

Her eyes glistened with her game. "And Browning, of course. And Keats."

"Sure. Those guys, too. So how many have you written?"

"I try to write one a day—half going in, half coming home."

"I'd like to read some sometime."

She shook her head. "They're not very good."

"Even if that's true, what difference does it make?"

Her brow knit thoughtfully, as though we were discussing cosmology. "I think if you decide to read a sonnet, you should read a good one."

"If I stick to Shakespeare, how would I get to know *you* better?"

She met my eye. "Why would you want to?"

"Because I like you."

She smiled shyly. "I'm glad. Despite what my father may have told you."

"Speaking of which, I've been a little rough on him. I apologize if he's upset."

Her back stiffened. "It's *good* for him to hear back talk for a change. Sometimes I think the reason he quit the machine shop was so he could have his own way all day long."

"Why is he so protective of you?"

She blinked and looked toward the house, as if the answer might appear like an apparition, mysteriously emblazoned on the siding. "Can we go somewhere?" she asked softly.

"Sure. Have you had dinner?"

"Sort of."

"Want some more?"

"Not really."

"Drink?"

"Yes," she concluded firmly. "One of those fruity things with lots of ice."

"Coming right up," I said, and put the Buick into gear and took the old highway into Danville. Since Ellen was an old-fashioned girl, I took her to an old-fashioned place— the bar of the Danville Hotel.

She ordered her frozen daiquiri—banana—and I ordered unfrozen scotch. We smiled at each other and took silent note of the unconvincingly rustic surroundings until the waitress brought the drinks. When she'd gone back to the bar, we picked them up and clinked our glasses. "Here's to happiness," I said.

"Yours or mine?"

"Both."

"Together?"

I blinked and swallowed and limited my answer to the ambiguity of a smile.

We both drank quickly, as if we had errands to perform and had to get to them. Because I still hadn't gotten around to asking my questions, I ordered another round. Because she seemed determined to obliterate her inhibitions pursuant to an agenda of her own, Ellen was more than agreeable—strawberry this time. Although I was intrigued by her élan, what I mostly hoped was that she wouldn't get sick—while I was a drinking man myself, Ellen was both by nature and nurture a teetotaler.

"You still haven't told me why your father is so protective of you," I reminded her when the second batch of booze had come.

"I don't *know* why," she said. "It's just the way he is. It's the way his father was as well, I think."

"Despotism runs in the family."

She squirmed. "Sort of."

"I think there's more to it than that." I waited till I had her full attention. "I think something happened to you back in high school. Around the time Tom Crandall went to Vietnam."

Her eyes flicked on and off my face. "I already told you something happened—I lost my virginity."

"I'm not talking about that."

"What makes you think there's anything else?"

"Reading between the lines, mostly."

She shook her head. "What's between the lines is only empty space." She fidgeted with her collar. "It's none of your business, anyway."

"It is if it has something to do with why Tom was killed."

"Who says he *was* killed?"

"I do. And you *used* to."

"You know everything about it, I suppose."

"I know a homicide when I see one. And I know a cover-up when I smell one, too."

"Cover-up," she sniffed. "You make it sound like Watergate or something."

I looked at her till she looked back. "Isn't it time the story came out? Maybe when it does, you won't have to hide at home for the rest of your life."

Her protest was shrill. "I live at home because my parents *need* me. They can't *cope* with the world."

"I think they're coping just fine according to their lights; you're the one who's dysfunctional."

A tear formed in her eye. I was sorry to be its architect, but I plunged ahead. "Whatever the truth is, I don't see how it could be worse if it came to light—you're already living like a prisoner on work furlough. Emily Dickinson may have been a great poet, but she wasn't a great role model."

It hurt her worse than I intended. To hide her pain, she closed her eyes and bowed her head. I looked out a window, at the Cadillacs and Mercedes grazing in the parking lot, untroubled by our contretemps.

"Look at this place," I said roughly. "Danville was a sleepy country town back when you were in high school, but now it's yuppie heaven—half the Oakland A's live out here, for God's sake. Do you or your family know *any* of these people?"

She sniffed defiantly. "We know *lots* of people. Old valley people, like us. We see them every Sunday at church."

"Then give your friends a chance to show what good Christians they are. Forgiveness, absolution, all that."

She dug a handkerchief from her bodice and wiped her eyes. "I don't know what you want from me."

"I want to know what happened between you and Nicky Crandall after Tom went to Vietnam."

"Who said anything about Nicky?"

"I did."

"Have you seen him?"

"No. Have you?"

She shook her head. "You don't know *anything*, do you? You're only guessing."

I kissed the back of her hand. "I'm a good guesser. I majored in it at college."

She didn't remove her hand from my grasp, but she didn't say anything, either.

"That's why your parents keep you locked away, isn't it? So Nicky can't get at you?"

Her hand grew as rigid as wood as she formulated a plan. When she had one, she withdrew her hand and drained her drink and looked around the bar. "How badly do you want to know all this?"

"Pretty badly."

"Badly enough to make love to me?"

I was the one who was reeling this time. "What did you say?"

"You heard me," she replied airily. "If you get a room in this hotel and take me there and make love to me, I'll—"

"This place doesn't rent rooms anymore."

"Then somewhere. Anywhere. If you do, I'll tell you everything you want to know. If you don't, I won't. It's as simple as that. You think I'm teasing," she added when I didn't respond.

"I don't know *what* you're doing. I don't think you do, either."

She pouted. "You're just saying that because you're not interested in the proposition."

"That's not it."

"Then what?—you're saving me from myself? Doing the honorable thing? Maybe you're afraid of my father. Or perhaps you're homosexual, asexual, unsexual. Please pick one before I start to cry."

As her emotions threatened to wreck her resolve, I tried to keep things from becoming more absurd than they already were. "Let's just say I don't want to take advantage of you."

"*I'm* the one doing the extorting, Mr. Tanner."

"You don't know anything about me. I'm old enough to be your father. I'm—"

"I know Tom liked you," she said softly.

I swore. "That's really what you want—to spend another night with Tom. I'm sorry, but I'm not him."

She stiffened in rebuttal. "I know that. I also know you're not someone who would hurt me."

"No."

"Or laugh at me."

"No."

"Or make me do something I didn't want to do."

I tried a smile. "'Maybe' is as good as you're going to get on that one."

Ellen swirled the slush in her glass, gazing into the strawberry floe that had become a match to her complexion, indulging fantasies I could only guess at. I felt sorry for her, at bottom, which made me leery: I make mistakes when I feel sorry for people.

With a final slug of her drink, Ellen raised her eyes. "I haven't had sexual relations for eighteen-and-one-half years, Mr. Tanner. My night with Tom has become pivotal—I marvel at it, I relive every second of it, I regard it as the defining moment of my life, I measure time from before and after that instant. *And I don't think that's healthy.* I think I ought to move beyond it, especially now that Tom is dead. Whatever it was that Tom and I were to each other needs to become history rather than float over me like a veil." The essay was so essential it left her no option but to beg. "What I was hoping was that you'd help me."

"I'd like to," I said truthfully. "I just don't think your idea is the best way to go about it."

She met my eye without defenses. "The time with Tom was . . . overwhelming." Her cheeks reddened even further. "I'd like to be overwhelmed once more before I die."

The craving was so candid I couldn't meet her gaze. "There must be men at the bank who would be happy to—"

She shook her head. "They would talk. Rumors would fly. People would speculate about me even more than they do now. They already think I'm odd; I don't want them to think I'm libertine as well." She made another pass at her daiquiri and seemed surprised to find it empty. "Let's face it," she went on, her words slurred with liquor and weighty with disappointment. "You don't find me attractive."

"I find you very attractive."

"I don't excite you. You're afraid you couldn't . . . perform."

"I'm a bachelor; I could perform with a stump. I'm just not sure I should."

She looked around, then leaned forward so she could whisper whatever it was she thought would turn the tide. "I have very nice breasts, Mr. Tanner. You'd be surprised."

I laughed to cover my embarrassment. "No, I wouldn't. Look, Ellen. Your offer is tempting. Maybe when this business with Tom is over we can get together and see how things develop. But I can't just waltz you off to some motel and screw you like a hooker. You're too nice a girl for that."

She made a fist and pounded the table. "To *hell* with nice. *Nice* girls sit at home and listen to their parents rant and rave about the evils of the world as if laughing and singing and dancing and loving were the most barbaric things on earth." She put down her glass and took my hand in fingers that were cold and damp. "Do you have any idea how badly I wish I could *be* like a hooker and offer myself to the first man who came along? But I can't do that; I don't have that in me. It has to be someone . . . nice." She smiled bravely despite it all. "And you're a nice man, Mr. Tanner. If you weren't, we'd already be undressed."

All I can say in defense of my decision is that it took me several seconds to reach it. "I haven't made love to all that many women," I said finally. "But I have to tell you that very few of them have called me 'Mr. Tanner' on the way to the bedroom."

Chapter
26

The motel was the first one I came to, on the south edge of Walnut Creek wedged between a hospital and a barbecue joint. It was unobtrusive and unostentatious, suitable for iniquity, a match to my mood. The clerk was smirking by the time we reached the desk—they always seem to be smirking when you're doing something to warrant it. "We'd like a room," I told him.

"Twins or queen?"

"Queen."

"That'll be ninety-seven dollars. Plus tax."

"My goodness," Ellen erupted behind my shoulder. "I had no idea."

I tried for a joke. "It keeps you from forming bad habits."

Ellen wasn't amused. "It's unacceptable. A hundred dollars for a bed? For *one night*? Outrageous. We'll just go to your—"

I put my hand over her mouth and tossed two fifties on the counter. "This is business, remember? I can write it off."

The smirk slid to a smarmy grin. He shoved a key my way, told us to "have fun," and watched as Ellen led me like an ill-fated lamb in the direction of an excessively mirrored elevator.

The room was adequate, I guess—I was too immersed in the shifting sands of morality to pay much attention. When we were enclosed within its pastel confines, we looked at each other with a blend of incredulity and mirth.

"I almost brought my nightie," Ellen said with a timid smile. "But it was too dowdy. I *did* bring my toothbrush." She patted her purse.

"So this wasn't a spur-of-the-moment thing."

She shook her head. "Spur of the week."

"I'm afraid there's still a problem."

A lip quivered. "You've gotten cold feet."

"Pretty much everything on me is hot, pedal extremities included, but I don't have a condom. Things are different than they were eighteen years ago. We shouldn't—"

"I'm not from Mars, you know," she said primly, and reached into her purse. When her hand emerged, it was holding the crimped edge of a foil-wrapped disk the way I hold the worm while I'm trying to bait my hook.

She held it so I could see the brand. "Is it all right? I didn't . . . the man said it was one-size-fits-all." Her cheeks could have served as landing lights.

"It's fine."

Her eyes sparkled. "I'm a very efficient person, Mr. Tanner. I anticipate contingencies and provide for them. I'm *very* underutilized at the bank."

"So that makes two things I know about you—you're efficient and you've got nice breasts."

Her response was brazen. "I'm five-six, I weigh one-twenty, I like silk scarves and frilly underwear, I devour Anne Tyler and Barbara Pym, and I've voted for Jesse Jackson two times." She blushed. "Does any of that disqualify me?"

"That makes you first in line."

"Good. Here. Or should I open it? Do you put it on now or later?"

"Later."

"Do you do it or do I?"

"Either."

She looked at it, turned it over, looked at it again, then thrust it toward me. "It looks like it could get tricky, and I don't have much practice." She tittered. "None, as it happens."

"I'll handle it," I said, and put the condom on the bedstand.

Ellen looked around the room as though she were the set designer on the remake of *Ali Baba*. "I'd like the lights on if you don't mind. A few, at least." When she looked at my face, she adjusted her demands. "One, if it's all right. Tom and I were in the back of his car halfway up Mount Diablo. It was dark and cramped. There wasn't much room for . . . perspective."

I turned on the light in the bathroom, closed the door most of the way, then turned off the overhead. "Satisfactory?"

She glanced at the bed. "Perfect." She blushed again. "I should wash up." Without waiting for a reply, she disappeared into the bathroom. Which was too bad, because it gave me time to think.

When all was said and done, I almost tossed some cab money onto the bed and left. Fled. Retreated in disarray, all of which I've done more than once in similar circumstances, not that the similarity was all that strong. But somehow it wasn't right. It wasn't entirely wrong, either, but despite Ellen's resolutely blasé demeanor, the musk of desperation clogged the room, an aura of ersatz ecstasy, the itch of the cheap thrill.

Given my solitary life, I could empathize with Ellen's physical desires, and I was egotist enough to approve her choice of partners. What I had trouble with was that to make it right it would have to be more than a physical experience for her, it would have to be transforming. As far as I knew, I hadn't provoked an epiphany in years, in or out of bed, and I didn't want to see my failure on this occasion reflected in Ellen's postcoital eyes. But when the door to the bathroom opened, and Ellen was naked in the doorway with backlight making her curves and hollows glow as if she were freshly glazed and being fired in a spotless kiln, my reservations vanished in the maze of possibilities and nothing beyond that mattered, certainly not a store of half-baked mores that didn't meet the needs of anyone.

"You've changed your mind," she said when she saw my sartorial status had remained quo.

"Not exactly."

"You've decided I'm a slattern."

"Not at all."

"You pity me. You think I'm a tease. You think I'm a sex fiend."

"None of the above. I just want to make sure you still want this."

She canted a hip and raised an arm. "What does it *look* like?"

I tugged at my belt and at whatever else was in the way.

When I was her mate in dishabille and had made my own trip to wash up, I faced her at the foot of the bed. In the crimped light from the bathroom doorway, her body was like soft sculpture, a Venus perfect in proportion, flawless in surface, infinite in opportunity. The difference was, this particular masterpiece was mine for the asking, at least for the evening.

Her skin was unsullied by the sun, her face still free of the etch of age, her breasts as advertised. For a moment, her hand lingered to mask her crotch, then that barrier was whisked away as well, and she waited for me to begin the rite. I reached for her hand and pulled her to me, trying not to notice that the hand was ice-cold.

The embrace was brief, at her insistence. "I want to touch you first," she said, and did, gently but utterly, as though her sole surviving sense were tactile. "It's blood that makes it that way, right?"

"Blood plus stimulation."

"You seem to have the requisite amount of both."

"No question."

She paused. "Some women do . . . things with it, don't they?"

"Yes."

She paused again. "I don't think I can."

"You don't have to."

"I think just the basics, pretty much."

"The basics are fine."

"But we can . . . hug for a while, can't we? When Tom and I were together, we didn't take time to—" She caught herself and became abject. "I'm sorry. I won't talk about that anymore. This isn't that, this is this."

"Ms. Simmons and Mr. Tanner."

Her smile was finally unrestrained. "That's it, exactly."

"We'll hug, and then we'll do a little more than hug, and then we'll hug some more." I bent and kissed a breast.

She responded as though I'd burned her, the reaction so electric it was impossible to tell whether the reflex was grounded in pleasure or pain. I left one breast and kissed the other. This time she clasped my head and kept me at it.

"They are nice, aren't they?" she said after a while.

I lowered Ellen Simmons to the bed and tried to become what she wanted me to be, which was the reincarnation of Tom Crandall.

Chapter
27

It was over before it should have been, of course—when
your sex life is as fitful as mine, ejaculation is by definition
premature. But Ellen was even more deprived than I, so she
rode the wave and crested with me.

When we were finished and cleaned up and back on the
bed though not in our clothing, Ellen turned onto her side
for a better view. "There's quite a difference, isn't there?
Before and after."

"Yep."

"An amazing mechanism. Hydraulic, almost."

"As good a metaphor as any."

"Have you ever not been able to . . . get it up? Is that
the term?"

"That's one of them."

"Well?"

"A couple of times."

"What happened?"

"I apologized, we told each other it didn't matter and
exchanged exceedingly polite farewells. And never saw
each other again."

"What I *meant* was, why do you think it didn't work those nights?"

I shrugged. "Guilt. Exhaustion. Intoxication. Boredom. More than one but less than all, probably."

"It's difficult for me to think of sex being boring. Frightening. Embarrassing. Disappointing, even. But not boring."

I looked to see if Ellen intended an implicit critique of my performance, but apparently not. I turned on my side to face her. "The truth is, Ms. Simmons, that the mechanics of my sex life wouldn't keep an insomniac awake. So why don't we talk about you."

She stiffened and flopped over onto her stomach. "The quid pro quo. I hoped you'd forgotten."

"Private eyes are forbidden to forget. There's a law on it."

She rolled away from me. "Since the fun seems to have ended, I'm going to get dressed."

She disappeared into the bathroom. By the time she returned, I was dressed myself and trying to look business-like in the chair beside the rumpled bed. Since the chair beside the bed was the only chair in the room, Ellen straightened the spread, fluffed and stacked the pillows, and sat back against them, lips in a matchless pout, arms crossed against my purposes. Her expression was not calculated to make me feel triumphant or even decent.

"Look," I began. "I'm sorry you're upset. The transition was too abrupt; I'll do better next time."

The last sentence was in the air before its implication registered. When it had, we regarded each other with a newfound shyness. "See that you do," Ellen said finally, halfway back to brazenness. "When do you suppose the next time will be?"

"How about next week? Dinner Friday night."

She looked at her watch. "I was thinking more in terms of twenty minutes."

I laughed. "I'm not a young man, you know. We can give it a try, but you might have to get a little . . . bawdy at first. Just to get the hydraulics going."

"I can do that," she said confidently, then reconsidered. "Can't I?"

"You're only as bawdy as you feel."

"Then there's no problem at all."

I got up and walked to the dresser and looked at Ellen's reflection in the mirror. "Let's talk about you and Nicky Crandall."

Wantonness drained out of her. Hurt, then petulant, she turned away from me again and curled into a ball, knees hugged to her chest, fetal with a vengeance. When she spoke, the words bounced off the plastic headboard and reached me in a brittle timbre.

"You're right, of course," she murmured softly. "Something did happen with Nicky."

"When?"

"About six months after Tom went away."

"And Nicky had gotten it into his head that you wanted to be his girl."

"Yes."

"How did that notion occur to him? Do you know?"

"Not really. Given Nicky's mental state, it could have been anything—a smile, a greeting—who knows what might have put the idea in his mind? At that age, even *normal* boys get wrong ideas."

To put it mildly.

Ellen fell silent, struggling to summon the past with accuracy, to deliver her part of the bargain—the whole truth and nothing but. In my experience, not many people made the effort, and I was flattered that she was making it for me until I decided that, as in the exercise we'd just completed, she was expending her energies for Tom.

"I think maybe Tom asked Nicky to look after me while he was gone," she went on after a long silence. "And Nicky misinterpreted. God, that was an awful time," she concluded, misery active in her eyes.

"What exactly happened between you and Nicky?"

She didn't answer.

"Was it rape?"

Her eyes moved my way with the lethargy of a snake in the sun. "That's what everyone *thought* it was."

"Why?"

"Because I let them."

"Why?"

"Because I thought that was what would hurt Tom the most when he found out—what would punish him most for deserting me."

"But rape's not what it was?"

She shook her head.

"Then what was it?"

She looked at me in turmoil. "Why do you need to *know*? Why do you have to dig at my troubles with Nicky?"

"Because I think Nicky Crandall may have killed his brother."

Rather than the surprise I expected, her response was as level as a pool table. "Then it might be of interest if I told you that twenty years ago Nicky tried to kill *me*."

At this point, the surprise was mine. "Tell me about it. If you don't mind."

Her look was fragile and disconnected. "Oh, I mind. I mind a *lot*. I've tried very hard to erase that night from my memory entirely. But it hasn't worked, so I'll tell you what you want to know. That way I'll have earned my evening."

"It wasn't like that, Ellen. You know damned well it wasn't."

"If you say so, John."

I hadn't been called John in years. That Ellen Simmons didn't know it made me sad.

Chillingly detached, she spoke as though we were tourists trading anecdotes. "Let's see. Tom had gone in the army in June. Nick had been put in Dr. Marlin's clinic about the same time. He got out in, oh, September, maybe. But he wasn't any better. If anything, he was worse—the tirades, the talking to himself, the odd behavior: The whole town was wondering when he'd do something violent and why no one was doing anything to make sure it couldn't happen."

"Had he done anything harmful before this?"

She shook her head. "Not that I know of. But people saw the signs. Some people, at least. I didn't think he was so bad, myself—odd, certainly, but not dangerous. Until I found out differently."

"What happened?"

She started talking before I finished the question, as though now that the die was cast, she was impatient to exorcise the nightmare.

"I saw Nicky uptown one night. It was late, after I'd been to a movie and dropped a girlfriend off at home. We waved, and I pulled over and offered him a ride. I didn't even think about it; I mean, I'd been with him a hundred times before without a problem. But this time he wanted to go to the high school. He said he'd left some books by the tennis court and needed them over the weekend. It wasn't far, so I drove him over there. When we were in the parking lot, and he could see there was no one else around, he attacked me."

"Did he have a weapon?"

"No."

"A knife, a rope—anything?"

Her eyes sparked. "What *difference* does it make? He had his hands around my *throat*. I couldn't breathe, he kept telling me I was going to die. I was afraid he'd rip my *eyes* out, I—"

I went to the bed and sat beside her and took her hands in mine. "I wasn't implying it wasn't a life-threatening situation, I was thinking about Tom. In his case, the murder weapon was unusual—a piece of drug paraphernalia—so if Nicky used an unconventional weapon with you, then it might indicate a pattern."

Ellen closed her eyes and shook her head. "No weapon. Just Nicky."

"You're sure it was attempted murder? Not rape?"

"Definitely. Nicky was trying to kill me."

"Why?"

"I don't know. Not then, not now. In some sense, I don't think Nicky knew, either."

"How did you get him to stop?"

"First I tried to reason with him. Then I . . . begged. Begged him to . . ."

"What?"

I had to strain to hear her. "Let me be nice to him." She raised her eyes. "I begged Nicky the way I begged you."

"You didn't do anything of the sort with me. We—"

She shook her head to stop me. "You wanted to know about Nicky. So ask about him."

There were a lot of reasons to console rather than interrogate her, but I did as she requested. "What happened when you told the police about it?"

"Nothing."

"You mean they didn't arrest him?"

"I mean I didn't tell them."

"Why not?"

"Because everyone told me not to."

"Who's everyone?"

"My parents. Mrs. Crandall. Dr. Marlin."

"Why didn't they want you to go to the police?"

"My parents didn't want to endure the scandal; Mrs. Crandall wanted the whole thing to go up in smoke like it always had before; and Dr. Marlin said Nicky wouldn't survive in prison, that he wouldn't get the treatment he needed and would be subjected to all sorts of brutality because of his weird behavior. He promised that if I cooperated, he'd put Nicky on medication that would make sure he wouldn't do that again. To me or anyone."

Her look turned wretched as she tried to make me understand. "I didn't realize what was happening until the very end. I mean, when he put his hands on me, I just thought he was . . . horny. That he would stop when he understood I didn't like him in that way. Nicky was so weird that all the girls were afraid of him. He didn't have any dates, and so I was . . . trying to be gentle with him, I guess, to explain my feelings and at the same time try not to injure his, and all of a sudden he was strangling me. So I told him I'd do what I thought he wanted. I was very specific, as specific as I could be, at least. I tried to make it sound delightful. But that wasn't what he wanted, it turned out. By the end, I knew absolutely that he wanted me to die."

"So your . . . offer . . . wasn't what stopped him?"

She shook her head. "Someone pulled into the parking lot. Nicky ran off when he saw him coming."

She put her hands over her eyes and began to cry. I started to embrace her, but she shook her head. "Just let me be. Please. What else do you want to know?"

"Did he tell you why he was attacking you?"

Ellen looked at me with what looked like gratitude. "No. But it didn't have to do with me at all. Not really. The person he was actually attacking was Tom."

"What makes you say that?"

"Because the last thing he said before he ran away was for me to tell Tom about it. 'Tell him what I did to you,' he said. 'Tell him this is what happens when you leave people to be captured. Tell him this is what they make you do.'"

"He thought he was being controlled by outside forces, it sounds like."

She nodded. "He repeated it several times. How Tom had deserted him. Left him without protection. It was as if the war wasn't in Vietnam but right here in San Ramon, and the enemy wasn't communists but some secret band of aliens." She sighed. "I suppose for Nicky that's how it was."

"Did he hurt you badly?"

She shook her head.

"How did Tom react when he heard about all this?"

She looked at me with an expression as bleak as the room. "That very night I wrote to Tom and told him, implying it was rape. And I never heard from him again. Not for a dozen years."

She started to sob once more. This time I took her in my arms and did what I could to calm her. "Surely he didn't blame *you* for what happened."

She shrugged. "I'm sure he blamed himself. But instead of punishing himself or his brother, he transferred the guilt and punished me. There was a very complex psychology between them; I'm not sure anyone understood it. Not even Dr. Marlin."

I sighed and shook my head. "When I kissed your breast, I thought you were shuddering with pleasure."

She smiled bravely. "Not at first."

"But later?"

"Yes."

"This was a home remedy you concocted, wasn't it? It had nothing to do with Tom."

She looked at me. "Are you mad?"

I shook my head. "Are you sorry?"

She rolled toward me, gave me a quick kiss, then reached for the button on her blouse. "Your twenty minutes are up. But I'm going to need some tips in bawdy, Mr. Tanner."

"I've got a million of 'em, Miss Simmons."

Chapter

28

Most of the lawyers I know don't have wills. Most of the doctors I know never get checkups. Most of the mechanics I know drive rattletraps. Which may be a clue to why a child with a tin shovel could break into my home.

I was tired, and out of sorts, and preoccupied. Part of me still wrestled with the ethics of my participation in Ellen Simmons' self-help exercise. Another part worried that Richard Sands might make good on his threat to destroy my livelihood if I kept probing for a reason for Tom's death, that I would be summoned by some regulator or administrator armed with a carefully scripted suspicion and become immersed in a bureaucratic proceeding that would cost all I had to get out of: It doesn't take much to destroy an innocent man these days, the courts and the media are too willing to become accessories to such a scheme. Yet despite these and other claims on my consciousness, I knew from the moment I opened the door that someone had been inside my apartment.

The scent in the air—sour and caustic—wasn't one of mine. The table in the entryway wasn't quite where it usually was, and the dust on its top was smeared. The door from the foyer to the living room was ajar, although to minimize the burden on the heating unit, I always keep it closed. I had been invaded.

The first question was whether my caller was still calling. I leaned against the doorjamb and tried to remember whether my gun, which was back in the bedroom a thousand miles away, was loaded. After I remembered it wasn't, I realized it didn't matter—for the moment, the only weapons at hand were my ears.

The refrigerator was humming. Traffic was still laboring to climb Telegraph Hill. The neighbor below me was listening to Marvin Gaye; the neighbor above was watching *Nightline*. My heart was playing hopscotch, and my body needed more air than I could give it. As far as I could tell, no one was lying in wait.

I took a step, made a noise without wanting to, waited for a reaction but got none. I reached for the switch and flipped on the lights. Nothing exploded, no one screamed, everything stayed put. Apparently I could leave or stay at my pleasure, so I chose the latter course.

My first trip through the apartment confirmed that I was its only occupant. My second was a quick inventory to ensure nothing had been stolen. The third established that the game wasn't to steal, the game was to bring gifts. And what they'd brought was poison: While I'd been rolling around in Walnut Creek, applying a poultice to Ellen's heartache and a treat to my own libido, someone had been contaminating every comestible I owned.

The adulterants numbered three. Most prevalent was a white powder that could have been anything from lye to strychnine but smelled more like Comet cleanser: I was supposed to assume it was some sort of nerve agent, I think. It had been liberally sprinkled where it would be most visible—in a jar of spaghetti sauce, over a slice of chocolate cake, on my stash of Oreos and in my bag of French Roast beans.

The second substance was even more unsettling. A yellowish unguent, a glutinous salve that put me in mind of mustard plaster, had been smeared across a pound of ground beef, ladled onto a loaf of bread, scraped into the open spout of a milk carton, even spread over the trays of ice cubes. As I evaluated it to no avail, the inescapable suggestion was of purulence and contagion.

Last but not least, a substance that could have been someone's blood had been added to selected items as a sadistic sauce. Ladled over a hunk of ham, dripped onto a tub of margarine and poured over a pint of Heavenly Hash, the effect was of mayhem and dismemberment, a limitless abandon. Bile burned in my throat as I completed the inventory. If the intent of the enterprise was to give me the creeps, the mission was accomplished.

My first impulse was to gather up samples to take to Charley Sleet for analysis at the police lab, but then I figured what the hell. They hadn't meant to harm me, after all—every jar, every can, every bottle, every box that had been both carefully and obviously sabotaged, had one of those little poison warnings stuck on to it, the labels with the skull and crossbones that help parents teach kids what things in the cupboard were dangerous. I wasn't supposed to die or even get sick, I was just supposed to believe that they could kill me at any time, in ways I would have no way of detecting without the aid of a chemist or a food-taster. As I imagined the Healthways boys reveling in a delicious sense of power as they moved through my apartment, sowing their decals of dread, I decided I believed just that.

I gathered up my foodstuffs not to test them but to throw them out—they didn't leave so much as a pristine potato chip to ease the anxiety. As I bagged up the last of the canned goods and emptied out the salt, I wondered how long it would be before I could make myself a sandwich without fearing it would kill me.

Then I pledged that Richard Sands would pay in some suitable way for the new notch of fear he had cut into my life.

Then I tried to decide what I had learned that had made me so dangerous.

Chapter

29

The next morning I called my client before I left for the office. While I waited for her maid to tell her I was on the line, it occurred to me that the personal and professional relationships that had surfaced during the Crandall case were as unlikely as any in my experience.

"Mr. Tanner," she enthused when she came on, panting as though she'd raced to the phone. "I was hoping to hear from you. Have you any news?"

What she meant was did I have enough on her husband to indict him. "Not really," I demurred. "What I'm after is information."

"I see." Enthusiasm was replaced by calculation. "I think I'd better call you back. It will take me ten minutes."

The line went dead; the woman suspected her husband had tapped her phone.

In the interim, I placed another call. I remembered only belatedly that it was early to be disturbing someone whose workday ended at 3:00 A.M., but when she answered the phone, Clarissa Crandall didn't upbraid me;

she didn't even sound annoyed. I hoped she was feeling chipper because her boyfriend was off on a toot to Toronto.

"How are you getting along?" I asked.

"I'm fine." She paused. "Well, not so fine, actually. I miss him. Quite a lot. My skin seems to miss him the most—I feel like I have hives or something."

"We're talking about Tom, I hope."

"Of course," she said stiffly.

"I've had that feeling a few times—overloaded nerve endings. An emotional hangover."

"That's it exactly. I feel . . . undeservedly decadent. How long do you suppose it will last?"

"A man I know who just got divorced told me his therapist said it would take him six seasons before he was over it. Death probably takes longer."

We were silent again—there was always more silence than communication between Clarissa and me—and when she spoke again, it was only after her emotions were strapped so she could manage them. "Are you learning anything I should know?" she asked, careful not to betray excessive interest.

"Not about Tom, I'm afraid. I have learned a few things about his brother."

"What kind of things?"

"Some violent episodes in his past, for example."

"What kind of violence?"

"It seems to have amounted to attempted murder."

Her voice rose. "Are you serious?"

"I'm afraid so."

"Who did he try to murder? Surely not Tom."

"A woman named Ellen Simmons."

"Ellen? My God. Why on earth did he want to kill poor Ellen?"

I suppressed my irritation at the adjective. "Do you know her?"

"I know *of* her—Tom mentioned her quite often over the years, more so once I started seeing Richard. I guess I was supposed to feel about Ellen the way Tom felt about Mr. Sands. Further evidence of our miscommunication."

"We're talking jealousy, I take it."

Her laugh was unattractive. "I believe we are. I don't like to be rude, but why did you call me, Mr. Tanner?"

I refrained from being rude in return. "Have you seen or heard from Nicky since Tom died?"

"No. Why would I?"

"Because it's conceivable he's a threat to your safety."

"Why would Nicky want to hurt *me*?"

"I'm not sure; he's not rational, so I don't pretend to be privy to his thought processes. All I know is, he's been behaving even more strangely than usual lately. Given the dynamics of his relationship with Tom, it's possible Tom's death could have sent him off the deep end. It's also possible he *killed* Tom. I advise you to take precautions."

"You don't really think Nicky . . ."

"I don't know what I think. I'm just listing possibilities."

"But why would Nicky be a problem for *me*? I still don't understand."

"Fifteen years ago, Nicky tried to kill the woman in Tom's life. The reason seems to have had to do with the fact that Tom had just gone away to war. Now Tom has gone away again, and since you're the woman in his life at this point, it's conceivable that—"

She sighed. "You don't need to complete the picture. What steps do you think I should take?"

"Ask Sands to have some of his muscle boys stick close to you for a while."

"They're already so sticky I feel like a refrigerator door."

"Your privacy is a subordinate consideration at this point. I'm talking day-and-night protection, at least for a while."

"Until what?"

"Until I learn who killed Tom and why."

"Will that really solve anything?" she mused softly. "Especially for poor Nicky?"

"Maybe not. It probably didn't even solve anything for Tom."

Her laugh was brittle. "I don't discuss theology anymore, Mr. Tanner; Tom's obsession with it pretty much wore the subject out for me. 'Amazing Grace' is as complex as I need that particular issue to get right now."

"You're ahead of me—I'm still struggling with 'Jesus Loves Me.'"

"Tom would have pitied both of us."

I didn't think so, but there didn't seem any point in saying so. "One last thing," I said instead. "I'd like you to do some thinking about your friend Mr. Sands."

Her tone was as defensive as always whenever his name came up. "What about him?"

"I'd like you to decide what your feelings for him really are."

"What possible business could that be of yours? And why would you suppose I haven't thought about that for weeks?"

"I may need you to decide what you're willing to do to find out what kind of man he is."

"Why would I have to do *anything*?"

"Because it's possible Sands is a monster. The scheme he's come up with to save his companies may be endangering far more people than your husband. I—"

"*Wait* a minute. Are you saying *Richard* killed Tom? Do you know how *ridiculous* that is?"

"I'm not saying that," I interrupted.

"Then what *are* you saying?"

"I'm saying I may need your help to find out what happened to Tom and whether Sands had anything to do with it. I'd like you to think about whether you'll give me that help if I need it."

Her breaths were static in the line. "You sound like something sinister is about to happen."

"Something sinister may have *already* happened. The question is how to put a stop to it."

"What would I have to do?"

"Get Sands away from his henchmen so I can confront him with my suspicions."

"When?"

"When does he get back from Toronto?"

"Tonight. Late."

"How hard would it be to get him alone with you at the club?"

"Not very."

"Check your answering machine this evening. I'll let you know if it's on."

My thoughts on schemes and plots, I hung up on her next question.

Deirdre Sands called me back a minute later. "The word around town is that your husband is on the edge financially," I said. "Is it true?"

Her voice fell. "This is confidential, isn't it? I mean, it doesn't redound to my benefit if Richard loses his shirt. Half of that shirt is mine, after all."

"This is just between us."

"Then yes. Richard's in trouble."

"How big?"

"The biggest. Bankruptcy. Maybe worse."

"He's in Toronto trying to line up a loan?"

"Yes. He gets back tonight."

"If he doesn't get the financing, the house of cards collapses?"

"I'm pretty sure that's so. Little gray men in little gray suits are making Richard dance a jig. And he just *hates* it."

"Why didn't you tell me this before? Why did you imply he's still flush?"

She hesitated. "I'm used to people doing my bidding only because of who and what my husband is. I was afraid if you knew he was in trouble you wouldn't take my case."

"Just for the record, that's nonsense."

"It's nice of you to say so."

I enjoyed the warmth of her comment for a moment. "One thing worse than bankruptcy is a criminal indictment. Is your husband under investigation by the U.S. attorney?"

She inhaled audibly. "What makes you ask that? Do you know something?"

"Not a thing. But anyone who's wheeled and dealed as much as your husband has must have violated half-a-hundred statutes along the way. I figure the feds may be honing in. Who's his lawyer?"

"Barrett Noland."

"Who's yours?"

She paused. "What makes you think I've seen a lawyer?"

"You know more divorce law than I do. I figure you're positioning yourself for a breakup in both the personal and corporate senses. I also figure some of your husband's tax dodges have included trusts and dummy corporations that list you as a beneficial participant, which could make you a target of the investigation, which should make you scared as hell."

The confirmation was in her timbre. "Jake Hattie," she murmured, which was more than enough to establish my suspicions.

"Does Jake think you're in trouble?"

"Jake says he'll handle it. I should just make sure there's enough in the account to cover the checks."

Jake's unbending avarice made me laugh, which made my client mad. I asked another question before she could scold me. "So how's your husband taking all this?"

"How do you mean?"

"Is he getting irrational? Behaving oddly?"

"You mean other than with his little thrush? He's not certifiable, I don't think, but he's definitely paranoid. I've started taking steps to make sure I'm not being followed."

"Is he doing anything else to keep from going under?"

"My expenditures are being monitored—anything above five hundred dollars has to be cleared with his secretary. My jewels are being auctioned off—some of them—discreetly, of course, so as not to start a panic. Two of our homes are up for sale." She sighed despondently. "We're under siege is what it amounts to. Given your populist inclinations, I imagine you take satisfaction in that."

"Not really," I said truthfully, but only because I never root against a client. "Tell me what you know about Tom Crandall."

She repeated the name. "Nothing."

"I mean it, Mrs. Sands. I need to know what you know."

"I know he was her husband, and I know he's dead. Period."

"Did Sands ever mention him in your presence?"

"Not that I remember."

"How about Nick? Nicholas Crandall."

"I've never heard of him."

"If you hear from him, or about him, let me know right away."

"Why?"

"Nick is Tom's brother. He's been mentally unbalanced for a long time, and he's probably even more so because of what happened to Tom. Anyone connected to the situation could be in danger."

"I'm hardly connected to the Crandalls, Mr. Tanner."

"Sure you are—you're paying the freight for the guy who's stirring things up, including aspects of the past that won't stay buried. Does the monitoring of your expenses mean your husband knows you've hired me?"

"No. I've squirreled away some money over the years—a slush fund, if you will. Richard knows nothing about it."

"So you hope."

"So I know. I'm quite canny when I need to be. Is that all, Mr. Tanner? I'm late for a lunch date."

"Tell me about Healthways," I said.

"What about it?"

"Does it come up much around the house?"

"Constantly."

"Why?"

"I don't know, but Richard is always on the phone with Lex about it. Lex Chadwick is the Healthways CEO."

"You don't know the gist of what they're talking about?"

"Not precisely. They're hoping Healthways will be the salvation of Sandstone, I do know that."

"How's that going to happen?"

"I have no idea."

"*When* is it going to happen?"

"As soon as Food and Drug issues its report."

"Report on what? A new drug?"

"I think so," she said eagerly. "I think Healthways has discovered something important."

Chapter
30

When I got to the office, I found yet another limousine blocking the alley—I was beginning to feel like a rock star until I remembered I didn't have any money or any fans.

The visitor cooling his heels in the outer office wasn't new business—Lex Chadwick had been there before. He hadn't liked it then, and he didn't like it now. When I entered the room, he whirled to confront me as though he was afraid I might be armed with something besides insignificance. Things were apparently on edge at the Healthways Corporation.

A frown puckered his face. "Banker's hours," he sneered as I flipped through the mail on the desk. Like a pair of miniature valets, his hands tended his person incessantly, adjusting the tilt of his tie and the angle of his collar, recurling his lapels, patting his pockets to make sure the drape of the ensemble was undisturbed. Natty in imported fabric and an Italian cut, he made me feel like an immigrant in my tweeds and twills.

When I'd finished with the mail, I gave him a hearty grin. "I drink my juice, I had a checkup three years ago, take a Centrum every morning, yet Healthways *still* keeps popping up. What am I doing wrong?"

Chadwick was not amused. "Why don't you tell me?"

"Okay, I will. I used to think Sands was bothered because of my interest in Clarissa. But now I think he wants to be sure I stay away from Nicky."

"Nicky who?"

"Nicholas Crandall. Tom's younger brother. Clarissa's crazy brother-in-law."

Chadwick shrugged. "Never heard of him."

"Someone at Healthways has."

"Who?"

"Dr. Marlin, for one. A couple of ambulance drivers, for another."

I waited for a comment, but Chadwick didn't have one he wanted to share.

"I think this is where you tell me to leave Healthways alone," I prompted helpfully, "or else the boys who ruined my Cheerios and my White Label will come back and do it for real."

His response was less a threat than a recitation. "Mr. Sands has asked me to inform you that your continued interference in the affairs of Healthways would be . . ." He fumbled for a word.

"Unhealthy?"

He crossed his arms. "Yeah."

"Tell me something, Chadwick," I said, hoping my manner was blithe enough to irritate him. "How do you list this kind of work on your résumé—public relations or preventive medicine?"

He answered the question with an oath and a motto: "Motivation."

"Ah, yes. Your specialty. Well, I hope you've got the old C.V. updated—they say Sandstone is about to crumble like a croissant in a food fight."

"That's crap," Chadwick pronounced.

"Toronto came through?"

"That's none of your business. I don't know anything about a brother-in-law, or Dr. Marlin, or anything else. I'm here to make you an offer."

"For what?"

"Your discretion."

"I haven't listed it for sale."

Chadwick rumbled with disgust. "Everything is fo sale."

"Only in your world, Lex."

Big shots don't like it when you disparage their values— it makes them insecure, and the only people who are botl rich and insecure are in show business. "If you're smart you'll hear what I have to say," he grumbled.

I shrugged. "Okay. What's the deal?"

Chadwick picked his briefcase off the floor, extracte what looked like a contract, and began to read from it "We—by that I mean both Mr. Sands and the Sandston Corporation—have certain security requirements that ar not being met under existing arrangements. Someone wit your expertise could be invaluable in designing an effectiv interface between the need to interdict both internal an external threats to our operational structures and program on one hand, and the needs of our staff professionals to fee unencumbered in their persons and their work on the other."

He needed time to catch his breath. "On a consultin basis or full time?" I asked, just to fill in the blank.

"Whatever you prefer."

"Consulting, I think. What's the remuneration?"

"Whatever you think is fair."

I laughed. "I'll bet that's the first time you've used *tha* gambit."

He decided my levity would go away if he ignored it "I can offer a thousand dollars per day for a period of on hundred and eighty days. That should be sufficient to ge the program up and running."

"Payable in junk bonds, I suppose."

"I can have a certified check here in twenty minutes When can you start?"

Our eyes tussled above the coffee table. "As soon a Tom Crandall's killer is behind bars."

He was surprised by the rejection more than the con dition. It took him time to summon the inevitable cliché "You'll regret this, Tanner."

"If Healthways is as evil as I think it is, you'll regre not paying more attention in Sunday school."

"I don't know what you're talking about."

"For your sake, I hope that's true. How much do you pay Dracula to pimp for the blood bank?"

Chadwick tried to look confused. "You're not making sense. Maybe you should stop in at one of our clinics for an examination."

I shook my head. "It won't wash, Chadwick. I saw you two in the parking lot. I know Dracula rounds up blood donors in the Tenderloin and herds them to Fremont Memorial. What I'm also pretty sure of is that he pays them surreptitiously even though no other bank uses paid donors. What I *don't* know is why. But I'm going to find out; you can make book on it."

Chadwick was shaking his head before I was halfway through my exegesis. "Healthways isn't involved in blood collection or distribution in any way. Our hospitals rely on the Red Cross and the other banks for a safe and certain supply of whole blood and components, of course, but that's it." Chadwick's look was nearly beatific. "The industry has gotten a bad rap—people are afraid to donate; inventories have been reduced to precarious levels. For some reason, you seem determined to magnify that misperception. For the health and welfare of the people of this city, I hope you'll keep your fantasies to yourself."

I was so moved by his selfless plea I decided to give him some solace. "I hear Healthways Pharmaceuticals has a new product in the pipeline."

He squinted. "So?"

"I understand it may be the salvation of the company."

"So?" he said again.

I got in position to observe any tic that might erupt after I played my hunch. "It wouldn't happen to be an AIDS vaccine, would it? Being tested on humans without the knowledge or approval of the FDA? And without the knowledge or approval of the guinea pigs themselves?"

The only response was a steely silence.

"You wouldn't be the first," I went on breezily. "Not long ago, some children in Zaire were inoculated with an experimental vaccine without either them or their parents consenting to the test, and that bit of business was supposedly perpetrated by one of the leading AIDS researchers in the world. Then there was the AIDS victim in Mexico who died after getting his blood removed from his body and heat-treated by a doctor who took his lab south of the border when the feds wouldn't let him perform that particular exercise in *this* country. Sub-rosa AIDS experiments seem to be booming—Healthways is just playing the game. Right, Lex? It's the American way—going for the gold."

Chadwick took two steps toward me, until his cologne almost put me to rout. "If I see a story to that effect in the public press," he pronounced with real ferocity, "you will be a dead man."

"Just like Tom Crandall," I reminded him, but I don't think he needed it.

Chapter
31

I had gotten ahead of myself in my duel with Chadwick, had been guessing, more or less, when I'd accused him and his company of illegally testing an AIDS vaccine in the Healthways clinics, and a guess wasn't anything I could take to Charley Sleet and expect him to do anything but laugh. But the guess had been educated, based on the fact that Healthways had something big to hide and Sandstone was counting on something big to save its financial skin and Tom Crandall's room had been full of tracts on the subject, so it was time to find some proof.

The closest thing to an informed source I had was Dr. Marlin. When I called Healthways headquarters, they told me he was in residence at the Turk Street Clinic that morning. Before I set out for the Tenderloin, I put in a call to Clay Oerter.

"Sorry to bother you while the exchange is open," I said when he came on the line.

"It's okay, but make it snappy," he admonished happily. "I'm writing orders for customers I haven't heard from since the crash."

"If you ask me, they're getting in just in time to take another plunge."

Clay laughed. "You're right to stay out of the market, Tanner. It's not a game for pessimists."

"What is?"

"Lo Ball," Clay said, then asked me what I wanted.

"You mentioned that Healthways Pharmaceuticals had some new drugs in the pipeline."

"Right."

"What are some of them?"

"I don't remember offhand. Let me punch up our research and see what they say about it."

I heard the clatter of a keyboard followed by the silence that meant Clay was scanning the report. "Let's see— transdermal arthritis analgesic, arrythmia medication, some antifungals, synthetic blood, fat substitute, Alzheimer's treatment, antidepressives—pretty much the same things the other guys are playing with, it looks like."

"It doesn't say anything about an AIDS vaccine or a new treatment for one of the opportunistic diseases?"

"Not here it doesn't, but these reports aren't all inclusive. I don't track the stock myself, so I can't tell you any more than I see on my screen; I'd have to ask one of our specialists."

"Would you? Some time today? I'll get back to you by five."

"That's all you want to know—whether Healthways is working on some kind of AIDS medication?"

"That's it," I said.

Professional to the core, Clay smelled a chance to make a buck. "Do you have any reason to think they're onto something? There are thirty thousand people with HIV in this city alone; ten million infected worldwide. If Healthways was first out of the chute with an effective vaccine, it would be a license to print money—a year's supply of AZT for one person grosses Burroughs-Wellcome close to five grand, and that's only a palliative." Clay's zeal dropped a notch. "Of course, someone with inside information could get his ass in a sling if he traded the stock."

I laughed at his nod to the Securities Act. "When did a little inside information stop anyone in *your* business

But you can relax; I have no idea whether Healthways has come up with something on AIDS or not. It's just that if they have, it might explain some things."

"Like what?"

"That *would* be inside information."

Clay laughed. "Okay. I'll do my best to get you some data, but it's pretty hectic around here these days. Based on the trend of the last month, if we end up nuking Baghdad, the Dow will go to five thousand."

I left the world of stocks and bonds and headed for the world of speed and crack. Just before I got there, I stopped at the Hastings College of Law and spent an hour in its library, in search of a little leverage.

The question was simple: When a corporation commits a crime—when Healthways administers unapproved drugs to unknowing recipients in order to test their efficacy, for example, and maybe kills someone in the process—who gets the blame and who gets punished? In other words, what were the chances that Richard Sands would face criminal penalties for the wrongdoing I was increasingly certain he and his cohorts were committing? The answer I came up with was both predictable and disheartening.

At common law, a corporation wasn't held responsible for the criminal conduct of its employees, under the theory that as a fictitious person a corporation could have no mens rea, the criminal intent that's a necessary element of virtually every crime. A corporation's officers were *theoretically* responsible for their behavior while acting in their corporate capacities, but in practice they usually escaped prosecution because of the difficulty of proving actual or constructive knowledge of the illegal course of corporate conduct, i.e., they got off by covering their asses in an organizational maze similar to the carefully crafted shell of deniability that let Reagan disclaim knowledge of trading weapons for hostages or illegally funding the Contras.

Centuries after their formulation, the common-law doctrines retain their potency. Under current precedent, when a corporation commits a crime, awareness of the misconduct must be traced to a specific individual in order to hold that person criminally responsible. The individual, in turn, can defend himself by asserting the defense of "objective impossibility," i.e., that he had no power to either detect or prevent the violation. Conviction for corporate misconduct under such a standard of proof has proved difficult over the years, a difficulty compounded by the phenomenon of "jury nullification"—the tendency of juries to acquit white-collar criminals regardless of the proof of their wrongdoing.

In sum, the history of criminal law didn't offer much encouragement that Sands or any of his lackeys, given the powerful attorneys and influential friends who would line up to protect them, would be imprisoned for their machinations at Healthways, even if I could prove them. Neither did the recent decision by the attorney general to withdraw the Justice Department's longstanding support for the U.S. Sentencing Commission's recommendation that tougher mandatory sentences be imposed on corporate criminals, a reversal that was reached after intense lobbying from defense contractors, oil companies, and other representatives of the Business Roundtable—the very people to whom the tougher sentences would apply. In other words, what I dug up was all too illustrative of the laissez-faire approach to business behavior currently in vogue—the little guys are jailed in droves, while the fat cats run amok.

Depressed and defeated, I spent a few minutes with the *Reader's Guide*. I was about to give up when I stumbled on a reference to California's brand-new Corporate Criminal Liability Act. Then I happened onto Section 331 of the Food, Drug and Cosmetics Act. After delving into its history and application, I left the library with something close to a smile on my face.

My luck held when I got to the bowels of the Tenderloin. Instead of having to wade through the intake bureaucracy at the clinic in order to get to my quarry, I ran into him in front of Glide Memorial as he was about to climb into his Town Car and call it a day.

I hurried to nab him before he could disappear inside the Lincoln. "Dr. Marlin, my name's Tanner. I talked to you at the clinic the other day. About Nicky Crandall."

He was still dressed to sell, still serene and self-possessed, still in a rush, but intrigued by what I had to say. "I remember. Did you find him?"

"Not yet."

"Then what do you want with me?"

"To tell you why you were lying to me." I looked up and down the block. "Is there some place we can talk in private?"

His laugh was careless and paternal. "Not in this neighborhood, there isn't. And I don't have time, regardless."

"I think you'd better make time, Doctor."

He bristled at my effrontery. "That's out of the question. I have a staff meeting in twenty minutes."

"With Chadwick?"

He raised a brow. "You know Lex?"

"He's one of the reasons I'm here."

Marlin looked at me for a long moment, reached a decision, then unlocked the car doors by pressing the button on a gizmo he got out of his pocket. I figured he was about to drive off and leave me, but he opened the passenger door and motioned for me to get in. "I can give you five minutes."

After he joined me in the sumptuous interior, we faced each other as best we could, traffic and transients streaming past us beyond the tinted barriers that remained as closed to the out-of-doors as they could get. My nostrils gorged on the smell of leather.

"What is the nature of your relationship with Mr. Chadwick?" Marlin asked when I didn't open the discussion.

"Let's just say it led me to reach certain conclusions about the R and D program at Healthways Pharmaceuticals."

Marlin visibly relaxed. "If that's your area of interest, you're wasting your time with me—I have nothing to do with the drug company."

"It may not show up on the organizational charts," I admitted, "but I think you're a vital part of their program."

He could have given lessons in indifference. "How so?"

"Maybe it would be best to tell you what I think has been going on at Healthways."

He shrugged and looked at his watch. "If you must."

I waited till I had his attention. "If I'm right, you're subject to federal criminal charges for your role in it, Doctor. Felony charges, for violation of the Food and Drug Act, which as far as I can tell is the only area in all of criminal law where a businessman is likely to do time if he plays fast and loose with safety regulations. And there's a new state law that punishes concealment of product dangers as well. In other words, Doctor, if I were you, I'd listen up. Then I'd start thinking of how you could distance yourself from the *real* bad guys when the feds come calling."

Marlin glanced in the rearview mirror. "Have you told anyone about this?"

"Only Chadwick."

"Not the police; not the FDA; not the medical examiners?"

I shook my head. "Not yet."

His brow got shiny. He glanced out the window, looked at his watch once more, then tried to look both innocent and exasperated. "I hope your tale is not an epic, Mr. Tanner. I'm leaving in two minutes."

I leaned against the door and spoke with all the assurance I could muster. "We know from the newspapers that there's an outbreak of AIDS among the homeless and destitute population in the city, a good portion of which lives here in the Tenderloin. We also know that over a hundred thousand people have died in this country from AIDS, and thousands more worldwide. The number of people infected with the virus is estimated in the tens of millions."

"The tragedy is well documented, Mr. Tanner. What's your point?"

"We also know that nothing resembling a preventive vaccine is on the horizon—the end of the century, at the earliest. Medications like AZT that slow the progress of the disease are both expensive and of limited effectiveness, and come with nasty side effects. Which means the company that hits on a vaccine that immunizes against the virus, or produces antibodies that destroy the virus once it's been contracted, will have themselves a gold mine. Do you agree, Doctor?"

His shrug was noncommittal. "It's obvious. But what does that have to do with Healthways?" The doctor was getting bored—more bored than he should have been.

"Given the spread of AIDS among the poverty-stricken," I said quickly, "it's inevitable that Healthways would get lots of HIV-infected people at its clinics, just as a matter of percentages. Most of them are people on their own, without families, or friends, or colleagues—in other words, without anyone who could raise a significant stink about what was being done to them."

"What *is* being done to them? Besides the administration of free medical care, which for some reason you seem to oppose?"

I tried to look as composed as my adversary. "At some point, someone at Healthways realized they had access to a valuable set of guinea pigs—a perfect test group for conducting secret drug trials outside the FDA test protocols. I figure it goes something like this—they identify a prime candidate for the presence of the virus, test him to make sure, then slip the patient an experimental drug while they're at the clinic for some other reason. Then later on, they use the wellness program and the ambulance follow-ups that Healthways is so proud of to track down these same patients and check on the efficacy of the drug— how well it produces killer T-cells to combat the virus, for example—and also to look for any side effects that might have resulted. All without FDA knowledge or approval or the knowledge or approval of the patients themselves. And all with only a slight risk that anyone would give a damn if the side effects turned out to be fatal."

I looked at Marlin. What I was hoping for was a complete confession. What I got was an elaborate smile that was the exact opposite of the reaction I'd expected to provoke. There was nothing to do but give him all I had, in the hope it would spook him.

"From what I read," I went on, "this type of thing goes on a lot, though usually in the Third World—multinational drug companies getting a jump on the competition and being first in line at the Patent Office by treating some poor peasant like a white rat. Well, the U.S. has a Third

World of its own these days; in San Francisco it's called the Tenderloin, and Healthways is the only game in this particular part of town. Which means once the feds turn loose, it won't be hard to come up with proof of what's been going on."

Marlin was shaking his head with synthetic compassion. I felt like a kid at Confession who can't for the life of him provoke an outrage. I tried to up the ante.

"I've done some reading on this, Doctor. I know there's a clamor for new AIDS medications, and that several of them are currently undergoing clinical trials and others have already been through testing and are awaiting FDA approval. Drugs like ddI that don't destroy bone marrow and maintain their efficacy for a longer period than AZT will be a big boon to their manufacturers if and when they're approved."

Marlin shook his head. "I still don't see the point."

"The tests run on new drugs developed by the big drug companies are usually done by the companies themselves, in their own labs. But Healthways doesn't have that kind of facility—it has to rely on the government. The problem is, even though they've tried to speed up the approval process by establishing an AIDS clinical-trial group and other accelerated processes, FDA procedures can take forever. Layer and layer of bureaucratic strata, and meanwhile the disease runs rampant. But you don't *have* forever, do you, Doctor? Not because so many people are dying, but because Sandstone is going down the financial tubes. So you're doing your *own* tests, then running the participants through the blood bank so their screening procedures will give you independent evidence that the virus has been eliminated. When you've got enough to make your case, I figure you'll go public. Not to the FDA, but to the media."

"Utter nonsense." Marlin started the car.

"You think you've got another pentamidine on your hands, I imagine, a drug that was administered to thousands of patients long before it was approved by the FDA because everyone but the FDA knew it was effective against AIDS-related pneumonia. But what if you've come up with another Suranim?—a drug that seemed effective in the beginning but turned out to do major and permanent damage to vital organs. Does it *bother* you that the race to put Sandstone in the black might be killing people right and left, Dr. Marlin?"

Marlin said nothing, so I answered my own question.

"I suppose not. I suppose all you can see are dollar signs. If the medication's any good, after you leak word that you've come up with a wonder drug, gay-rights groups like ACT UP and Queer Nation will bring so much heat on the FDA to let you release it, you'll never have to go through the normal testing protocols at all, and the profits will start rolling in immediately. Even if the FDA does its job and makes you test it properly, black-market sales in Africa alone would put Sandstone in the chips for good."

I swallowed and took a breath. "How do you like it so far, Doctor?"

Marlin was as cool as slush. "Your paranoia is quite advanced, isn't it?—I'm surprised someone hasn't petitioned to have you committed."

"Speaking of which, this is where Nicky Crandall comes in."

The doctor remained serene. "I'm sorry; I don't get the connection."

"The connection is, you've been on the payroll of the illicit drug business for years. Way back when Nicky first came to you, out in Walnut Creek, I figure you were already taking under-the-table payoffs from drug companies to administer unapproved medications to your psychiatric patients much the way you're doing now, though probably not on as wide a scale. I'm guessing that's why Healthways hired you in the first place, because of your reputation on the fringes of the medical profession for not being scrupulous about the rules."

Marlin raced the engine and fumed in silence.

"Come on, Doc. The generic drug industry is *littered* with fraud. They routinely fabricate their product-approval applications—over a hundred generic drugs have been approved for marketing based on phony test results. One congressman said he'd never *seen* an industry as broadly corrupt as the generic-drug business. I figure you've had a part of that action for a long time, Doctor. Even before you took your greed to Healthways."

"You really are insane, Mr. Tanner," Marlin said with impressive aplomb. "If you will allow me to do so, I can refer you to someone who can help you."

"You persuaded Tom to help you get Nicky committed to your clinic just before Tom went off to war. While he was institutionalized, you gave Nicky some experimental drug for mental illness, one with a side effect that provoked the violence Nicky committed on Ellen Simmons once he was released."

"Perhaps you can give me the name of your witnesses. Or provide me with documentation. Or suggest any *other* method by which you intend to prove your charge."

His self-control was infuriating. "I don't have proof of that part, I admit. I could probably get some if I notified the right authorities and they checked the right records, but maybe not—you no doubt covered your tracks. But if you play your cards right, no one is going to go into that at all."

The doctor pouted. "What a shame. Not that I admit anything of the sort was occurring, you understand, but it would make a wonderful story, wouldn't it? Virtually a metaphor for the times."

"You're pretty calm, Doctor; I suppose I admire you for that. But there could be murder charges involved in this, remember."

"How so?"

"I think Tom Crandall guessed what had happened back when Nicky was first committed to your care. When he learned that Nicky was in your clutches again, he looked into the situation and discovered what was going on in the clinics with the AIDS experiments, probably by talking with some of his colleagues in the Healthways EMUs. Which is why Sands had him killed." I paused for effect. "You really should consider cutting yourself a deal with the U.S. attorney before this all comes out, Doctor. Sands is the one I'm after."

The doctor put the car in gear. "If you make any of these charges against any of the persons you have mentioned, myself included, I can assure you that slander will be the very *least* you will be prosecuted for."

I forced a smile. "That's what they all say, Doctor. Only no one ever seems to follow through once their lawyer tells them that truth is a complete defense."

The doctor rolled down his window, then regarded me with what looked like sympathy. "Let me make a suggestion."

"Sure."

"A person like you must have friends in law enforcement. Or in the Medical Examiner's Office."

"Both, as a matter of fact."

"Fine. Let me suggest that you arrange for one of them to examine one of these . . . *guinea pigs,* as you call them. Give them Nicholas Crandall himself, if you can locate him. Better yet, have them perform an autopsy on a recent AIDS victim who was formerly a patient at our clinic—I would be happy to give you a name that corresponds with the records at the morgue: Doctor-patient confidentiality terminates upon death, after all."

Marlin checked for oncoming traffic. "If you dare to follow such a procedure, you will find that no drug that even *remotely* resembles the type of medication you describe can be found in the blood or tissues of the subjects you have chosen."

"You sound pretty sure of that, Doctor."

His look was arrogant and dismissive. "Oh, I am. As sure as I am that your reputation as an investigator and a prognosticator is about to be revised. To your detriment, I'm afraid." He actually managed a laugh. "Take a good look around the neighborhood, Mr. Tanner. You may be about to become a resident."

Chapter
32

Sometimes you're right and sometimes you're wrong and sometimes you don't know where the hell you stand. This time I'd been wrong, not on a trivial point but on the central thesis I'd developed to explain Tom Crandall's death. Dr Marlin's tranquillity in the face of my accusation told me as much, as did his suggestion of an autopsy on former Healthways AIDS patients to establish the absence of experimental drugs in their system. Since his challenge seemed a definitive rebuttal to my charge, either Marlin was running a bluff or he wasn't part of the scam that Healthways was running out of its health-care system. Because I couldn't accept either hypothesis, there was nothing to do but go back to the beginning and reason it out a second time.

I was doing just that, strolling down Eddy Street toward my car, trying to decide where I'd gone wrong, when I felt a sudden pain in my side—sharp, searing, insistent. Tension, cramp, heart attack—a series of organic calamities streaked through my mind before I felt the pain a second time, more penetrating than before, and knew its origin was external. As I turned to see who and what had stuck me, a hand clamped my shoulder, the knife inched closer toward my innards, and a voice ordered me to keep moving and not look around. I did what it said, but not before catching a glimpse of my assailant.

He had probably been stalking me since I'd left the office, had come up behind me as I was lost in thought, and had shoved a knife in my side at the approximate level of my kidney for reasons at present unknown. For the moment, Dracula had me in his spell; I felt like a bit player in a spatter film, and in that genre bit players don't fare too well.

"I hear you been looking for me," he rasped in my ear, his tone and phrasing an amalgam of every movie tough he'd ever seen. He no doubt reminded himself of Robocop; he reminded me of the hapless gunsel in *The Maltese Falcon.*

"And now I've found you," I said, trying to hide my apprehension behind a breezy manner. "No wonder I'm so highly paid."

Dracula didn't like it that I wasn't terrified. "Keep on till I tell you," he ordered roughly, and gave me another jab in the side. Luckily his knife was as blunt as his sensitivity— I was scared as hell.

"I don't like being trolled for," he went on as we tangoed down the block. "Down here *I'm* the one does the fishing."

I was as affable as a con man reeling in a mark. "That's what I wanted to talk to you about."

"What?"

"Your business."

The pressure above my kidney eased; Dracula sensed a deal. "You looking to sell a pint?"

I laughed.

"Maybe you're trying to cut me out?" He cackled like a jackal. "Last guy that tried it needed some blood *himself* when I got through with him." The knife returned with a vengeance.

"I'm interested in the financial aspects," I said.

"Yeah? Why?"

"I'm getting into a similar line of work, and I could use some tips."

"Like what?"

"Like who pays your salary?"

He hesitated. "They don't like me to talk about that."

"Are you on straight time or commission?"

"Ah . . ."

He didn't know what a commission was. "Do you ge more money the more people you recruit?"

"Yeah."

"Do you go after everyone or do you have a list?"

"I got a list."

"Who gives it to you?"

"Don and Ron."

"The ambulance guys."

"Right."

"How much do you pay the people you line up?"

Like any entrepreneur, Dracula took pride in his pricing policy. "More than those bitches at the *plasma* center."

"What, fifteen a pint?"

"We go twenty for whole blood. That's sixty-six percen more than plasma pays."

I wondered who'd done the math for him. "You pay u front or only after they pass the screening?"

"Half and half," he bragged, a balloon of pride in hi voice: Dracula was top-of-the-line.

"You hustle for all the blood banks or only Fremon Memorial?"

I had pressed him far enough. "I send them where I send them," he grumbled. "This is it."

Dracula grabbed my arm and tugged me into an alley way, narrow and dank and lined with a ribbon of trash tha looked as if it had been pawed through by several dozer street people in search of an ounce of sustenance. Nothing good was going to come of a trip in that direction, but th tip of the knife still bit into my flesh like a mongoose. Wha I needed was a diversion.

I was still looking for one when Dracula tugged me to a stop in front of a padlocked doorway beneath a tilte sign that said VINNY'S VIDEO; from the look of it, Vinn had been out of business as long as the Beta format. Th poster in the window was a come-on for *Heartburn*; th expression on Nicholson's face made me wonder if he an Dracula had sprung from the same gene pool.

"Hold it right here," Dracula demanded. "Put your hands on your head. Come on; lift 'em and lock 'em."

I did as he said, which gave Dracula time to give the door a shove. The padlock held, but the hinges didn't, and the door careened open in reverse to the tune of a wrenching squeal. A moment later, the knife was back in my back and Dracula was urging me inside. I ducked and entered the dungeon. When I bumped my head on the tilted door, my psyche seemed to see it as my due.

From the look of the place, Dracula was the last in a long line of outlaws who had used it as a refuge—the fixtures were ripped out and piled in a corner to make a kind of fort; remains of edible garbage littered the floor; a tattered blanket and some sodden pillows formed someone's idea of a bed. Additional posters fluttered across the room like the remains of the film festival of hell; a cardboard cutout of the Terminator gave it all a crazy context. The light through the window was as thin and eerie as my young assailant—as with every other time I'd entered the Tenderloin, I wished I had brought my gun.

"Against the wall," Dracula demanded, and jabbed me again, this time in the stomach—if he did it again, I would have to try something foolhardy. I backed to the wall and wondered how something good was going to happen.

"Some people don't like you fucking around down here," Dracula said when I was sufficiently far from him to get a good look at my nemesis.

His smile advertised crooked and jaundiced teeth. His pores had oozed a stream of bilious acid long enough to erode and encrust his cheeks; his hair hung as limp as a mop that had just swabbed the men's room. His tiny eyes shone too brightly to be powered by normal circuitry.

"I'm only working a gig," I said by way of explanation. "Just like you."

"Yeah, well your gig and mine don't mix." He seemed almost apologetic now that we were face-to-face. "I got to take you out."

"You'd be making a mistake. Homicide is a rough rap."

It didn't faze him. "I'm covered to the max on this; the only way I lose is if you keep breathing."

At this point, the only thing I could think of to do was to rush him or to stall for time. Given my age and the skill with which Dracula brandished the knife, I opted for the latter. "How much are they paying you to stick me?"

He hesitated, then decided what the hell. "Five hundred. There's guys in Scanlon's who'd do it for fifty, but they know I get the job done and keep my mouth shut."

"They're likely to shut it for you, aren't they?"

The suggestion didn't take. Dracula merely cursed and wiped his knife on his sleeve, a butcher preparing to quarter the next side of beef: Although he intended to gut me like a heifer, Dracula didn't want me to get infected.

"Five hundred's good, but I'll do better," I said.

"How much better?" he asked without much interest.

"A thousand."

"To do what?"

"Walk out of here and give me half an hour to get lost."

Dracula examined me as carefully as his namesake had inspected the lissome necks of his victims. "You ain't got a grand," he concluded.

"Not on me, no."

"Not anywhere."

"I can have it by the end of the day. Anywhere you say. What does it cost you to give me a few minutes? In the meantime, you can tell Chadwick you couldn't track me down."

He blinked. "Who said anything about Chadwick?"

"I did."

"Yeah, well you don't know much, do you? So I get an extra five large; when they see I fucked up, they'll, like, take the blood trick away from me."

I scrambled for an answer. "I can set you up in a better business than blood."

"Like what?"

"Body parts."

It was the first thing that came to mind, and like most things that leap to my mind unedited, it didn't make much sense. But Dracula seemed intrigued.

"Body parts? Like arms and legs, and shit?"

"More like eyes and livers and kidneys. Huge market for that stuff; thousands of people waiting for transplants. They can't freeze livers and kidneys and store them, so there's no way to build up an inventory, which means there's always a demand, which means there's a lot bigger profit in parts than blood. A kidney goes for ten grand in Egypt."

Dracula tried to fathom it. "So how does it scope?"

"Just like boosting cars—we give you an order, and you fill it. We don't ask questions, you operate wherever and however you choose. You'd be just like you are now—an independent contractor."

His pigeon breast swelled at the resonance of the title. "Independent contractor. Yeah. But what about Don and Ron?"

"They're going to be out of the picture."

"How?"

"The cops are about to be all over them like a body bag." It was the only truthful thing I'd said since we hit the alley. Truthful if I managed to stay alive.

Dracula seemed to be considering my proposition, which was as good as I could hope for. While he did, I looked around for something that would give me the edge I needed to jump him, but there was nothing in the place but trash. Even the Terminator was sitting this one out.

"Tell you what," I said when he didn't respond, trying to portray myself more as friend than foe. "You think it over. To help you decide, keep in mind that my people pay a thousand bucks for eyes alone."

He blinked. "One or both?"

"One."

"Wholesome, man."

"You'd have to hustle a hundred barrels of blood to come up with the same amount."

Dracula nodded pensively, presumably relishing the prospect of removing someone's eyes and getting paid for the pleasure, but after a minute his expression began to cloud. "Can't do it," he said.

"Why not?"

"Healthways is King Shit down here. They find out I had you and let you go, *I'm* the one'll end up in an alley, and someone'll be boosting *my* fucking liver."

"I told you, Don and Ron are going to take a fall."

He shrugged. "They got other guys as bad. I got to stick you, man, that's all there is to it. No hard feelings. I stuck people before when I didn't really want to, but business is business." His brow lifted. "Hey. You probably got some parts your people can use. Tell you what—you tell me who to call to make the connection, I do you a favor and make it quick."

My charade had boomeranged, and the scenario had turned grotesque times two.

There was only one thing to do, so I told him what it was. "I'm going to take that thing away from you, Dracula."

His cracked-up eyes staged a riot. "Don't call me that. I *hate* that crap."

"You don't like Dracula? How about Vampire? How about Leech? How about Maggot? All bloodsuckers, just like you."

He was mad but not mad enough. "You crossed it, man." He got into a Bruce Lee crouch and advanced on me with purpose, except Bruce Lee didn't pack a knife and I didn't know any martial arts more sophisticated than a kick to the balls. Which is what I was about to do when the door to Vinny's Video creaked on its severed hinges.

Dracula turned toward the sound, squinting in the lance of sunlight that pierced the room, raising his knife hand to shade his eyes. Half-blind myself, I leaped for him and chopped his arm at what I hoped was a point just above the elbow. What I hit was bone, hard and unyielding. My shoulder throbbed, my hand went numb, the knife clattered to the floor.

We both bent to retrieve it, but all we came up with was each other. Breathing with effort, locked onto me in an awkward and profane embrace, grimacing from the pain in his arm, Dracula suddenly freed a hand then swiped at my eyes in an effort to rip them out. "You just made me a thousand bucks, you fucker." The prospect of trafficking in my organs made him giddy.

I grasped his wrist and tried to roll him over. I managed it with effort, but my place on top was momentary—momentum carried us across the room. When we hit the wall we strained and grunted but remained at impasse until he spit in my face. It was a sufficient distraction for him to wrench a hand away, grasp at something on the floor, then raise it overhead. The knife blade caught the light and held it—the fire of final judgment.

The knife descended. I parried with a forearm. We rolled again, this time away from the wall toward the center of the room. I lost sight of the knife for a moment, then felt it rake my shoulder. From within a bath of pain, I summoned everything I had and prepared to heave him off me.

"Are you my contact? Huh?"

Dracula froze at the words, which gave me the chance I needed. As powerfully as I could, I shoved with my arms and legs. When he flew into the air, I rolled from under him and was on my feet by the time he had recovered enough to come again. As he was gathering himself to rush me, I kicked him in the head, then followed with a chop to his neck and a fist to his jaw. The combination put him out.

"I figured they forgot to send you," a voice behind me said. "They're totally incompetent."

Chapter

33

Emerged from the shadows by the door, looming over Dracula like a buzzard over a road kill, Nicky Crandall's delight arced like lightning across the gray and haggard contours of his face. His movements jerky and perpetual, his eyes alive with childish guile, his attire neglected and absurd, Nicky was the embodiment of a tortured soul, imprisoned within his wayward mind, unable to escape the nightmare.

When we satisfied ourselves that Dracula would remain harmless on the filthy floor, we regarded each other for a moment of confederacy and assessment. "Got him," Nicky said, bouncing on his toes like a lightweight skipping an invisible rope. "Huh? Got him." His paranoia was palpable enough to make me attuned to doom myself.

"Got the Blood Man," Nicky repeated, still enraptured by the deed.

When he looked at me again, it was an afterthought. When he spoke, words came with a rush, as though each syllable were in the way of all the others. "They must be trying to erase you, too," he raved. "Huh? Beware. Dracula is an entry-level agent, but now he's neutralized, so they up the grade. Huh? Survival becomes precarious—they don't like it when an agent goes down. You see the significance? Huh? The battle rages at a higher level."

Satisfied that he had alerted me, Nicky began to explore the room the way a setter explores a thicket with a bird in it. As I brushed dirt off my clothing, I considered how to communicate with someone who lived in a different world and spoke in a different language. "I didn't realize they were that close," I began, hoping to join his crusade, whatever that crusade might be. "Thanks for the help."

"Premature," Nicky said brusquely as he pawed through litter. "Huh? Win the battle; lose the war. They like you to think you've set them back, so you'll lower your shields. Huh? Then wham. They come from another direction."

"Well, I'm glad you showed up when you did. My name's Tanner. I was a friend—"

"*Man and Superman,*" he interrupted—Nicky could only bottle up language for so long; I began to wonder if I'd complete another sentence. "Which are you? Huh?"

I was surprised he'd made the connection with Shaw's creation. "I—"

"Maybe both. Huh? Multi-oriented. Double-identified."

"I'm not—"

"A useful device. I'll consider a similar tactic." He looked at me and smiled as though he'd caught me trying to trick him. "Huh? Or a variation."

"I was a friend of Tom's," I blurted when I had the chance.

Nicky's look turned sly. "So was I," he said. "Until he betrayed me and became my enemy."

"Betrayed you how?"

Like the offspring of ancient royalty, he gave me a look both lordly and insane. "Tom assisted their design. Huh? He pointed them my way, then aided in invading my essence."

"That doesn't sound like Tom." But it did sound like *Dr. Strangelove.*

"I hoped he would be wise enough to resist. Huh? When I saw he wasn't, I took pity, but I also took precautions."

"By doing what?" I asked, thinking it might have been just that simple after all, that Tom had been killed pursuant to a paranoid fantasy of his brother's, an agenda no one would ever understand or punish.

"Putting distance between us," Nicky was saying. "Huh? Breaking the link; removing the specimen; stunting the research. Huh?" At this point, Nicky's mood approached the ecstatic.

"Did you do anything else?"

He outlined some possibilities. "Dismantle the conduits? Destroy the invasive agents? Disable the hardware? Huh?" He laughed mordantly. "Not yet. But operations are being mounted."

"I was wondering if you took any steps against Tom. To keep him from betraying you again."

Nicky shook his head. "Negative. He's my brother. Huh? I'm his keeper. Huh? One day he will see the light."

For the moment, it served as a sufficient explanation for both of us, even though it was a reversal of everything I'd heard about the nature of their relationship.

The one thing I had been certain of was that Nicky knew that Tom was dead. Now even that seemed doubtful. "I'm afraid I have bad news," I said.

His mind twitched as rapidly as his limbs. "Good news is no news; bad news is glad news, bought and paid for to deter me. Huh?"

His jerks and jitters, his puzzling references, his urgent, singsong speech, his guttural punctuation, all were so removed from his brother's precise nature I had trouble keeping the bond in mind. "Tom is dead," I said. "I'm sorry to have to tell you that."

I don't know what I expected him to do, but I expected him to do something. Instead, the news, if it was news, hardly seemed to penetrate. "They want me to carry certain concepts so I will oblige them and retreat," he said blandly, pleased at his insight. "Self-nullification is what they're after. Huh? I'm surprised you don't see it. If you are who you say you are," he added cryptically. "Huh?"

I didn't know I'd said I was anybody.

What I decided was that Nicky knew that Tom was dead, but he didn't believe it. "Tom was buried last Sunday," I said, to try to get at least that much through to him.

"You lack awareness of their reach. Huh? They can fabricate anything—birth, death, health, wealth. A hole is a hole no matter what they call it. Huh?"

"What if someone makes it an altar?"

The reference was to the artifacts Nicky had placed atop Tom's coffin—I thought it possible that Nicky had both murdered and enshrined his brother—but Nicky's mind was trained on his enemies. "When it suits my purposes, I play along. Huh? So they won't know what I know."

"Who's 'they'?" I asked. "Who has all this power? I need to know so I can resist them."

His look turned sly once more. "A good question—who's at the top of the pyramid? Huh?" He looked around the room to make sure we were unobserved. "I trust you know the field operatives."

I shook my head.

My ignorance made him angry. "You haven't been paying attention. Huh? Each of us has a nemesis. My opposite is Marlin—in deep cover as a physician. Huh? He was assigned to me many years ago; he's penetrated me several times."

"What's he after?"

"First my blood, then my life. Huh?"

"Why do you think he—"

Before I could complete the sentence, Nicky seemed to hear something somewhere outside the building. He glanced at the window as a mix of glee and cunning warped his face—Nicky was terrified, and he reveled in it.

After one last look at Dracula, he started toward the door. "They've implanted a transmitter on my person," he said by way of explanation. "Huh? They can triangulate on me in seconds, from receivers on the bridge towers and Mount Sutro. I have to keep moving. Huh?"

I took a stab at a joint venture. "They're tracking me, too. Thank God they take Sundays off."

Nicky stopped near the door. A long moment went by as I underwent a complex evaluation. I don't know if I passed or not; all he said was, "Yes."

"It helps them to be seen as devout, doesn't it?" I went on. "Religiosity aids subversion."

"You know more than I thought. Huh? We can help each other."

But instead of confiding further, he squeezed through the broken door and set off down the alley in a simian shuffle. I started to go after him, then thought of something and returned to Dracula instead. He was starting to regain consciousness by the time I found what I was looking for and put it in my pocket. As his eyelids began to flutter and his throat struggled to form a word, I slipped through the door and ran after Nicky.

When I reached his side, he didn't encourage or discourage my presence. We jogged together for a while, a race that put a premium on awkwardness. When we reached the street, he came to a stop. "It will be better if we split up," he said. "Huh?"

"We should rendezvous later."

"Where and when?"

I thought about it. "Midnight. Steps of Glide Memorial."

"Public place. Huh? Good tactic. The Glide people are secure." He glanced up and down the street, ready to set out again.

"One more thing," I said. "What methods are they using against you? How are they attacking?"

He frowned dubiously, as if reconsidering his earlier appraisal. "Contamination. Huh?" he pronounced finally.

"Right. Contamination. I thought so." I turned in the direction of my car, then looked back. "Your brother wasn't one of them," I said. "He was working with me. We had them vulnerable to countermeasures, but he was killed because he knew too much."

"Too much is never enough. Huh?"

Nicholas Crandall looked at me with what appeared to be a mix of skepticism and hope, then ran off into the clutter and clamor of the Tenderloin. As I watched him go, I had no idea what we'd said to each other or if we'd said anything at all. But when I remembered Tom's final telephone message, I decided Nicky's obsession wasn't entirely irrational, that somewhere within those paranoic ramblings lay a core of truth that had triggered his brother's death.

Chapter
34

When I got back to the office, I telephoned Scanlon's and left a message with Gary the barman for Jan to give me a call as soon as she had a chance. After I gave him my name, he asked if I'd located Nicky Crandall yet. When I told him I had, he asked about the timing of Nicky's inheritance. I told him that was up to the courts. He didn't regard it as encouraging.

My next call was to Clay Oerter. The market was still spiraling upward on the immaculate news from the air war, so he could only give me a second.

"Nothing in the Healthways pipeline on AIDS, Marsh," he said quickly. "Not a direct application, at least. There could be fallout from other research, of course, but the specialist didn't know of anything offhand. You need me to dig deeper?"

"I don't think so," I said.

The dead end at the brokerage firm left me with another call to make, this time to Dr. Lodge, the man whose wife had been rescued from their crumpled home courtesy of the courage of the late Tom Crandall.

The doctor got back to me in ten minutes. "I need to know something about blood," I said when he came on the line. "I thought maybe you could help me."

"Does it have to do with Tom?"

"Yes."

"Then I'll tell you whatever I can." He cleared his throat. "Blood is a fascinating subject: the Egyptians used to bathe in it, the Romans drank it at orgies, and someone had the idea of injecting sheep's blood into sick people as far back as 1667—transfusions have been a part of medical practice ever since. What is it about the subject that interests you, Mr. Tanner?"

"The transfusion part. Blood banks, plasma centers, that kind of thing."

"The blood supply; is that what we're talking about?"

"I guess it is."

"What do you want to know about it? That's a pretty large subject."

"First off, what's the difference between blood banks and the Red Cross and the plasma centers you see around?"

"Blood banks and the Red Cross are similar—nonprofit organizations that collect whole blood from unpaid volunteers, then sell the blood or its by-products to hospitals for use in transfusions. The Red Cross supplies roughly half of the blood used in this country; the blood banks provide the rest. The Red Cross blood services gross half a billion a year."

"But none of these outfits pay their donors?"

"Not anymore."

"Why not?"

"Back in the early seventies, it began to be felt by hospitals and others that the accumulation of a blood supply that relied on people who *sell* their blood introduced too much risk into the system. The fear was that poor people who needed money would lie about their health status in order to pass the screening procedures, and the supply would become contaminated. Although this view was a bit alarmist in my judgment, most hospitals stopped buying paid-for blood, which forced the Red Cross and the blood banks to rely on voluntary donation only. Then when AIDS came along, California made it illegal to transfuse paid-for blood and blood products."

"But not plasma."

"Transfusing paid-for plasma is prohibited in California as well, but there are still collection centers that pay the donors and ship the product out of state."

"What is plasma, exactly?"

"More than fifty percent of the volume of whole blood is plasma. The other primary components are red cells and platelets, which are collected and sold separately as well. The basic approach is for plasma to be collected at plasmapheresis centers, then broken down by pharmaceutical companies through a process called fractionation into plasma derivatives such as albumin and immunoglobins and the factor VIII clotting agent and the like. Frequently what is commonly called a blood transfusion is in reality the transfusion of one of these derivatives rather than whole blood. In current practice, whole-blood transfusions constitute fewer than ten percent of all transfusions."

"How safe *is* the blood supply, Doctor? From contamination, I mean."

Lodge hesitated, then repeated the litany of Nurse Glad. "The blood supply in this country is as safe as it can possibly be."

I laughed. "I used to be a lawyer; I know an evasive answer when I hear one. The kind of answer people give when they're afraid someone is going to sue them."

"There *have* been a host of lawsuits against the blood industry of late," Lodge replied. "Several hundred of them, in fact; Irwin Memorial's liability insurance premium is half a million dollars a year. Many banks fear bankruptcy."

"Are we talking about people who've gotten AIDS from a transfusion? Then sued the blood bank that provided the blood?"

"And the doctor and hospital and anyone else they could think of, too," Lodge answered.

"But you say these lawsuits aren't successful."

"Most have not been, though there have been some large verdicts quite recently—a court in Boston just awarded a military man almost three million in a transfusion AIDS case, for example. Which is why legislatures in many states have enacted laws that limit the dollar amount of recoveries for bad blood just as they limit recoveries in medical malpractice actions. There are also laws that declare that a blood bank which sells blood to a hospital is providing a service rather than selling a product."

"Which means product-liability principles don't apply— the blood banks don't face strict liability for selling defective merchandise or for breach of warranty."

"Correct. The only claim the victim has is negligence, which is hard to prove in these situations since it usually requires finding carelessness in the screening or testing procedures."

"Carelessness exists though, right?"

"Unfortunately, that's true," Lodge acknowledged. "Recent FDA studies of both Red Cross and private blood center operations have unearthed a number of processing deficiencies which have led some people to conclude, among other things, that the incidence of transfusion AIDS has been seriously underreported. Others dispute that, and proving it is a difficult matter. Incidentally, the Red Cross is about to announce a major reorganization of its blood program to eliminate the kinds of errors and inconsistencies the FDA turned up. The goal is to give the public increased peace of mind about the safety of the system."

"Let's back up a minute," I said. "Is AIDS the only disease you can get from a transfusion?"

"Hardly. Transfusion hepatitis, which can lead to cirrhosis of the liver, has been a far greater risk than AIDS over the years. But a test for types A and B hepatitis has been employed by blood people for quite a while, and a new test for so-called hepatitis C will reduce the remaining risk substantially. A host of other viruses—everything from Epstein-Barr to malaria and Lyme disease—can be transmitted via transfusion as well. The most promising solution for *these* problems is a method of blood cleansing through laser and chemical-heating techniques that destroy the viruses before the blood is used in transfusion."

"These blood baths don't work with AIDS?"

"Not so far."

"So the blood supply *isn't* safe."

"Not completely, but what *is*? Few procedures in modern medicine entail no risk whatsoever. What's ironic is that AIDS may have been introduced into the human population during efforts to understand malaria by injecting researchers with the blood of mangabey monkeys, to see if the parasite was transmittable in that manner. Benign intentions; catastrophic results."

"I thought there was a test for HIV in blood, so the bad stuff got screened out."

"There is. But it isn't one hundred percent effective."

"Because the lab people screw up sometimes."

"That's the greatest risk, to be sure, but a second problem is with the test itself—ELISA it's called: Enzyme Linked Immunosorbent Assay. It involves using a goat antibody to human IgG that has been tagged with horseradish peroxidase, then—" Lodge stopped himself, then laughed. "I won't bore you with the science. The problem is, the test doesn't detect the virus itself but rather the antibodies the body has produced to *combat* the virus. Even when supplemented by the so-called Western Blot test, ELISA results are not conclusive in terms of identifying every sample that contains HIV."

"You can have the virus but not the antibody, in other words."

"Precisely. Initial estimates were that antibodies didn't begin to form until two to fourteen weeks after infection. After further research, the period was extended to six months. A recent UCLA study suggests that antibodies may not occur for up to three *years* after contraction of the virus, though those results are widely disputed."

"In the interim, blood from those people will test as safe."

"Yes. But there *is* initial screening for the high-risk groups, don't forget. The chance of infection with AIDS or any other virus from a transfusion is really quite small."

"How small?"

"Current estimates from the Centers for Disease Control say the chance of contracting transfusion AIDS is one in forty thousand. Others say the risk is larger—more on the order of one in eight thousand—because the average transfusion uses blood from more than one source, and thus

the possibility of exposure is increased. Others put the odd
at more like one in one *hundred* thousand."

"There's no way to test for the virus itself—not ju
antibodies?"

"There is such a test—a DNA polymerase chain-reactio
assay. But it's too difficult and too expensive to administ
on a mass basis. Other efforts to detect the virus are sti
unproven."

I thought over what I'd learned. "You don't hear to
much about all this, Doctor. Everything I read seems to sa
the blood supply is okay."

"The blood supply *is* okay, in large part; there a
fifteen million transfusions per year in this country, an
most people survive the experience just fine."

"That's a lot of blood."

"This is a two-billion-dollar-a-year business we're tall
ing about, Mr. Tanner. All the major drug companies ar
involved with blood in one way or another."

"Which means they all have an interest in downplayin
any problems with the product."

"There's no doubt that the blood people are reacting t
the losses they've suffered from the panic of both dono
and recipients because of the AIDS scare. Supplies ar
alarmingly low in some areas because of the concerns abor
safety. The nation's largest blood bank gets twenty-fiv
percent of its blood from abroad."

"More balance-of-payments problems."

"Among other things. And if the Gulf War goes the wa
many people fear it will, the demands on the blood suppl
will increase manyfold. We could be facing a crisis."

"How long does blood last? I mean, after it's bee
removed from the body?"

"Refrigerated whole blood lasts just over forty day
although a recent recommendation would reduce the storag
period to half that because of fears that bacterial contamina
tion can develop in the longer period. Red cells and plasm
are usually frozen upon collection, which means they ca
be stored much longer."

"One last thing, Doctor. What's the deal with *artifici*
blood?"

"That's the new frontier, of course, but the news

mixed. Although dozens of pharmaceutical firms are working on it, there is as yet no FDA-approved blood substitute. Experiments in the 1970s with a fluorocarbon-based product and with artificial hemoglobin were not promising, although a fluorocarbon product has been approved for use by Jehovah's Witnesses because they refuse human transfusions on religious grounds. Recent testing of genetically engineered clotting proteins holds the promise of freeing hemophiliacs from reliance on plasma-derived factor VIII, which has been the major source of the spread of AIDS among hemophiliacs. Just within the last few weeks, human tests of Hemopure, which is purified cow's hemoglobin, have been authorized, though it's too soon to tell whether adverse reactions will be too severe to make that a viable substitute."

"*Cow's* blood, Doctor?"

Lodge laughed. "It has its advantages. One is that purified hemoglobin can be made without the outer shell of the red cell that envelops it, which means blood typing isn't required and adverse reactions are reduced. Another advantage, at least in the public mind, is that cows don't have AIDS."

"Cows just have anthrax," I said, and we shared a morbid moment and hung up.

Two minutes later, Jan called me back. "Did you find him?" she asked breathlessly, the bleary noise of the bar in the background.

"For a while."

"Is he okay?"

"He seems to be."

"What's he doing? When's he coming home?"

"I'm not sure *what* he's doing—keeping a step ahead of the Other Side, it sounds like. We didn't have much time to talk."

"If you see him again, will you ask him to call me at Scanlon's?"

I told her I would. "Listen, Jan. The stuff Nicky has been storing in your refrigerator—the stuff that was too creepy to talk about?"

She hesitated. "What about it?"

"Is it still there?"

" . . . Some of it."

"How much?"

"I . . . Why?"

"Several bags?"

Her voice was leaden, as if the subject evoked images she would rather forget. "Yes. What about it?"

"Tom got some from you not long ago, right?"

"Yeah. What did he *do* with it, anyway?"

"He had it tested."

"For what?"

I ignored her question. "I'm going to need some, too. Take three or four bags from the fridge and let them warm up. Don't use a microwave or anything, just let them reach room temperature. I'll be by tonight to pick them up."

"Are you *serious*?"

"Totally. I'll need you to come with me, if you can. It'll be late. It could also be dangerous. Are you up for it?"

"Will it help Nicky?"

I couldn't tell her what I really thought, so I made do with an evasion. "All I know is it's the only way to learn what happened to his brother."

Chapter
35

Guy Heskett had the easiest job—to stay awake and near a telephone. Because he smelled a breaking story and wanted an exclusive, he'd put on a pot of coffee while he was still pumping me for details. I put him off with a promise that he'd be first in line for whatever I had by tomorrow's deadline.

Jan had gone along because she'd do anything for Nick and I'd implied my charade would help him in some vague way even though I knew that by the time the night was over I might be forced to tell her that the man she loved was doomed. I had been hoping I could at least put her in touch with him again, but true to his nomadic ways, Nicky Crandall didn't show for our rendezvous at Glide Memorial, so he wasn't a part of it at all. Which was probably just as well.

Clarissa was essential to the enterprise; I'd reached her as she was about to leave for the hotel. As usual, we sparred like club fighters in the beginning, but eventually she agreed to do her part, only because I told her this would end it, one way or another, and I'd be out of her life for good. I also

promised no one would get hurt, which was one of man
straws I was clutching at.

Tony had been the hardest to convince. I began b
appealing to his regard for his fallen partner, but ultimatel
I had to threaten blackmail in the form of airing the mor
unsavory aspects of his days as a Healthways paramedi
to convince him to go along. I also had to front the C-not
he used to persuade the Atlas dispatcher to take his un
off-line for a couple of hours, purportedly so Tony coul
use it to "nail some nurse."

By the time he honked for me in front of my apartmen
Tony seemed eager to get at it, an instinct for adventure tha
explained his vocation and an inclination toward larcen
that explained his willingness to steal an ambulance an
provide the necessary equipment for a one-act drama
hoped wouldn't take more than an hour. As we rolle
through the Tenderloin on our way to pick up Jan, h
regaled me with tales of murder and mayhem whose mon
ments were all around us. By the time we came to a stop i
front of Pluto's, I felt I'd been on a tour of Sodom unde
the guidance of the Marquis de Sade.

When the ambulance was snug against the curb, Ton
glanced out the window. "Pluto's, huh? Knew a lady worke
a booth there once. Her thing was pudding. Stuffed a scoo
of tapioca up her cunt, then let it drip into a beer mug an
charged twenty bucks for a taste. Sandra was her nam
Nasty."

I told Tony to honk his horn.

A few seconds later, Jan emerged from the door t
Pluto's left. She was wearing a denim miniskirt and a
orange top and was carrying a shopping bag with MACY'
branded on the side. The way they moved as she trotte
toward us made the bulbous contents of the bag see
reptilian and alive.

I got out of the ambulance, thanked Jan for comin
relieved her of the bag, then gestured to my left. "This
Tony. Tony, Jan."

In tribute to the miniskirt, Tony flashed his smile. "Y
Little Mama. Some fun, huh? Bet you never went partyin
in an EMU before."

Pale and frightened, Jan was beyond the courtesy c
a smile.

"Do you mind riding in back?" I asked her. "It won't be far."

She shook her head, then climbed in the cab without a word and squeezed between the seats and sat on the floor beside the stretcher. When I was back in the cab myself, I put the Macy's bag on the floor between my legs and told Tony to head for Cleveland Street. I took one last look at Jan. As we got under way, she reached for the oxygen cylinder at her side, embracing it as though it would save her from whatever was coming next. If I was anywhere close to the right answer, it might take a lot more than oxygen to save her.

I told Tony to park on Seventh Street within sight of the entrance to the Sandstone Club, then wait for further developments. The wait was long enough for me to learn more than I wanted about Tony's sexual prowess and to worry that Jan was going to have second thoughts.

When her anxieties seemed about to erupt in flight, I told her she was the only one who could give my scheme the verisimilitude it needed, and that she'd be free to look for Nicky in an hour. When I finished my pitch, she rested her head against the stretcher and nodded reluctantly—Jan was used to quixotic behavior. A few minutes later, she asked Tony how the resuscitator worked, initiating a seminar that carried us over the minutes until RS-1 turned into Cleveland Street the way the Yorktown used to turn into Hunter's Point.

It was *déjà vu* all over again. The limo glided to a stop beside the awning; Lex Chadwick got out and helped Clarissa Crandall to the street as well; the limo vanished around a corner; and Lex and Clarissa hurried inside the club. When Tony reached for the ignition, I told him to wait, then got out of the ambulance and walked to the corner. The Escort was about where I figured it would be; I walked up to it and knocked on the window.

Predictably, Garth Standish was already asleep—it took three taps on the window and a bang on the roof to wake him. In the grip of panic, he was tugging at the strap on his shoulder holster before he finally recognized me. I smiled and waved and made a face.

Standish rolled down the window with a grunt. "What do you want?"

"I'm relieving you again."

"Like hell—you hung me out to dry the last time, asshole."

"Sorry about that—I told her it wasn't your fault."

"Right."

"You're still on the job, aren't you?"

"You bet your ass." His brow furled in imitation of thought. "Why do you want rid of me?"

I came up with an answer Standish could understand. "I need to bill for my time, and Deirdre won't like it if we double up."

"You keep the whole fee, is that it?"

"I'll split it with you."

He was inclined to dicker some more, but the prospect of sleep was too good to pass up. "If she bitches, I'm going to tell her you called me off," he threatened bravely.

"Tell her something else while you're at it."

"What?"

"That this would be a good time to junk her marriage."

I left Standish to wend his way to Slumberland and returned to the ambulance and listened to Tony and Jan discuss a succession of medical procedures that had me half-nauseous before they were finished.

Half an hour later, two limousines materialized beneath the Sandstone awning. Six minutes after that, five people exited the club and were whisked away in style—two couples and my old friend Lex. A moment later, the carriage lamps flashed off and on.

"This is it," I said to Tony. "Put on your mask and gloves, then pull up in front of the awning."

Macho to his core, Tony resisted disguise. "Someone got the plague, or what?"

"If this goes bad, the guy in there can have you in jail in a minute if he knows who you are."

"So how come *you're* not making like a bandit?"

"Because he knows who I am already."

Tony shrugged. "It's your show, man; just don't make it an opera—I got to get the rig back by four."

Tony and Jan put on their masks and rubber gloves,

and Tony eased the ambulance into Cleveland Street and stopped in front of the club. Gear in neutral and engine idling easily, he looked at me for instructions.

"Where's the IV stuff?"

Tony reached under the seat and pulled out an oblong package wrapped in a cotton towel. "You know how to use this thing?" he asked.

"Not really."

"Then I better handle it."

"It's a battery, Tony. I'd better do it myself."

"Better that than a homicide. I'll handle it."

I nodded, then pointed toward the rear of the rig. As Tony scooted into the back to open the rear doors, I reached for the Macy's bag between my feet; it was as warm as mother's milk.

After the rear door squeaked open and Tony had dragged the stretcher onto the walk, I joined them under the awning. "Follow my lead," I said. "I'll do the talking until I hand it over to Jan."

Her eyes were moons of apprehension. "What am I supposed to *do*?"

"Tell the truth."

"About what?"

"This." I held up the favors she'd brought to the party. "All set, boys and girls?"

The nods were hesitant at best. I walked to the door and turned the knob. It opened without resistance. I paid silent homage to Clarissa Crandall and motioned for the others to precede me. By the time Tony and his stretcher were rolling toward the library, it was 3:15. I was tired, Jan was scared, and Tony was Tony.

I got out my gun. When I got to the door, I opened it. The lights were low; the fire was well on its way to coals. The music was Sinatra, and the mood was a match for the game being played on the couch.

Richard Sands was shoeless and in shirtsleeves, which was a break—businessmen feel vulnerable without their brogans. The spaghetti straps of Clarissa's gown had slipped from her shoulders, and only the jut of her heavy breasts kept the bodice from falling to her lap. Her hair was as mussed as her dress, but her eyes seemed lit less by lust than artifice.

Sands was so intent on seduction he didn't hear me, but Clarissa knew the moment I came through the door. The expression that began as relief that I'd arrived on time turned to misgiving when she saw the masked marauders in my wake.

Her gasp alerted her swain. Thwarted, then startled, Sands looked over the back of the couch. "Tanner," he said as he squinted me into focus. "Who let *you* in here? What the fuck do you think you're—"

When Tony rolled the stretcher out from behind my back, Sands lost his train of thought.

"Sorry about the osculation interruptus," I said. "It's time to talk."

Sands abandoned Clarissa with a dispatch that disconcerted her and bent to slip on his shoes. "I don't do business down here. Call my people and make an appointment."

When his wing tips were knotted and his attentions were back my way, I held my gun where he could see it. "Let's be spontaneous tonight."

His eyes flicked toward the desk.

I wriggled the hand with the gun in it. "I'm sure there are a dozen alarm systems within reach, but leave them be till you hear me out. I'm not going to hurt anyone, or steal anything; I'm just going to tell you a story and then ask you some questions. If you answer them, that will be the end of it."

"And if I tell you to go to hell?" The words were crisp and unconcerned.

"My assistant will perform a minor medical procedure." I looked at Tony. "This gentleman is a trained technician, just so you'll know."

"A *what* procedure?" Sands said, his voice rising like a kite.

"We'll get to the specifics in a minute. First, you need to lie down on the stretcher."

Sands' brow became a thunderhead. "Like hell."

I waved the gun again. "Don't make me tap your skull and drag you—it wouldn't be healthy for either of us."

Sands could barely rein his pique. "You spend too much time watching TV. Do you know what I can *do* to you for this?"

Probably because she was afraid her boyfriend was nearing apoplexy, Clarissa whispered something in his ear. Sands fumed for a moment longer, then looked at me again. "What happens when I'm on the stretcher?"

"We strap you down."

"Then what?"

I looked at Jan. "She tells you a story."

"What kind of story?"

"A true story."

"What about?"

"Nicky Crandall and the Healthways Corporation."

His sneer slacked a bit. "I know all about the Healthways Corporation. I *own* the damned thing."

"That's why we're here."

He decided to try the benign approach. "Now look. I don't know what you're up to, but you've clearly gotten some misinformation. Lots of people resent the hell out of me, you know. They spread a dozen rumors a day trying to bring me down by making me sound like some kind of crook. So if that's what this is, let's calm down and discuss it. I'm sure we can straighten out any—"

I shook my head. "No discussion. This is a monologue. For once in your life, you're not the star."

Sands reddened to the color of rhubarb. "If this is some kind of *kidnapping,* I warn you I have—"

I was so used to his threats I finished it for him. "You have a veritable army at your disposal, and they'll hunt me to the ends of the earth and I'll never get away with it. Well, kidnapping isn't what this is about—after you hear us out, we'll leave you to your business." I winked at Clarissa. "If your partner is so inclined."

Sands was finally operating at speed, and he had a revelation. "You're part of this," he said to Clarissa. "You *have* to be."

She was so hurt by his charge I tried to come to her rescue. "She doesn't have any idea what this is about. Neither do the others. I'm the only one who's read the script, and that's because I wrote it." I looked at my watch, then flashed the gun again. "Stretcher, please."

"You must be insane."

A rage that had been festering for a long time, from long

before Tom Crandall died, erupted without warning. "You know what I hate most about guys like you?" I asked, then answered my own question. "You don't have the guts to do the dirty work yourselves. You hire guys like Chadwick to do it—fleece the little guy out of his job or his retirement plan or his life savings—while you hide in the penthouse and the boardroom, so if someone blows the whistle you can pretend you didn't know about it. Well, that may wash with the government, or the courts, but it doesn't wash with me. You're responsible for every trick the Chadwicks of your world come up with, Sands, because you hire them for one thing—ruthlessness. You know it, and so do they. What you want is for them to sacrifice anything and anyone for the bottom line, and that's exactly what they do. Well, this time you went too far." I let my outburst simmer before I finished up. "Now get on that fucking stretcher." My revolver was aimed at his sternum.

Sands thought about it for so long I thought I was going to have to get rough. As I was trying to remember how hard you have to hit someone to render them unconscious but not for very long, Sands walked to the stretcher and lay down on it. "This better be quick. And you'd better be lucky, because after it's over, I'm coming after you with all I've got."

I looked at Tony. "Strap him."

With consummate ease, Tony flipped the restraints across Sands' limbs and chest. When Tony signaled all was well, I put my shopping bag on the floor and took out one of the smaller bags inside it. The slick and sloppy feel was so repellent it made me want to change my mind.

I looked at Jan. "Tell him what this is."

She blinked and cleared her throat, making her mask a balloon of white. "Blood." The word was blunt and portentous.

"Whose blood?"

"Nicky's."

"Who's Nicky?" Sands grumbled from his litter, eyes locked on the eddying blob of blood I cradled in my hand.

"My boyfriend. He's . . . got a thing about his body. He saves, like, his fingernails, and hair, and piss and stuff."

"And this," I prompted, jiggling the bag like Jell-O.

She nodded. "The fridge is full of it."

"When did he extract this particular batch?"

"It's marked on that piece of tape. A few weeks ago, I think."

I nodded to confirm it. "Tell Mr. Sands a little more about Nicky, so he can see how he fits into the scheme. For example, Nicky has a mental problem, doesn't he?"

"He's a schiz," Jan said simply.

"Does he have a job?"

She shook her head.

"So you don't have a lot of money."

"Not after rent and medication. Clozapine costs a fortune."

"But Nicky has a doctor, doesn't he?"

She shrugged. "Sort of. He saw Dr. Marlin after we got back to town, I know."

I started warming to a role I'd once played in court. "Dr. Marlin is a Healthways psychiatrist, right?"

Jan shrugged. "I guess so."

"How long ago did Nicky see him?"

"About three months."

"How did Nicky feel about Dr. Marlin?"

"He didn't like him."

"Why not?"

"He *said* the doctor was trying to poison him. Fill him with microbes and stuff. I don't know if it's true or not," Jan concluded ingenuously. "It's hard to know what Nicky means, sometimes."

Sands' laugh was bilious. "You're *all* crazy. Jesus. Why don't we just adjourn to Langley-Porter?"

I looked at Jan again. "Dr. Marlin did some follow-up with Nicky, didn't he?"

"He sent Ron and Don around to see him, if that's what you mean."

"A Healthways ambulance crew."

Jan nodded. "They wanted Nicky real bad, but I don't think they caught him. Nicky's tricky when he has to be," she added proudly.

"Someone else has been looking for Nicky, am I right?"

Jan frowned, then brightened, glad to be accomplished. "Dracula was after him, too."

I reached in my pocket with my free hand, then looked at Sands. "If the nickname doesn't ring a bell, maybe it will if I tell you that Dracula is the young man Healthways sends out into the Tenderloin to hunt up donors for the Fremont Memorial Blood Bank. He doesn't hustle just anyone; he works from a list given to him by Lex Chadwick. Here's the current crop of recruits." I showed Sands the paper I'd taken from Dracula as he lay unconscious at Vinny's Video. "See? There's Nicky, right near the top."

Sands read the paper, then looked at Clarissa. "What's this guy to you?"

The words were lemony in her mouth. "My brother-in-law."

"How does he matter?"

"I don't know."

Sands looked back at me. "Am I supposed to know what this blood stuff means?"

"Yep."

"Well, I don't." The words were thick and too believable.

"I guess that remains to be seen," I said, then held out the bag of blood. Tony reached in his shirt and took out two plastic packets. After he tore them open, he extracted tubes and clamps and needles and a second plastic bag.

When the paraphernalia was laid out on the coffee table, I handed Tony the bag of Nicky's blood, and he began the transfer to the bag he'd brought along. "That's an IV unit," I said to Sands. "When he's ready, he's going to stick a needle in your arm and hook you up to the IV system. When it's set, I'll turn that little blue valve, and then *this* blood—Nicky Crandall's blood—will start mixing with *your* blood. A special transfusion, just for you."

Sands was unnerved enough to writhe against his restraints. "You do that and I'll see that you rot in jail for life."

"I forgot one thing," I interrupted pleasantly. "The valve stays closed if you tell me all about it."

His eyes rolled, desperate and disbelieving. "Tell you about *what*?"

"The horror story you're perpetrating at Healthways.

The scheme to save your company from ruin." I let my anger linger. "The plot that got Tom Crandall killed."

"*What* scheme?" Fear assaulted him headlong. "*What* plot? I don't *know* any—"

I waved the gun again. "The pharmaceutical breakthrough. The new product that's going to pull Sandstone's fat out of the fire."

"The *Alzheimer's* thing? It's going to restore some memory, sure, but it's not a *cure* or anything."

I shook my head. "Not Alzheimer's."

"But that's the only breakthrough I *know* about."

"Then I guess I'll have to do to you what you've been doing to those poor souls in the Tenderloin."

I nodded to Tony. He plucked some paraphernalia off the table and walked to the stretcher and swabbed the back of Sands' hand with antiseptic, then wound a tourniquet around his forearm. After slipping the cap off the needle, Tony inserted it into an engorged vein just below Sands' left wrist, then tugged off the tourniquet. After fitting an adapter to the needle, he hooked the adapter to a cannula, which led to the little plastic valve that dangled just below the bag that bulged with Nicky's blood, which Tony held aloft.

"You can't put any blood into *anyone,* you moron," Sands cried. "It has to be typed and cross-matched and—"

"I'm not going to use it all. Just a little. Just enough to do the job. Of course, I won't use any of it if you admit to what's been going on at Healthways and to having Tom Crandall killed to cover it up."

Sands fumed in silence, looking for a way out—guys like Sands never believe they'll be caught, never concede that there isn't a bribe, a payoff, or a threat that will erase the mess their greed has made. What puzzles me is why we've let guys like Sands become our gods.

Time was as thick and languid as the blood. Sands closed his eyes and seemed to sleep. When he opened them again, he looked at Clarissa, less with cunning than with sorrow. "Is that what *you* think? That I had your husband killed? For something to do with *business?*"

Except for the tear that traveled down her cheek, Clarissa Crandall was as immobile as a stone.

Sands sniffed and blinked and looked at me. "You're

saying the only way I can prove I didn't know what wa
going on is to let you go ahead with this blood business."

"That's about it."

He regarded me with a primacy I couldn't have dupli
cated on the best day of my life. "Then go ahead." He
thrust his arm and then his jaw. "Not for you, you bastard
For her."

I put my hand on the little blue valve.

Rather than recoiling in terror, Sands seemed to feed o
the moment. "You thought I'd cave, huh? You thought yo
could run a bluff. Well, I don't bluff, Tanner. When you g
against *me,* you play all your cards."

I turned the valve. A snake of red slithered from the ba
and crawled toward the hand that lay naked and impaled o
his chest. Clarissa started to sob; Tony emitted a sarcasti
laugh. Sands and I appraised each other.

"I had a friend who died from AIDS last year,"
said softly. "Fungus, fevers, sarcoma, blindness. And hug
amounts of pain. I've seen a lot of death, but I've neve
seen anything as bad as that. Just so you know why I'n
doing this."

Sands didn't say a word. Clarissa Crandall said a prayer
I looked at the lengthening asp of blood.

When it was an inch from his hand, I squeezed it off
then tugged the tube off the needle and the needle out o
his vein. Careful not to spill on the rug, I gathered up the
entire apparatus and tossed it in the fire. As the blood an
rubber and plastic began to smoke and stink, I told Tony
to let him loose.

Clarissa's eyes were wet, and her chest heaved wit
relief. "I needed to know whether he was the monster Ton
thought he was," I said to her, "and this was the only wa
I could think of to find out. It looks like the monster wa
someone else. I'm sorry."

After a moment of reflection, she looked at Richard
Sands. "I think it's going to be all right," she said.

Although she wasn't talking to me, I told her I hoped
so.

I like to think I meant it. I like to think Tom Crandal
would have meant it, too.

Chapter
36

"Why the detour?" Guy Heskett asked, his irritation barbed by his lack of sleep.

"It's not a detour, it's a pilgrimage. I told Sands I'd give him twenty-four hours to go public and clean house," I added as I pulled into the early-morning traffic on the bridge. "It will take you that long to do the background work and write it up. If you're lucky, you can have it on the streets five minutes after his press conference."

"I'd rather have it five hours before."

"You would have if Sands had done what I expected. Since he didn't, I had to give him time to wash the dirty linen himself."

"When do I find out what that linen is?"

"When we get where we're going."

"Which is?"

"A little house in Danville."

"Whose house?"

"The woman who can tell you how it all began."

The woman in question was standing beside the highway waiting for her bus, trying to keep her bank attire in place as a stream of cars whizzed past at illegal speeds. She wore flat shoes and a plain green coat, but there was a flower pinned in her hair and a smile on her face when she saw me. I took a bit of credit for both of them.

"Mr. Tanner!" she exclaimed. "What are *you* doing here?"

"I'm here to take you to a telephone."

"Why?"

"So you can call in sick."

"But I'm not—"

"Sure you are. The symptoms are perverse—hallucinations of good health. Very serious if allowed to fester. Dr Tanner advises the day off."

"Why?" she asked again.

I pointed toward my car. "So you can tell that man about Tom and Nicky. And about them and you, if you want to."

"Why would I do that?"

"Because I know why Tom was killed, and part of i has to do with the early days. Not a big part, but a part."

She put a hand on my arm. "You look awful," she said "Like you've seen a ghost."

"They aren't ghosts yet, but I'm afraid they will be."

She frowned. "Am I supposed to understand?"

I shook my head. "Not yet."

She squinted into the morning sunlight. "Who's the man in the car?"

"A reporter for the *Chronicle*."

She looked more closely. "He's cute."

"That's something you have in common. Another is tha he's a big admirer of Tom's."

Just then her bus rolled up. I looked at Ellen, and sh looked at me. When the door swished open, she steppe toward it. I was about to reach out and stop her when sh smiled up at the driver and spoke with the sweetness of th *Sesame Street* people. "I think I'm coming down with th flu; I'd better stay home today. Sorry to make you stop fo nothing."

The driver shrugged; the door closed; the bus trudge off to Oakland, and Ellen Simmons took my hand. "I don know what this is, but it's already better than the bank."

I helped Ellen into the backseat and made brief introductions. Both she and Heskett seemed to regard them as a cut above pro forma.

When we were under way, I launched my spiel. "I'm going to begin at the end. When I'm finished, Ellen can tell you the beginning."

"It usually works better the other way around," Heskett objected.

I ignored him.

"It ends with Richard Sands. More precisely with his holding company—the Sandstone Corporation. Sandstone has been breaking down under its debt load, along with a lot of other highfliers of the eighties." Heskett started to interrupt. "I can give you sources for this," I said. "Check with me when you're ready to write it up."

"If Richard Sands is involved, I'd better check with you *before* I write it."

"We do it my way or not at all."

"Like I said," Heskett grumbled, "I'll check with you later."

Ellen's laugh seemed more elaborate than the amendment warranted.

"When the company began to fall apart," I went on, "someone came up with a scheme to save it. That someone was Lex Chadwick, president of Healthways Corporation, one of Sandstone's subsidiaries. What Sandstone needed was a ton of cash to service its debt, otherwise it was going to have to auction off its assets and file for reorganization under the Bankruptcy Act. What Chadwick learned was that the pharmaceutical division of Healthways had a hot new product in the pipeline, a substance so revolutionary that in the right market conditions it could generate the cash flow necessary to put Sandstone on solid footing."

"What was it?" Heskett asked.

"At first, I thought they'd come up with an AIDS vaccine and were using the Healthways clinics to test it on humans without authorization from the FDA."

"Jesus," Heskett blurted. "Is that true?"

I shook my head. "That wasn't quite it."

"What *was* it?"

"What Healthways had come up with was synthetic blood. I don't know the science behind it—apparently it involves a mixture of something called perfluorochemicals, along with a detergent and some kind of molecules from egg yolk. Because of the way it's engineered, synthetic blood can perform the primary function of real blood, which is to oxygenate the body, while freeing transfusion recipients from the rejection problems of real blood and from transfusion disease problems as well. The point is, Healthways may have developed the first blood substitute that really works."

"I know blood is big business," Heskett said with more than a little paternalism, "but I have to tell you, I don't see this as a story unless and until Sandstone is ready to go public with the stuff. Maybe a science-page spot, though; I can put you in touch with our guy on that beat."

"Why don't you wait till you hear the whole thing?"

Heskett shrugged. "I seem to be a captive audience." He looked at the woman in the backseat. "Not that I'm complaining."

When Heskett's eyes were on the road, Ellen grinned at me in the rearview mirror. I hurried to wrap it up.

"Even though Healthways had a breakthrough, they also had a problem. Sandstone couldn't wait for them to put the blood substitute through the FDA testing protocols and approval process—that could take years, and Sandstone needed income now. Chadwick decided the way to get it was to create such a massive demand for the product that the normal testing procedures would be waived even if it was discovered that Healthways had failed to follow them."

"Where was this demand supposed to come from?"

"From the people who normally need blood—hospitals and their patients. That demand is substantial normally, but in a few weeks the need may be far greater than anyone estimated—if the War in the Gulf turns into a quagmire, demand for blood will skyrocket. If the Healthways synthetic is any good, they can name their price."

"But why would people need *synthetic* blood? Why not use the real stuff?"

I paused for effect. "Because Healthways is sabotaging the blood supply. Not all of it, just enough to start such a panic in Bay Area blood circles that hospitals will embrace *any* alternative to the local supply in order to meet demand, even an unproved synthetic."

Heskett's head jerked left. "How do you mean, 'sabotage'?"

I took a deep breath. The adrenaline of the evening had evaporated—fatigue fell over me like snow. "As you know, donated blood—whether at a blood bank or the Red Cross—is tested for contaminants, including the AIDS virus. But there's a problem—the AIDS test doesn't react to the virus but to the antibodies the body produces to *fight* the virus. Between the time the virus is contracted and the time antibodies form, there's a gap—several weeks for sure, maybe as long as several months. What Healthways did was send the Fremont Memorial Blood Bank a select number of donors who had the virus but not the antibodies, people with HIV who would pass the screening tests and compromise the Bay Area blood supply by slipping infected units into the inventory."

"They did this on *purpose*?" Ellen asked.

"Yes."

"That *Sands* person?"

"It was his company that did it, but I don't think he knew what was going on," I said. Then the events of the evening took a new shape in my mind and I decided to amplify my answer. "Either that or he and I just had a game of chicken and I lost. But whatever Sands might have known himself, his people certainly knew about it, which to me is the same thing."

Ellen's voice was hollow. "Did that *woman* know?"

"Definitely not."

"So what happened after the bank got the bad blood?" Heskett demanded, his notebook in his lap.

"Sandstone leaked word that the Fremont inventories were compromised. The FDA decided to investigate; their report is due any day. When it comes out, all the local blood banks may have to discard their inventories to make sure they don't have the same problem. When the public gets wind of the situation, no one within fifty miles of San Francisco will accept blood from a source that isn't certifiably safe. When Healthways pops up with a substitute, they'll be welcomed with open arms."

"What's to keep this from becoming a national crisis?"

"What I *hope* is that Healthways knows whose blood was bad, and that those units can be traced into the inventory and extracted."

"But some may have been used already."

"Possibly. But those people should be able to be identified. With luck, the panic will be localized and short-lived."

"You *hope*," Heskett repeated, then considered what he'd learned. "How did Healthways know the people they lined up to give blood really *had* HIV?"

"That's not the question."

"What *is* the question?"

"The question is, how did they know the donors had the virus but not the antibodies?"

"Well? How did they?"

I looked at him. "This is where it gets evil."

"I thought it might."

I honked at an errant driver.

"Healthways knew the blood donors had the virus but not the antibodies because Healthways gave the donors the virus in the *first* place. Massive doses of HIV, injected into destitute patients who visited Healthways clinics for other purposes and got an injection that would supposedly make them well but in reality flooded their system with the virus. A few weeks later, when the virus was rampant but the antibodies hadn't had time to form, these same people were rounded up by a kid named Dracula and paid to go to Fremont Memorial and donate blood. The recruit would pass the screening procedures, of course, since they weren't in the risk groups—they had been given the virus deliberately. I should emphasize that the donors weren't collaborators, they were victims—they had no idea they'd been turned into HIV carriers and no idea they were being used to destroy a vital part of the health-care system. Fremont was a victim, too."

"That's fucking diabolical," Heskett mumbled.

"Is it starting to look like a story yet?"

Heskett swore. "You can *prove* all this?"

"I expect Sands to lay it out by the end of the day. If he doesn't, I can tell you how to flesh it out yourself."

Ellen's voice was ethereal in the rear seat. "I don't understand what this has to do with Tom."

I found her in the mirror. "Tom was killed because he uncovered the scheme I just mentioned."

"Killed by whom?"

"A couple of Healthways paramedics."

"How did he learn about it?"

"Nicky was one of the guinea pigs. Tom figured out what was going on because despite the lunacy of his ramblings, Nicky knew what had been done to him and was telling Tom about it in his own warped way. When Tom put it together and started asking questions, he was killed to shut him up."

I explained to Heskett. "Tom Crandall's brother was one of the people injected with HIV. The guy who did it was a Healthways psychiatrist named Marlin. Nicky wasn't chosen at random like the others—Marlin wanted to get rid of him because of what had gone on in the old days out here in the valley, back when Marlin ran a psychiatric clinic and Nicky was one of his patients."

"Is Nicky still alive?" Ellen asked.

I nodded. "I saw him yesterday."

"But he has AIDS."

"He has the virus. He didn't seem symptomatic, but I'm not a doctor."

"If you have the virus, doesn't it mean you're going to die?"

"I don't know," I said truthfully, then thought of people I'd known and stories I'd heard, of Acyclovir and Iscador, of ddI and ddC, of T-helpers and PZ4. "A lot of people hope it doesn't, and they go through hell trying to fight it off. Some people have lived with the virus for years. Tough years, but years."

"Nicky has a girlfriend, doesn't he?"

I nodded. "Her name is Jan."

"Then she has the virus, too."

"Possibly."

"Does she know it?"

"Not yet."

I pulled to a stop in front of a coffee shop. "Ellen can give you the first chapter," I said to Heskett, then got out of the car and waited for him and Ellen to join me.

Ellen grasped my hand. "You're not staying?"

I shook my head. "I've got to see some people."

"Jan."

"And my client. Tom's wife doesn't know the whole story yet, either. She isn't a bad woman, by the way. She and Tom just messed up their marriage. It happens sometimes, even to people who love each other."

"Hey," Heskett said in what sounded like distress. "I don't have a car. How am I going to get *out* of here?"

I kissed the back of Ellen's hand. "When it's time to go, you'll find a way. Right, Ms. Simmons?"

Her smile made mincemeat of the sun. "Absolutely, Mr. Tanner."

Then I drove back across the bridge.